# Murder and the Muse

Also by Alexei Bayer

*Murder at the Dacha*

*The Latchkey Murders*

# MURDER
## AND THE
# MUSE

ALEXEI BAYER

Russian Life
BOOKS

ISBN 978-1-880100-49-3

Library of Congress Control Number: 2016958700

Russian Information Services, Inc.
PO Box 567
Montpelier, VT 05601-0567
www.russianlife.com
orders@russianlife.com
phone 802-223-4955

Cover image: Altered portion "Olga in an Armchair," by Pablo Picasso.

For Natalia Alexeyevna Zolotnitskaya-Scriabina
*That your name and your story live on*

Born in Moscow in 1894, Natalia Zolotnitskaya-Scriabina escaped from Crimea in 1920 and was an exile all her life. A citizen of Venezuela, she lived in many countries and died in Rome in 1975.

She is buried at the Cimitero Acattolico in Rome, resting in one of the most peaceful and poetic corners of the city, in the shadow of the Pyramid of Caius Sestius, along with the English Romantic poets.

# MOSCOW

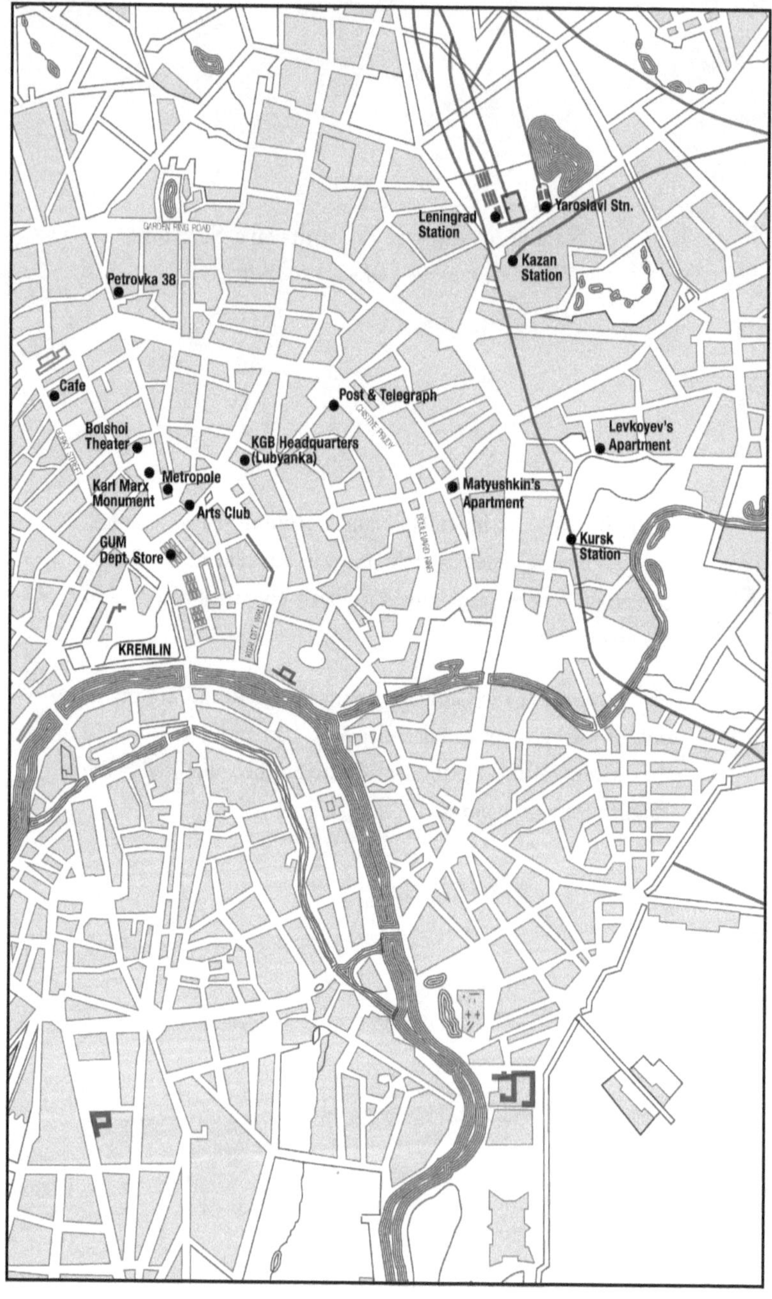

GARDEN RING ROAD
Leningrad Station
Yaroslavl Stn.
Kazan Station
Petrovka 38
Cafe
Post & Telegraph
CASTYE PALEY
Levkoyev's Apartment
Bolshoi Theater
KGB Headquarters (Lubyanka)
GORKY STREET
Karl Marx Monument
Metropole
Matyushkin's Apartment
Arts Club
BOULEVARD RING
GUM Dept. Store
Kursk Station
KREMLIN
RIGA CITY HALL

В эту ночь мы ушли от погони,
Расседлали своих лошадей;
Я лежал на шершавой попоне
Среди спящих усталых людей.

И запомнил и помню доныне
Наш последний российский ночлег,
Эти звезды приморской пустыни,
Этот синий мерцающий снег,

Стерегло нас последнее горе, -
После снежных татарских полей, -
Ледяное Понтийское море,
Ледяная душа кораблей.

Николай Туроверов


Tonight we shook off the chase,
Unsaddled our horses;
I stretch on the rough horsecloth
Among my exhausted men.

I'll think back to this day and remember
This night, our last in Russia,
These stars shining upon the coastal desert,
This snow, glowing dark blue.

Our last misfortune still lies ahead,
Beyond the snow-covered Tatar fields:
The Pontus across the frozen waves,
The frozen soul of departing ships.

Nikolai Turoverov

Nikolai Turoverov was a White officer who evacuated from Crimea, lived in France, became a poet, fought for the French in 1940, and died in Paris in 1972.

# AUTHOR'S NOTE

Nonfiction has invaded storytelling.

This is certainly not a new development. *The New Yorker*, America's premier literary magazine, thrives on quality reportage, and literary titans Truman Capote and Norman Mailer wrote highly acclaimed nonfiction novels half a century ago. Yet the tagline "Based on a true story" seems to be an obligatory claim of every Hollywood movie, no matter how far-fetched its plot. And a work of literature can't be simply magical – it has to be magical realism. Last year, nonfiction received the ultimate imprimatur as Belarus writer Svetlana Alexievich, who weaves indelible portraits and stories from first person interviews, was awarded the Nobel Prize for Literature.

Art has become a pale imitator of life.

However, if real life is allowed to supplant the realm of literary imagination, there is no law against literary imagination invading real life, altering it, and, perhaps, even improving on it. This is especially important in detective novels. Indeed, where would they be without artifice? There were all of 250 murders in Britain in 1960 and probably none in the sort of sleepy towns where Agatha Christi's mysteries take place. Dame Agatha would have died in obscurity had she been forced to wait for a real-life murder to take place in St. Mary Mead, Miss Marple's hometown.

So, in *Murder and the Muse*, the third novel in which Senior Lieutenant Pavel Matyushkin of Moscow Criminal Investigations is confronted with a series of daunting crimes, I invade and embellish reality. But, rather than basing the story on real-life events, I base it on real people, for whom I do the favor of ascribing – post factum – a couple of imaginary adventures.

The characters in *Murder and the Muse* are mostly fictional, with three exceptions – Olga Khokhlova, Alexei Zolotnitsky and Yuri Andropov. Olga Stepanovna Khokhlova was a real-life ballerina born in 1891 in the small Ukrainian town of Nizhin (or Nezhin in Russian, since back then it was still the Russian Empire). She was indeed married to Pablo Picasso, with whom she had a son. However, by the time the Bolsheviks took power in Russia in 1917, Khokhlova, along with the rest of Sergei Diaghilev's Ballet Russe troupe (of which she was a member), had already settled in France. She had none of the misadventures in Crimea described in the novel. And, even though she had family in the Soviet Union and Pablo eventually joined the French Communist Party, she never revisited her native country. Nor could she have done so in 1964, the year the novel takes place, since she had been dead for nearly a decade.

Alexei Zolotnitsky is a real life character, but not a historic one. I never met him. He fought in World War I and joined the Whites in the Russian Civil War. Some of the events described in the novel were recounted to me in 1974 by his widow in Rome. I can't vouch for her veracity.

Finally, there is Yuri Vladimirovich Andropov. Certainly he is a historical figure, since he led the Soviet Union for a little over a year. Before succeeding Leonid Brezhnev in 1982, Andropov had been the head of the KGB, the notorious Committee for State Security, or the Soviet version of the CIA and the FBI wrapped up in one. He was appointed to that position in 1967, not 1964, but since he never met Olga Khokhlova – much less escorted her around Moscow – this inconsistency seems minor.

What is true, however, is that Andropov was a ruthless and cunning man. He earned his wings – so to speak – by being in the right place at the right time. He was Soviet ambassador to Hungary in 1956, when a revolution against Soviet rule erupted in Budapest. He made sure that the uprising was brutally suppressed by Soviet tanks and that Imre Nagy, the Hungarian party leader who dared disobey Moscow, was executed. Many other Hungarians met a similar fate or were given lengthy prison terms. Andropov was therefore nicknamed "the Butcher of Budapest."

But he was, apparently, a charming man who wrote poetry in his spare time.

MOSCOW, 1964

# PROLOGUE

He had not expected it to be this easy.

It's a hotel for foreign tourists, for God's sake. You would have thought they'd have taken the trouble to install something more sophisticated on hard currency-paying guests' doors. But no. It is the same crappy spring lock they've got in hotels all across the country, the ones where five or more guys share a room. Perhaps it made sense – with all the security personnel hanging around this place, you probably don't have to even bother locking your door. But, then again, most of the security was there to keep foreigners from talking to ordinary Russians, not to protect them from thieves. So, installing more sophisticated locks would have been a good idea, and his presence there was the best argument in its favor.

Still, none of that would have mattered because he had yet to see a lock he couldn't open. Given enough time, he could open anything.

As usual, he was losing himself in thoughts about stupid things. He had to clear his mind and get down to work.

He gave the heavy wooden door a slight push, opening it a tiny crack. The door was old, and he worried the hinges might squeak. There was no sound, and the suite was dark. He opened the door a little wider. All quiet. The crack was now wide enough for him to squeeze his skinny frame through. He pulled the door shut. The lock clicked.

On the inside, the door was painted white and separated from the room by a heavy velour curtain that smelled of prosperous old age and dust. The fabric probably hadn't been cleaned since the Revolution, he thought. He stood motionless for a few seconds, his hearing keenly tuned. The room had two large square windows. Their curtains were drawn, letting in light from the illuminated façade of the Bolshoi and intermittent green and red neon flashes from the building directly across Karl Marx Avenue. There was a steady hum of cars and buses passing three floors below. Otherwise, all was quiet in the hallway behind and the suite before him. He felt safe enough to exhale, then he slipped the passkey into his pocket.

He had committed a detailed plan of the suite to memory, and now mentally charted the shortest route to the bedroom. He entered the living room. Yet as he surveyed his surroundings in the half-light, everything looked different. Suddenly he was no longer sure which direction it was to the bedroom, whether he needed to turn right or left. He crouched down, pulled the plan from his pocket and shone his flashlight onto it. For a second, a yellow circle played across his right hand, illuminating dirty fingernails and a cross tattooed on the proximal phalanx of the index finger. He cupped the light with his palm, training a narrow ray onto the sheet of paper.

There was a couch with side tables at either end. He would have to go around it to get to the bedroom. The question was which way. There wasn't enough light to read the plan – or, for that matter, to tell whether he even had it properly oriented. He was never very good at reading maps.

He could feel himself starting to panic.

To the left, all was dark. To the right was a room with a window. He couldn't remember if the bedroom had a window or not, but decided to go that way anyway. If it wasn't the bedroom, he'd be able to tell right away.

Shielding the ray of the flashlight with his palm, he tiptoed to the right. The tiny bright sliver of light trickled through his fingers and danced over the furniture. His practiced eye made out objects as he passed them, calculating their value. A couple of glossy foreign magazines on the coffee table – definitely something to think about. People paid good money for such things. A jacket with a fur collar thrown carelessly over the back of a chair – far more valuable, but also bulky. Bric-a-brac here and there – nothing interesting, just part of the hotel's decor. The Japanese transistor radio on top of the grand piano – wow, a grand piano in the room – was both the most expensive thing he saw and the smallest, too. The easiest to pick up. It would fetch a small fortune on the black market, and he even knew who would fence it.

But first he had to get what he had come for. He was getting paid extremely well. Better than he had ever been paid. He had never done a job like this, not at a hard currency hotel. It was a dangerous job, no doubt. If he got caught, he'd probably get a sentence twice as long as if he were caught doing this at any other hotel in the country. Then again, it was not a difficult job, technically speaking. It didn't require his exceptional skills at breaking and entering.

So he was being paid for the high level of risk. Make that *very* high level of risk. Was he being paid enough, or had he sold himself short? Good question. From where he stood – and he now stood in a hard currency hotel suite, his knees weak and trembling and his heart in his throat – he certainly would be justified in rewarding himself with a little something extra, and no one would be the wiser. A bit of a premium for the extra risk.

But his client had said not to touch anything – only what he wanted him to take. This client was a tough customer. Not one to be taken lightly, despite his efforts to seem polite and humane. He was a tough guy, even though he pretended to be a member of the intelligentsia.

On the other hand, what could he do, this tough guy? The job would be done, and he would have gotten what he wanted. Why would he make a stink about a few things missing from the suite? Would he even know about them? How would he find out? And even if he did find out, what could he do? Make him return them?

The idea made him chuckle softly.

Wait a second. He had now arrived at the door of what he had thought was the bedroom, only to find it was a small study. He remembered this from the plan. The bedroom was larger and didn't have windows. It was at the opposite end of the living room.

Then he spotted it. A silver jewelry box sparkled green and red in the blinking of the neon sign across the street. He shone his flashlight on it, opening his fingers a bit more. He picked up the box and examined it closely. Did it have a lock? Was it a music box with a loud movement that would wake up the occupant of the suite? No, nothing. A plain jewelry box, crafted of solid silver and weighing heavy in the palm of his hand. Still careful, he slowly pushed the lid open. His hand began to shake with excitement, and he had to set the box down. He knew it was very valuable. Very expensive.

Boy, how lucky could you get?

He turned off the flashlight, but there was still plenty of light coming in through the windows. He emptied the jewelry box, stuffing the baubles into his pockets. He thought of taking the box too, but it was too bulky. He put it back down on the desk and started toward the front door.

Then, at the last moment, he remembered that he had not done what he had been told to do. He grinned, shook his head, and turned back.

# ONE

She was tall for a woman of her generation, taller than most men. Her height had kept her from getting into classic ballet in prewar St. Petersburg, but it delighted Sergei Pavlovich.

"Look at Mademoiselle Olga, everyone, look at how delightfully tall she is," he declared as he introduced her to the rest of his Ballet Russes company, as though she were an example for them all to emulate.

Both men she married were short, which was a paradox because as a young girl she dreamed of an exceptionally tall Prince Charming arriving on a ship with scarlet sails and coming ashore to take her into his arms.

But the whole world was one huge paradox – a paradox that was funny or amusing only if your sense of humor tended toward cruelty.

Her two husbands were a paradox as well, especially when compared to each other. One was a military officer named Alexei Zolotnitsky. Like many Russians, inside his gruff, war-hardened shell he was as gentle as a lamb, almost effeminate. He had fought in a bloodbath some called the Great War, which went on for three years. That was followed by two revolutions and a Civil War that was an even greater orgy of bloodletting than the Great War. He had seen men, women and children die by the hundreds, and killed some of them himself – not women and children, she was sure of that, at least not intentionally, but certainly many men – yet nothing could alter his childlike naiveté and basic compassion for every living thing, from an ant carrying a stick on its back to a captured commissar.

That act of mercy, saving a woman commissar from hanging, was probably the cruelest thing he ever did. That too was a paradox.

Alexei Zolotnitsky was her first husband. Her second husband –

Well, her second husband was a very different story. He stood only one meter sixty-five centimeters tall and had big ears, and, as far as she knew, he had never killed anyone. But there was nothing funny about his fierce determination to take everything life had to offer – by force if need be, and at the expense of everyone else he came into contact with.

She considered her second husband for a few minutes. Perhaps you wouldn't call him short. He was compact, true enough, but many of his constituent parts seemed to belong to a much larger man. His nose, eyes, feet, and mouth were far too large for his body.

He had outsized balls, too, both literally and figuratively. He was afraid of nothing. He had enough courage in his stocky frame for a dozen military men.

And then there were his hands. Craggy and knobby, with thick fingers and prominent metacarpals radiating from his wrists like the rays of a rising sun. His skin was dark and freckled and so thick (again, both literally and figuratively) it made you think of a pachyderm. Nothing bothered him, ever.

There is a popular belief that for a visual artist it is all about the eyes – the vision, the power of observation. But her second husband perceived the world through his hands. He also thought with his hands. When he painted, drew, or sculpted – which he did constantly, every waking moment – his fingers did all the observing, all the probing of the world around him and all the creating. That was why, perhaps, his work had such striking immediacy.

He didn't fall in love with her until his hands had. The path to his heart lay through his fingers.

And when their marriage ended, it was his hands that fell out of love with her first. She could tell exactly when it happened, by the way his fingers touched her, how they lost interest in her, became bored with her shoulders and breasts, poked around inside her incuriously, as if he had on the rubber gloves of a gynecologist.

Two short men don't make one tall one. Another paradox was that she was married to both these short men at the same time. Not knowingly, no. She had been certain that her first husband was dead when she married her second. But he was actually off doing the only thing he knew how to do, making war. In the Foreign Legion.

A greater paradox was that she was *still* married to both men. She and her second husband had been split for a long time, but they were still officially married. She had no intention of giving him a divorce. *Parbleu*, while courting her he had made so much noise about his deeply ingrained Iberian Catholicism and devotion to the family. It was only fair that she made him stick to his principles. There were certainly other women waiting in the wings, hoping to assume his world-famous name (something she had never done, incidentally), but let them wait. He had so much vitality, she was sure he'd outlive her. As to his libido, it would outlive even him.

As for her first husband, she was surely his widow now. Most definitely. There was simply no way he was still alive.

She hadn't thought about him in years, but now, as her Aeroflot TU-104 jetliner sliced through the cloud cover and began its descent into a blinding whiteness below, into a landscape punctuated by copses of bare-limbed trees, steel pylons of high voltage power lines and a handful of half-buried peasant huts spewing white smoke from their chimneys, she wondered whether his bones were buried somewhere in this enormous expanse of a country, beneath the ten feet of snow that seemed to stretch for thousands of kilometers to the east, in some unmarked grave beyond the Urals.

Her plane touched down on the icy tarmac and maneuvered to the side of the terminal. The flight attendant instructed other passengers, Russians and Frenchmen alike, to remain seated until Olga was off the plane. A dozen or so men huddled at the foot of the stairway, waiting for her – all with nondescript, well-fed faces, in identical grey overcoats. Their apparent leader was tall and slightly stooped. He was the only one not wearing a fur hat, letting the airflow from the turbines ruffle his receding grey pompadour. He stood apart from the welcoming committee, between two plump women in parodic Russian dress. Their faces were generously rouged and frozen in fake smiles; each held aloft an embroidered hand towel, one with a loaf of bread, the other a dish of salt.

As she came down, the hatless man bowed, made a big production out of kissing her hand, and declared, "On behalf of the Government of the Soviet Union, the Central Committee of the Communist Party of the Soviet Union, and the entire Russian people, allow me to extend our wholehearted welcome on your return to your native soil, Olga Stepanovna. Here, on the soil of your beloved Motherland, the land of your forefathers, Mother Russia, we greet you in a hallowed tradition of Russian hospitality with bread and salt, the symbols of our open hearts. Welcome home, Comrade Khokhlova. It's been too long."

The man's hand was surprisingly small, flaccid and damp – the hand of a duplicitous person. Not a hand with a direct connection to the man's heart. A blind hand – so unlike Pablo's.

Perhaps she had been thinking of her second husband too much. She should be focusing on the long ago and far away – and, for that, thinking of her first husband was more appropriate.

"*Qui est-il, ce cornichon?*" she asked softly of the Russian embassy employee who had made the flight from Paris with her. He had been assigned to her as her escort – as if she needed one. Apparently, his job entailed asking her every ten minutes whether she wanted a cocktail and, once she declined, ordering one for himself.

Every time he had a highball, he would remove the swizzle stick and slip it into his jacket pocket. He must have quite a collection by now.

"Hush," the man said quickly, turning pale. "This is Comrade Yuri Vladimirovich Andropov. He's just been appointed the chief of the Committee for State Security."

He stopped and spelled it out in an ominous whisper: "The K-G-B."

# TWO

"What do you think of our magnificent capital?" Andropov asked, half-turning in her direction from the front seat.

She had been asking herself this question since they turned off the rutted service road of Vnukovo International Airport and onto a busy highway, heading northeast in the central lane reserved for government limousines such as theirs. After about a twenty-minute ride, they reached a thicket of unadorned concrete high-rises, many still under construction. As they plunged deeper into the city, the broad avenue began to be lined with pompous apartment buildings with over-the-top decorations. They looked sort of like Bavarian Rococo but were rendered, if possible, yet more ludicrous by the fact that some architectural genius had replaced their angels and nymphs with workers and peasants holding hammers and sickles and hoisting overflowing baskets of fruit.

A procession of black limousines containing the other members of her welcoming committee kept pace with them, forming an impressive motorcade.

"It's changed," she replied after giving it some thought.

"Oh, it certainly has. And for the better, of course. This gorgeous street is named after General Kutuzov. You are, of course, still a Russian patriot, even though you have been living in the land of Napoleon."

He gave her a condescending smile to let her know that it was a joke.

Next, he pointed to a construction site in the middle of the avenue.

"Here we're building a Triumphal Arch to honor Russia's victory. It will rival the one in Paris – and it will have a stronger claim, too, since we actually defeated Napoleon. Over there, across the street, is the panoramic exposition of the Battle of Borodino. As you can see, we have great respect for Russia's glorious past, even as we're building its bright communist future."

Two minutes later, he indicated a tall building on the embankment. The genius architect had been at work there too, cross-breeding a New York skyscraper with a Protestant church.

"Lily Brik lives in this building. You know, she's Vladimir Mayakovsky's widow. We would love you to meet her. To bring together the brilliant widows of two of the century's artistic geniuses."

"My husband isn't dead yet," Olga said coldly. "At least not to my knowledge."

She was getting annoyed by the man's ceaseless prattle. Besides, she'd met the Brik woman. She was Louis Aragon's sister-in-law.

"Oh, yes, of course, I know that," Andropov said, unexpectedly flustered and blushing as though she had caught him in a lie. "Comrade Picasso is a great friend of the Soviet Union. In any event, it's a beautiful building with a panoramic view. The front part is the Hotel Ukraine."

"Is this where I'm going to stay?" she asked.

She loathed tall buildings and detested panoramic views.

"Oh, no. This hotel is reserved for Soviet citizens. For you, we have a different place, one reserved for tourists from capitalist countries. It's called the Metropole. It's more central and very beautiful. Art Nouveau, mosaics by Vrubel and others. Perhaps you remember it from the old days."

They were now entering the central part of the city, one she was more familiar with, and she wished he would be quiet. She wanted to take in the streets in silence, concentrating on her thoughts and waiting for her memory to stir in recognition.

What a fascinating place – and how different from the Moscow of her youth. In those days, Moscow had been an upstart – full of energy, dynamic, hip, modern. It had changed from a sleepy backwater into a boomtown almost overnight, and continued changing rapidly, along with the rest of the country, up until the accursed Great War. In its rapid growth it had become more democratic and almost European. Everyone from the great empire had flocked there – workers, merchants, artists, and writers.

Moscow had always been connected to Russia. Even the modernist apartment buildings that arose after the turn of the century in imitation of Vienna and Berlin hadn't made it any less Russian. St. Petersburg, on the other hand, had always been brilliantly, beautifully, hopelessly foreign. Cold and remote, it was an alien civilization on the empire's edge.

Now, as she looked out of the car window, she was seeing a very different Moscow. The city that looked back at her was both too busy with mundane tasks and too concerned with the opinion of others. Like the KGB chief in the front seat, it was too eager to impress.

And yet, beneath this strange new skin the same old city remained. She was like an old friend – or perhaps an aging, distant cousin – trying to play a part for which she was poorly suited. You want to scold her, to tell her to take off the shabby five-and-dime tinsel hat and imitation imperial purple dress, to wash off the face paint and to stop embarrassing herself. And, above all, to stop fussing.

And something else, too. It made her think of her first husband again. She had a sudden flash of riding with him on these streets, past mounds of snow carefully gathered along the curb. It had been the winter before the war, and, running into one another by accident in Moscow, they had had no way of knowing that six years later they would run into each other once again, in a different place and under different circumstances, and would get married. He was a school friend of her older brother, and he gave her a thrilling ride in his father's new English motorcar. She was just seventeen and very naive.

He got into a lot of trouble with his father for that, he later confessed, but it was worth it.

Suddenly, she recognized the Bolshoi on her left and her heart skipped a beat. The Bolshoi had been a part of her as far back as she could remember. Then, on her right, she noticed a monument to a man with a wild mane of hair that was completely covered with snow and ice. All you could see was a carved figure sinking into a hunk of roughly hewn granite.

Intending to please her host, she complimented the monument. What a great idea, she observed, to show Beethoven struggling against the silence that was slowly enveloping him and still being determined to write his music, as implied by a fist that he was forcefully bringing down upon the monolith. And a great location, too, smack across the square from the Bolshoi. A wonderful homage, even though he never wrote operas or ballets.

"Beethoven?" the KGB man repeated in surprise. "Where do you see Beethoven? That's Karl Marx."

Oh, well, she thought. It must be the snow covering the statue's beard that caused her confusion. But then who would expect to see Karl Marx facing the Bolshoi? The man had a tin ear for music.

# THREE

The driver hit the brakes, throwing me forward against a stocky, middle-aged woman. The woman wore a pair of felt boots and had a long grey headscarf tied across her chest. The thick padding of her winter coat absorbed the impact of my fall, and, even though she wasn't holding on to the handrail, her short, sturdy body didn't budge. The bottles in my shopping bag clicked loudly against each other.

"What have you got in there, young man?" she asked suspiciously. "I'll bet it's vodka."

"Are you kidding, grandma? It's far too early in the day to be drinking. It's a bunch of milk bottles for my baby."

"Oh, that's a good one."

Everyone on the bus burst out laughing.

"Driver, why the hell have you stopped in the middle of the street?" a man sitting in front demanded to know. "I waited in the cold for your goddamn bus for half an hour, and I'll have you know I've just recovered from a bout of the flu."

He was a middle-level office clerk wearing a soft, wide-brimmed fedora instead of a fur hat with earflaps tied on top like the rest of the nation's men. His preference for a fedora suggested that he thought of himself as a non-conformist.

"We all had to wait for half an hour, or even longer," said the woman to whom I had given up my seat at the previous stop. "You're the only one complaining here, citizen. Don't you see a traffic cop is holding us up? There must be an important reason for the delay."

"That's right, no one is complaining," a voice piped in reproachfully from the back of the bus. "Everyone else is waiting patiently, except for one person."

The other passengers were in agreement.

"He must think he's better than the rest of us."

The non-conformist bit his tongue. It's never a good idea to go against public opinion in Russia.

It soon became clear why traffic had been stopped. A cortège of four black Volga limousines with miniature red flags fluttering on their hoods had made an illegal left turn across four lanes of oncoming traffic into the driveway of the Metropole Hotel. A traffic cop had left his booth at the corner near the Maly Theater and was standing in the middle of the road with his striped baton raised, freezing us in place. An unusual number of bellboys and doormen were rushing out to open the car doors. Several men emerged, all wearing identical grey overcoats and fur hats. The coats, along with their black limousines, revealed their status as high government or party officials, but they acted like little kids, running to form a kind of receiving line from the front car to the entrance of the hotel. Once they were lined up, another man jumped out of the car and hastened to open the back door. He looked youthful and energetic, despite his grey hair.

The passengers on the bus were glued to the windows. The stocky woman next to me bent down, leaning over the top of a seated passenger to get a better view.

"Who do you think they're greeting?" the woman in my old seat asked, addressing no one in particular.

"Comrade Brezhnev, who else?" said my stocky neighbor.

"I'm sure it must be him," another passenger agreed.

"Brezhnev for sure."

"I put my money on Comrade Kosygin," opined the non-conformist.

The other passengers ignored him.

"Kosygin comes here much more often," he added. "It's a hotel for foreigners, German businessmen stay here, and he comes to personally welcome them. He's very democratic."

If he was trying to curry favor with the others, he was wasting his time. No one paid him the slightest attention.

We were all doomed to be disappointed. For all the pomp and circumstance, the person who finally emerged from the back seat of the limousine was neither Brezhnev nor Kosygin. It wasn't even a man. A tall woman – old, but well put together and still attractive, albeit a little too skinny for my taste – stepped out of the car. She was dressed in a red half-length coat and a scandalously short skirt. Her hair was dark – or perhaps dyed – and closely cropped, and she wore no hat despite the cold. Her earrings sparkled emerald green as they caught the rays of the low winter sun.

Clearly a foreigner.

She marched to the front door, where she paused for a moment while three or four bellhops tripped over one another rushing to open it. The receiving line moved forward, forming a perfect semicircle around her. For a moment, the group was like some strange flower set against the snow – a blood-red center in a corollary of black petals.

Everyone on the bus was angry and disappointed. It was one thing if we had stopped for Comrade Brezhnev's cortege, or, worst case, Comrade Kosygin's. But not for some foreign bird.

"When the hell are we going to get going?" my stocky neighbor inquired, her voice turning nasty.

I too felt let down. I was hoping to see someone I could tell Tosya about. A foreign lady, no matter how tall or elegant, could not compete with the sighting of Brezhnev or Kosygin.

Thinking of Tosya reminded me of the milk bottles in my shopping bag and what I considered an unfinished conversation with the stocky woman. When all the excitement started, I had been about to demonstrate a milk bottle as proof that she had maligned me in front of the entire bus.

Besides, I was exceptionally proud of myself. Having risen at six in the morning, I had taken this very same bus all the way across the river, to Pyatnitskaya Street, and then stood in line at the infant nursery for two and a half hours in order to refill eight milk bottles. Everyone behind me started to complain about the number of bottles I was getting refilled, and kept asking sarcastically whether we had quintuplets. I was forced to explain then that we only had one son, little Nikola, but that he was eating if not five times the normal quantity, then certainly at least twice as much, and that my wife was running out of milk to feed him. That got them started, and for the next hour they were telling me what Tosya needed to do to increase lactation, prescribing all sorts of folk remedies and silly solutions. I made a detailed list of their recommendations in order to keep them happy, and tossed it in the garbage pail once I got the bottles refilled.

Still, talking with the strangers had increased my pride as the father of a boy who was eating so much. We had named him Nikola in honor of my father, who had been killed two weeks before the war ended.

But what I told those mothers at the baby nursery was a fib. Not the eating part and not the lactation part, either, but the part about Tosya being my wife. She wasn't yet. She was headstrong and kept refusing to marry me.

Why? I had no idea.

But at least she agreed that we should move in together, exchanging our two rooms in two separate communal apartments in the same building for two rooms in the same communal apartment somewhere else. Tosya spent the late stages of her pregnancy scouring the weekly lists of residential properties, but with no luck. Everything she found was either too small or too far from the center. Or the two rooms on offer were in huge communal apartments in old buildings, full of bedbugs and quarrelsome neighbors.

In the end, it required a little help from someone in the business. Eduard was a black market wheeler-dealer specializing in real estate, one of those shady characters who operated out of dark stairwells and back alleys who could help you find an apartment rental or get an advantageous exchange of your property for an appropriate fee.

I had once helped Eduard get rid of a nasty character who had been extorting and blackmailing him. Eduard was now only too happy to repay the favor. He promptly found us a place that was almost too good to be true, two rooms in an apartment on Chernyshevsky. Not only was it centrally located, but it was only a fifteen-minute walk from our old building on Kirov Street.

"You always get us involved in some illegal deal, Pavel, even though you're supposed to be a cop," Tosya protested. "Don't you see that this is unfair? Thousands of people who don't have your connections to the underworld are doomed to live in awful apartments."

Having grown up in an orphanage, Tosya had a finely developed sense of justice.

"We're not going to help them much if we too ended up living in an awful apartment," I said.

Despite her objections, Tosya liked our new place. I too was pleased. We were sharing it with only one neighbor, a guy my age, with whom I was sure I would be able to get along. But the happiest of all was Tosya's son Sevka. He got his own room and no longer had to share living quarters with his mother. True, his room was small and more like a glorified hallway that offered a passage to ours, depriving him of any real privacy. And he would have exclusive rights to that room only temporarily, as long as we kept Nikola's crib alongside our bed. Once his brother got older, Sevka would have to share. But that was some time in the distant future. For now, Sevka had his own room, which Tosya allowed him to decorate as he pleased, with a poster of his favorite Torpedo soccer players and a reproduction of a painting showing the defense of Sevastopol, clipped from the *Ogonyok* illustrated weekly.

Sevka was also happy because he didn't have to change schools. He had an easy commute by tram, and he could even walk the three stops if he wanted to save the three kopek fare and was willing to get up twenty minutes earlier.

# FOUR

"You have a busy schedule the next few weeks, Olga Stepanovna," the collector of swizzle sticks from the Paris Embassy said. "You need to rest."

Busy was an understatement. Merely looking at the list of activities and meetings typed out on the sheet of paper he handed her was making her head spin. And she realized that the grey-haired KGB chief had expressed an interest in escorting her to almost all of them. That was supposedly a great honor, judging from the Embassy man's tone. In addition, she was going to have two people attached to her, a man and a woman, whose singular job it was to make sure that she lacked for nothing during her stay in Moscow.

The KGB man had departed, but had left her in the care of one Igor Ivanovich, whom she was informed would be in charge of her security at the hotel.

Igor Ivanovich clicked his heels and stood at attention. He was a bear of a man, and his broad Cossack face could have been handsome, had it not been for the black patch over his left eye and the scar that ran like an open wound from temple to chin. She found it hard to keep her eyes off the repulsive purple line that sliced through the man's upper and lower lips and came to a point at the center of his chin. It looked like a rough-edged exclamation point drawn across his face, a road sign warning of imminent danger. She wondered where he had gotten it and under what circumstances.

She would have to try to remember their names. The one with the scar was Igor Ivanovich, while his boss, who was going to escort her to all the cultural events and meetings, was Yuri Vladimirovich. Having lived in France for so many years, she had lost the knack of remembering long Russian names and patronymics. She practiced saying them when she was finally alone in her suite, making sure they rolled off her tongue easily, "Igor Vladimirovich. Yuri Ivanovich. No, the other way around, damn it."

She probably wasn't supposed to know that Yuri Vladimirovich was the head of the KGB. He had introduced himself as a Candidate Member of the Politburo. Did that mean he was running for the Politburo? Did they have elections? It was all fairly enigmatic.

Back in Paris, she had been told that she was going to be a guest of the Soviet Ministry of Culture and that her host would be someone with a long name and patronymic and a title that sounded something like Deputy Minister for Cultural Heritage. Apparently, she was part of that heritage. She had met the deputy minister while he was on a trip to Paris and had had a brief talk with him. He was also a bore, but at least he wasn't KGB.

After the first day, the Paris Embassy man who had flown with her to Moscow never showed his face again. He faded into the ether without so much as a goodbye. Presumably, he had to return to his diplomatic duties in Paris, whatever they might be. He was more amusing, despite his excessive fondness for highballs and swizzle sticks. She could have pumped him for more information about Yuri Vladimirovich and Igor Ivanovich.

Had she finally gotten their names right?

"Igor Ivanovich. Yuri Vladimirovich."

Candidate Member of the Politburo Yuri Vladimirovich called on her the first night to take her to the Bolshoi. *Swan Lake*, of course. What else?

Tchaikovsky's music always struck her as kind of easy. But the ballet somehow succeeded – you couldn't help being moved by it. Except, sitting in the Emperor's Box she couldn't rid herself of the sensation that she had seen it all before, lots of times. Not from the Emperor's Box, of course. That was a new and unexpected experience. But everything else was familiar to the extreme: the gold, the sparkling crystal, the red velvet, the nine muses dancing on the ceiling with apple-cheeked Apollo and, above all, the staging and the dancing. It all was – how best to express it? – a bit moth-eaten. As though the past ninety or so years hadn't happened. As though there had never been Sergei Pavlovich and his Ballets Russes. Her Ballets Russes.

She had always known that her visit to the Soviet Union would be a journey into the past, but the time machine had transported her a bit too far. *Swan Lake* had its first performance at the Bolshoi back when Tsar Alexander II ruled Russia. It was a few years before his assassination, and perhaps he too watched it from the Emperor's Box, occupying the same chair that she was sitting in. Or did they have to bring the throne in for the occasion? Stalin used to watch performances from the Emperor's Box, too. Did Stalin like *Swan Lake*?

*Swan Lake* had been frozen in time like a fly inside a chunk of amber.

Still, it was a joy to see. The Great Hall of the Conservatory and the Barshai Chamber Orchestra were a treat, too, and so was the new Tchaikovsky Hall on Mayakovsky Square. Meetings with cultural figures, on the other hand, were torture. They wore terrible clothes and had bad teeth and body odor, even though she didn't give a damn about that. No, the worst of it was their smarminess. Male cultural figures kept trying to kiss her hand, grabbing it in their moist palms and holding onto it far too long.

She couldn't understand why Pablo actually liked these people. Pablo could be deadly sarcastic when he wanted to be. He could laugh at people with his hands, and he could ridicule their foibles like no one else. His wicked sense of humor was concentrated in his fingers and his art was always on target. His sarcasm knew no pity. But as a person he could be simple-minded and vain. He could be dead earnest about small things, strange things. He had been very proud to have been awarded the Stalin Peace Prize in 1950, and then a second one a couple of years ago, when it was renamed the Lenin Peace Prize, because in the meantime Stalin had turned out to be a bloody two-bit dictator and not the greatest man who ever lived.

Pablo was a tangle of contradictions, and his own hands would have savaged their owner if he had ever let them. But then again, isn't every great artist a tangle of contradictions? She was one herself, come to think of it.

Pablo always took these officials seriously and had even joined the Communist Party at the end of the war, along with his friends Aragon, Elouard, Sartre and other pompous French intellectuals. It had always been a mystery to her how he could stand them. *Comme bien des intellectuels, ils sont d'une extrême stupidité.*

Be that as it may, every cultural figure she met in Moscow reminded her how Pablo was a "great friend" of the Soviet Union. They were especially eloquent on this subject in Yuri Vladimirovich's presence. It was the way they looked at him – that mixture of outward sycophancy and desire to please, with a fear and loathing they tried desperately to hide. After every such meeting she had a strong desire to take a hot bath, to wash herself clean of the sticky, slavish filth.

At least her first husband had had no illusions about the Bolsheviks. He had had his share of illusions, too, about people, but not about the Bolsheviks.

Yuri Vladimirovich took her to the Pushkin Museum of Fine Art. It was another paradox in that city of paradoxes. Why was it named after a poet? Pushkin was not an art collector, like Jacquemart-Andre or Frick. Sure, he doodled in the margins of his manuscripts and some of his impromptu pen drawings and self-portraits were excellent, but he was not an artist. He was a quintessentially Russian poet, and not particularly well known or loved abroad. He didn't translate well into other languages. Why name a museum after him that contained a collection of Western art?

She remembered when the museum had been opened to the public. She was a young woman then, still in her teens. It was a big deal back then, an art museum in Russia's second capital. It was called the Alexander III Museum – which also didn't make much sense.

Perhaps Russia was a giant paradox even then, she thought.

The ground floor contained plaster replicas of famous statues. Michelangelo's *David* made the KGB chief blush and turn away. The man's prudishness amused her, and she stopped in front of the statue, inspecting every detail closely.

"Let's go see your husband's works," he urged. "We have wonderful examples of his earlier periods. I've always been an admirer. But not of the blue period. His blue period is too depressing. No hope at all. All those ladies of the night, none of them beautiful, all of them debauched and ill with venereal disease. It's disgusting and not our kind of art. We're optimists, enthusiasts, our people are brimming with hope for the future. We're building a new kind of society in which everyone will be happy. We're different from people in capitalist countries, and I hope you have had a chance to see that. I like your husband's Minotaurs better than his Harlequins. They project so much vigor."

Maybe he was deliberately taking revenge on her for making him stand under *David*'s genitals, but his mention of Pablo's Minotaurs was not especially tactful. Pablo had begun painting them when his love for her faded, and their vigor was a reflection of the passionate sex he was having with a teenager.

"And I don't much care for your husband's more recent paintings," Yuri Vladimirovich added. "They are too abstract. We like traditional art in this country. This is what the working man understands best. What they call 'modern art' in the West is nothing but self-indulgence."

The worst disaster was seeing Lilly Brik. They had met before, in Paris, where everyone had also been eager to bring together "two great Russian beauties," and had never hit it off.

It was no different in Moscow. Being put down by an old witch, and watching her fondle a young lover on a sofa, wasn't Olga's idea of a pleasant dinner party. It was all she could do to keep herself from saying something like, "Well, yes, darling, I did share my bed with a major artist of the twentieth century. And yes, I'm so sorry you had to make do with Mayakovsky. Yes, I remember him from before the revolution, a big lug with an oversized inferiority complex. Who knows why he has become such a big deal here? Maybe because Gumilev was executed, Mandelshtam died in the camps, Tsvetaeva hung herself, and Bunin went into exile? Anyway, he is a complete unknown outside the Soviet Union. But calm down. My Pablo left me for another woman, whereas your Vladimir blew his brains out on your account. You win."

She should have had the courage to say it. Her first husband would have been proud of her. He hated the Bolsheviks, their "great proletarian poets" and their poets' lovers.

Everywhere she went in Moscow she couldn't help feeling his presence. They had only spent a couple of hours together in this city, but as she moved around Moscow, driven about mainly in Yuri Vladimirovich's black limousine, she felt as if Alexei Zolotnitsky was slipping in and out of her grasp.

If he was somewhere here – it was madness to think that he was, but even if by some miracle he were alive and living in the Soviet Union, or even here in Moscow – he would not have been able to visit her at the Metropole. The only Soviets allowed in were hotel staff and a couple of very good-looking young ladies she would see in the elevator on her way to breakfast, their clothes rumpled and looking out-of-place in the morning, their pale faces and lifeless eyes bearing testimony of the sordidness of sex for money.

And of course the ubiquitous Igor Ivanovich, who was in charge of her security and who came and went as he pleased.

She amused herself by thinking of Alexei Zolotnitsky trying to come to her suite unnoticed. He'd have to pass through many layers of security. There were doormen manning the front door and an old man operating the elevator, as well as a number of interchangeable concierges in black dresses and white aprons. One of them sat behind a small desk on her floor around the clock.

Her suite was on the third floor. Most rooms in the back, past the elevator, were occupied, but none of her neighboring, more luxurious suites. Apparently, they had been reserved for some VIP delegation that failed to show up. She would have felt a little lonely in her part of the third floor had it not been for all the security personnel protecting her from God knows what danger.

The rest of the hotel was quite full. At breakfast, she met an Italian trade union delegation of noisy men who all spoke at the same time, complaining about the quality of the coffee, and a very quiet, middle-aged couple from English-speaking Canada – he, professor of Russian history at Kingston. There were also some Turkish and South American businessmen, Japanese tourists, and a few Indians and Arabs. The Arabs were humorless men in suits, with thin moustaches and an unmistakable military bearing.

The most exotic group by far were a trio of Cubans – two men and a young woman. The men had bushy beards, and that was the only way they differed from their female companion. All three wore khaki fatigues and berets and seemed to have walked off the cover of *Life Magazine* from the late 1950s. All three smoked cigars at breakfast. Unlike the Italians, they didn't complain about the coffee – but they did frown stoically when they had to drink it.

The rest were various Eastern European types – Hungarians, East Germans and Poles. The East and the West, *pace* Kipling, met at breakfast but showed their divisions in their attitude to sausages, which were the only food served to them day after day after day. The Easterners wolfed theirs down, whereas the Westerners preferred to keep their distance from them, the Italians being particularly vociferous in their disgust.

The atmosphere at the Metropole reminded her of a luxury hotel she once stayed at in Berlin in early 1939 – similar, hard-to-place characters from murky countries without an obvious reason for being there. Except in Berlin there had been a palpable sense of dread. At the Metropole, everyone soon struck up a silent friendship born of solidarity in the face of privation, and winked at each other across the heavily starched expanse of tablecloth when the sausages were once again brought out.

Someone said that everything in history occurs twice – once as tragedy and next time as farce. Who was it? Oh yes, it was Karl Marx, whose monument outside the hotel she had mistaken for Beethoven's.

That trip to Berlin had been the last time she had seen Alexei. They made love in Berlin, for the first time after Crimea. He was tender and loving and happy making love to her, but he was in a terrible mood. He was mad at himself for his stupid illusions about Hitler. She urged him to come to Paris with her. He dithered, and soon it was too late. In September, Hitler struck a deal with Stalin and they divvied up Poland. Another European war was begun.

There she was, thinking about Alexei again.

She asked Yuri Vladimirovich about the tight security at the hotel.

"Oh, that," he gave an airy reply. "It's not really that tight. It's just to keep our foreign guests safe."

"I see," she giggled. "You're quoting a French fairy tale to me. It's called *Little Red Riding Hood*."

"Why do you say that?" he asked apprehensively. He seemed to be offended by her light-hearted tone.

"You know, 'Why do you have such big ears, Grandma?' 'It's to keep our foreign guests safe.'"

"I see nothing funny about it," he said. "All these people are working to protect you."

"But didn't you tell me that crime doesn't exist in Moscow? That it only survives where there is private property, and that Soviet workers and peasants have no need to steal from each other?"

"Well, that is the theory. That is what Marx and Lenin wrote and, objectively, it's absolutely true. Under communism there won't be any crime at all. But we haven't yet built communism. We're working on it. And while we're working on it, some capitalist vices have become exacerbated. This is also true because Marx and Lenin wrote about it. This is why we must provide tight protection for our foreign guests. Not only because it is the first commandment of hospitality, but also because if something happens to one of our foreign guests, Western propaganda will try to use it against us. We must not allow that to happen."

"I see," she said. "But what about the concierge on my floor who's there around the clock? Are you afraid that I may be visited by a lover?"

He definitely was a prude, this Candidate Member of the Politburo. He turned deep crimson at her mention of a lover. Did he consider sex another capitalist vice? Were they planning to put an end to it, too, once they built their communism?

She had an uncomfortable feeling that Yuri Vladimirovich had a crush on her. It was a ridiculous idea, she realized, because she was almost twice his age. Or was he trying to recruit her instead? Was it entrapment, the way she had heard intelligence services operated? She wouldn't be a valuable asset for them, would she? A former Diaghilev ballerina and the estranged wife of a major contemporary artist? But, then again, there is no knowing what spooks want. It's all just a game. We spy on you, and you spy on us.

It's too bad they didn't all look more like Sean Connery. Actually, they couldn't have looked any *less* like Sean Connery than they did.

If Yuri Vladimirovich did have a crush on her, she felt sorry for him. It was very unlikely she was going to reciprocate, to fall for him. He had told her that he wrote poetry. She had to work hard to suppress a smile. A KGB man writing poetry. Moderately funny, but mostly pathetic.

# FIVE

Little Nikola slept through the night when they had lived in Tosya's old room, but he seemed to have left the ability behind on Kirov Street. The move to new digs must have frightened him. He started to wake up at two in the morning and then take a long time to calm down.

"Is he teething?" I muttered on the fourth night as I pressed my face against the wall and pulled a pillow over my head. I had to be at work early, and Tosya tried to let me sleep, taking the baby into our other room to feed him and lull him back to sleep.

"Get serious, Pavel. He's barely two months old."

"When do they start teething? Is it not at two months?"

"Go back to sleep."

Nikola would wake up hungry and reach for Tosya, but her lack of milk made him frustrated. He would try to twist his tiny body out of her grip, arching his back, and screaming even more loudly.

"I'm going to take him to the kitchen," Tosya said. "You need to get some sleep."

She went out, with Nikola still testing the limits of his lungs, and I sank into a deep sleep. I was woken up almost immediately by Sevka, shaking my shoulder. He wore a pair of old pajama bottoms that were way too short on him. He'd had a growth spurt over the summer.

"Wake up, Uncle Pavel," he shouted into my ear. "Wake up."

I sat up in bed, rubbing my eyes and trying to get my bearings.

"What's the matter, Sevka? What do you want?"

"Just listen."

We fell silent, listening. A loud, ugly exchange reached us through the open door. A male voice was shouting profanities in our communal kitchen, and Tosya was answering, giving as good as she got. It sounded like two dogs barking, one in a lower register and the other in a higher, while Nikola was doing his best to provide the orchestration by screaming his little head off.

I jumped out of bed. Like Sevka, I only wore my pajama bottoms. Squabbles in communal kitchens were part of life in the city, and it looked like we were not going to avoid having them in our new apartment.

Except this one was taking a nasty turn.

"You shut him up right now, woman," our neighbor Boris screamed as I rushed down the long corridor. "Or else I shut him up myself, your little red piece of shit."

"You lay a finger on him, and I'll rip your balls off," Tosya responded.

Tosya grew up in an orphanage, or, as it was called, a State School for Orphaned Children, and she could be pretty tough when provoked. And not just with her words. She had a nice pair of fists that she knew how to use.

Tosya was sitting on a wooden stool next to our kitchen table, rocking Nikola. It was having no effect. Boris was standing in front of them, hovering over the baby. His face was purple with rage, and a vein was pulsating on his forehead. I barely recognized the nice young guy I had chatted with just a few hours before. We had talked of having a drink some day when we weren't busy. Now, it seemed, he had gotten drunk on his own, without waiting for me. The kitchen reeked of liquor.

I stepped in between them and pushed Boris lightly in the chest.

"What's the problem, Boris?" I asked. "What's all this screaming about?"

When you deal with drunks it's best to stay calm and steady.

"Hello, Lieutenant."

Boris laughed as he eyed me. It wasn't a happy kind of laughter, more like a challenge he was throwing in my face, and I decided to focus on the challenge rather than on the fact that he knew my rank. I did not recall telling him what my job was, and it was not the kind of information you could readily obtain.

"I've been telling your woman to keep her spawn quiet and not disturb people in the building. Now that you're here, you can give her a hand shutting the little fucker up."

"Get out of the kitchen," I said. "Go to sleep. We'll talk in the morning."

Boris leered at me.

"Oh yeah? Maybe you can make me leave?"

When I was a kid growing upon the wrong side of the tracks, in a neighborhood full of other kids whose fathers didn't come home from the war, I used to fight almost every day. We fought each other almost as often and as ferociously as we fought our mortal enemies from the ball bearing plant dorms two streets over. I liked fighting back then, but as I grew up I had come to distrust physical violence. It is a distraction in any argument, and it doesn't prove anything. But in some cases it can't be avoided. Boris was out of control, and he had managed to get under my skin. Besides, I was jumpy and irritated from getting so little sleep for the past two weeks. I stepped up and took a swing at his drunken face.

It was a mistake.

Boris wasn't as drunk as he had led me to believe, and he was no pushover. He deflected my blow, catching my arm at the elbow and twisting it behind my back. Sharp pain flashed through my shoulder, blinding me for a second as the kitchen exploded red and white in my eyes. He kicked my feet from under me, sending another jolt of pain through my body. In three quick, precise motions he had turned me around and dropped me to my knees in front of Tosya. Still holding my arm behind my back and now pushing on it gently – and extremely painfully – he kept bending me down until my face was pressed against the cold linoleum.

He held me, gradually dialing up the pain until I started to thrash about on the floor. There was no way for me to slip his iron grip. I was helpless, unable to resist. I was also suffocating. After what seemed an eternity he let go of me, watching me as I gasped for air at his feet. All the while, Nikola went on screaming as loudly as before.

"What the hell are you doing?" Tosya shouted at Boris, finally regaining her ability to speak.

"First off, you scum," Boris said, ignoring her and addressing me. "I want you to know your place in this apartment. You may think you're a hot-shot detective, going around shooting State Security officers, but in reality you're nothing but a piece of shit. Do I make myself perfectly clear?"

I kept panting, now exaggerating my need for air. I needed time to think it over. I knew perfectly well what he was referring to. A year ago, while investigating a murder, I had shot and killed a KGB colonel. It had been a cut and dried case of self-defense, and the guy had been as corrupt as they got. The fact that Boris knew about that was disturbing. Clearly, the guy was KGB.

"You deaf or what?"

He gave me a kick. It was a gentle kick, more like a warning.

I said nothing. He kicked me a lot harder. He must have studied anatomy, either in a classroom or in the basement of Lubyanka prison, and he knew exactly where to place his kick to get to the kidneys. The pain was severe and sharp. I clenched my teeth and moaned.

"When I ask you a question, you give me an answer. You say 'Yes, sir' or 'No, sir,' depending on the context. Understood?"

"Yes, sir," I moaned in response.

I was pretending to be hurting, but only a little.

"That's better. What you need to understand is that I can beat the shit out of you any time I want. This is my apartment, and you are second-class citizens here. Now, the first thing I want you to do is shut this little bastard up. I don't care how you do it, that's your problem.

You can strangle him if you want, I don't care, but he's going to be quiet this minute."

Tosya tried to say something, but Boris interrupted her.

"And your woman too. She's got a dirty mouth. It doesn't look good on a pretty young thing. Are you going to shut her up?"

He pulled back his foot ready to kick me again.

"I didn't hear an answer. Are you going to tell her to shut up, or do I have to do it myself?"

"Yes, sir," I said.

I was trying to organize my thoughts. Boris was KGB, and he had looked up my file, including the old Polishchuk case. I had always known that killing a KGB colonel would come back to haunt me sooner or later, but I could never have guessed that it would come in this form, in my own kitchen and in front of Tosya and my baby. Boris had also been trained in hand-to-hand combat. That was important to know. When you fought a man like that, you needed to use everything you could lay your hands on against him. And you had to watch out. He could kill you with his bare hands, with a single blow.

"Did you hear what this bastard said, Pavel?" Tosya asked.

"Yes, woman, he heard me. I told him to keep you quiet. You only talk to me when you're spoken to. And if you give me any more of your lip, I'll stick your words back into your dirty mouth. I don't give a damn if you're a member of the weaker sex."

He turned to me.

"Will you keep her quiet yourself, or should I do it for you?"

"Yes, sir," I said. "I'll do it myself, sir."

"What did you say, you bastard?" Tosya screamed at me.

Her voice was full of hurt, disbelief, and anger. She had never seen me so humiliated, and she hadn't thought it possible. The thing was, if it had been her in my place, she would have died rather than reply "yes" to Boris. And she expected nothing less of me.

"Go ahead," Boris said. "Do it now."

"Do what?" I asked.

"Tell her to shut up and never talk to me until I address her. "

I said nothing, and Boris kicked me again. This time I didn't have to exaggerate how much it hurt.

"Yes, Tosya," I said once the pain receded. "You'll have to be polite to Boris and not speak to him unless he has spoken to you first," I said, looking up at Tosya from the floor. "And now you'll have to stand up and apologize to him."

"Good man," Boris grinned at me.

"What?"

Tosya still couldn't believe her ears.

"Get up," I bellowed at her.

It was a measure of her shock that she actually obeyed, getting up from the tall wooden stool. This allowed me to grab it by one leg and swing it in a wide arc at Boris's knees. It was a vicious blow, and he had no time to react. He dropped as though his feet had been cut off from under him – which wasn't far from what had happened.

There was silence in the kitchen, and even little Nikola had stopped crying. Sevka, who had followed me to the kitchen and had witnessed the scene, was the first to recover. He inhaled noisily and declared, "I'll be damned, Uncle Pavel."

Boris was lucky. Or maybe that's how they were made, the KGB men. After all, Felix Dzerzhinsky, the founder of the political police, used to be known as Iron Felix. Maybe they were all like that, indestructible.

We eventually got him off the floor and sat him down. Tosya staunched the bleeding and washed the long gash on his face where he had cut himself on the edge of the stove while falling, having been thrown across the kitchen by the force of the blow.

All during the improvised medical procedure, he continued cursing and threatening me. Actually, all four of us, including Sevka and Nikola.

"You have no idea who you're fucking with. You don't know the trouble you're in."

"First off, we'll need to see if you ever walk again," Tosya observed sagely.

"Fuck, woman, watch what you're doing," he cried out, wincing as Tosya daubed iodine onto his cheek.

Nikola was no longer crying. He was staring wide-eyed at the bleeding man with an orange face, sitting on the very stool with which he had been felled. Tosya patted Nikola on his back, afraid that he would start screaming again at any moment, telling Sevka to go back to his room. She didn't like him hanging around the kitchen, listening to the avalanche of highly inventive profanities Boris was hurling at us.

"Take the baby back to our room," she told him at last. "And stay there with him. Make sure he doesn't start crying."

# SIX

Nikola began howling with redoubled energy the moment Sevka took him back to our room, demanding to be taken back to the kitchen. Once there, he calmed down right away and resumed watching with morbid fascination our efforts to patch up Boris.

It was then that the telephone began ringing. Tosya and I shuddered involuntarily, not expecting a call at such a late hour.

"It's for me," said Boris.

"You can't get it," I said.

I went over and picked up the receiver.

"It's for me I tell you," Boris yelled after me, gnashing his teeth.

"Matyushkin," the Boss's familiar voice came over the line. "Get over to the office. On the double, lieutenant. You've got fifteen minutes."

I knew better than to ask him stupid questions, such as what this was about or whether it couldn't wait until the morning. If he called – and if he was at the office at that hour – it was an emergency.

However, I was reluctant to leave Tosya – and little Nikola – alone with an enraged KGB officer. Those guys had all kinds of dirty tricks up their sleeve to lull you into a false sense of security.

"Are you going to be alright?" I asked Tosya.

"Don't worry about me. I could have handled him better than you, Matyushkin. Had I clocked him with a stool, we would have had to call an ambulance for him – if not a hearse."

"I would like to see you try, you fat whore," Boris growled.

His face was red and sweaty, but whether it was from pain or impotent rage, it was hard to tell.

"Behave yourself," I said to him before leaving.

Tosya went out into the hallway with me. I leaned close to her and warned her to be careful.

"He's dangerous," I said. "He can hurt you if you get too close to him."

"I know. I'll watch out. You be careful, too."

Ever since Nikola was born, she had been unusually concerned about my safety.

I had to hail a cab to get to the office. Public transportation had been shut down for the night and didn't reopen until five-thirty in the morning.

I could have arrived within five minutes after his call, and the Boss would have still found reason to give me hell. That was his management style, to keep us on our toes. But not this time – even though it took me twenty minutes just to find a cab on the deserted, snow-covered street, then travel the length of four boulevards along the Boulevard Ring. This time, the Boss greeted me with an ingratiating smile that clung uneasily to his gruff facial features.

"There he is, Senior Lieutenant Pavel Matyushkin," he said, introducing me to a tall, grey-haired man. The man, an official of some kind, wore a tie and a crisply starched white shirt, even though he looked tired, showing the puffy eyes of someone who had not been to bed all night. He looked vaguely familiar.

"One of my best operatives," the Boss went on. "As I told you, he gets results, even though for the life of me I have no idea how he does it."

The Boss was praising me, and even though his compliment was of a back-handed variety, it could only mean one thing: his nocturnal visitor was a very big boss and, moreover, a big boss from a competing law enforcement agency. Regardless of how he treated us behind closed doors, in front of his colleagues from other agencies, the Boss always maintained that his detectives were all top notch.

The visitor gave him a dismissive nod and a frown.

My Boss's real name was Ashot Modestovich Martirosyan and his rank was colonel. But no one ever referred to him as Colonel Martirosyan behind his back. Around Moscow Criminal Investigations he was known by his nickname, Budyonny – on account of his luxurious mustache, which resembled that of the legendary Red Cavalry commander Semyon Budyonny.

The real Budyonny was a Cossack, while our Budyonny was an Armenian. Russian wasn't his native language. He spoke it extremely well, except when he was angry, excited or, as was the case now, nervous. Then his speech became so accented as to be almost incomprehensible.

"Good morning, lieutenant," the Boss's visitor said, eying me through the lenses of his wire-rimmed glasses. Usually, thick lenses tended to make the wearer look soft and vulnerable, but not this man. His grey eyes were steely and unblinking. "Thank you for getting here so quickly at this hour. I appreciate that."

I saluted him.

This was a sharp contrast with Budyonny, who felt that thanking his subordinates or apologizing to them diminished his authority. It was a nice way to start a working relationship.

I was struggling to place the man. Was he one of those Politburo members whose portraits graced the facades of public buildings for the November 7 Anniversary of the Revolution and the May Day holiday? That would explain the Boss's nervousness and ingratiating smiles. But it was more than that. There was something familiar about his whole stooping figure.

"I need you to help me investigate a burglary," the man said. "I want you to come with me now. Except I want you to be properly dressed, in your police uniform, the way your partner is."

Only now, turning to look behind me, did I spot my partner Valera Tumakov, standing at attention at the back of Budyonny's office. He wore his police uniform, complete with a starched blue shirt and a clip-on tie. The senior lieutenant's small stars on his epaulets had been polished and sparkled brightly, reflecting the light of the Boss's overhead light fixture. He had been standing motionless – perhaps not even breathing – and the grey of his uniform had been camouflaged, chameleon-like, against metal filing cabinets.

"You'll be meeting a foreign woman, lieutenant," the visitor continued. "I don't want her to get wrong impressions of our police force."

"My uniform is at home, sir. I didn't expect—"

"No need to apologize, lieutenant. Your superior officer should have told you to wear it. My car is waiting downstairs. We'll take a detour to your place along the way."

"Damn it, Matyushkin," the Boss hissed as we filed out of his office. "Why is it that Tumakov knew enough to wear his uniform while you show up here dressed like a lousy civilian?"

"I'm sorry, sir," I said as I squeezed past him.

The Boss wasn't a mean person. He knew that it wasn't my fault. I'd gotten plenty of night calls from him in the past, and usually it had been a murder or some other crime that required our immediate attention. It meant a lot of work for the next 48 or 72 hours – dirty work without sleep. A police uniform was rarely required on such occasions and, on the contrary, was usually an impediment. As to how the hell my partner Valera had known to wear his, I had no idea. I could only say that he had a sixth sense when it came to anticipating what our bosses wanted of him – sometimes he even knew what the bosses wanted *before* they themselves had figured it out.

That was one reason Valera and my late partner, Lenny Urumov, never got along when they had worked together. They were both good detectives, but their personalities were just too different. Lenny was a rebel, while Valera had an almost unnatural respect for all manner of rules and regulations.

"So, you're the two best detectives at Moscow Criminal Investigations?" the man asked as we sped through empty streets back to my apartment. "Your boss seems to think the world of you."

I didn't rush to respond, detecting a note of irony in his question, but Valera quickly took the bait.

"Colonel Martirosyan is a top level professional and, as such, an excellent judge of character. Our entire team has been hand-picked by him."

"And you are the best?"

"Well, it wouldn't be modest to say that, and the other guys are all great," Valera said.

"Then how come both of you are only senior lieutenants?" the man asked. "Your boss doesn't put anyone forward for promotion?"

"Senior Lieutenant Tumakov would have made captain long ago," I said. "But at Moscow Criminal Investigations, we're wary of rank inflation, which I've heard is rampant in other services."

Valera, who was completely devoid of any sense of irony, smiled stupidly, but the man, riding on the front seat next to the driver, turned and gave me a sharp look. As was typical of big bosses, he enjoyed taking the mickey out of his subordinates, but didn't like it when he got a dose of his own medicine.

"I think I've just heard the reason why," he said sharply.

"Why is that, sir?" Valera asked.

"Because smartass officers get promoted last."

The man fell silent. I wasn't keen on continuing the conversation, either. During our short ride, I was wracking my brain, trying to figure out where the hell I had stowed my police uniform when we moved. I had stuffed it into either a box or a suitcase, and it should be somewhere at our new place, but there hadn't been any time to unpack, what with taking care of the baby, going to get milk and washing diapers, while also continuing to show up for work.

I also had a moment of panic in which I didn't remember actually packing it. What if I had left it in my old armoire, the one I had inherited from my aunt? Tosya had judged it too big and ugly for our new place, and so I sold it to the family moving into my room. If it was still hanging in my armoire, there was no way of avoiding a huge embarrassment in front of this sarcastic boss and a major dressing down by Budyonny.

These worries occupied my head completely, so that I had forgotten about Boris, my fight with him less than an hour before, and the fact that Tosya was there alone caring for his injuries. I was startled to be greeted by a lengthy tirade, which my temporarily incapacitated neighbor laced with choice obscenities and threats. He was still sitting in the kitchen, his face swollen and yellow from iodine. But at least he was no longer bleeding, and Tosya had transferred him to a more comfortable armchair.

Ignoring him, I riffled through all the stuff that was still in boxes and, by the time the doorbell rang insistently twenty minutes later, our rooms looked like a marauding army had just marched through.

"Yes, Valera, I know," I shouted as I went to answer the door. "You want to ask me what the hell is taking me so long."

There was no answer from the other side.

"You'll see in a moment that I'm not sitting in the kitchen making myself a cup of tea," I continued as I undid the lock. "I'm trying to figure out where the devil—"

I stopped short. The grey-haired man, the big boss, stood on the landing in front of me, stooping characteristically.

That left me speechless for a moment. All I could think of was that there's going to be hell to pay when Valera reported to Budyonny that the man had to go up to my apartment to tell me to get on with it.

"I'm sorry, sir," I mumbled. "We just had a baby. I mean, we have just moved in, and we had a baby. I mean first we had a baby. Anyway, I'm looking for my uniform. I don't know where I packed it."

"Congratulations, lieutenant. Children are the flowers of life. But we're on duty, and we're pressed for time. Do you think you'll be able to locate your uniform any time soon?"

"Yes, sir," I roared, snapping to attention. "I'm almost done looking through the boxes."

"Very well then. Hurry up. I'll wait here."

He stepped into the foyer and I ran to get him a chair.

Now not only Tosya but Sevka, too, who had been trying to stay asleep, joined the search. In the end, my uniform was found in the first place I should have looked – in Tosya's armoire. Sevka was the one who spotted it, and he was literally glowing with pride.

"Some detective you are," said the man, shaking his head. "Now put it on please. And do hurry up, won't you?"

He yawned, stood up, and started to pace the hallway. He looked around our apartment with a great deal of interest, as though he had never seen anything like it. He opened the door to the bathroom, looked inside, and then poked his nose into the kitchen. By then I had finished putting on my uniform and come out.

Boris's behavior managed to shock me for the second time in the course of one night.

He had been sitting in the armchair where we left him, having forgotten about him while searching for my uniform. Seeing the visitor, he stared at him for a few seconds with his mouth open, then jumped up and tried to stand at attention. His face convulsed, tears welled in his eyes, and his face blanched under the layer of iodine. He stood for a few seconds fighting bravely against the pain, but finally sank to the floor. Still, he managed to whisper hoarsely before passing out, "Good morning, sir, Comrade Andropov."

# SEVEN

Nights are dark in Moscow in late January, and mornings come late. The darkness drags on, reluctant to give way to thin, half-baked daylight. There was still no sign of light when we finally reached the Metropole Hotel. Some guests were already up. A window here and there shone bright yellow through the cracks in the heavy curtains, but the building loomed dark under the layer of snow and ice on its mansard roof and on top of its ornate bay windows.

We had done the last leg of our trip, from my new apartment to the hotel, in just a few minutes, speeding through the empty city. I was wondering about being in the car of the head of the KGB and what it meant for the burglary we would be investigating.

As to Andropov, he had given curt instructions to the driver once we got back into the car and then sank deep into thought, drawing on his cigarette and blowing the smoke out the crack in the car window. I lit up one of my own non-filtered Primas, and Valera gave me a sidelong glance. He no doubt thought it was the height of impertinence to smoke in a boss's car without being invited to do so. Especially since Andropov was smoking some sweet-smelling foreign brand and had made a face when he caught a whiff of mine. Well, I was sorry to cause him discomfort, but after little Nikola was born, and our household expenses escalated, I had switched to a cheaper brand and even started to think about quitting.

The moment the car turned into the driveway on the side of the Metropole, slithering across the sparse early morning traffic, I remembered where I had seen Andropov. I had been on the bus a few days ago when he was taking an older woman into this hotel. I also remembered being disappointed that it had been some unknown foreign woman and not a member of the government who had emerged from Andropov's car. Still, if the KGB chief was giving her a ride, she had to be an important character. I now wondered whether it was she who had been robbed.

If so, the question was why the KGB, which took pride in its ability to know everything about every last one of us, ordinary Soviet citizens, needed assistance from our underfunded and undermanned agency, and why it thought that a pair of underpaid and overworked Criminal Investigations detectives would do better than a bunch of its own agents. The KGB had all the resources it needed to investigate any crime.

Its formidable resources and plentiful manpower were on display as we drove up to the entrance. Across the street, two figures were silhouetted against the brightly lit Karl Marx monument. They were the same height and dressed identically, and from the distance could have been taken for twins. Andropov gave them a quick hand signal as he got out of the car, and two fur hats inclined in synchronized acknowledgement.

There are several hard currency hotels in the city, along with special apartment buildings for high-level government officials and Communist Party *nomenklatura*, as well as their dachas. There are also apartment buildings for Western journalists and diplomats. The KGB keeps watch over all of these. And the same pantomime is repeated every time an officer drops by to inspect any of these important surveillance posts.

At the Metropole, the twins lurking next to the Karl Marx monument were only the tip of the iceberg. As Valera and I got out of

Andropov's Volga and headed for the entrance, our way was blocked by a mountain of a man in a doorman's uniform, complete with a gold-braided peaked cap and gold piping running down the sides of his trousers. Two rows of freshly polished brass buttons gleamed on the front of his coat, and the thick wool fabric was stretched across his pectorals to the point of tearing.

"Your papers, citizens," he barked. "Only hotel guests permitted."

"Open your eyes, Mustafa," Andropov said wearily. "Can't you see they're with me?"

Mustafa's eyes were narrow and mean, and were almost hidden by a pair of fat cheeks. But they were wide open, regarding us ominously from their owner's great height.

"I'm sorry, boss. I've got my instructions. I'm to ask everyone I don't know for their papers. You told me so yourself, boss, 'No exceptions.' Especially after what happened last night."

If it had been Budyonny in Andropov's place, there would have been plenty of yelling and screaming – not to mention name-calling. But the KGB chief remained calm and icily polite. He produced his red card and showed it to the enormous Mustafa.

"I sure know who *you* are, boss," Mustafa said, laughing stupidly. "It's those two."

He pointed at us.

"Aren't you shutting the stable door after the horse has been stolen, buddy?" I asked Mustafa.

The display of extra zeal on the part of the enormous doorman was fairly typical after a screw-up, and it suggested strongly that the KGB was no different from any other organization.

"You're trying the man's patience with your smart aleck comments," Valera said to me in a theatrical whisper, which he fully intended for Andropov to hear.

Andropov grinned.

"That's the problem of dealing with morons," he said not worrying that Mustafa could hear him. "They can't think. I hope you two are different."

A clean-cut young man at reception jumped to his feet and stood at attention as we passed. The elevator had the hours of operation posted on the door of the cabin, and it hadn't yet started running. We took the stairs to the third floor and walked down a long, dimly lit hallway, making right angle turns.

The place was quiet and expensive-looking, with oil paintings of the Kremlin, the Bolshoi, the Convent of the New Virgin and other Moscow cityscapes hanging on the walls, and potted plants placed every few steps. The hallway smelled of sleep and shoe polish. Moscow winters were tough on people's shoes, especially on quality leather footwear, and guests had set them out to be shined overnight. As we walked, Valera stumbled over a gleaming leather boot, kicking it down the hall. Apologizing to God knows who, he replaced it on its doormat.

A man wearing the uniform of a KGB major sat at the concierge desk. A middle-aged woman in a dark dress with a broad lace collar and a white apron stood in front of him. They didn't hear our approaching footsteps on the thick-napped runners.

"You might as well confess," the major was saying. "You were fast asleep. You can't trick me."

The woman was short, and her round, wrinkled face, which looked a bit like a Shrovetide pancake, was almost level with the sitting major's. She batted her eyes stupidly as she looked at him, but she didn't sound at all timid as she responded, "Oy, Igor Ivanovich, don't you have any shame? What are you saying? You know I'm a good, conscientious employee. I didn't sleep a wink the entire night."

"Then you must have left your desk," the major insisted. "How else did they get in?"

"Of course I left my desk, Igor Ivanovich. More than once, too. I drink tea all night to stay awake, and the staff bathroom is on the second floor, all the way in the back. How else do you expect me to—"

She broke off. The major had finally seen us and jumped up. He tugged at his shirt and saluted Andropov, clicking his heels.

"Here we go, boss," he said as we passed. "Doing a bit of investigating."

His voice became meek and ingratiating as he was addressing Andropov – in sharp contrast with his ferocious appearance and bullying tone when speaking with the concierge. His appearance was indeed intimidating. He looked like a pirate or a villain from an illustrated edition of *Treasure Island*, thanks to a black patch over his left eye and a purple scar running the length of his face.

"At ease, Yershov," Andropov said coldly, dismissing the major with a wave of a hand.

The pirate remained standing and followed Andropov with his one eye. But the doglike devotion and adoration extinguished the moment his boss had passed. The concierge stared at the floor and stood with her hands linked over her apron, the way servants did in the presence of their maters in films about capitalist countries.

We turned another corner in the labyrinthine hotel, and Andropov stopped in front of the door of Suite 318. His knock was indeed answered by the same foreign woman I had seen the other day. She was fully dressed and made up despite the early hour. She stood ramrod straight in the threshold, eyeing our group angrily.

Up close, she was even taller than she had seemed from a distance – approximately the same height as Andropov and me and taller than Valera. She was also older than I had thought, but still very attractive. And, despite a completely foreign appearance, she spoke excellent Russian.

"Well, Yuri Vladimirovich," she said. "There go your famous security arrangements. As they used to say when I was little, it's the case of seven nannies watching over a one-eyed baby."

I chuckled inwardly, thinking of the one-eyed pirate interrogating the concierge around the corner.

She was polite, but beneath her sarcasm was an unmistakable anger. Her Russian was precise and a little old-fashioned, her words clipped. She took great care to enunciate every syllable. That and a cotton-wool "r" that she pronounced in the French way made her sound haughty.

"I don't understand how it could have happened," Andropov said, spreading his arms wide. "It's an outrage. I'm sure it's a provocation meant to smear the reputation of the Soviet Union in the eyes of our foreign guest."

The all-powerful KGB chief was definitely on the defensive. I wouldn't go so far as to say that he was afraid of the woman, but he certainly had a lot of respect for her. After all, it was for her sake that he had had us put on our full police uniforms.

"Please, Yuri Vladimirovich, let's not overdramatize it. It's an ordinary hotel theft, the kind that happens every day in every country of the world."

"Not here, Madame. Not in the Soviet Union. Not on my watch. But rest assured, the perpetrators of this vile crime will be caught and punished to the full extent of the law. Your property will be returned to you – you have my word it."

"I don't care a hoot about a couple of trinkets. Had I known you'd make such a big deal about it, I wouldn't have bothered to report the burglary. And I certainly do not want you to pack some poor wretch off to Siberia for twenty-five years."

"We don't give out such long sentences any more, Madame," Andropov retorted tersely. "Our justice system is just but humane. Please, Madame, may we come in?"

As we filed into Suite 318, it came to me where I had heard the lady's accent. A few years ago, in the course of an investigation I had come across a very old woman. We had a long chat, and at the end I asked her about her strange accent.

She laughed.

"It's you who have a strange accent, young man. This is the way we used to speak when I was young. At least some people did. They were called nobility. Hardly any of us around any longer. There was a time you could get shot in the street just for having this kind of accent. And many were, believe me."

She turned her head, put an arthritic forefinger to the side of her head as though it were the barrel of a gun and pulled an imaginary trigger: Bang!

And now the occupant of Suite 318 turned out to have the same kind of accent.

Once we were in and the door was closed behind us, Andropov did the introductions.

"These two comrades are police detectives," he said, nudging Valera and me forward. "They are the best men Moscow Criminal Investigations has to offer. Comrades, please meet Olga Stepanovna. Olga Stepanovna is a compatriot of ours, but for one reason or another, she's been living in Paris, far away from her native land. Olga Stepanovna will fill you in on what happened."

Olga Stepanovna inclined her head and actually curtsied.

"Very pleased to meet you, Messieurs," she said.

I couldn't vouch for Valera, but I was certain that no one had ever addressed me as *Monsieur*.

Suite 318 consisted of a living room with a small study on the side and a windowless alcove that served as a bedroom and was large enough to contain a double bed, two night tables, and a dresser. The suite was filled with large, bulky old-fashioned furniture, most of it original, dating back to the time the hotel was built and much of it scratched and scuffed. A mirror in a massive gold frame hung on one wall, reflecting a painting in a matching frame on the wall directly opposite, showing an early spring landscape somewhere in central Russia, complete with crocuses popping up around melting piles of snow. Somewhat incongruously, a grand piano sat ponderously by the window, looking a bit like a beached whale. A tall floor lamp, still burning despite a gradually brightening morning outside, hovered over the music stand and a vase filled with live carnations. The study was almost entirely taken up by a desk and an armchair. A pewter inkstand was positioned in the middle of the polished redwood surface of the desk, next to a stack of Metropole Hotel stationary and envelopes. The only other object on the desk was a silver jewelry box, its lid thrown open and its red velvet inside emptied out.

The suite overlooked Karl Marx Avenue, which had come to life in the quarter of an hour since we had arrived at the hotel.

"Well, there isn't much to tell," Olga Stepanovna said with a deep sigh as Valera and I got the lay of the land. "At approximately two o'clock in the morning, a man came into my room and took my jewelry. As I said, it's not a very exciting tale."

At last, Valera and I heard why we had been dragged out of bed in the middle of the night, and it was far from a life-and-death situation. It sounded like the sort of ordinary burglary that happened every day and on account of which local police precincts did not bother to call in Criminal Investigations. The only thing that made it different was that it had happened in the fancy Metropole Hotel, and the victim was someone KGB chief Yuri Andropov knew personally. And a foreigner to boot.

But that brought me back to the question as to why he wasn't relying on his own men to find the perpetrator.

Valera, meanwhile, threw himself into the questioning of the victim, producing a notebook with a stiff cardboard cover on which he had already printed in meticulous block letters:

Case No__

Metropole Hotel

He began bombarding the woman with the usual array of questions to which she responded with a crooked smile on her face, meant to make him understand that she had little faith in his investigation. She also made several snide comments that were way over Valera's head.

"Where were you when the burglary took place?" Valera inquired.

"Why, I was in my bed, of course. Where else would a woman my age be found at two o'clock in the morning?"

"Do you know how the intruder got in?"

"Of course I do. Through the front door. He had a key."

"Or else he was handy with a jimmy?" Andropov suggested.

I opened the door and stepped out into the hallway to examine the lock. Valera and Andropov joined me. There were no scratches.

"The chain had not been thrown?" Valera asked once we returned.

"Of course not. I generally don't fear burglars, and I'm too old to be of any interest to a rapist." Andropov blushed, and she giggled, very pleased with herself. "Besides, this place is crawling with security personnel. I was sure I had a better chance of being arrested than robbed."

Andropov said nothing, but it was clear that he didn't find her frequent references to his security arrangements, arrests and Siberia particularly amusing.

"How do you know that the intruder came in through the door?" I asked. "You said you were asleep."

"Young man, I said I was in bed. As to whether or not I was asleep, I can't really tell. I'm such a light sleeper I often can't tell whether I'm asleep or awake. You'll know what I mean when you get to be my age."

"Did you hear him come in?" Valera asked.

She stumbled.

"Not exactly. He must have been very quiet. I became aware that someone was in the living room when I saw a light flash across the ceiling. I don't know how long he had been there."

Valera took a step toward the alcove.

"There is no door here," he said. "Just those draperies?"

"Yes, as you can see."

"And they were open last night."

"Yes, of course. I have no one to hide from."

"So you did see the intruder?"

"Not really. Or not very well. It was fairly dark in the living room, and he had a flashlight in his hand which made it difficult to see him."

"But you're sure it was a man?"

She hesitated, thinking it over.

"Well," she said. "I assumed that a burglar would be a man, but now I'm not so sure."

"Do you mind if I take a look into your bedroom?" I asked.

She shrugged.

"You're from the police. One can never have secrets from the police. You're like gynecologists."

She cast a quick glance at Andropov to see whether he would blush again. He obliged.

I walked into the alcove. Both lamps were on. All the lampshades in the suite were identical, dripping with lace. I wondered whether they were a fire hazard.

"Was your bedroom completely dark?" I asked. "I mean do you have a night light?"

"I don't like night lights. I like to keep my bedrooms dark. It makes me sleep better. When I do manage to sleep."

"And your valuables were where?" Valera resumed his questioning, his pencil suspended in mid-air and ready to take notes. "Over there in the study in your jewelry box?"

She nodded.

"Isn't that a strange place to keep your jewelry?" Valera asked.

She shrugged. "Not particularly. I don't use the desk much. I put my jewelry box there so that it didn't get in my way."

"Who else knew where you kept your jewelry box?"

"The cleaning staff did, naturally. And Yuri Vladimirovich."

"What do you mean?" Andropov asked, turning crimson. "Are you implying that I come into your room when you're not there?"

"Not at all," she giggled. "And I'm not saying that the KGB chief has tipped off the burglar. It's just that you have so many people working for you here, I'm sure you have found out everything about me, including where I keep my jewelry box."

Andropov said nothing and stared straight ahead, his jaw set.

"Other than that, nobody," she said, turning serious once more. "I'm not in the habit of letting strangers into my hotel rooms."

"Did you see the intruder go into the study?"

"I didn't. I only saw the light in the living room, that's all. I told you I didn't get a good look at him."

Now Andropov, who had been standing behind Valera, interrupted the questioning.

"I'll leave you to it for a moment," he said. "I'll be out in the hallway if you need me."

Valera became visibly relaxed with Andropov out of the room. The voice was suddenly less strained, and his next question was much sharper.

"Why didn't you raise the alarm?"

"Naturally, the thought crossed my mind. There is a concierge desk in the hallway and it's always manned, but I couldn't be sure she'd hear me screaming. And in any case by the time she got here he would've strangled me three times over."

"So you thought it was a man?" I asked.

She eyed me.

"Are you trying to catch me in a lie, monsieur? I told you that I had *assumed* it was a man."

"Did he come into your bedroom at all?" Valera asked.

"God no. I would have died of fright if he had."

I was sure she would not die of fright under any circumstances, but I said nothing.

"So, you waited until the intruder left before alerting the staff?" Valera asked.

"Yes," she replied after a moment's hesitation. "But not immediately. I must have been in a state of shock. I continued to lie in bed for ten or fifteen minutes. Maybe a little longer."

"Did he leave by the door?"

"I assume so. He couldn't have climbed out the window."

"But you didn't see him leave?"

"I can't see the door from my bed."

"I assume the intruder didn't relock the door?" I asked.

She stared.

"Of course not. Why would he?"

"Did he spend a long time looking around the living room?" Valera asked, having given me a reproachful look for butting into his interrogation.

The thing about Valera was that he always did everything by the book. Even though his questions seemed random, they followed an order prescribed by our interrogation manual, designed on the one hand to jog the crime victim's memory, and on the other to make sure the victim was not trying to hide something. But it was one thing to ask the right questions and quite another to spot inconsistencies in a testimony. In this particular case, I thought there were, in fact, a few inconsistencies that needed to be explored.

"I couldn't tell. I told you already that I don't know how long he had been here before I became aware of his presence."

"So he didn't go directly to the study?"

She shook her head.

Valera asked a few more questions and got some fairly bland answers.

"Is there anything else you can tell us about the intruder?" I asked when he was done.

"Like what? I told you several times that I didn't get to see him."

"Like whether he was wearing gloves."

"I don't know. I'm not sure. I have no idea."

"Was he wearing a mask?" I asked.

"Come on, Pavel," Valera said. "You're being unreasonable. She didn't see the intruder."

The foreign woman gave him a smile. She was practically old enough to be Valera's grandmother – but she had a charming smile that made you feel like you were a knight errant. I could see he had all but melted.

"Was your jewelry valuable?" Valera asked.

"Yes, certainly. Some of it. Actually, most of it. Some unique pieces. Impossible to replace. Some made by my husband. My former husband that is."

It was her turn to blush.

"Actually, we're still officially married, but we don't see much of each other," she concluded.

"So if your pieces were unique, they are not going to be easy to fence?" I asked.

She shrugged.

"I have no idea. This is not the side of the jewelry business I'm very familiar with."

"Did you have any other valuables, aside from the ones that were stolen?"

Olga looked at me. Her reply came after a long pause and was quite halting.

"No, I don't think so. I kept everything I had in my jewelry box and I'm not in the habit of pinning diamond brooches on my nightgown. Why do you ask?"

"Well, I would have thought that the intruder, whether it was a man or a woman, not being familiar with what jewelry you had and where you kept it, would have naturally assumed that it was in the bedroom, on your night table. And even after finding a small jewelry box in the study, he or she still would have thought there might be more on your night table."

"But he didn't come into my bedroom," she exclaimed. "Why would I lie to you?"

"I don't know," I shrugged. "You tell me."

"Come off it, Pavel." Valera was developing a taste for coming to her rescue. "The lady has told you that the intruder did not come into her bedroom. That should be enough."

I actually didn't mind Valera taking her side. Without planning to, we were doing a good cop-bad cop routine. It felt more natural when unrehearsed.

"Are you sure you are not missing anything else?" Valera asked. "Your papers, your passport, your wallet?"

"Nothing," she said.

"Money? Clothes? Did you check all your belongings?"

She nodded.

Valera insisted on taking a more thorough look around the suite and inspecting the windows. The window frames had been glued shut for winter. He produced a magnifying glass and examined the desk for fingerprints. When he returned, he pulled out his notebook once again and started to make a list of stolen pieces, insisting on a thorough description and even attempting to make a little drawing of each bauble.

While he was at it, I came up with another question. Unlike Valera, I didn't have a system and asked my questions based on my intuition, in the order in which they popped into my head.

"Do you wear a lot of jewelry when you go out?"

She smiled.

"Do I look like I do? Jewelry is a garnish on a woman, not the main course."

I too was starting to like it when she smiled at me. Was I falling under her spell?

"Could you do me a favor, monsieur," she asked me after describing another one of her jewels to Valera and commending him on the accuracy of his drawings, "Could you go out and get Yuri Vladimirovich?."

I went out. The hallway was empty, but I heard the sound of two voices, the louder and angrier of the two belonging to Comrade Andropov. I rounded the corner and walked onto an ugly scene.

The concierge was gone. The scar-faced major, whose name I recalled was Yershov, stood at attention in front of his boss. The KGB chief's face was beet red, and his hair, once so carefully combed, was dark with perspiration and stuck to his furrowed forehead. The top button of his shirt had come undone, and his tie was riding half-mast under his trembling chin. "So you want me to think she imagined everything?" Andropov inquired, his voice dripping with anger.

"No, sir," the major barked in response. "A capitalist trick, sir. Hid her baubles and accused us of stealing them. To make an international incident. To defame the Soviet Union."

"Oh, shut up."

"But sir, it's obvious—" the major started to object.

Before he had a chance to finish, Andropov took a quick furious step towards him and slapped his face. The sound was as loud as a gunshot, reverberating up and down the empty hallway. It was a powerful blow, making his head jerk sideways The man absorbed it without blinking his one eye.

"Don't you ever try to make a fool out of me," Andropov hissed.

He stood glaring at the major and then turned on his heels, almost as though he had felt my eyes on his back.

"What do you want, lieutenant?"

"The foreign lady asked to see you, sir," I said.

"Dismissed," Andropov commanded to Yershov, who saluted him, adjusted the eye-patch, which had gotten slightly dislodged, spun around and goose-stepped down the hallway.

It took Andropov only a few seconds to take hold of himself. He tightened the knot of his tie and passed his hand through his hair, wiping a few drops of perspiration off his forehead in the same motion.

"This is why I called on you, lieutenant," he said as we walked back to Suite 318. "I can't rely on these men. Olga Stepanovna has a point. I have seven nannies to watch over her, and all of them are one-eyed."

He grinned at his own joke, but it was a bitter grin.

"They're a bunch of incompetents," he continued. "Obviously they screwed up and missed a man breaking into Olga Stepanovna's room. I can't have this happening. This is a high-priority site, protected by what is supposed to be my best-trained agents. And all this idiot can suggest is that Olga Stepanovna invented the robbery."

He stopped in front of Suite 318 and added softly before going in, "All they know how to do is to beat confessions out of prisoners. Don't get me wrong, lieutenant, it's a useful skill, but it's not enough in this day and age. And I don't want them to scare our guest. I want her to like everything she sees in the Soviet Union, to fall in love with her mother country. Imagine if she decides to come and live here permanently. It would be a huge propaganda coup."

"If you say so, sir. I don't know who she is."

"Are you kidding me? She's Olga Khokhlova, the wife of Pablo Picasso. I suppose you have heard of him."

"Yes, sir, he's an artist," I said, but I wasn't sure about that.

Inside, Valera was finishing with his list of stolen jewelry.

"Yes, Olga Stepanovna," Andropov said. "Did you want to see me?"

She hesitated, then shook her head.

"No. It's not important. I'm sorry to have taken you away from whatever you were doing."

But there was a worry lurking in the corners of her eyes. I had a strong feeling she wasn't telling us the whole truth. She was hiding something, and that something was bothering her.

# EIGHT

The pale winter day had finally gotten started. The light brought into focus the room's dusty furniture and the deep wrinkles on Olga Stepanovna's face, making both the room and its occupant look old and tired. She reached out and turned off the lamp by the grand piano.

"Anything else, messieurs?" she asked.

There wasn't much else. We had gotten all the answers she was going to give us, and we were finished there for the time being.

"I know you've been shaken up, Olga Stepanovna," Andropov said before leaving. "You should try to calm your nerves and get some rest. I'll be back to pick you up at five in the afternoon."

"What do we have tonight?" she asked in a weary voice.

"Olga Stepanovna, you have the schedule. We'll start with a supper at the All-Soviet Economic Exhibition, at the Collective Farm Culture Pavilion with—"

She rolled her eyes. "Oh, no. More cultural figures? Now from collective farms?"

"I'm afraid it can't be avoided. Our cultural figures are so eager to meet you. You're an inspiration to them."

She sneered. "I suppose I'm an inspiration to them because I slept with Picasso. Do they want to try that too? They might succeed, you know, but only if they're young and good-looking."

"Please, Olga Stepanovna. Such words do not become you. Comrade Picasso is a giant of modern art and a great friend of the Soviet Union. And you're part of our cultural heritage as well. Ballets Russes, Marc Chagall, you. You're our national treasure. That's why our artists, poets, theater directors, and other citizens active in the artistic field are so interested in you."

"Well, they've got a strange way of showing their interest. They never ask me anything about either Ballets Russes or Pablo. All they seem to be interested in is how much various consumer goods cost in Paris. As if I pay any attention to such things. Or else they keep telling me how happy they are living and working in the Soviet Union – as if I have ever questioned that."

Andropov was instantly uncomfortable with the turn the conversation had taken – even more so than when she had mentioned sleeping with Picasso.

"Be that as it may," he said tersely, "we'll have to be at the Maly Theater by seven. It's just across the street from here, as you know. We're going to see *Tsar Boris* by Tolstoy. You will like that."

"Oh, yes, I will," she exclaimed, clapping her hands.

In her enthusiasm, she looked like a little girl.

"I want to see every production at the Maly. They're doing more Tolstoy and Ostrovsky and two plays by Pushkin. Damn the cultural figures, this is what I want to do every night until I leave."

"I'm afraid it's not possible, Olga Stepanovna. We have our schedule and we need to stick to it."

Once we climbed into the back seat of his Volga, Andropov turned to us.

"I want you two to start working on this case right away. It has to be a priority. I want this burglary solved."

"Yes, sir, Comrade Andropov, we'll get to it right away," Valera responded readily. "We'll—"

"Let me finish, lieutenant," Andropov said, cutting off my partner's effusions. "You have got to understand that this is a sensitive assignment. Just because Khokhlova speaks Russian doesn't mean she's any less of a foreigner. In fact, because she speaks Russian we have to be even more careful with her. I don't want you to bother her. I don't want you to talk to her at all without me being present. Understand?"

Valera nodded his vigorous assent and wanted to say something but restrained himself.

"That's one thing," Andropov went on. "The other is I want to be informed about every detail of this case. Whatever you dig up, get it to me first. Not to any other member of my staff – not here at the Metropole and not even at the headquarters. I'm a new broom at the agency, and I plan to do a lot of sweeping. There's plenty of deadwood here. It's not the Committee for State Security our nation needs. They became demoralized when Josef Vissarionovich died and the party came down on us with a lot of criticism. So there need to be personnel changes, and if you do a good job—"

He let the sentence hang before adding, "Here is how you can get in touch with me. It's strictly for your use and only for emergencies."

He scribbled a telephone number in a small notebook bound in soft brown leather, tore out a page, and passed it to Valera.

The car looped around the statue of Felix Dzerzhinsky, founder of the secret police, standing thin and upright like a stela in the middle of the vast square at the end of Karl Marx Avenue, and headed for the back of the KGB building, to the driveway reserved for official vehicles. I wondered what Valera had made of Andropov's hint that, if we solved the burglary at the Metropole quickly, he might recruit us into the KGB. At least that was how I understood him. It was not a prospect I relished. Especially since there would not be an easy way to refuse such a job offer.

The driver stopped the Volga in front of a closed gate. It was solid steel, covering the entire width and height of the arch and leaving no cracks though which to peer into the courtyard. The gate was guarded by two Internal Ministry soldiers armed with Kalashnikovs, one of whom ran to open the gate at the sight of Andropov's vehicle.

"Wait till they get out, Ivan," Comrade Andropov said to his driver.

"I was wondering, sir—" I began.

"Yes, lieutenant?"

Andropov turned around once more.

"When can we question hotel personnel, sir?"

"Never. I'll talk to them myself, and I'll let you know if anything pertinent comes up."

"And what about other hotel guests? Is someone going to question them?"

"They are foreigners."

I nodded.

"I see. How about information about past robberies at the Metropole? It may be pertinent."

"It is not, lieutenant."

"Yes, we understand," Valera said quickly. "It's classified."

I didn't like it.

"It will be a hard case to investigate," I said. "We'll be fighting with one hand tied behind our backs."

Andropov glared at me.

"You won't need any of this information, lieutenant. Hotel personnel have been thoroughly vetted by the KGB. And I can assure you that it is highly unlikely that another hotel guest broke into Khokhlova's room. Not because I think that there can be no criminals among foreigners, but their luggage is always thoroughly searched at customs when they leave. They know they won't get away with smuggling anything out. In any case, your job is not to poke around the hotel, but to look for the stolen jewels. They are expensive, and they are unique. They will be fenced by a professional. I assume you have good contacts in such circles – informers, moles, what have you. Find the loot, and it'll lead you to the burglar. Stay out of the hotel, stay out of Khokhlova's way, and keep me informed of every step you take. Good day, comrades."

Valera had opened the door while Andropov was lecturing me, and was halfway out of the car as though he were trying to run away.

"Yes, and one other thing," Andropov added. "You must keep this whole business confidential. Not even your family members should know what it is about. I don't want rumors to spread that foreigners are being robbed at hard currency hotels."

I couldn't resist it. "So there have been other robberies at the Metropole?

"Goodbye, lieutenant," Andropov said coldly as Valera stepped on my toe. "Just keep in mind what I told you. That's all."

I was glad Andropov hadn't offered to drive us back to the office. I wanted to stop at home and change out of my uniform. More importantly, I had been nervous about leaving Tosya and the boys alone with Boris, and wanted to check on them.

As I neared home, my heart ached. I should have locked him up in his room before leaving, I thought.

Naturally, I had expected Boris to go on heaping insults and threats on Tosya in my absence. What I found when I got back took me completely by surprise.

"It's strange," Tosya whispered when she met me at the front door. "He's changed his tune completely. He's like a different man. The moment you were gone, he turned all polite and respectful. He even admitted that he had been in the wrong and said he wanted to apologize to you personally. I nearly fell over when I heard that. It's eerie, the change that has come over him. He's like a dream neighbor all of a sudden. Sevka helped him to his room, and he's sleeping now. "

Sevka was just leaving for school. He looked like he hadn't had enough sleep – none of us had – but he was cheerful and full of energy.

"It's the beating you gave him," he declared while putting on his winter coat and hat. "I've always said that physical violence works best on bullies. It's the same way at school."

"It's a great theory, Sevka, but you're dead wrong," I said. "Do you know who the guy was who came in while I was looking for my uniform?"

"Which guy? The old one who looked like a stuffed suit?"

"First of all, he's not that old," I said. "He just seems old to you because you're a kid, and everyone over thirty seems old at your age. As to calling him a stuffed suit, I'd watch my mouth if I were you.

Because that was Yuri Vladimirovich Andropov, the new chief of the KGB."

"Phew," Sevka whistled, expressing simultaneously his admiration and disbelief. "You're kidding me, Uncle Pavel."

"Not in the least."

I leaned back to enjoy the full effect my words had made on both of them. Sevka was clowning a little for effect. He stood as though transfixed, dropping his jaw halfway to the floor, exaggerated awe written all over his face. He remained like that until Tosya shook him by the shoulder and told him to hurry up and leave for school. But she was no less surprised.

"Are you serious?" she asked. "The head of the KGB was here in my kitchen?"

I nodded.

"Oh, my god. Why didn't you tell me that when he was here? At least I would have taken a better look at him. I've never seen anyone so important so close up. Imagine me, a girl from an orphanage standing next to a man like that. You should have warned me in advance that he was coming. I would have changed out of my old bathrobe. He must have thought of me as a slovenly hag."

"I doubt it," I said. "I'm sure you made a good impression."

"So you're working on something with the KGB, Uncle Pavel?" Sevka asked, resisting his mother's efforts to physically push him out the door. "It must be an important case involving spies and traitors. It has to be, what with the head of the KGB telling you to hurry up."

"It's you who's got to hurry up now," I told him.

"I bet it involves at least one murder," he said. "Am I right?"

"You're close," I said.

"Promise you tell me about it when it's over?"

"I will, certainly. And now please go already. You'll be late."

# NINE

Valera was waiting for me at Budyonny's office. He looked drained after a sleepless night, and the strain of being in the presence of a very big boss told on him, too. His uniform looked the worst for wear, hanging on his frame like a potato sack to which some prankster had attached a pair of epaulets for laughs.

Having caught the reflection of my own pale face in the bathroom mirror, I had to admit that I hadn't come out of our nocturnal visit to the Metropole in much better shape.

The Boss, by way of contrast, looked great. While we were making the acquaintance of Madame Khokhlova, he had had time to go home to take a nap and shave. The whole situation was getting him energized, too. He was tickled pink to have the mighty KGB call on us to help with an investigation. The KGB was at the apex of the Soviet law enforcement pyramid – except it was an inverted pyramid so that Andropov's agency had all the resources and manpower, and we, the lowly agency in charge of solving heinous crimes and keeping Soviet citizens safe, were at the bottom, barely making ends meet.

"You think you can do it, boys?" he kept asking us, rubbing his hands. "You think you can get to the bottom of it? Can we show those State Security hotshots what Moscow Criminal Investigations is capable of? Did I not pick the right pair of detectives for the task? Let me hear how you're going to go about it."

Valera and I expressed our respective views, and it quickly emerged that we were not at all on the same page. I was convinced it had been an inside job, while Valera thought otherwise. But even before we got to that point, we had had an argument about Khokhlova. In my opinion, she hadn't told us the whole truth.

"What makes you think so?" Valera asked.

"Didn't you see how she hesitated while answering your questions, Valera? She obviously didn't know whether she should tell you everything she knew."

"Give us an example, Matyushkin," the Boss said.

"Look, she claimed she hadn't seen the intruder. Sure, it was two o'clock in the morning and there was no light except for his flashlight. But the curtains were drawn, letting plenty of light trickle in. Karl Marx Avenue is always well-lit. She was looking into a better lit room from a dark alcove. How could she *not* see the intruder? How could she *not* be sure whether it was a man or a woman? How could she *not* notice whether he or she was wearing a mask?"

"Very easily," Valera objected. "She had been asleep, or at least dozing. She gives the impression of being cool and in control, but she's still only a woman. She was scared."

"That's right," the Boss said. "You never know, when it's women you're dealing with. Let's assume she's telling the truth. And now let's hear why you think it's an inside job, Matyushkin."

"Probably because he thinks that the Metropole is such a well-guarded place that no one can sneak in unobserved," Valera interjected before I could reply.

"Let him speak," said the Boss.

"It's the other way around," I said. "The more KGB agents there are, the less responsibility each feels for doing his job properly. The reason I think it's an inside job is timing. Why break into a hotel suite when the guest is certain to be in the room? Most likely because it's the only time your associate is on duty. That's why I want to see the files of everyone who was working last night."

"You can't see them," Valera objected. "You heard what Comrade Andropov said."

"Fine," I said. "But the point stands. Then, the key. The intruder might have picked the lock. However, the victim, who says she was awake or at most dozing lightly, didn't hear anything. This means that he got in quickly and fairly silently. Finally, where he found the jewels. It seems he knew exactly where she kept them, even though the study was not an obvious place. Normally, a burglar would have headed straight for the bedroom. But this one never went there."

I was looking at Valera but saying all this for the Boss's benefit. He was the arbiter in our professional discussions.

"So far so good," the Boss said.

"But it's nonsense," Valera protested heatedly. "The only person who would be suspected of being the thief's associate is the concierge. She'd be stupid to have a burglary take place on her watch. Do you think Comrade Andropov would have needed our help if he had thought it was an inside job? You heard him. The staff have been vetted, which means they are all KGB informers."

"Still, for a burglar to go into a hard currency hotel at night, when the guest is in her room, would be a huge risk," I said.

"Not if he's a pro," the Boss said. "It's just one of a whole range of risks he's running."

He was coming down on Valera's side, and my partner could not hide a triumphant smile.

"There is another possibility," Valera said. "What if he was looking for a special piece of jewelry? Something the woman always wore during the day and thus he had to wait for her to be in the room, in order to take it."

"A fair point," Budyonny said. "Why don't you ask her next time you talk to her, whether there was something she always wore."

"I can't," Valera replied. "Comrade Andropov doesn't want us to bother her. Besides, it doesn't really matter. We still have to look for all the stolen pieces, and that's what I'm proposing."

"Very well," Budyonny said.

"And I would like to talk to the KGB major," I said. "The one who was interrogating the concierge. I'm sure he questioned others on the hotel staff, as well."

"Comrade Andropov will not be pleased," Valera said.

"I don't give a damn," Budyonny said, glaring at Valera. "If he wants our help, he'll have to fall in with our methods. At least some of the time."

In other words, the Boss was giving me unstated permission to talk to the scarred Major Yershov, even though I had to approach him without Andropov's permission. His willingness to cross the KGB chief was a measure of his desire for us to solve the case.

For his part, Valera was planning to work the case the way Andropov had wanted us to. He would start that afternoon, despite being tired and irritable. He would make the rounds of jewelry stores, pawn shops and consignment outfits with his list of Khokhlova's baubles and his own drawings, and then go on to various known fences, jewelry thieves, collectors, informers, and other people inhabiting the city's seedy underside. Valera always did everything systematically.

I had my own private source in the trade. I wasn't crossing into Valera's territory – and yes, all of a sudden there was his territory and my territory in this investigation. All I wanted to do was to get a professional opinion – and to get a sense of how likely my partner was to succeed.

Once we were out of the Boss's office, I took the metro to the recently opened Kuntsevo station. Until it was incorporated into the city about five years ago, Kuntsevo had been a suburban town. And, for no apparent reason except for the fact that it was both close to Moscow and out of the direct gaze of the city authorities, it was where the best consignment shop in the country had once been. And the reason it had been the best was August Karlovich Nuremberger, the world's foremost expert on second-hand clothing, vintage jewelry, antiques, rare books, paintings, etchings and so on.

In the meantime, clouds had gathered, and a blizzard had begun. The Kuntsevo line was above ground, and as the train chugged out of the tunnel midway down Kutuzov Avenue, its windows instantly became swathed in melting slush. Streetlights went on despite the early hour, and the windows of nearby apartment buildings lit up against the winter gloom.

Nuremberger was brilliant. No matter how cleverly something had been made, he could tell a fake from the real thing by looking at, touching, and smelling the object. He knew the market and could tell you right away how much any object would fetch. He was also a legendary skinflint and a stick-in-the-mud. Once he gave you a price, he never added a single kopek on top. It was always take it or leave it. But it was always a fair price; there was never a reason to complain.

He also knew every collector in the city. If something valuable or rare was brought into his shop, it never made it into the store's display case. The authorities, who frowned on all manner of wheeling and dealing and, for that matter, on all private selling outside official state channels, had tried many times to put him behind bars, but he knew influential people who always got him off the hook. Rumor had it that he was as rich as Croesus, but in his retirement he lived modestly in a tidy two-room apartment overlooking a local park.

Perhaps not surprisingly for a man who had spent his life surrounded by all kinds of objects, his apartment was sparsely furnished and remarkably uncluttered.

Mindful of Andropov's gag order, I said nothing about the burglary and limited myself to the description of missing items, which I had copied from Valera's notebook. I had not copied his drawings.

Nuremberger pulled a wrinkled handkerchief from the pocket of a moth-eaten tweed jacket, wiped his thick lenses and blew his nose. He squinted nearsightedly out the window, which at that moment was nothing but a square white sheet concealing the park and the street below. Even the banister of his balcony had been nearly obliterated by the orgy of whiteness.

"What's the rush, young man?" he asked. "You couldn't have waited until the blizzard blew over?"

"I would like to get the answers quickly, August Karlovich," I said.

He batted his dark hooded eyelids, rubbed his eyes, and replaced the old-fashioned tortoiseshell frames on the bridge of his prominent nose.

"Picasso, eh?" he said after a long silence. "Lots of original jewelry by Picasso?"

"It would seem that way," I said evasively.

"The objects you are describing, young man, do not exist in the Soviet Union. I don't say they don't exist somewhere else in the world. All I'm saying is that they definitely don't exist in the Soviet Union. Whoever told you they have them was taking you for an idiot, if you pardon my expression. Or else they are dealing in fakes. Bring them to me, and I will tell you right away what they are."

"But if they do exist here and are not fake?" I insisted.

"Then they are extremely valuable. Even the ones that were not made by Picasso. Every single one is custom-made by a world famous jeweler. All unique works of art, artistic masterpieces. Whoever put together this collection, I congratulate him. They have exquisite taste. Not *nouveau riche*, if you know what I mean, but the real thing. I don't wish to pry, but I would be lying if I said all this did not intrigue me."

I ignored his last remark because I could not satisfy his curiosity.

"So it would be easy to find a customer for things like that?" I asked.

"I wouldn't think so. On the contrary. If you want to get anywhere near what such objects are worth, I would advise you to take it abroad. To Zurich, to London, to New York. I don't think there is anyone in this country who can afford to pay their real price. Maybe some underground millionaire could buy some of the cheaper individual items, and only if you gave him a discount on account of it being here in the Soviet Union and not in Zurich, London, or New York. But I don't believe this collection is here. I would have known about it."

"So you think that if someone were to steal those jewels, he would only be able to sell them off gradually?"

"If he's not a complete idiot, yes. Still, ultimately, there are only a limited number of people who can afford to buy things like that and who would appreciate them. The trick is to know who they are. You know, they are not listed in the telephone directory."

"And who does know those people?" I asked. "Someone like you?"

"Exactly. Someone like me."

I didn't mention my visit to August Karlovich to Valera. Let him go about his investigation his own way. Sometimes his sheer persistence and diligence paid off. Like the time several years ago when we were investigating a series of children's murders. It was one of the first cases I worked on with my late partner Lenny Urumov, and we hadn't hit it off. While the two of us argued over a bunch of clever theories, Valera kept his nose to the grindstone and systematically questioned everyone who could have had even a remote possibility of glimpsing the murderer. Eventually he stumbled upon a valuable witness, and that became the first tenuous thread that allowed us to untangle that case. Sometimes playing by the rules was the best way to go.

I had my own line of inquiry to pursue. I stalked Major Yershov outside the Metropole, taking care not to be spotted by three sets of Andropov's identical twins who, relieving each other at eight hour intervals, kept a round-the-clock watch over the front door of the hotel. The blizzard that persisted for another two days was my ally, forcing the gumshoes to shelter behind Karl Marx's pedestal.

When I finally waylaid the scarred major, he proved uncooperative. He might have been warned by Andropov not to speak to me, but he hardly needed such a warning. KGB officers were disdainful of us, ordinary cops, and, besides, I had been an accidental witness of the slap in the face he got from his boss. I was sure he hadn't forgotten it.

"If I knew anything about it, we wouldn't need your assistance, lieutenant," he declared.

"What about the concierge who was on duty that night?" I asked. "I take it you questioned her."

"I did," he said. "As you can imagine, the idea that she had something to do with the burglary crossed my mind as well. You're not the only one who's so smart."

He chuckled.

"What about the one who was on duty the day before? She could have let the burglar in on her watch, and he could have concealed himself somewhere and waited. This way the suspicion wouldn't fall on his associate."

The major grinned. "You *are* a smart one, are you? Soon enough you'll make everyone who works at the Metropole a suspect. What about the elevator man? Or the restaurant manager? Come to think of it, I could have done it, too."

He was making fun of me. Talking to him was a waste of my time.

But talking to the concierge would not be a waste of time, even though it took me another two days to figure out when she got off her night shift and what route she took home.

I waited for her in front of the Bolshoi, kitty-corner from the hotel. It was early and half-dark. The snowstorm had finally ended and the street sweepers were hard at work liquidating its aftermath. I positioned myself on a bench facing the Metropole, having first cleared the snow off the seat. Looking at the whitened façade of the Metropole, I spotted three lighted windows on the third floor. I wondered whether they were Number 318 and, if so, what Olga Khokhlova was doing up so early.

My wait was getting to be longer than I had expected. A steady stream of people crossing the park on their way to work – to the State Planning Agency around the corner and the Central Department Store on the opposite side – kept turning their heads to look at a man on a park bench, sitting alone and chain-smoking Primas. It sort of defeated my attempt to be inconspicuous.

Eventually I got too cold and took a brisk walk around the frozen fountain. Only the top spout was sticking out of the pile of snow dumped into the circular pool by street sweepers clearing the pathways.

It is one of those spots in Moscow that reminds you what an intensely beautiful city this is. Behind me was the portico of the Bolshoi, painted white and pale yellow and with a bronze chariot galloping out of the two converging pediments. Across the avenue was Revolution Square with another park, anchored by the Karl Marx monument. The monument was also completely swaddled in snow, as if it had been wrapped in cotton wool in preparation of a move. Behind it, a surviving section of the medieval Kitai Gorod wall was coming into view as the day dawned, and behind its crenelated battlements, as if soaring over the rooftops, two ornate bell towers caught the rays of the rising sun on their onion domes. Everything was soft and white and light blue, with a touch of red, green, and gold peeking tentatively out of the snow.

I had circled the fountain a dozen times, spent some time clearing another bench, and sat on it long enough to smoke another cigarette before the concierge finally appeared. She was nervous when I approached her and kept casting frightened glances around. She eyed every passerby as though she was having a tryst with a lover – and yet she was willing to talk to me. She even gave me her name.

"Daria Shubina. But please, let's walk. It's a bad place to meet. Someone may spot me from the windows of the hotel."

We crossed the square to the Bolshoi, walked past the service entrance – through which streamed skinny young women in fur coats and ballet tights, their identity cards at the ready – and crossed the street to the Central Department Store, and walked along its plate glass windows toward Kuznetsky Bridge.

"How long have you been working at the Metropole?" I asked when we got far enough from the hotel for her to stop looking back and trembling.

"Three years."

"And before that?"

"The Northern on Basmannaya Street."

I knew the Northern well. It was a seedy, rough-and-tumble place where geologists, oil and gas engineers, gold and diamond prospectors, and others working in the Far North lodged when they came to Moscow on business. The guys were hard-drinking and tough – some of them had done time. They were paid well, and there was nothing to spend it on in the North except vodka, and so they took full advantage of the enticements of the big city – most notably, the fairer sex.

"A tough place to work," I said.

"You can say that again."

"Is it better at the Metropole?"

She shrugged. "It's the same. The problems are different, that's all."

I was trying to put her at ease, but it wasn't working. She was stingy with her words and clearly wanted to get the conversation over with. Yet, strangely, she continued to talk even though nothing would have prevented her from cutting it short.

"What exactly is your job there?" I asked.

She shot me a glance. "You really don't know?"

"I do. In general terms."

"My job is to make sure no outsiders bother our guests. That means other Soviet citizens, of course. They are not allowed in unless accompanied by a hotel guest – and even then not every kind of Soviet citizen will be let through. I have other duties, too."

I was pretty sure that those other duties included informing Major Yershov about the guests' activities. That went without saying. As to visitors, hard-currency prostitutes were always allowed in if they were from the KGB's pool.

"It's too much responsibility," she sighed. "You always worry that something will go wrong. And, as you see, something always does. That is what makes this job hard. It was easier at the Northern."

"Tell me what you did on the night of the burglary."

"You're the fifth person asking me that," she said. She sounded weary of the whole business.

"It's an important case," I said. "Lots of people are interested in what happened that night."

"That's the thing," she said. "Nothing happened. I mean nothing out of the ordinary. None of the suites in that part of the third floor were occupied, except Number 318."

"Why was that? Is it normal?"

"We were expecting a big delegation from Vietnam," she said. "But they were delayed. They'll be coming next week. They are a strange bunch, the Vietnamese. Skinny and quiet. And they all look alike. But they're better than the Cubans. The Cubans are worse than our Russian guys at the Northern. They sing and dance when they get drunk and sneak into each other's rooms at night. It's not allowed, but there is nothing anyone can do about it. A promiscuous bunch, even though they are our friends."

We crossed Kuznetsky Bridge and walked up Neglinka toward the Boulevard Ring. She stopped by the Hunter's store at the corner and stared at a stuffed silver fox in its window, surrounded by a dozen hunting rifles. The fox's wide-open, glassy eyes gave it a permanently bewildered look.

"Poor devil," Daria observed, shaking her head.

"About that night," I said, steering her back onto the subject. "You said there was no one on the floor except the woman in 318 and nothing happened. Absolutely nothing?"

"Well, obviously something did happen," she said. "But I didn't see or hear anything."

"Were you asleep?"

"So what if I was?" she bridled suddenly. "Maybe I dozed off for a moment or two. Everybody sleeps there at night. Especially when it's so quiet. Then Semyon the shoeshine shows up at five. I would drink a lot of tea to stay awake, but then I've got to run to the toilet."

"I see," I said.

"But never mind if I doze off. I always hear what's going on. I would have heard if someone tried to sneak by me."

"Is there another way to get to Number 318?" I asked. "I mean without passing by you?"

"Hell no," she said. "You can get to the floor by using the stairs or the elevator, and either way you have to pass by my desk."

"Except someone could have snuck in while you were in the bathroom?"

"That's a possibility," she conceded. "There is nothing I can do about that."

"What happened when the guest in Number 318 raised the alarm?"

Daria shrugged. "Nothing. She came out into the hallway and told me she had been robbed by an intruder."

"How was she? Nervous?"

"Not at all. Cool as a cucumber. I didn't believe she was serious at first. She asked me to call the cops, but I didn't, of course. Your kind, the regular police, are never allowed into the Metropole. I'm surprised they called you in this time."

"Have there been any other burglaries at the Metropole?"

"Not to my knowledge. Now and again a guest complains about things missing, but most of the time it's because they have misplaced them themselves. Foreigners are finicky and get hysterical about minor things."

"And when the missing items are not found?"

"Who knows. They say the cleaning staff picks up things every once in a while, but I don't believe it. Comrade Major Yershov would crush you if he caught you stealing. Everyone is scared to death of him."

I took note of that. It cast a slightly different light on her willingness to speak to me.

"Can you remember how long after you had gone to the bathroom that she raised the alarm?" I asked.

"Not for a while," she said, after thinking it over. "A couple of hours."

"So the burglar could have gotten away by then?"

She shrugged. "He could've hidden in one of the other suites. If he could break into one suite, he could have gone into another. That's what Comrade Major Yershov said."

"Did he search the other suites?"

"Of course he did. First thing after he arrived. He thought that the burglar might still be hiding there."

For the hundredth time, she looked around and pulled her head into her shoulders.

"I had better be going," she said hastily. "I shouldn't be talking to you in the first place."

# TEN

Olga's first husband was never meant to be a soldier. When a man becomes something he was not meant to be, everything he does turns out for the worse.

Alexei Zolotnitsky once saved a commissar from hanging. It was probably the worst thing he ever did.

It was in the summer of 1920, in August or September, at the southern fringe of the old Empire. Except by then there was no Empire left, no Republic, and whatever government there was, was going to hell. All that was left was a vast expanse of land on which nightmares were being brought to life. The best you could do was to fall in with the nightmares. If you tried to do good, or even just stand aside from the nightmares, you made matters worse.

On a hot day in the summer of 1920 in Northern Tavria, an advance guard of General Barbovich's First Consolidated Cavalry Division under Alexei's command broke away from the front lines and intercepted a Bolshevik commissar on the road to Ivanovka. His men cut down most of her escort and sent the rest scampering down the dusty road, then dragged her out of her carriage. She was a tiny fireplug of a woman – a small, ridiculous and yet strangely threatening figure with thick lenses set in horn-rimmed glasses. Her straight black hair was cut boyishly short.

Excited by the chase and the smell of Bolshevik blood, his men removed her oversized leather jacket and tore away a filthy, sweat-soaked undershirt. By the time Alexei caught up with them, they were having a good laugh fondling her breasts.

"I swear to God," Junior Lieutenant Osipov shouted to a burst of guffaws. "I've never even seen such a flat-chested Bolshevik. Man or woman. You sure she's not a boy?"

"No way," someone called out. "That's the new Bolshevik breed. A Jewess with no tits. They won't screw anymore and will procreate by reading Trotsky."

"The Jews breed like rabbits, however they do it. It's exhausting just slicing their heads off."

There was more laughter, more obscenities and more ribald humor.

"Let me take a better look, boys," Osipov said, making his way toward the commissar.

Wachtmeister Boyko, meanwhile, had pulled out a rope from under his saddle and was tying a noose.

"Stand back," he said curtly. "The fun is over, boys. This is my good rope on which I string commissars."

He dismounted, propelling his heavy frame gracefully over the side of his horse, and elbowed his way past his comrades.

"Wait a while, Taras," came a protesting chorus. "You'll have plenty of time to string her up yet. Let the boys have some fun with the Jew commissar. Wait at least until we find her tits."

The commissar stood in the midst of the red and black rumps of the men's horses, scarcely taller than their front legs. As he placed the noose on her neck, the wachtmeister accidentally knocked her glasses off. She was squinting nearsightedly at him and smiling, making no attempt to remove the noose. She was scared. Her face was pale and her left cheek was twitching nervously, but her hatred was stronger than her fear. Perspiration glistened on her forehead in the full brightness of a midday southern sun.

"Don't you worry about a thing, girl," Boyko said to her softly, almost tenderly, adjusting the noose on her scrawny neck. "It won't hurt a bit. Trust me, I'm an expert. I don't like to make it any more painful than it has to be."

Dismounting, Alexei came over. He removed the noose from the commissar's neck, catching a whiff of the acrid stench of her body, a mixture of sweat, leather, mold from the carriage, and fear, and ordered his men to disperse.

"You should have been chasing down the rest of her men," he told them. "Now they'll be back with reinforcements. And remember, we don't fight women."

It wasn't, strictly speaking, true. During General Denikin's advance, the soldiers under his command had raped and killed plenty of women and young girls, especially Jews, and there was nothing he could do about it.

"This one is not a woman," Osipov replied. "This one is a she-Devil."

The men laughed.

"Well, all the more reason to let her go. It's a bad omen to string up a she-Devil."

The men laughed some more, but they were angry at him, too. He picked up the commissar's glasses, wiped off the dust and handed them to her.

"You're free to go," he said.

She put her leather jacket over her tattered undershirt, buttoned it up and said coldly, *"Vous avez fait un grave erreur, capitaine."*

Her French was excellent.

"You mean by letting you go?" he asked.

He responded to her in Russian. Osipov probably understood some French, but the rest of his men didn't and he didn't want them to think that he was having a friendly chat with a commissar – especially after saving her from hanging. Nerves were frayed, and being suspected of Bolshevik sympathies could be dangerous.

---

* You're making a big mistake, Captain.

"Of course," she continued in French. "You should never waste an opportunity to kill your enemy. But an even bigger mistake was not letting your men have some fun with their prisoner. I'm their prize, you know, they won me fair and square. They need something to break the routine of fighting, and nothing fits the bill like raping and stringing up a Jew – and a commissar to boot. Two for the price of one, so to speak."

She was taunting him. Not only did she speak perfect Parisian French, but she even had the tough, ironic Parisian sense of humor. He shrugged and turned away. His men got back on their horses and watched as she scurried down the road. She was favoring her left leg and, aware that she was being watched, tried to hide her limp.

When she had covered some distance, one of Alexei's men fired a shot, deliberately missing her but hitting the road at her feet. The bullet raised a splash in the dust. Alexei turned and glared at his ragtag detachment, but whoever had done it had already put his revolver away.

She stopped and turned.

"This is why we're going to beat you," she shouted back at all of them, speaking Russian now. "You believe in mercy while we believe in what we're fighting for. We don't play cat and mouse with you. Our cause is too important for that. When we catch you, we shoot every single one of you. And if it's me who catches you, captain, don't expect me to spare you in return. If I did, I'd deserve to be put before the firing squad myself."

In the weeks that followed, White forces tried in vain to dislodge the Reds from their Kakhovka bridgehead, wasting manpower they didn't have. The Reds, meanwhile, shifted troops from the Polish front, where a truce had been signed in early October, and brought their overwhelming numerical superiority to bear.

Alexei never gave a second thought to the tiny commissar he had saved. All that time, he hardly slept or had a full meal, and he lost count of the engagements in which he took part and the units he commanded.

Soon after that encounter on the road to Ivanovka, he was ordered to attack the left flank of the Kakhovka bridgehead at Nizhny Serogozy.

The idiots on General Barbovich's staff gave them no information as to what to expect, either in terms of the Reds' strength or how entrenched they were on the left bank of the Dnieper. Alexei's men were cut down by the thick machine gun fire before they could even come within sight of the Reds' trenches. Osipov and Boyko were killed. His losses would have been far greater had Alexei not reassessed the situation in time and ordered a retreat.

After that, his badly depleted unit, still ambitiously called a Hundred, was sent to defend Konstantinovka, where the Red cavalry had broken through and was rampaging the Whites' supply lines. Replenishing their ranks was out of the question. Peasants in Tavria, whether mindful of the threat of Bolshevik reprisals or responding to their appeals, refused to be pressed into service by the Whites. Worse, they kept killing Baron Wrangel's men whenever they could lay their hands on them. For much of October, Alexei and the survivors of the Konstantinovka defense chased them around the Tavria steppes, burning farmhouses and stringing up resisters. It produced no new soldiers and generated plenty of hatred, but it hardly mattered any more. The war was lost.

In the haste and confusion of the Red advance during early November, Alexei and a dozen of his men found themselves cut off from the retreating main force. By the time he got back to Crimea – on foot, avoiding the Reds and Makhno's thugs roaming the countryside, killing and torturing any White officers who had the misfortune of falling into their hands – the Bolsheviks had occupied all the major ports of the peninsula without encountering further resistance.

The last steamers, loaded to the gills with evacuees, had put to sea. One of them carried Olga into exile. A staff officer serving with General Balbovich told her that Alexei had been killed and that she had been a widow for two months. There must have been confusion in the records, or else the staff officer had simply lied to her.

Alexei returned to the rooms in Feodosia they had been renting. The house was on the outskirts of the city and now it stood empty and shuttered. The landlady and her other tenants had had the good sense to flee. The signs of their hasty departure were everywhere – from a half-finished plate of cooked bulgur wheat on the table to a few dozen high-denomination Kerensky banknotes scattered under the benches on the veranda, soaked by the autumn rains.

It had rained a lot that year. Alexei changed out of his faded, mud-splattered uniform and into his civilian clothes. At first he thought of throwing his Colt into the well, but then changed his mind and buried it in the soft black soil of a flower bed, among some nasturtiums.

He stayed indoors, not daring to go into town. He was waiting to see what was going to happen next – to Crimea and to him. The Bolsheviks had promised amnesty for Wrangel's soldiers, but only a fool would trust them.

Indeed, it was a strange kind of amnesty. The executions began the day the Bolshevik takeover was complete. There was no pause, no boundary to separate the end of fighting and the start of the Red Terror.

When the last steamer was departing, a detachment of Kuban Cossacks was left behind in the confusion, even as a frantic crowd of civilians got on board. The Cossacks surrendered to the advance detachments of the Reds and were disarmed and stripped naked. Their clothes and footwear, though filthy and worn, were fought over by their captors.

The Cossacks were kept under guard on the same pier where they had been found, shivering in their underwear in the early morning cold and starving. A few days later they were taken to a muddy ravine behind the port, where port workers had been ordered to dig a shallow trench. The Cossacks were then shot with two German machine guns positioned diagonally, so as to rake through the huddle of naked boys more efficiently. Those who survived the bullets were finished off with bayonets. Their bodies were covered with a thin layer of earth. The port workers were lined up next. A death sentence for loading steamers for Wrangel was read out to them by a 20-year-old in a leather jacket – the bosses of the Terror all wore leather jackets – and were shot in the same way, their bodies dropping on top of the still warm bodies of the Cossacks.

The next night, with freezing rain falling on the cobblestones of the service road, another group was marched to the same ravine. The engine of terror had been set in motion and had to be fed nightly. The machine guns worked overtime.

Alexei got all this news from their housekeeper Anfisa, and it seemed so horrible that he dismissed it as phantasmagorical gossip of her own invention. Anfisa had been hired by an artillery major who appeared out of nowhere in the company of a morbidly obese soprano from the Kiev Opera and her nine-year-old daughter. They started off on a grand scale, renting three large rooms on the second floor and hiring Anfisa, but ran out of money two months later. They disappeared just as quickly, and were replaced by a young couple from Samara, a former seminary student and his very pregnant wife. Even though none of them could afford to pay Anfisa's wages, she kept coming to the house and going about her chores, and she came to work even now, braving the drunken Red and Makhno soldiers in the streets to bring Alexei a loaf of bread one day and a pinch of homegrown tobacco the next, for which – especially for the rough tobacco to fill his cigarette shells – he was eternally grateful.

Many years later, Olga thought of her first husband – whom she had believed to be dead and lying unburied, like so many others, somewhere in the Tavria steppes, his fine bones picked clean by vultures and bleached white by the sun – staying in that creaky, shuttered house with its overgrown garden bordered by a rusty cast-iron fence, shrouded in autumnal mist, and separated from the muddy road by a row of cypresses that rose gently into the hills.

He stayed in the room they had once designated as his study, lying on the sofa in his shirtsleeves and cavalry boots, beneath all the wool blankets he could find, reading books from their landlady's library and rationing his tobacco and bread.

In the streets, civilians were shot daily, and no one knew if those were deliberate executions by the leather-jacketed Cheka men or random killings by drunken soldiers. It didn't make any difference, anyway, because in both cases the victims were stripped of their clothes and their naked bodies were left in the ditch, to be gnawed on by stray dogs.

The Reds, having entered Crimea hungry and in tatters, owning nothing but their guns, looked more prosperous by the day. They now had gold watches swinging on thick chains, new clothes, and leather boots.

Houses were robbed, too. Soldiers simply entered any house that caught their fancy and took anything they liked. They would turn out the owners and stay for a while, wrecking and befouling the place before moving on. The new authorities declared this to be class justice. Let the moneybags get a taste of their own medicine.

It was only a matter of time before they came to his house, but by some random piece of good fortune, it was spared for three full weeks.

In the end, it was Anfisa who turned him in. Not counting her, his first visitors were men from the Cheka, wearing leather jackets and accompanied by a detachment of soldiers. His was an orderly arrest, which was the reason he wasn't killed outright. They asked to see his papers. Since he had none, they took him away. His guards, two young peasants from Yaroslavl Gubernia with rifles and fixed bayonets, looked back wistfully, where their comrades were ransacking Alexei's house.

Alexei was glad he had finished the last of his tobacco the day before. There was some bread left in the pantry, but it had gone moldy in the humidity of the Crimean winter.

As he was being led away shivering under a cold rain, he was not thinking about the bespectacled, boyish commissar whose life he had saved an eternity ago on a hot dusty road in Tavria. He was thinking instead of the long Pisemsky novel, *A Thousand Souls*. He was in the middle of it and sorry he would never know how it turned out.

## ELEVEN

It's important to keep an open mind when you investigate a crime, to not dismiss anything out of hand. I always say this to Sevka when sharing the pearls of wisdom I've acquired while working at Moscow Criminal Investigations – in case he doesn't change his mind when he grows up and still wants to become a detective.

Another thing I should have told him was this: when giving advice to others, don't forget to heed your own words. I had been so sure that Valera's rounds of the consignment shops and jewelry stores and meetings with informers and fences in the alleys around Tishinka Market would be a waste of time, and that looking for an inside angle would be much more promising, that Valera's success took me completely by surprise.

Actually, it wasn't a total success. At best, it was a step in the right direction – and a faltering one at that. And it raised more questions than it had answered.

Later that same morning when I had my talk with Daria, Valera and I were sitting in our cramped office. Our office had been nicknamed TU-104, like the world's first passenger jetliner, because Valera Tumakov and Lenny Urumov, my late partner, had been its original occupants and the first letters of their last names were T and U. But the name also fit because the space in our tiny office was as scarce as on that jetliner. We were comparing notes, trying to figure out our next step, when the phone rang.

The phone was on my desk because Valera hated clutter and preferred the top of his desk to be clear. Mine was usually piled high with files – a habit I had picked up working with Lenny, the world's sloppiest detective – so it had been decided that our shared phone would sit on my desk, among the files. But that also made it easier for Valera to pick up the receiver from where he sat, by simply extending his left arm.

He listened briefly, said nothing, then handed me the receiver.

"For you," he stated laconically.

Captain Gordeyev, Valera's old partner, was on the line. The two of them had had a huge fight, which was the reason Valera and I had been partnered up. They still weren't on speaking terms, even though the Boss had threatened to fire both of them if they couldn't start working together like professionals. They pretended to make peace, then made me the unwilling intermediary in their ongoing spat.

"I've got something you might be interested in," Gordeyev said.

"Which is what?" I asked.

"A dead body," he replied.

"That's very good news," I said. "And other than that?"

"Plenty. But it's too difficult to explain over the phone. You'd better get over here."

He dictated the address, which was on a side street behind Kursk Railway Station. While I jotted it down, Valera stared out the window. His pose suggested that my conversation with Gordeyev was of no interest to him.

Other landmarks in that neighborhood included the State Institute of Physical Culture and, on the same street that bent to the right, the Gogol Drama Theater. I knew the neighborhood well because Tosya was a fanatical theater-goer. She attended her first live performance in the course of one of my murder investigations a couple of years ago and became hooked on drama theater. The Gogol was her favorite theater. It wasn't popular. The critics regularly panned its productions and the city's snobs rarely set foot there, and that meant you could get tickets even if you showed up five minutes before curtain time. Tosya didn't care about reviews – she never read *Theater Life*. She cared about the experience.

"Misha Gromovsky and I will be here for another hour," Gordeyev said, referring to his partner. "They'll probably remove the body by then, but it's not the stiff that I want you to see. And make sure to bring your partner, too."

I would have liked to get more information, but it was no use trying to get anything more out of Gordeyev.

"He wants us at a crime scene," I told Valera when I hung up.

I got up and started to put on my coat.

"You go," Valera said. "I'm busy."

"You'd better come," I said. "I'm pretty sure it has something to do with our case."

"Oh yeah? Well, I'm pretty sure it's one of Gordeyev's false positives. He oversells his discoveries, and everyone ends up wasting time. But he doesn't care, because he's a captain."

Gordeyev's career success was one of the things that kept Valera up at night. He was ambitious and envious of other people.

I was fully dressed and holding my hat. Valera had not moved. I had had about enough of the both of them.

"As you wish," I said curtly. "But you realize, don't you, that if it's something serious and you aren't there, and then Gordeyev reports that to the Boss, I'll have to back him up."

It wouldn't have worked with any other cop in the world. A partner has got to have your back and be on your side, no matter what. Lenny Urumov would have punched me in the face if I had threatened to back another cop against him. Valera was different. Valera was a stickler for the rules, and in his frame of reference, the rules were more important than the brotherly bond between partners.

"Very well," he conceded, rising reluctantly to his feet. "What the hell is this about?"

I opened my mouth to tell him, but he interrupted me.

"Actually, I'd rather not hear. It'll only make me more upset."

I had my war-booty Zundapp motorcycle parked outside headquarters. I'd left it there before the snowstorm, but now that the roads were clear, I brushed off the snow and the machine was ready to be ridden once more. You had to be careful riding on wintry streets, but my Zundapp was safer than other motorbikes because it was a hunk of heavy pre-World War II German steel and, moreover, it had a sidecar and three wheels.

It was a short ride down the Garden Ring to Kazakov Street and from there over a narrow railroad bridge to Lower Susalny Lane, which ran along the side of the Moscow Gas Plant. I checked the number on the side of a two-story clapboard house and killed the engine.

Only half an hour had passed since Gordeyev phoned. We were perfectly on time – which wouldn't have happened if we had taken public transportation.

"What the hell is going on?"

Valera had thrown off the blanket and climbed out of the sidecar. He stood on the sidewalk in front of the house glaring at me.

"What's the matter, Valera?"

"I was here just the other day," he said, shaking his head and frowning. "What is Gordeyev up to?"

"He said it was a murder," I replied. "He didn't elaborate.

"A murder? Who was killed?"

I shrugged.

"As I said, Gordeyev didn't elaborate."

"Typical. And yet I was just here the other day."

"So you said."

Valera headed confidently toward the back of the house. I followed behind.

"This is exactly where I was," he repeated, turning toward me. "Is it the second floor apartment?"

"Look, I really have no idea," I said as we turned the corner, walking single-file on a narrow footpath cut through a deep snowdrift.

The path ran past the back of the house and continued on, around a children's playground with a broken swing and a slide half-buried in snow, to a hole in the fence that offered a shortcut to the suburban platforms of the Kursk Station. There were car tracks and our departmental all-terrain "GAZik" stood by the front door of the house. The driver was inside it, but whether it was the old one, Zhorik, or the new one, Sergei, was impossible to tell because the interior was thick with cigarette smoke. A uniformed cop was leaning against the GAZik, also smoking a cigarette.

"Go on," the cop waved us in once Valera showed him his ID. "It's the second floor apartment."

"Oh, damn it," Valera muttered. "It's Levkoyev's place."

It was an old, decrepit clapboard house. The wooden stairs were rickety and creaky, and the stairwell smelled of mold, rotting wood and cooking. The rusty radiator on the landing between the floors hissed as we passed, spewing out a cloud of grey steam.

"Let's stop for a second," I said. "We're not in a rush. Who's Levkoyev?"

I figured I should find out who Levkoyev was before we visited his apartment and viewed his dead body. Assuming it was Levkoyev's dead body.

"Levkoyev is an antiques collector. And of course he deals in art and antiques on the side, in the black market. He might also sell some smuggled consumer electronics, and they say he fences stolen goods. But he doesn't have a police record."

Valera winked at me.

"Which means what?" I asked.

Valera grinned.

"It means that he has another sideline working as an informer."

"That's why you came to see him? The Metropole case?"

"That's right. I was here only two days ago."

"And? What did he tell you?"

"He told me he knew nothing about any major jewelry heists," Valera said. "There had been no buzz on the street, as he put it."

"Did you believe him?"

Valera's reply came slowly.

"On the whole I did. I think he was telling me the truth. He became really interested when I mentioned a jewelry heist. I didn't give him any particulars of the case, of course, but the fact that I had gone to the trouble of seeking him out was in itself an indication that something serious had happened. He kept asking me about the missing jewels, as if he was going to help me, but I think he was interested in it for himself. He's a collector and collectors are a crazy bunch."

"So he was no help?" I asked.

Valera shook his head. "Not much."

The door of the second floor apartment was unlocked, and we wandered around for a minute or two before finding our colleagues in the back room. It was a large place.

"Come right in, friends," Gordeyev said, playing a gregarious host. "Welcome to our little art museum. Make yourselves at home. Enjoy our beautiful collection."

He shook my hand and ignored Valera, who also refused to greet him.

The second-floor windows faced the tall brick wall of the gas plant. Behind it, you could see a bunch of guys in black work clothes pushing a piece of heavy equipment between two circular buildings, while another man, wearing a suit and tie under an unbuttoned overcoat, was running around issuing commands. It wasn't much of a view, and the windows had steel bars over them that were thick, rusty, and ugly, but the man's three-room apartment was unexpectedly luxurious and filled with various expensive objects. It was like some provincial museum that became the repository of assorted collections requisitioned from local landowners after the revolution. Every surface was crowded with vases, crystal goblets, porcelain figurines, and marble and bronze statuettes, all mixed together. The furniture was also old, heavy and, by the look of it, valuable. There were also a couple of late-model Japanese television sets – a jarring contrast to all the cute knick-knacks. A large bookcase with sliding glass panels contained antiquarian volumes in leather bindings. Central Asian rugs covered the floors, placed in layers of two or three, one on top of the other. Paintings, etchings, decorative plates, and ornate Persian swords completed the picture, occupying every inch of available wall space.

There wasn't much room for the body to fall. Judging by the chalk contour traced by forensics, it had been squeezed between a foldout couch – also covered by an Oriental rug – and a dining table with removable leafs.

"This is where the body was found," Gordeyev announced.

"I see that," I said.

We looked around. There wasn't anything else of note – or at least nothing that seemed relevant to the murder.

"Forensics must have spent a good long time here dusting for fingerprints," I said.

"They did," Gordeyev confirmed. "They cursed a lot while they were at it."

"Was it Levkoyev?" I asked.

Gordeyev nodded.

"But that's not the reason I wanted you to come," he said.

He went down the hall, motioning for us to follow. I did, but Valera, wishing to impress upon Gordeyev that he wasn't interested in whatever he was going to show us, lingered in the room. Gromovsky stayed behind as well, scribbling in a notebook.

"How did he die?" Valera asked Gromovsky, who pretended to be immersed in his notes. He was being loyal to his partner.

It was an old house. It was cheaply built and must at one time have been a dormitory for gas plant workers or a hotel for migrants, given the proximity of the railway station. Levkoyev must have liked living there. No outsider would guess that its decrepit façade concealed such riches.

The apartment had a long, narrow hallway with rooms strung along its length. The bathroom and the toilet were at the end of the hallway, separated by a brick chimney against which a stepladder had been leaned. Up high, under the blackened beams of the ceiling, several bricks had been removed, revealing a small hole.

"This is one of his secret hiding places," Gordeyev said. "I'm sure there are others. But this one has yielded some interesting stuff."

"How did you find it?" I asked.

Gordeyev's face spread into a self-satisfied smile.

"Our famous deduction methods. We're Moscow Criminal Investigations detectives, are we not? It's like that joke about Sherlock Holmes and Dr. Watson—"

He took a look at my face and caught himself. It was clear that I wasn't interested in hearing the joke right then.

"I'll tell you some other time," he said. "Actually, Gromovsky discovered it. He spotted some brick dust on the floor and then saw a stepladder in the hallway. He put two and two together, and the rest was easy. This is where we found what I wanted to show you. Let's go back to the dining room."

A frosty draft was blowing along the floor of the hallway.

"It's cold in here," I said.

"I'm not surprised. One of the window panes has been knocked out."

He opened the middle door, and we walked into another large, cluttered room. One of the barred windows was broken.

"It looks like someone put a brick through it," I said.

"A bronze candelabrum," Gordeyev corrected me. "And it didn't come from the outside. It was tossed from in here. It got caught in the bars."

We went back to rejoin the others and found Valera hard at work. There was a stainless steel tray on the dining table of the kind used by forensics, but instead of body parts or a murder weapon, it contained pieces of jewelry – earrings, rings, two pendants, and a large brooch in the form of a woman's face. The face looked like it had been modeled by a kid, but there was something in its irregular features that made it sweet and tender, and it was the most beautiful piece in the cluttered apartment.

Valera had taken out his notebook and was making marks in it, lifting his eyes to the jewelry every few seconds. He and Gromovsky were standing side by side, looking more like insurance adjusters than police detectives.

"I guess your partner has figured it out already," Gordeyev said.

He sounded disappointed.

"Are these the pieces from the Metropole?" I asked Valera.

He was absorbed in his task and didn't hear me the first time. I had to repeat my question. He nodded without interrupting his task. Gordeyev and I waited for him to finish. After a few more minutes he turned to me and, ignoring Gordeyev, declared proudly, "A perfect match. One for one. A complete set. Now, where did it come from?"

"Come, I'll show you," I said.

I took him back into the hallway and showed him the hiding place on the side of the chimney. The hallway was very cold by then, and we both shivered.

"So, whoever murdered Levkoyev must have done it soon after he got the jewels," Valera observed. "I wonder if the two events were connected."

"Well, the killer didn't take the loot, did he?" I said. "And the place shows no sign of having been ransacked. It's possible that something else was taken, but the killer wasn't after Khokhlova's baubles. He either had no idea they were here or wasn't interested."

"I wonder," Valera said, shaking his head. "It would be a huge coincidence. In any case, let's go get them."

However, when we went back to pick up the baubles we ran into an unexpected complication.

"You can't remove evidence from a crime scene," Gordeyev said.

Valera, ignoring him, attempted to get to the tray, and Gordeyev barred his way. Suddenly, the two of them were toe to toe.

"Is he trying to prevent me from restoring stolen property to its rightful owner?" Valera asked me, still ignoring Gordeyev. "Does he realize it is a high priority case assigned to us by the head of the Committee for State Security?"

Gordeyev didn't budge. He stood stone-faced, pretending not to hear.

"He doesn't know it's a high priority case," I said. "He says we have no authority to remove evidence from a crime scene, and he won't allow it."

I felt like an idiot being their go-between. Gromovsky lifted his face from his notebook and gave me a wink behind their backs.

"Then I'll have to go directly to the Boss," Valera said. "Or even to Comrade Andropov. Let's see how Gordeyev likes that."

I turned to Gordeyev.

"We'll have to go directly to the Boss then," I said.

"That's right," Gordeyev said. "You can go directly to the Boss or you can go to hell, but I won't allow you to remove anything from the apartment."

"I understand," I said. "Anyway, how did he get killed?"

I thought it would be a good idea to change the subject and to diffuse the tension. But Valera, getting more and more irritated, turned to me.

"Look, Pavel, this is a matter of national interest. We should not be wasting any more time here. Returning the jewels is our highest priority. Once they're safely back in Madame Khokhlova's possession, we can start investigating the murder."

"What do you mean you'll start investigating the murder, Tumakov?" Gordeyev bellowed, turning crimson with rage. "This is my case. Stay out of it, d'you hear?"

# TWELVE

"Well, well, well," Budyonny repeated while pacing up and down his office. Valera and I stood facing his desk like two third-graders summoned into the principal's office over failing grades. "Lucky for you two that it was our team on the job and that Gordeyev was alert enough to recognize the foreign lady's jewels. It easily could have been someone else, a different group, a local cop, anybody. What would Comrade Andropov have said then? You have no idea? Let me tell you then. He would have said 'Why the hell did I ask Colonel Martirosyan for assistance?' That's exactly what he would have said and that would have made me very mad."

But he was picking on us. He didn't seem mad, and his accent was under control.

"So," he said finally settling in behind his desk. "Who was this Levkoyev character?"

We both looked at Valera.

"Levkoyev was a collector and a black market dealer in antiques," he said.

"Is that all you can tell me about him?" the Boss asked.

"And he was also one of the most valuable informers of the Department for Combating the Theft of Socialist Property," Valera added. "They let him stay in business, and he gave them his list of clients. They would then check them out to see how they got their money, and if it wasn't legitimate they would haul them in."

"Did he have any legitimate customers?"

"He did. Figure skaters and classical musicians, the ones who perform abroad."

"Was he married?"

"I don't know, sir. I don't think so."

It was my turn to step in. I had had to get all the details about Levkoyev's personal life from Gromovsky since neither he nor Gordeyev would talk to Valera.

"Divorced," I said. "A daughter, a 12-year old, lives with her mother. He had a woman who came twice a week to clean and cook."

"And he died how?"

"Stabbed, sir," I said. "Very competently, a blade to the heart from behind. Quick and efficient. No sign of a struggle. Except for a smashed window. That's how the murder was discovered. The neighbors saw broken glass on the ground."

"Is that how the killer got in? Through the window?"

"No, the windows have bars. The locks on the door are solid – lots of valuable stuff in the apartment – and no sign of a forced entry. Most likely the victim let the killer in."

"And nothing stolen," Valera added. "At least not anything that we can tell. And no sign that the killer searched for Khokhlova's jewels. Apparently he didn't know about them or didn't care."

"What do you think happened then?" the Boss asked.

We were silent for a moment, and Valera was the first to answer.

"I'd say it was a personal matter. The broken window, the professional stabbing, everything intact in the apartment. It looks like they had a quarrel or, even more likely, that someone was settling a score with him. Gordeyev should check who had been jailed because of the information supplied by Levkoyev – and who had recently gotten out."

"I hope you told him that," the Boss said, winking at Valera. He was not taken in by the two ex-partners pretending to be on friendly terms.

Perhaps he had his own Levkoyevs in the department, reporting to him what was really going on.

The Boss turned to me.

"What's your view, Matyushkin?"

I shrugged.

"I don't know," I said. "The jewels appeared out of nowhere in Levkoyev's apartment two days after Valera had gone to see him. Apparently Levkoyev didn't know that a valuable collection of jewelry had been stolen and first learned about it from their conversation."

"Right," Budyonny said, sitting up in his chair. "Let's talk about that for a moment."

His tone had changed suddenly, and his eyes flashed. He gave Valera a withering look.

"So, lieutenant, you visit Levkoyev and talk to him about the missing jewels. It's news to Levkoyev, but then, less than two days later, the man turns up dead and in possession of the same jewels. Am I missing something here?"

"No, sir."

"Louder, please. I can't hear you."

"No, sir," Valera repeated, but his second try didn't come out much louder than his first.

"Let me ask you a question, then. Where is your pride as a detective?"

Valera stared at him.

"I'm asking you a question, lieutenant. What I mean is, how did you allow the man to hoodwink you like that? How could you not have put him under surveillance?"

"I don't understand, sir. I left his house convinced he'd never heard of the jewels."

"And he twisted you around his little finger," Budyonny concluded triumphantly, as though he had always known that Valera was a failure as a detective and that this case had been assigned to him to prove the point.

Valera was a sorry sight. His face was pale, and he looked like he was going to cry. He was not a coward, and he was not a sycophant. He simply couldn't stand it when his superiors were displeased with his work. That was, perhaps, why he was such a stickler for the rules. Going by the book might not always be the best solution, but you had a ready excuse if things didn't work out. Doing it your way, as Lenny Urumov used to do, was a high-risk strategy. But Lenny was thick-skinned and didn't give a damn if the Boss occasionally yelled at him.

Budyonny watched Valera squirm with a satisfied grin on his face and concluded, "Well, let that be a lesson to you. Where do we go from here? Matyushkin, what do you think?"

I was reluctant to speak with Valera standing there absolutely quashed.

"I think we should let Gordeyev focus on people who might have had a grudge against Levkoyev," I said slowly. "Just as Senior Lieutenant Tumakov has suggested. But I would like to continue working the Metropole angle. Levkoyev may not have known about the burglary at the hotel two days ago, but you know how quickly rumors spread. Just because Comrade Andropov told everyone to keep the incident confidential doesn't mean that people did. Levkoyev might have had connections and quickly learned about the jewels once he had been tipped off about the burglary. That would explain why he got Khokhlova's jewels so quickly. I wonder whether there was any connection between him and someone on the staff at the Metropole. Perhaps now that the jewels have been found, Comrade Andropov will be more forthcoming with information."

"You don't give up, do you?" the Boss asked sarcastically. "You can certainly talk to the staff, but not without Comrade Andropov's permission. And if he doesn't give it, forget about it. What I certainly don't want you to do is to tangle with State Security."

He didn't mind me going against Andropov's orders while we were looking for the jewels, but now that they had been found – and found, albeit accidentally, by his department – he didn't want any problems with the chief of the KGB.

Budyonny began to pace the office again. Valera, meanwhile, was starting to regain his composure. Some color had returned to his face.

"Speaking of Comrade Andropov," the Boss said. "He wants to see both of you. Apparently, the foreign lady wants to thank you personally."

"It wasn't us," Valera exclaimed. He was now sufficiently recovered for his sense of fairness to be outraged. "It was Gordeyev and Gromovsky. She should be thanking them."

"I'm aware of this, lieutenant, thank you very much," the Boss said coldly. "But Comrade Andropov says he wants to see *you*, and the victim wants to thank *you* for recovering her jewelry. Neither he nor she has ever heard of Gordeyev and Gromovsky, and I'm not going to bother them with useless details. Your job is not to set them straight, either. Your job is to click your heels and accept the lady's thanks in silence, and speak only when you're spoken to. Understood?"

"Yes, sir."

"I'm glad we're on the same page, lieutenant. Go downstairs. Comrade Andropov's driver is on his way here to pick you up. Don't make him wait."

As we filed out of his office, I thought I heard the Boss softly say, "Good job, boys."

But I couldn't swear that I didn't imagine it.

# THIRTEEN

The black Volga limousine arrived a few minutes after five. As we got into the back seat, Valera and I discovered that Comrade Andropov was sitting in the passenger seat next to the driver. To make sure our heads wouldn't spin from the great honor of having the KGB chief personally coming to pick us up, he said, staring straight ahead, "I wanted to give you instructions for your meeting with Olga Stepanovna."

Ivan, Comrade Andropov's driver, was a pleasure to watch at his job. He drove fast, but in his hands the car was moving with an exceptional smoothness. He had a magic touch that ensured complete control over the road. We picked up speed, squeezing into a small opening between a bakery delivery truck with BREAD spelled out in orange letters on its side in Church Slavonic-style letters, and a beige Moskvich hatchback pottering close to the curb, then moved to the central lane that separated the flow of traffic and was reserved for black limos like ours with their government tags.

"She may wish to speak to you two alone. You never know what comes into these foreigners' heads. We must try to humor her, but you need to know what you can say to her."

"I thought you said she was Russian, Comrade Andropov," I said innocently. "She speaks Russian so well."

Valera gave me a quick shove in the ribs. He didn't think it was appropriate to interrupt a big boss like Andropov.

"Of course she's Russian, lieutenant. She was born here, and her blood is Russian and Ukrainian, which is the same thing really. Blood is thicker than water. It makes no difference that she lives abroad. She's our cultural treasure. A couple of years ago, we had a visit from Prince Alexander Romanov. He lives in England, but he's Russian, too. One day, all these Russian people will return. But none of this should concern you. All you need to do is listen to me."

"Yes, sir," Valera responded for both of us.

Andropov spoke softly, still facing away from us. Even though the sound of the Volga's fine-tuned engine was as gentle as a cat purring, and the custom-built cabin admitted no outside noise, we could hardly hear him. We had to lean forward, our heads touching as we crowded the space between Andropov and Ivan.

"She wants to thank you for solving the case and recovering her property. You will accept her thanks by saying, 'Thank you very much, Madame, we're only doing our job.' If she decides she wants to talk to you about crime in the Soviet Union, tell her it's practically nonexistent and, when it does happen, it is solved promptly. As you have done in this case."

"Yes, Comrade Andropov," Valera said.

I winked at him. He was clearly not going to inform Andropov who had really recovered Khokhlova's jewels. Nor was he prepared to dispute Andropov's assertion that the crime had been solved.

"If she asks whether any special effort was made to solve her case because she is a foreign guest, tell her absolutely not," Andropov continued. "It was a routine investigation that would have been conducted exactly the same way had an ordinary Soviet citizen been involved. Tell her that was why you were called in and not the KGB."

"Yes, sir," Valera and I responded in unison.

"Good. Make sure you decide beforehand who says what, so you don't sound like you've been coached or that you have rehearsed your answers."

There was a traffic jam at the turnoff from the wide Gorky Street to Karl Marx Avenue. The traffic cop spotted us and promptly waved us past a line of waiting cars and delivery trucks. The sidewalk in front of the Metropole had been cleared of snow, but a pair of women in padded coats and white aprons were waving their brooms just in case. They scurried away at our approach.

"One more thing before we go," Andropov said, staying in the car for a moment longer. "Under no circumstance are you to mention that anyone has been killed. Not a word that her property was in the possession of a dead man. If she asks you who the thief was and how you recovered the jewels, tell her that the investigation is ongoing, that the thief is yet to stand trial, and that you can't talk about the case because you may prejudice the court against him. Tell her that in our legal system a person is presumed innocent until proven guilty."

He chuckled. Apparently, being the chief of the secret police, that last notion amused him.

"Are we to continue working on this case?" I asked.

Andropov now turned around and gave me a surprised look.

"It's up to you. My concern was that the stolen property should be recovered and restituted to Olga Stepanovna. It has been, very promptly, and that's a great relief. Even though it wasn't you who recovered it."

It was now my turn to poke Valera in the ribs, which I did with great pleasure as he was getting out of the car. So it turned out that Andropov knew all along how the baubles had been found.

We rode up in the elevator, which was piloted by an elderly attendant who took us to the third floor without even asking where we were going. Just before we got out, Andropov said, "Keep in mind that, even though I may not be present while you speak with Olga Stepanovna, it doesn't mean I won't know what you say to her."

The concierge's desk had been moved around the corner, so as to keep the door of Number 318 under observation. Major Yershov was manning it, and he saluted us smartly as we passed.

"She's in," he whispered.

We knocked and waited for several minutes before Khokhlova's voice asked, "Who's there?" Only then did she undo the lock and remove the chain. She had become more careful since our previous visit.

Andropov noted that as well.

"I'm glad you're starting to take our security arrangements seriously," he said as she let us in.

Khokhlova invited us to take a seat, which we eventually did – but not before assuring her that we could easily remain standing, since both Valera and I thought that standing on ceremony was a sign of good upbringing.

Andropov's fears that she would want to see us alone had been exaggerated. The thought of sending him out of the room didn't seem to have entered her mind. Instead, she offered him a seat next to her, and the two of them sat facing Valera and me as we sat next to each other on the couch.

She thanked us for recovering her "few trinkets," as she dismissively put it, and declared that she was amazed by how promptly and efficiently we had done it.

"I can assure you that if it had happened in Paris, the police would be just finishing compiling the list of stolen items. And they would have dragged me to the commissariat at least ten times, to answer the silliest questions you could think of. And in the end, they would have still got everything dreadfully wrong. They would have insisted that I file an insurance claim – just in case they didn't recover my property – and that would be a waste of another week, struggling with red tape in yet another suite of offices. After that, a fat *commissaire* would say to me something like 'By ze ooay, Madame, have you checked all your drawers carefully? You might have simply misplaced your jewelry, you know.'"

Valera and I laughed politely.

"I'm so very surprised to hear such things about the inefficiency of the Paris police force," Andropov said, shaking his head. "And here I am, a gullible Soviet reader of Georges Simenon's detective novels. I have been led to believe that Commissaire Maigret solves all crimes in France by page 25. Please do not tell me it is not true, Olga Stepanovna."

"Oh, I believe Commissaire Maigret is a perfect French policeman," she said. "All he does is smoke his pipe and drink beer. He's never in any hurry to solve crimes."

She laughed, but her eyes were not laughing. They were worried and watchful.

"By the way, may I offer you something to drink, officers? I don't think I have much here at the bar, but there is Armenian cognac, whiskey, and of course vodka."

Valera and I shook our heads vigorously, even though I wouldn't have minded a drop of whiskey. You hear so much about it without ever having an opportunity to try it.

"No thank you," Andropov replied sternly, raising his hand for emphasis. "I never drink alcohol. A kidney complaint, you know."

So far, the meeting had gone well. We started to relax, and that was when the glitches started.

First she asked us whether we always solved crimes so expeditiously as we had solved hers. Valera, in his zeal to carry out Andropov's instructions to the letter, assured her immediately that it was always the case, whereas I, speaking at the same time, uttered a much more ambiguous "More or less," which to my mind also sounded a little more plausible. Sitting next to her, Andropov gave us a stern look.

Then a real disaster struck.

"I assume you have caught the thief," the woman asked.

Her tone was casual, but I thought I could sense tension in her voice.

We had not been given specific instruction about that by Andropov, and so there was an awkward pause as both Valera and I racked our brains what to reply.

"Oh, yes, of course they did," the KGB chief said, coming to our rescue. We nodded in sync like two idiots.

"May I know who he is?"

She kept staring at us, even though it was once again Andropov who answered.

"A petty criminal. One of those lost souls who hangs around foreign currency hotels asking Western tourists for chewing gum and such things. There are some such characters in Moscow, but very few indeed, I can assure you."

He had a smile on his face that looked as fake as a thirteen-ruble banknote. She gave him a quick look and turned to us.

"Now that you have arrested the thief, gentlemen," she said, addressing the two of us pointedly, "what do you think will happen to him?"

There was more confusion on our end, and we started to give various cagey replies, with Valera not looking at her but staring apprehensively at Andropov as though looking for his approval, which of course he was.

"There is something I want to make absolutely clear," she said abruptly, interrupting our long-winded explanations. "I do not want the man to rot in jail because of me. Who knows, he might have been put up to it by others. He shouldn't be taking all the blame."

"No, of course he won't," Valera exclaimed. "He certainly won't be taking all the blame."

"So he *was* put up to it by someone?" she asked quickly.

That got Valera flustered. "Well, yes, of course."

"Do you know who?"

Andropov gave Valera a venomous look.

"There was no one else involved, Olga Stepanovna," Andropov said sharply, cutting Valera off. "As I told you, it was a misguided young kid who had been listening to Western propaganda broadcasts and broke into a hotel for foreign tourists in the hope of stealing a pair of blue jeans and some rock 'n' roll records. He made the mistake of burglarizing your room instead. He realized too late that you had none of that silly stuff here. So he took the first thing he could get his hands on, which was your jewelry. Rest assured, he is not going to be severely punished. We don't punish our citizens, especially young ones. We try to rehabilitate and re-educate them."

There was a long silence after that, which I broke almost in spite of myself.

"Did we recover everything that was taken from your room?" I asked.

I knew immediately that I was on to something.

"Why?" she asked quickly. "Did you find something else?"

"Was there anything else to find?" I asked.

She was flustered, but then she quickly recovered.

"No," she said coldly. "Everything that was taken from me has been recovered. I'm very grateful for your help, gentlemen. And now I would like to get some rest. It's been a difficult couple of days."

# FOURTEEN

They were kept in the refectory of the Convent of the Virgin, desecrated and befouled back in 1918, at the time of the Tauride Soviet Socialist Republic, re-consecrated after the arrival of the Germans and the Whites, and most recently transformed into a Cheka jail. The long narrow hall with low ceilings and bars on the windows was filled with so many prisoners that there was no room to sit on the stone floor. They had to stand, pressing hard against each other. More people were shoved into the rectory every night – Wrangel's officers who had been either unable or unwilling to evacuate, or had trusted in the Reds' promised amnesty, arrested all over Crimea and gathered in one place, exhausted men nursing bruises, broken bones and burns sustained by torture.

Zolotnitsky had been lucky. They beat him only once after his arrest, and they had gone easy on him. But they had pulled his boots off and taken his cavalry trousers. Other men also stood there in their filthy white undergarments. The guards joked that they already looked like the Lord's angels they were about to become.

It was cold and wet, a dreary Crimean winter having finally settled in for the long haul. The rain fell on those who were closest to the smashed windows, but it did provide some relief and a breath of fresh air. You could also open your mouth and catch tiny raindrops. The refectory was hot, and the hot stench of humanity was unbearable. Condensation glistened on the brick vaulting overhead, gathering into droplets and dripping down on them like foul dew in a rain forest.

He had been placed with civilians first – priests, merchants, doctors, engineers, and others the new regime didn't like. Out of habit – he had been a frontline officer for six years – he had assumed command and made rules for everyone to follow. They were also crowded, but at least they had a couple of wooden benches. He drafted a schedule for women and older men to take turns sitting or lying down on them, and a pregnant girl in her seventh month got priority. A man complained – what was the point, they were all going to be shot anyway – and was told to shut up. When he didn't, Zolotnitsky slapped his face. He was a gentle soul, but he knew that a challenge to his authority had to be put down pitilessly.

No command structure was possible in the tightly packed refectory. It was a Hobbesian state of nature. The strong won spaces by the windows and fought off challenges in order to keep them. The weak and the injured were pushed closer to the door, so that their bodies could be removed easily once they died. Subordination had broken down. Older, senior ranks stood no chance in the struggle for better spots. They were no longer military officers. It was every man for himself, and there was no honor.

They weren't given any food and drank from a rainwater barrel like pigs at the trough whenever they were let out into the courtyard. The courtyard had been turned into an open-air toilet, its lush flower beds once lovingly tended by nuns, churned up and thick with excrement. The chapels and cells had been befouled, as well, and stood with their doors wide open. They had been stripped of everything of value, their icons smashed to splinters and murals defaced.

At night, the sound of machine gun fire behind the convent walls kept them awake. Zolotnitsky couldn't tell what time it usually started, but on a clear night he determined that it had to be around two o'clock. The shooting went on for a few minutes at a time, followed by silence and then scattered gun shots.

It went on almost every night and became a kind of lullaby –
bratatatatatata, bratatata, bratat, bratatatatatatatata, and then – tchup,
tchup, tchup-tchup-tchup – echoing through the silent halls. The men
in the refectory would stop arguing, groaning, and praying, and listen
to other human beings being murdered. They would stay quiet even
after the gunshots had died down, until the executioners' ribald songs
reached them through the windows. The Reds were drunk on sweet
Crimean wine and the blood of their victims.

Other cells continued to be emptied and restocked with new
prisoners who, once some critical mass had been reached, would be
taken behind the convent wall and the bratatata of the machine gun
would be heard anew. But the refectory remained filled to capacity,
with even more officers added every day and dead bodies removed
every morning.

And then their time came. Except it didn't come at night and that
took them by surprise.

They were herded out of the refectory and made to stand in the
stinking courtyard. The guards tied everyone's hands behind their
backs. They filled up the entire courtyard. There was only a small
space left in front of the rusty convent gate. It was filled by a miniature
commissar in a leather jacket.

By then Zolotnitsky had been at the convent for at least two weeks.
Maybe longer – a lot longer. He had lost count of the days. The faces
of other prisoners had become pale, unshaven blurs. All of them were
identical and stripped of any distinct personality.

He was starving and thirsty and exhausted from having to
constantly stand. He had a cold, and his feet were swollen and
covered with sores that oozed blood. His mind was coming loose
from its moorings. All he knew for certain was that he had been there
for a very long time, longer than most others, and that he was still
alive. Or at least it seemed that he was.

The pregnant girl, her unborn fetus, and the man who had objected
to her sitting on a bench out of turn were already over there, behind
the convent wall – bratatatat, bratatatat – in a shallow ditch, their

bodies gnawed by the homeless dogs and piled beneath other bodies. Come to think of it, being dead wasn't that unpleasant, but waiting to be dead was.

The undersized commissar read some sort of text from a sheet of typewriter paper. She spoke very proper Russian, without a shadow of a Ukrainian accent. Zolotnitsky wasn't listening. It was a cold, sunny winter morning. The weather was wonderful. The southern sun was tepid, but still it felt pleasant on his back. He felt like a plant, starting to revive under its rays. It was nice to be outside, especially if you could make yourself ignore the stench of excrement.

The commissar called out Zolotnitsky's name, and she called out other names, too. Those called were told to step across the courtyard and form a column. Those not called formed a column against the refectory wall. The two groups were more or less equal in size, facing each other across the courtyard. The one by the refectory was to stay behind, and the one in which Zolotnitsky now found himself was to march. He obeyed the orders with indifference.

The guards tied them into pairs, making them stand back-to-back. When this strange column started, they walked sideways, slowly and awkwardly, stumbling on a rock-strewn road with their bare feet. There was a detachment of soldiers guarding them, commanded by a couple of commissars who walked alongside them with guns drawn.

"Hurry up, will you?" the soldiers spat, hitting any who had trouble walking or who stumbled with the butts of their rifles.

Goodbye, Convent of the Virgin. Zolotnitsky would have liked to make the sign of the cross but his hands were tied. He did it in his mind, and he thanked the Lord for granting him a short, tragic and yet wonderful life.

After the rains of the previous days, the sky was newly washed and crisp. Dark rocks rose on both sides of the road, and the sea gleamed before them. Zolotnitsky filled his lungs with the fresh morning air. It smelled sweet after the rotten stench of the refectory. There were hills in the distance planted with cypress trees, pear and quince orchards, and long rows of vineyards. A Tartar in a distinctive hat was riding in a cart through a muddy field, pulled slowly forward by a donkey.

Back in the refectory, he had learned to ignore other men, and he had initially ignored the man to whom he had been tethered. He merely tried to keep in step with him, because that was the only way they could walk. Now, however, he heard a sob and turned his head as far as he could. He saw that he had been tied to a kid of nineteen or twenty. The kid was crying, tears streaming down his face, wetting the blond fuzz on his cheeks.

"Don't cry," Zolotnitsky told him. "Look around. The world is so beautiful."

"That's why I'm crying," the kid replied.

Indeed, it was a beautiful place. How strange to be dying in this setting, on such a nice winter morning. Zolotnitsky felt a sudden rush of gratitude to the guards for not taking them out in the dead of night, so that they could enjoy a glimpse of this beauty one last time.

"It'll be even more beautiful where we're going," Zolotnitsky said to the kid.

"I know," the kid replied, still sobbing.

He had expected to be taken to the hills behind the convent, but they kept going. His hands, tied roughly behind his back, began to ache. He moved his wrists and flexed his biceps. It was like bidding farewell to his body. Never before had he felt so strongly the presence of a soul, of a divine spark that the Lord had breathed into the clay of his flesh twenty-seven years before. The clay was comfortable to inhabit but it wasn't the limit of who he was. He was the tiny, divine spark immanent in his body.

They marched for almost half an hour and along a rocky shore, by a long narrow pier jutting out over the water. It was a natural harbor pressed between two sheer cliffs. The water was calm and aluminum grey beneath the sun. A pair of old rusty barges were moored by the pier, lolling on the gentle surf. Another commissar was waiting for them, surrounded by a group of sailors. He and the tiny female commissar exchanged greetings.

The sea was clear all the way to the misty horizon line and the unseen Anatolian coast beyond, and eerily empty. No pleasure craft, yachts, steamships, fishing sloops, or commercial boats traversed its expanse. Life had come to an end. Hungry gulls cawed overhead, happy to see a barge and hoping for food to come their way.

By the time Zolotnitsky's turn came to be loaded onto the barge, most of the other officers were sitting on the deck, back-to-back. The water had seeped through the rotting boards and was sloshing around their bodies. As he and the blond boy stepped off the pier, Zolotnitsky stumbled and stubbed his toe. He fell heavily, hitting his knee and shoulder against the edge and dragging his mate down. In an instant, one of the sailors was upon him, prodding him in the ribs with a bare toe.

"Get up, Your Excellency," he shouted and, since both prisoners were still down, pulled them unceremoniously by the hair. He was a huge man – perhaps a village blacksmith in his past life – and he lifted the two emaciated frames as easily as if they were a pair of rag dolls. "I can't let you two sleep here," the huge sailor laughed. "Go sit down with the rest."

There were about two hundred of them on the barge, Zolotnitsky reckoned.

"Wait a minute, Panteleyev," came a high-pitched voice from the pier. "I want to see him. No, the older one. Let me have a closer look at him."

The huge Panteleyev got hold of Zolotnitsky's hair again and twisted his head toward the pier. The commissar laughed.

"*Bonjour, capitaine,*" she said cheerfully. "*Vous devez me pardonner, je ne vous reconnais pas tout de suite. Mais maintenant je me rends compte que nous sommes de vieux amis.*"*

Zolotnitsky shrugged.

"Aren't you pleased to see me?" she asked, switching back into Russian. "Don't you think you deserve special treatment?"

---

* Hello, captain. Forgive me, I didn't immediately recognize you, but now I realize that we're old friends.

He was too weak to speak, and he didn't care. He wasn't happy to be waylaid. His aching, battered feet and injured knee made him want to sit down on the deck. But through the fog enveloping his brain, he finally recognized the tiny commissar.

"I was so much hoping we'd meet again," she went on. "Do you remember our conversation back there on the road to Ivanovka?"

She turned toward her men, who had eyed her suspiciously when she spoke a foreign language.

"This man," she shouted, her voice unexpectedly loud and strong. "This White scum spared my life in Tauria a few months ago. He probably thought he would get mercy from us if he fell into our hands. That is the code those bluebloods live by – they call it chivalry. But workers and peasants can't afford such niceties. They have seen too much misery in their lives. We have our own code of honor. We're sworn to fight for the victory of the Revolution until our last drop of blood and to show no mercy to the class enemy. That's our code of honor."

"That's right," her men shouted. "They never showed us any compassion. Down with him! Hurray for She-Devil! Long live the Revolution!"

"That's right, officer," she turned to Zolotnitsky. "That's what they call me, She-Devil. Do I look like a person who would ever spare an enemy, comrades?"

The cutthroats guffawed.

The officers on the barge were straining their necks to see what was going on.

"Comrades, I want to show you how compassionate I can be," she shouted. "Cut the other one off of him, Panteleyev."

The huge Panteleyev used his bayonet to slice the rope that tied the kid to Zolotnitsky and pushed him onto the barge.

"Go sit down," he ordered the kid. "And don't try any tricks if you don't want to have your neck broken."

The commissar turned to Zolotnitsky once more.

"You see, captain," she said softly, addressing him. "The Crimea Revolutionary Military Soviet sentenced all these men to be shot. But when they put me in charge of carrying out the sentence I didn't want to waste ammunition on them. We can get rid of some old barges and a whole bunch of officers at the same time."

She glanced at the officers on the barge who were listening to her intently. "As to you," she explained with a crooked smile, "you're going to get special treatment. I'll make you watch the others go down first. After all, by sparing my life you bear responsibility if not for their death, then for the manner in which they'll die."

"Let's get on with it, comrades," she commanded.

The sailors jumped onto the barge and, using crowbars, began crushing the rotten boards. It had already been taking on water under the weight of so many men, and now the waves flooded in and the barge began to keel over. The sailors jumped back onto the pier and gave the barge a push. It drifted off, travelling a dozen yards, and began to sink. There was panic among the officers as the rapidly rising sea began to cover them, they attempted frantically to get to their feet, which was when the purpose of tying them together became clear. All the desperate drowning men could do was crawl or roll helplessly on the deck, splashing in the rising water.

The sailors and the guards found it very comical. They pointed to some who were struggling especially desperately and laughed until tears ran down their rough faces. Zolotnitsky turned away. He was used to the sight of death. He just didn't want to see it.

"You're not watching, captain," the commissar said. "You don't find it amusing?"

Suddenly a figure separated from the squirming mass, and Zolotnitsky recognized his former mate. The kid was running awkwardly with his hands tied behind his back and his feet splashing in the water. He reached the edge of the barge and leapt overboard. The commissar was ready for him, picking him off with a shot from her Mauser before he hit the water. The gun looked huge in her tiny hand.

"Are you a good shot, captain?" she asked, putting the gun into a wooden holster dangling on her side.

Zolotnitsky recoiled from her in disgust. As he did that, he felt the rope tying his hands loosen a little. He wriggled his wrists some more and felt his hands almost come free. Perhaps while cutting the rope that tied him and the kid together, Panteleyev had accidentally freed Zolotnitsky's hands as well.

The officers continued to squirm and scream as the barge gurgled and sank and the sea covered them. The soldiers on the pier kept roaring with laughter. It was all over.

Zolotnitsky sighed. He knew it was his turn now, and he didn't want to die with his hands tied. They weren't anymore. But he stood with his hands behind his back as though they were.

The tiny commissar, turning suddenly toward him and giving him a push, took him by surprise. He nearly threw his hands out in front of him before he hit the water. He managed to fill his lungs at the last second and fell into the water sideways, creating an enormous splash.

The cold took his breath away. The salt water began to burn the sores on his body and feet. Opening his eyes, he saw dark shapes in the distance, suspended and swaying softly. The sea around him was muddy with the sand and slime that the barge had lifted from the bottom. His brain made a note of it while his body stayed motionless, sinking out of sight of the people watching him from the pier.

He would have drowned like the others if his hands had been tied. But now, suddenly, he desperately wanted to live. For one, he wanted to prove She-Devil wrong. But mostly he wanted to live for his own sake.

The challenge energized him. He strained his muscles, propelling himself upward, under the welcome shelter of the pier. He came up for a split second, just enough to get a breath of air, and went below the surface once again. After a while, he swam behind the second barge and, shielded from the shore by its bulk, waited for the soldiers to leave. He was frozen stiff by the time dusk fell, and he felt it was safe to wade onto the shore.

Six months later he made his way first to Warsaw and then to Berlin. He had friends in both cities who sheltered him and gave him money to get to Paris. Once there, he made no attempt to look up Olga. If she had felt she could leave Crimea without him, it could only mean one thing, and there was nothing for them to discuss.

Within a month of arriving in Paris, on the recommendation of an old buddy from the Austrian front, he enlisted in the Foreign Legion. March or die was their motto. By then, he knew that dying wasn't easy for him. That left marching as his only option.

# FIFTEEN

"So, lieutenant, what was that all about?" Andropov asked, shaking his head and staring steadily at me.

I shrugged. I couldn't tell him why I had asked Khokhlova that question. Call it intuition. I honestly knew nothing about anything else being taken from her, something that was not among the baubles we had found in Levkoyev's apartment.

"Don't play games with me, lieutenant," Andropov said, his voice threatening.

Andropov may have been a new breed of KGB chief – polite and businesslike, and determined to bring a new style of work to the organization. He certainly was different from the grim cutthroat types who still, despite the purges of the past ten years, endured in its ranks. Yet, just below the surface, he was still KGB. They were the aristocracy, the knights-errant of communism – and you played games with them at your own risk.

"I don't know," I said. "I can't put my finger on it, but I'm sure she's not completely honest with us. She's hiding something."

"And yet she says everything has been recovered. Why would she lie to you? And to me, too?"

"I don't know, sir. This is what I would like to find out."

We were having this conversation in Andropov's Volga parked at the curb on Dzerzhinsky Street, on the side of the massive KGB complex.

"I didn't ask you to find that out, lieutenant," Andropov said. "The task I set to you was to make sure that Olga Stepanovna's jewels have been returned. You were lucky. You found them very quickly. Olga Stepanovna has declared herself satisfied. You are done, thank you very much."

"The burglary has not been solved," I said. "The thief has not been caught. And now we have a murder on our hands."

"It's entirely your affair. I don't care about any of that."

I was catching horrified looks Valera was giving me. He couldn't believe I was arguing with the head of the mighty KGB. If truth be told, I too was cursing myself inwardly for my own stubbornness. I should have just said "Yes, sir, thank you very much, sir" and moved on.

Instead, I said, "First of all, unless we catch the thief we won't know how he got here. The security breach which allowed him to get into the victim's suite will not be discovered, and a similar crime could happen again at any time."

Andropov gave me one of his superior smiles. That was also a KGB hallmark – to be certain that they're smarter than the rest of us.

"I didn't say that you shouldn't be catching the thief. When you do, I'll certainly want to hear who he is and how he got into the Metropole. But I specifically asked the two of you to work on this case because I didn't want to scare Olga Stepanovna. In any civilized country, a theft from a hotel room is a routine police investigation. And now you're harassing her with your questions. I hope you noticed how upset she got."

"I did," I said. "This is what makes me think she is not at all satisfied with the results. She did get her jewelry back, but something is still bothering her."

Andropov sighed.

"Even if you're correct, lieutenant," he said coldly. "There are plenty of other explanations why she would be unnerved. She was probably frightened to find an intruder in her suite more than she showed. It may be a delayed reaction to that fear. What makes you think it's a missing piece of jewelry?"

"It may not be," I admitted. "This is what I would like to find out by questioning her some more."

"It's absolutely out of the question," Andropov said sharply. "You're not to approach her or any member of the hotel staff. I told you this before, and I know you disregarded my orders. I let it go once, but I will not tolerate a second instance of insubordination."

So Andropov was aware of my interview with Daria Shubina. That was yet another problem of dealing with the KGB. You couldn't hide anything from them. This made me mad, and so I said, "If you don't allow us to interrogate anybody who could have had a hand in the burglary, how do you expect us to catch the thief?"

"I can do it," Valera suddenly butted in. "I don't need to talk to Olga Stepanovna or the hotel staff. I'll work through Levkoyev's connections. His murderer was probably someone he had known, because he let him in himself."

"Good," Andropov said, smiling at Valera. "And I'm pretty sure you'll find that the murderer and the Metropole burglar are one and the same person."

I wasn't so sure that the murderer and the burglar were one and the same person, but I kept my own council. That was the thing. In every other civilized country, the equivalent of our KGB, if there was one, didn't get involved in police investigations. Their KGB didn't tell the police what to do, didn't hover over their cops' shoulders – or, at the very least, didn't impede their work so that they had to conduct investigations with one hand tied behind their back, as it were.

"Perhaps it makes sense for the two of you to work separately," Andropov said, sneering. "Or rather, I'd like Lieutenant Tumakov to go on working on the burglary and Lieutenant Matyushkin to do something else. I'm sure there are other crimes to work on at Moscow Criminal Investigations. I'll ask your superior officer to reassign you."

I was sure the Boss would be angry with me, but Valera liked the idea very much.

"Yes, sir," he cried out readily. "I've already been talking to people in the trade, including antique collectors, police informers, and buyers of stolen goods. I visited the dead man's place thirty-six hours before he was killed. I've been trying to determine whether his murder and the burglary were connected."

"Weren't they?" Andropov asked.

"It's not clear, sir. Not completely. Or at least we don't know in what way. Levkoyev knew nothing about those jewels when I mentioned them, and then they turned up in his apartment less than two days later."

Andropov made a face. "And then he turns up dead. It's too much of a coincidence, lieutenant. What if Levkoyev knew about the jewels when you came to see him? Your visit was most likely the reason the thief decided to kill him."

"Then why didn't the thief take the jewels back?"

"Plenty of reasons. Levkoyev might have misled him by telling him that he had already sold them to a third party. Or else he knew that Levkoyev had plenty of hiding places in the apartment and didn't want to risk lingering at the scene of the crime for fear of being caught. As I recall, during their altercation one of them broke the window and the neighbors could have called the cops."

I was paying close attention to their exchange, and I was surprised to find out that Andropov was remarkably well-informed about the case.

"Let's think why Levkoyev could have been murdered, lieutenant," he continued. "Let's look for the motive. Suppose the thief sells him the jewels having assured him they were legitimate, or at least safe – stolen them from some old Russian lady. But then out of the blue, Levkoyev gets a visit from Lieutenant Tumakov. All of a sudden it looks like the jewels were stolen from someone important enough for Criminal Investigations to be involved. Levkoyev gets mad. He invites the thief back, and they have a nasty argument. One of them throws a candlestick at the other, misses and breaks the window. Plausible so far?"

"Extremely," I admitted.

"The thief doesn't like to see Levkoyev scared. If the cops put Levkoyev's feet to the fire, he might turn the thief in, guaranteeing him ten years' hard labor. So he does away with Levkoyev. A nice and simple solution. It may not even have been premeditated. In fact, it looks more like a spur-of-the-moment decision. As to searching for the jewels – why bother? He's been paid for them once, and he doesn't want to take the risk of being caught with them – especially now that a murder is involved."

I had to admit that Andropov's version of events made a lot of sense.

"Very well, then, you've got plenty to work on, Lieutenant Tumakov," the KGB chief concluded, then turned to me. "And I'm sure Colonel Martirosyan will find an assignment for you."

The conversation was over. As I was getting out of Andropov's Volga I caught Ivan's eyes in the rearview mirror. He was looking at me, and it was as though he was sizing me up, assessing what I was capable of. It was a strange stare, and it left me uncomfortable and vaguely worried.

## SIXTEEN

To have been taken off the Metropole investigation had its advantages. While Budyonny, who, as I had expected, wasn't pleased with my removal from the case, was still looking to get me usefully employed, I got to spend more time at home. Nikola was sleeping a lot better, much like he had been at the old apartment, as though having provoked a massive fight between me and our new neighbor Boris, he could now revert to his usual self with a clear conscience. That also meant that Tosya was getting a lot more sleep, too, and that was reflected in her greatly improved disposition. She was no longer short-tempered with Sevka every time he got underfoot, which went a long way toward improving his mood as well.

Peace reigned in our apartment.

Of course, Tosya still yelled at me now and again, but I didn't mind. I knew she loved me – passionately in the beginning, when we first met, and more tenderly now, since little Nikola had been born. It was as though she was grateful to me for him, even though she would never have put it that way. In her perverse way, she yelled at me because she didn't want to show how tender she felt.

Complicated? You bet.

Tosya never knew her parents. Her life experience, growing up at a state orphanage, had taught her to trust no one. If you were stupid enough to fall for a guy and get attached to him, it was your own fault. It's you who made yourself vulnerable. Don't cry then when you are betrayed or taken advantage of. You should be strong enough to break the attachment before you have anything to regret.

She had let down her guard just once, with the man who became Sevka's father. She was too naive to know he had been toying with her, seducing a 17-year-old with a couple of trips to a restaurant and a few inexpensive gifts. He would come to see her with a bouquet of flowers and her heart would melt because no one had done anything like that for her before.

He disappeared as soon as she told him about her pregnancy, which she only discovered four months in.

"How do I know it's mine? You'll never be able to prove it. It's your word against mine. No one will believe you, because you're a nobody. An orphan trying to hit up a man for child support."

That was all he said.

Later, when Sevka was a couple of months old, he waylaid her at the entrance to a metro station. As she walked past him, ignoring his attempts to talk to her, he stuffed a few banknotes into her pocket. She threw them into a trash can and then had the satisfaction of seeing him try to fish them out.

She had been stupid once, and she wasn't going to fall for it again.

"Don't worry, Uncle Pavel," Sevka said to me after one of Tosya's outbursts. "She is the way she is because she just had a baby. My biology teacher says that when wolves have cubs their females are ferocious and dangerous. You've got to watch out for them."

"I will," I said. "I promise. I'll do my best to stay away from her teeth and claws."

Nikola was a big boy, solid all over and kind of slow-moving. It was clear that he was going to be a bruiser when he grew up, judging by his outsized hands and feet. Tosya is a large woman, as tall as me, and also very solid. Nikola was already turning into a male version of her. He ate nonstop, sucking Tosya dry and devouring all the milk Sevka and I could get at the nursery, to which we took turns traveling nearly every day. Nikola gained weight quickly, making the doctor at the neighborhood children's polyclinic very happy. Sevka was eating a huge amount, too, but he wasn't getting nice and round like his brother. He was starting to shoot up, but stayed as skinny as a bean – a typical Russian kid – despite spending half an hour every morning lifting weights in his room.

Most of the day, Nikola sat in his crib staring at his toys. He would lift one of them every once in a while, stare at it and put it down. We are not a fast-thinking nation, and Nikola, too, was a typical representative.

Sevka was great with him. On Wednesdays, the only day of the week he didn't have after-school activities – which included boxing at the Burevestnik Stadium, swimming lessons in the open air pool on Kropotkinskaya and, upon his mother's insistence, a drawing and sculpting class at the Young Pioneers Palace on Stopani Street – he took Sevka for a walk in his carriage.

"Take a look at my brother's hands," he would tell his buddies playing pickup hockey on the frozen pond on the boulevard. "When he's five, I'm taking him straight to the Soviet Wings Hockey School. His hands are made to hold a hockey stick."

The Soviet Wings were an obscure team who once managed to come out of nowhere to win the national title. They were the kind of underdog Sevka loved. I was different. I liked winners.

Fortunately, our new neighbor Boris was not badly hurt after all and quickly recovered from his injuries. He still stayed home from work and was on his best behavior. He was especially polite and almost differential to Tosya. I once overheard him noting that Nikola seemed to sleep a lot better.

"Of course he does," she replied. "All he needed was to get used to the new place. There was never any need for you to carry on like you did. He probably would have calmed down even sooner."

Tosya still held a grudge, and Boris didn't like being reminded of our fight. He was going to give her a sharp reply, but somehow restrained himself.

He and I were now on friendly terms once more. The first time we met in the kitchen after the fight he offered me his hand and suggested we let bygones be bygones.

"No hard feelings, neighbor? What's a couple of bruises between guys?"

I shook his hand and he limped back to his room, reemerging with a bottle of brandy and two glasses. He filled them to the brim, handed one to me and raised a toast, "To peace, friendship, and good neighbors."

We clicked glasses. The brandy was smooth on my tongue, but it began to burn my throat the moment it hit it.

"Good stuff," I said.

I had not had breakfast yet, and the alcohol went to my head almost immediately.

"Only the best. Three star Armenian. Like your boss."

He gave me a wink.

He was obviously referring to Budyonny, an Armenian by birth. And, since he was a colonel, he had three stars on his epaulets. In other words, Boris was making me understand that he had looked me up in his agency's files and knew everything there was to know about me. He probably knew more about my work than Tosya, because the KGB was that kind of organization. We had drunk to peace and friendship and what have you, but his eyes were watchful. I wasn't at all sure he'd be such a good neighbor going forward, no matter how much he pretended to be in the wake of Andropov's visit.

"By the way," he said, as though to confirm my observation. "What are you doing for Yuri Vladimirovich?"

"I don't know what you're talking about," I said.

Andropov had told me to keep the investigation secret, and that was what I was doing.

"Understood," he replied quickly.

That was the best way to behave around KGB guys: be cagey. The less information you give out, the more they think you have to hide.

I made a note to tell Tosya to be careful with Boris and to not mention our fight anymore. But it probably made no difference. We had made an enemy, and we needed to keep that in mind, even if outwardly we were on friendly terms.

# SEVENTEEN

I got to headquarters early in the morning and found Valera already hard at work.

"Guess what I found out," I said, removing my jacket and draping it over the back of my chair.

Valera was becoming a regular at the semi-illegal art and antiques market in Izmailovo Park, where on Saturdays nonconformist artists peddled works that looked like they had been hastily smeared on used canvases with cheap paint. On other days, he visited the racetrack on Begovaya, where he said some art collectors and antiques dealers liked to spend their leisure time. Late at night he made copious notes about all his activities, then reviewed them the following morning, before departing to meet a new bunch of fly-by-night characters.

"The strange thing about Levkoyev," he said, lifting his head from a manila file, "is that he didn't seem to have any associates. A couple of young women – one a student at the graphic arts school and another a flutist at the light opera – whom he was apparently seeing at the same time. They had no idea about each other."

"Don't you want to know what I found out?" I asked. "It may have something to do with Levkoyev."

"I'm sorry, Pavel. You're no longer involved in this investigation. I just find it hard to believe that a guy would see two beautiful young women at the same time. Why would he do that? It's dishonest."

"Remember the concierge at the Metropole?" I asked, ignoring his righteous outrage in the face of Levkoyev's duplicity and immoral conduct. "The one who was on duty on Khokhlova's floor the night of the burglary?"

"Sure," Valera shrugged, looking at me apprehensively.

"Her name is Daria Shubina. Her shift ends at seven. Since I have no work right now, this morning I took the trouble of trailing her home."

"You can't do that, Pavel. You've been told by Comrade Andropov in no uncertain terms to lay off this investigation and, specifically, to stay away from Metropole employees. It's my investigation now."

"That's right. But all the same, wouldn't you like to know where she lives?"

"Sure," he shrugged, making a show of resignation.

"She lives in Maly Demidovsky Lane."

"Where is that?"

I always forget that Valera grew up outside the city, in a small town beyond the Ring Road. Even after working for Moscow Criminal Investigations for several years, he still barely knew the city. I also grew up in a neighborhood on the outskirts that was probably just as far from the center, yet we would spend all day knocking about the city, exploring neighborhoods and picking fights with local kids.

We were the postwar generation, and we grew up without much supervision. Most of my friends' fathers didn't come back from the war. Those who did drank bitterly, while their mothers worked long hours at some factory or other. We grew up unsupervised, and, as a result, many of us ended up dead or in jail.

But the war also produced kids whose parents were overly protective. They wouldn't let them play outside and kept them home after school doing their homework. Valera must have been one of those kids. We would taunt those types, and they would run to the teacher to complain, then we would be summoned to the principal's office and branded as bullies – which only led to more taunting and beatings for the teachers' pets. It was a tough time to be a kid.

"It's around the corner from the late, lamented Levkoyev," I said. "I wouldn't be surprised if they stood in the same grocery store line twice a week or ran into each other in the street now and again."

"Did they know each other?" Valera asked. He looked dubious.

"I don't know whether or not they did," I said. "But it is worth exploring. She could even have been the burglar. Remember, Khokhlova wasn't initially sure whether the intruder was a man or a woman."

Despite himself, Valera was getting interested in our conversation.

"Could she have stabbed him though?" he asked. "Such a cool, professional job, it's unlikely to have been done by a woman."

"Why not? She could be a KGB officer who received basic training. There must be a reason Andropov doesn't want us to talk to anyone on the staff, much less see their files."

"Nonsense," Valera protested. "You said it yourself that Olga Stepanovna had to have seen the burglar and that she was certain it had been a man."

I shrugged.

"Maybe I was wrong, and she didn't get a good look after all."

"If Levkoyev bought those jewels off the concierge from the Metropole, you hardly would have expected him to be surprised to find out that they had been stolen there."

Valera was a pedant, but he had a point. Still, I wasn't about to give up.

"He may have been spooked by your visit," I said, "you coming to see him so soon after the crime. In any case, I still think you should include her in Levkoyev's circle. I admit it's a long shot, but you've just said that it's surprising how few people he knew. I doubt you need to check out the two women he was juggling. Unless of course you think he was stabbed by one of them in a fit of jealous rage."

"Actually, it's a possibility," Valera said. "I may look into it."

"What about Daria Shubina?" I asked.

"I'm not going to talk to her," he said. "Comrade Andropov told us to stay away from hotel employees, and I think we should do as we were told. And if you want my advice, I think you should stay out of this case."

We sat in silence for a while, Valera reorganizing his files and me twiddling my thumbs. Then, after a perfunctory knock, Budyonny's secretary squeezed into our tiny office.

"Hello, Della," Valera said, immediately returning to his files.

Years ago, Budyonny used to change his secretaries every year. The general opinion was that he had to do that because they tended to get too friendly with my late partner, Lenny. That hypothesis had been confirmed by Lenny's death. The usual secretarial turnover period came and went, but Della stayed on, outstripping all previous longevity records. In the meantime, she got married and had a child, and Budyonny held her job for her while she was on maternity leave. She had by now established a symbiotic relationship with the Boss, which all secretaries do after working for the same person for a long time. Unfortunately, it also makes them think they have a right to order people around.

"To the Boss's office," she commanded. "On the double. Follow me."

She started down the hall without waiting for us, confident that we would scramble after her – which of course we did. Valera was a few steps ahead of me, since I wasted a few seconds putting on my jacket.

The Boss hated it if we didn't come immediately when called. Every one of his summonses was extremely urgent, and it never paid to get him angry at you. But as I sped down the long hallway, trying to catch up with them, Della suddenly stopped and turned around, so that Valera nearly ran into her.

"Where are you going, lieutenant?" she asked, eyeing Valera coldly and, I thought, malevolently.

"But, you said—" Valera began. He was taken aback by Della's hostile tone. Ordinarily, she was better disposed toward him than me, because he made her job easy, while I always caused all sorts of complications.

"The Boss wants to see him," she said, pointing to me with her brightly manicured finger. "Alone."

Having turned against my partner, she apparently had not developed any warm feelings for me either.

The Boss was leafing through a file on his imposing desk. I waited for him to finish, standing at attention and, since the Boss didn't give any indication that he was aware of my presence, keeping my eyes on the panoramic window of his office. There were two men in torn sheepskin overcoats and cloth hats clearing the snow off the roof of a three-story building adjacent to headquarters. Their shovels scraped on the sheet metal and, every time they were about to toss a shovelful of snow and ice off the edge, they shouted a warning to the street below. Neither the scraping nor the shouting could be heard through the thick double panes. The men opened their mouths like fish in a fishbowl, releasing a cloud of steam and making pedestrians jump off the sidewalk in panic or cling tremulously to the façade as an avalanche came tumbling down the side of the building.

Behind the two men, on the cleared section of the roof, a black cat was stalking a pigeon. The cat was moving stealthily toward its prey, bending low and placing its paws down with utmost care. But the moment the distance between them narrowed enough for the cat to ready his pounce, tensing every muscle on its supple body, the pigeon nonchalantly hopped a few feet away, forcing the cat to start his hunt all over again.

I had become so absorbed in the scene, rooting for the cat and growing mad at the insolence of the stupid, fat pigeon, that I missed the moment when Budyonny raised his eyes from the file and started watching me watching the cat.

"Fascinating, isn't it, lieutenant?" he asked at last. "Would you rather I left you to it?"

"Yes, sir," I responded, taken by surprise.

Budyonny laughed.

"You would, wouldn't you? Unfortunately, I'll have to intrude. I want you to take a look at this."

He handed me the file he had been studying.

"It's a murder case," he said. "Here are the directions to the place where they found the body. Which is most likely not where the victim was killed. You'll figure that all out when you read the report by the local cop. It's southeast of the city, but not far. On the Moscow River."

"I know the place, Comrade Colonel," I said, glancing at the directions.

"Oh, you do? So much the better. You need to go there right away. Or at least as soon as you can tear yourself away from the window."

I was glad to have a new assignment and wanted to start on it right away, but the Boss held me back.

"I have to admit, Matyushkin, that I wasn't happy to take you off the Metropole case. I have no doubt that Tumakov will be able to handle the robbery investigation on his own. But he has a lot to atone for. I still can't get my mind around the ease with which Levkoyev twisted him around his little finger. He should have at least put the guy under surveillance, tapped his phone – something. This is why I would have liked you to be working with him."

The Boss's criticism of my partner went a long way toward explaining why Della had treated Valera with such contempt. She always shared the Boss's sentiments. And thus her attitude toward any of us could shift from moment to moment.

I picked up the file, saluted the Boss, and was about to go out when he added, his Armenian accent suddenly becoming much stronger, "These KGB guys, I don't know about them sometimes. I don't understand what they want. They have all their resources, secret agents and informers everywhere. Let them turn their attention to it. Why us?"

He sighed.

"You start on this new investigation, see what it is all about, and if you need help, I'll get you someone else. Gromovsky or one of the young guys. But I may also pull you back on the Metropole case if Tumakov doesn't get results. Off you go now. Dismissed."

To be honest, I was happy to be done with the Metropole burglary. What I didn't like was how the Boss was coming down on Valera. He, no doubt, had sensed that the Boss was unhappy with him, and that would be upsetting to him more than to any other detective on the force. I wasn't fond of Valera, but he was still my partner. Besides, it was unfair. How was Valera to guess that Levkoyev was connected to the burglary?

## EIGHTEEN

Ivan Rublyov was convinced that his little daughter Lenka would one day be a Soviet figure skating champion. She was just ten years old, yet she could already do amazing twists and pirouettes with all sorts of funny names, and it sort of gave you a headache if you watched her for more than ten minutes at a stretch. She had long, skinny, and very flexible legs that were like boiled noodles. Ivan scratched his head as he watched her, wondering how her legs didn't get tangled or tied into knots whenever she spun.

His buddies at the bus depot, where he was a shift supervisor in the repair shop, liked to tease him about his passion for figure skating, but he didn't care. What did they know? They were drivers and mechanics and had no joy in life except breaking into groups of three after work and splitting a half-liter of vodka out behind the bus depot. Their interest in sports was limited to soccer, which they could argue about for hours. Ivan didn't get it. Figure skating was beautiful. He had watched it just once on TV and fell in love with it. A year later, the American team died in a plane crash, and even though Ivan would never admit it to anyone, he felt tears welling up when he watched the tribute.

Maybe his daughter would grow up to compete in one of those tournaments, in Stockholm or Paris. She was dedicated and worked hard, which was more important than talent, yet in his eyes she had plenty of that as well.

A woman at whose dacha he was doing some carpentry work on the side told him about a school for figure skaters at Sokolniki Park, where you could skate year round on artificial ice, and where figure skating champions were churned out in an assembly line. Ivan took his daughter there one day after school. The woman coach watched her skate for about a minute and said that, even though the girl had potential and was exceptionally musical, her students had all started when they were four or five, and it may just be too late for her. However, she said that if she got a pair of real figure skates, instead of her brother's ill-fitting hockey hand-me-downs, and then practiced every day through the winter, she, the woman coach, would be willing to take another look in the spring.

Ivan left the woman coach's office crestfallen, and his mood didn't improve as they lingered at the Sokolniki school for an hour, watching the magic that the seven and eight-year-olds were performing. But his Lenka was not deterred. On the contrary, she was inspired.

"I can learn to do this stuff on my own, Dad," she declared. "If I have a place to skate through the winter, and if I get a good pair of skates, I'll be better than them."

The following Sunday, Ivan picked up his brother Savva, who lived across the river in the village of Zakharikha, Savva's older son Ilya, and his own son Pyotr, and the four of them went down to the Moscow River armed with brooms and shovels. They marked out a large rectangle on the frozen surface, cleared it of snow and assorted debris, poured a layer of water on it and, when it turned to ice in the sub-zero weather, polished it so well it glistened blindingly in the winter sunshine. They worked all day, and at dusk, while Ivan and Savva enjoyed a well-deserved glass of vodka and were warming themselves by a campfire on the shore, Lenka began her training regimen.

After that, she skated regularly, for an hour every morning before school – in the predawn darkness and in a cold so brutal that her brand-new figure skates got no traction on the rock-hard ice – and then for another two more hours every afternoon. Other Sofrino kids began skating on the rink as well. But Lenka didn't mind as long as they didn't interfere with her routine. At first they laughed at her, but her determination ended up earning her their grudging respect.

Every morning, Ivan got up before dawn, woke up Lenka, and while she dressed and had some tea, walked down to the river to sweep off the snow that had fallen during the night, along with any cigarette butts and broken bottles that idiots might have thrown onto his daughter's rink, just because it was there. He wished he could catch them in the act and give them a good belt.

That morning nothing unusual happened. He woke up at the first crowing of the rooster in his neighbor's coop and put on his work clothes, along with a pair of felt boots and galoshes. By the time he tiptoed into the room that Lenka shared with her two brothers, she was awake too, and he could see her eyes against the white outline of her pillow, blinking away sleep. Her eyes glowed in the dark like a cat's, burning with a passion for her sport.

While she was getting dressed, he took a drink from the full bucket by the door, after using the edge of an aluminum mug to break the thin crust of ice that had formed in the night. Then he walked outside.

The frigid air made his nose itch with every breath. He lit up a cigarette he had rolled before leaving, in the warmth of the house. The yellow smoke of his strong, home-grown tobacco mixed with his steaming breath. He stopped and coughed the deep-throated cough of a lifelong smoker, then spat into the snowdrift on the side of the footpath before continuing.

It was still dark, and the early morning stars made the sky glow silver. Chipped on one side, the moon hung pale over the horizon. But winter had already moved past its midpoint, and bit by bit the mornings were getting lighter earlier with each passing day – one sparrow's step at a time, as the old folks used to say.

Lights were on in some of the houses. His neighbors were country folks – still peasants at heart, though no one was tilling the soil and most had city jobs earning real wages. The single long street of the village was empty. The thin layer of freshly fallen snow creaked beneath the rubber soles of Ivan's galoshes.

He got down to the river, moving cautiously on the slippery bank, and got to work. His shoulders, stiff after a night's sleep, began to limber up. He walked the length of the rink, scraping the snow with the metal edge of his wooden shovel. Reaching the end, he gathered the snow onto the blade, lifted the heavy load and tossed it away. Then the same thing the other way. Then back again. After a while, he started to get warm, and about three quarters of the way into the job, he had to stop, wipe the sweat dripping from beneath his hat, and remove his quilted jacket.

He was a little ahead of schedule, which gave him time to roll and light another cigarette. The sun was rising slowly over the opposite bank of the river. He drew deeply on the cigarette and immediately was bent double by another coughing fit. Then, as suddenly as it had started, the fit stopped. He opened his eyes wide. A distorted mask of a human face stared at him from the river, tinted blue by the thick ice.

Ivan threw away the cigarette, breathed in and sat down on a frozen snowdrift at the edge of the rink. He removed his mittens and rubbed his eyes. Of course, in the deceptive, early morning half-light he had mistaken a snow-traced pattern on the ice for a human face. He breathed out, braced himself, and looked down again. The face was still there. The current under the ice was fast, and the ice was clear and polished, and Ivan could now see that the face was bobbing up and down in the water. It seemed to be leering at him.

And now Ivan became aware of a soft, rhythmic sound. It was the face, tapping gently on the underside of the ice.

He remained motionless for a long time, staring at the face, his blood running cold and his heart beating.

"What's happened, Papa?" Lenka shouted from the high bank of the river, starting her descent. Her skates, tied together by their long laces, swayed back and forth on her shoulder. "You haven't finished."

Her voice bringing him out of the stupor, Ivan jumped to his feet and ran to intercept her.

"Stay where you are," he shouted, waving his arms and shielding the grotesque blue mask from her view. "Don't go down there, girl."

# NINETEEN

It was early afternoon when I arrived at the village of Sofrino. Looking down from the high bank of the river, I saw a large rectangular clearing in the snow, roughly the size of a hockey rink. All around its edges the snow had been churned up by countless feet. A large hole had been chopped in the ice. An ax lay nearby, next to a pair of a child's figure skates. The water in the hole was green, and the current was rapid, gurgling and spewing a spray that had frozen white around the edges.

The only thing in the Boss's file was a telephone message taken down by Della, which simply stated that a body, apparently of a murder victim, had been pulled from the Moscow River. The sight of the figure skates made me sick to my stomach, reminding me of a series of child murders I had worked on when I first joined the Boss's team. I had no desire to see another dead child.

A short distance away, a body was lying on a stretcher, its outline showing through a grey wool blanket. A group of men in police uniform and civilian clothes stood near the hole in the ice, casting short purple shadows in the sunlight. They were having an animated discussion, gesticulating and pointing at the water. One of them crouched and touched the current. The others watched him, stomping their feet to drive away the cold.

Another cop was keeping a small crowd of locals gathered at the edge of the river under control. They were craning their necks in the direction of the stretcher. A pair of kids kept trying to sneak closer whenever the cop wasn't looking. But he was alert. Every time they stepped onto the ice, he turned and wagged his finger.

It had taken me a little over an hour to arrive and to locate the place. I was glad Tumakov wasn't working with me, as he would have refused to ride my Zundapp. He didn't think it was safe.

I came down to the river, got past the cop who saluted respectfully once I showed him my ID, and joined the others by the hole in the ice. One of the civilians turned out to be a medic from the town of Zhukovsky, which had an Air Force base and a top-notch forensics lab. Another was his assistant, whom I had at first taken for a teenage boy, but who in reality was a very pretty young woman with freckles and spiky blonde hair sticking out from beneath the ear-flaps of her fur hat.

The three uniformed officers were from the nearby town of Ramenskoye. Yet another man in a suit and tie was their boss. All four got a little flustered at first by the sight of a big city detective, but relaxed once they learned that I was a mere senior lieutenant. The boss was Major Snegiryov. I didn't catch the names of the other three.

The introductions and handshakes over, we got down to business. First they called over a square-shouldered, unshaven local by the name of Ivan Rublyov. He was wearing a padded jacket and a pair of felt boots, and he was the only one in our group who didn't seem to be bothered by the cold.

"Yes, comrade officer boss," he announced, nodding solemnly. "It was me who found the body. Early in the morning it was, comrade officer boss."

He went on to explain, very slowly and in great detail, that his daughter was a figure skater and he had made a skating rink for her to practice on, which she did every morning for an hour before school, and that he got up early in order to clear the ice for her. The pair of figure skates belonged to his daughter and the ax lying nearby belonged to him, and he had used it to get the body out from under the ice when the cops arrived – but that was getting a bit ahead of the story, because naturally he had found the body first and only after that had he called the cops.

I was relieved to find out that the pair of children's skates were not the murder victim's. I also knew better than to interrupt a local when he was telling a story. Their tales may be convoluted and move up and down the timeline freely and occasionally stray off on tangents, but there is always a flow to the narrative and interrupting it risks causing the narrator to lose his train of thought. The Ramenskoye cops and the doctor showed no impatience at what, for them, must have been a third or a fourth retelling. Only the doctor's pretty assistant fidgeted nervously. Eventually I heard how he had gotten up, gotten dressed, had come down to the river. He had started clearing the snow and had stumbled over the dead man's face. Not literally, of course, because it had been under the ice.

"I was scared out of my wits at first," Rublyov said. "I'm glad they told us at school that old wives' tales about river spirits were all nonsense, because I could have sworn it was one of them spirits right down there, winking at me. What I kept asking myself was how come he was hanging in there, not floating away with the current, which is so swift around here, and him being so dead."

"Did you find out?" I asked.

"Well, comrade officer boss—" Rublyov began, scratching his head, but the doctor's assistant cut in impatiently.

"The body was caught on the branch of a submerged tree, lieutenant," she explained.

"That's exactly how it was," Rublyov confirmed earnestly. "She hit the nail on the head, this girl. I couldn't have put it better myself."

He went on with his story, telling me how his daughter had come down to the river and how he had chased her away so that she would not see the ugly mug that would have given her nightmares, and how he had sent her to get Mikhalych while he, Rublyov, had stayed there by the river to make sure the dead man didn't get away.

"Who's Mikhalych?" I asked.

"He's the one over there."

Rublyov pointed to the cop who was still struggling to keep the onlookers in line.

"That's Sergeant Okopko," one of the Ramenskoye cops explained. "He's in charge of the village up there."

"That's right," Rublyov confirmed. "He even lives in a house next door. His wife keeps chickens."

"Get over here, sergeant, will you?" Major Snegiryov shouted.

The cop shook his fist at the two boys by way of a warning, then started to run toward us, wobbling awkwardly in his felt boots. Under his police overcoat he wore a pair of quilted pants and a heavy wool sweater. The moment he was gone, the locals surged forward. He turned around without breaking stride and yelled something at them that stopped them in their tracks.

"Tell us how you found the body, Okopko," the major ordered him. "This is an important detective from Moscow."

The major was getting back at me for the scare I had given him and his subordinates, somehow making them mistake me for a big boss from the city.

The sergeant was completely out of breath from his short run. He had to pause for a moment, panting heavily, before responding.

"It wasn't me, comrade major. It was Ivan Rublyov. I got here after the body had been discovered."

That was very typical of the locals. It's remarkable how they hate to accept responsibility for anything – because if something goes wrong, they might get blamed for it.

"We know that already, Okopko," the major said. "Let's start with when you got here."

"Sure," Okopko shrugged. "I don't care. If that's what you want."

Unlike Rublyov, he spoke reluctantly. The major kept asking him questions, and he kept giving hoarse, monosyllabic answers. It was painful to watch, like pulling teeth.

Yes, sure. He had come as soon as Rublyov's little girl ran up to his house to tell him that he was wanted by the river. No, she hadn't told him there was a body. She didn't know that at the time. Sure, there had been a body under the ice. Sure. Not a body but a face. But he had assumed that there would be a body attached to it. Yes, he had sent Rublyov to get an ax. Why hadn't they extracted the body before the cops got there? They had feared that they would do something wrong and be blamed for it. What if it had broken away in the meantime? There was nothing he could have done about it.

He sounded defensive. He kept shaking his head as if to say we get blamed for everything. Damned if you do and damned if you don't. But, in each and every case, the blame is smaller if you don't take the initiative than if you do.

"But what if the body had been lost?" the major insisted.

The sergeant shrugged and spread his arms wide. Apparently, that would have been God's will.

"Well," Rublyov broke in. "We talked it over, and I said what if we lose the poor devil? To my mind, it would have been a lot better for us if he had kept drifting the whole time, instead of parking himself right here in the clear section. But Mikhalych didn't agree with me. He said we could get into real trouble if we set him free and if someone found out about it. As to him breaking loose on his own, who knew what was holding him up? He could have hung around here for a month. We put our heads together and in the end decided not to touch him."

Rublyov broke off suddenly, catching a nasty look from the sergeant.

When the cops came, Rublyov got an ax and a rake – to make sure the body wouldn't slip – and that was how they pulled it out. It was pretty straightforward, but it took Rublyov about twenty minutes to get through his description.

"Let's go take a look at the body," I said.

Much relieved, the sergeant went back to his crowd control duties. He had his hands full by then, as the locals were getting excited, seeing that we had approached the stretcher and removed the thin wool blanket. He had to deploy a convoluted string of invectives to get them back into line. He called some of them by name, threatening retribution.

"It looks like he got it bad," I said.

The victim was a skinny young man with dark hair and Asian features. His face was intact and his body – naked, frozen stiff and yellowish-white – wasn't bloated and showed no signs of decomposition, having been in near-freezing water. But the corpse was badly damaged nonetheless. The flesh on the chest was almost all gone, baring sinews and the white bones of his rib cage. The stomach had been opened up and the intestines were gone, leaving a gaping black pit. On his thighs, the skin hung like shredded tissue paper around the knots of purple musculature.

"All this happened while he was in the water," the doctor explained, leaning over the stretcher and pointing at various parts of the body with a gloved finger. "It's nature red in tooth and claw, as they say. There are still fish in this river, although not many. The tree branch caught him on the stomach. He was hanging on it pretty solidly, like a pig carcass on a hook. Eventually something would have given, either the branch or the body, and he would have been dislodged. But not for some time."

He walked around to the other side. "Over here," he pointed at several parallel scratches running along the man's right shoulder, "is the damage we did with the rake, pulling him out. These are the freshest wounds, inflicted this morning. He hardly felt them at all."

He was cracking jokes with a straight face, and the Ramenskoye cops didn't realize he was trying to be humorous. They maintained earnest expressions. The boyish assistant didn't laugh either. It probably wasn't the first time she had heard these lines. I didn't find them funny, either, but I grinned in order to humor him.

"What we can also conclude," the doctor continued, "is that the victim did not drown. He went for a swim as a corpse."

"How did he die then?" I asked.

"One moment. I'll get to it. Give me a hand, will you?"

He removed his leather gloves, revealing elegantly manicured fingers with a gold wedding band and the glimmer of a gold watch nestled under a French cuff, and gripped the body by its shoulders. He signaled to me to take the feet.

"Turning to your left," he commanded. "One, two, three – done."

We turned the body on its stomach – or whatever was left of it. It was stiff as a log, except a lot lighter. The back was more or less intact, and the wound under the left shoulder blade was so small and neat in contrast with the damage inflicted on the front of the body, that I didn't notice it at first.

"A very skillful job," the doctor said admiringly. "There is no blood, of course, it has all been washed away, but I doubt there would have been much to start with, given the quality of the work. Surgical precision. Actually, better than that, not meaning to insult my surgeon friends. More like a bullfighter's skill. Very accurately between the seventh and eighth rib."

The doctor looked like he was going to wax lyrical for a while about the skill of the killer. The assistant made a face as though she had a sudden toothache.

"How long has he been in the water?" I asked.

"I can't tell. The water is too cold for the body to decompose. I'd say around a week, judging by the fish bites, but I'm no ichthyologist."

"That's not very helpful," I said. "And of course we have no idea how far he's travelled."

"None. What I can tell you for sure is that he began his journey downstream soon after he was killed. He was probably still warm."

"I see."

"That's the best I can do. I'm a scientist and not a magician. You can take him to Moscow, but I doubt your people at Criminal Investigations will do any better."

"Can you tell me at least how long he's been here hanging on that limb?"

The doctor shrugged and spread his arms wide.

"Your guess is as good as mine," he said.

"He wasn't here yesterday, that's for sure," the local, Rublyov, announced from behind our backs. He had been hanging around, listening to our discussion, as though he too was a member of the investigative team. "I would have seen him."

"That's something," I said. "If he had been drifting for a week, for example, he must have been dropped into the river somewhere north of the city."

"But at least he didn't come through the Moscow-Volga canal," Major Snegiryov quipped. "It's got locks."

The doctor's attempts at humor seemed to have put everyone in a mood to make jokes.

"The body could have been caught on that branch for a number of days," the doctor's assistant said. "They could have been drifting down river together. It would have been a very slow progress."

"That's right," Rublyov observed. "That tree is no longer there. It got moving the moment we pulled out the body."

"In other words, he may have been dropped half a kilometer away from here the other night or on the other side of the city a week ago," I summed up.

"The body could have also been weighted down with something," the assistant said. "To make sure it goes down. But the weight could have come off."

"Unlikely," said Major Snegiryov. "The body has been stripped naked and sent to float under the ice. This suggests that whoever did it didn't want it to be identified and didn't want it to be found until some time in the spring, when the ice is gone. And at that point, even if it were found, it would have been impossible to tell where it came from and when it had been dumped."

He was right, I thought. And by then the fish would be done with the flesh, only the skeleton would remain, and the stabbing wound would no longer be discovered.

"That's right," Rublyov declared. "Had I not cleared the ice, no one would have found the poor sucker for months, surely not before he had floated into the Oka.

He looked very proud of himself.

"One thing we know for sure," I said, "is that there has to be another hole in the ice through which the body was dumped. Somewhere upriver. The question is where."

An ambulance had now arrived, announcing itself by a piercing wail of its sirens. It was waiting on the high bank while two beefy attendants clambered down the slope. As the body was being hauled up, the locals kept trying to get closer, keeping Sergeant Okopko busy.

# TWENTY

Early the next morning I was back at the same spot, except this time I was wearing a track suit and, under my motorcycle helmet, a knitted wool hat. My cross-country skis and poles stuck out of my sidecar like spears. Major Snegiryov, similarly equipped, was waiting for me down by the river.

The night before, when I finally found my skis and boots among our still-packed odds and ends and was getting my old equipment into shape for the next day's expedition, Sevka, an avid cross-country skier, hovered around, peppering me with questions.

"Isn't it a work day, Uncle Pavel? Are you really going to go skiing? Is it part of an investigation you're working on? Can I go with you? You can call the school and tell them I'm sick."

I didn't like lying to him, nor could I tell him the truth. I hemmed and hawed instead. In the end, I told him that I had been roped in to compete in a police department race. Right after that, I had to tell him that I wasn't going to lie to his teacher, because lying was bad.

Boris came out of his room, still leaning on a walking stick, and watched my preparations in silence.

"Not a bad job you've got yourself, neighbor," he observed thoughtfully. "I'd love to do that on government time, but I'm afraid we've got too much serious work to do at State Security – like catching spies, wreckers, and other scum."

I'd met enough State Security people over the years to have my doubts about that, but I kept my mouth shut.

"You've got your methods, and we've got ours," I said. "Staying in shape is a duty of every law enforcement officer, whether he works for State Security or Criminal Investigations."

"Of course, it'll be a while before I get back on skis," Boris added, hobbling back to his room.

Tosya, who had overheard our exchange, whispered, "You're right, Pavel, he's not forgiven us. He's dangerous."

"I know," I replied, glancing at Boris's door.

Indeed, that short and seemingly innocuous conversation with Boris had me worried. I slept poorly, lying awake for a long time, thinking. He was pretending to be friendly, but to what end? I also suspected he was spying on me – but again, why? I had a nasty feeling about him. I didn't fear for myself, but it did worry me what he might do to Tosya or Sevka, or even to little Nikola – the three beings I cared about more than anything else in the world.

I woke up with a bad headache and in a foul mood. I felt hung over, except I hadn't drunk anything the night before. I was angry at Boris for making me worry, but I was even angrier at myself for allowing him to get under my skin. I was sure that was what he'd intended, something KGB officers were particularly good at.

It was another bright day. The air was fresh, the snow was crisp and soft, and it sparkled white and silver around us. On the opposite bank of the Moscow River there was a field covered with snow and, in the distance, a forest and, silhouetted against that, another village – a handful of houses with smoke rising above their snow-covered roofs. My head had started to clear the moment I left the house with my skis over my shoulder. And when I actually got on my skis, my mood began to improve, as well. We were on a hunt, and we were dealing with a pretty smart murderer who had a clever scheme for covering his tracks. We had to outsmart him.

Snegiryov and I had decided to start at Rublyov's rink and ski upstream, exploring every likely hole in the ice where a dead body could have been dumped into the river. Going on skis was the most efficient way to explore the frozen river. Sure, it might turn out to be a wild goose chase. If the victim had been killed elsewhere and stripped naked, it would have to be a place where a car could have been driven close to the river, and yet fairly secluded. The problem was, there were lots of places like that.

There were tracks running down the middle of the river and the skiing was easy. About half a kilometer upstream we came to the first hole. It was larger than the one Ivan had made and had a railroad tie floating in it.

"This is where the Walrus Club has its gatherings," Snegiryov said as he skied to the edge, poking at the tie with the tip of his pole. "That's what the guys who dip in the river in winter are called. Walruses. I call them nuts. They jump in and then come out as red as a boiled crawfish. They say it keeps them healthy. Look, there's the tracks of their bare feet. It makes me shiver just to look at them."

A couple of glasses had been buried discretely in the snow, under the bare limbs of a willow tree on the shore. An empty bottle of vodka sat next to them. Members of the Walrus Club liked to have a shot or two, to warm up after their extreme bathing.

"I don't know about the health effects," Snegiryov continued, "but I can't tell you how many times a Walrus goes in for a dip and never comes up for air. At first I thought the guy we fished out yesterday was one of those."

"He wasn't there by choice," I said. "I'm sure he'd have rather been somewhere else."

Snegiryov grinned. Cops like dark jokes about the dead.

Whether or not this hole was used to dispose of our body was impossible to tell. There were too many tracks around it, and the snow was tightly packed and iced over. We looked around for a few minutes and then examined the shore. There was a road nearby, but again the path connecting it to the shore was too well-travelled to have left any evidence. We decided to reserve judgment and to move on.

We continued our trek upriver, now skiing alongside each other. Now and again we would detour to examine an ice fishing hole. Ordinarily they would be too small, but each one still had to be checked. The dead man was fairly slim and had a small frame.

The next major stop was more than five kilometers away. We were skiing hard, no longer talking in order to save our strength, but I got winded anyway, given that I was not in particularly good shape. Along the way, we were overtaken by a half dozen skiers in bright red Spartak sweaters. They passed us as though we were standing still. As the last one zipped by, Snegiryov clapped his gloved hands, cheering him on.

"Go get 'em, killer," he shouted.

The guy turned around and gave us a thumbs-up, picking up speed.

The next hole was near another village. There had been a lot of pedestrian traffic around it as well, since it was where the locals came down to get water. Someone had even placed a wooden park bench nearby. The bench was crudely hammered together, and it was currently occupied by a young couple. The boy was smoking a rolled cigarette, talking loudly and gesticulating. The girl wore a quilted work jacket, in which she had contrived to look elegant and pretty, and a bright red floral kerchief. She was listening to him breathlessly and burst out laughing every now and again. When he saw us, the boy went silent and watched our approach with apparent suspicion.

"Good morning, comrade major," he said to Snegiryov when we got closer.

"How is it going, Petrov?" the cop responded. "Working hard to stay out of trouble?"

There was a path leading up the steep bank. It was a large village and an unlikely place for a dead body to be dumped in the river. The opposite shore was flat; there was a lot of pristine, deep snow on its banks and no road nearby.

"Let's move on," Snegiryov said and, turning to the kid, added, "Take care of yourself, Petrov."

Petrov and the girl sat on the bench in an uneasy silence, waiting for us to leave.

"That kid is bad news," Snegiryov explained once we were sufficiently far away. "He and his gang got caught burglarizing summer homes. He got off easy because Daddy is a collective farm chairman, but his buddies are serving time."

He was going to add something, but checked himself. For the next few minutes we rode our skis in silence.

"They would have locked him up, too," Snegiryov continued a bit later. "Because they also broke into a country store, and as you well know, stealing from the state is a different sort of crime than burglarizing private dachas. But his Dad had pull, so they ended up hanging the store robbery on some bum they got to confess. The whole thing pisses me off."

We were now in the summer cottage region and even though many of them were shuttered for the season, there were more people on the river – pensioners skiing at a very slow pace or strolling. Kids were sledding down the steep bank, screaming and tossing snowballs at each other.

The next two holes were both a possibility, but neither was conclusive. They had been cut in the ice for no identifiable purpose, and one had already frozen over. I tried to break the ice with the sharp tip of my ski pole, but it was too thick. That didn't mean anything, as far as disposing of the body was concerned, since we had no idea when it had occurred, and in the sort of cold we'd been having, it could have frozen back over in just one night.

Once again we conferred and decided to reserve judgment.

"One thing I can tell you, lieutenant," Snegiryov said. "Each and every one of the holes we have seen so far could have been used to dump the body. Looks like we'll never know for sure."

And then we hit the jackpot.

We were 20 kilometers upriver from where the body had been found, but it felt like a lot more. We were both exhausted – and we still had to make it all the way back. And we would not be able to use the excuse of inspecting holes to stop and catch our breath.

Here, the city was encroaching on the rural suburbs, sending forth its advanced guard of squat, five-story apartment blocks. We passed an industrial plant that had a concrete wall running along the edge of the river. It was topped by thin lines of barbed wire, and behind it a couple of smokestacks were belching orange smoke into the sky. Both banks in this section of the river were flat, and just as the factory wall ended, a road swerved from behind it toward the river. It was busy with truck traffic and suburban buses, and at that point one of its shoulders widened, forming a parking space. A truck was parked there, the driver sitting in his cab, taking a lunch break.

Someone had cut a hole in the ice for truckers to get water, and had even left a rusty bucket next to it, on the narrow path leading to the parking space. The thicket of young trees on the shore was well used as an open-air toilet.

While we were looking around, the driver finished his lunch and stretched out for a nap. He didn't get to sleep long, however. After about five minutes, Snegiryov hopped on the running board of his truck, reached into the cabin and shook the man by his shoulder. That was because, while examining the hole, we had discovered a few dark stains frozen into the ice that could have been blood. There hadn't been too much snow over the past week, and they were clearly visible under a fresh dusting.

The evidence was by no means conclusive, but it made us search the area a lot more carefully. It actually appeared as if something heavy had been dragged along the footpath. But, again, it could have been our overactive imaginations at work.

While I stayed behind guarding the scene, in the unlikely event that someone decided to tamper with the evidence, Snegiryov got the driver, once he was sufficiently awake, to drive him to Ramenskoye. He then returned in an official GAZ off-road vehicle accompanied by the doctor and his tomboy assistant.

"So we meet again, lieutenant," the doctor said as we shook hands. "No, you did the right thing bringing us in. You've got to be thorough when you conduct an investigation."

His assistant ignored my hand and got down to business examining the footpath, measuring the thin layer of snow on top of the brown stains and collecting everything into plastic bags. While the doctor probed the ice at the edge of the hole, shaking his head dubiously, she wandered off the path into the befouled thicket, where she made the most important discovery of all – a white bedsheet that had been folded and buried in the snow.

"This is what they dragged the body on to the river," she declared.

The sheet was frozen stiff. There was a reddish-brown stain in the corner and a few reddish-brown streaks running down it, also frozen.

"This looks like blood," she said. "We'll let you know if it's a match with your guy."

The two of them loaded all their trophies into the GAZ. We caught a ride back with them, sitting under the canvas top in the back, our skis and poles sticking out of the sides. It was clear that Snegiryov was as happy not to have to ski another 20 kilometers as I was, even though he repeatedly expressed regrets about having to cut our expedition short.

And while we were both happy to have made our discovery, in truth it didn't add much to the investigation. We didn't know where the victim had been killed, by whom, or why. The neat knife wound in the back did allow me to make some assumptions, but it didn't bring me any closer to knowing the identity of the victim.

Still, I now had plenty to report to Valera when I returned to the office the following morning, starting with the knife wound the guy in the river had received. The way I saw it, it looked too much like the wound that had killed Levkoyev. Whether I liked it or not, I was back on the Metropole robbery investigation, even as it was growing with new, gruesome ramifications.

# TWENTY-ONE

Alexei Zolotnitsky was not meant to be a soldier. He was born to be a musician, an artist, a scientist, or an athlete. He was a champion rider at his school. His father wanted him to be a public servant. His own dream was to be an engineer and to build motorcars, but then, when he first saw one of those clumsy, lumbering, plywood and canvas flying machines, he decided he wanted to build those. And fly them, of course.

He had small, delicate hands, which seemed to come alive on the piano keyboard and to know just what to do in the innards of any motor.

He was small in stature but perfectly proportioned, athletic and elegant – the genes of some nomadic ancestors from the eastern steppes expressing themselves many generations later. He was one of the best dancers Olga had ever lit across the floor with. And that was something, coming from a ballerina who had danced with some of the best of her generation.

He was not meant for war, but he got to be good at it, too, once he became a soldier. Soldiering was a waste of remarkable potential, but soon there would be so much talent wasted in Russia that the waste of Alexei's talents was a minor matter, a drop in a vast sea of waste. And now, after all the talent that had been wantonly flushed down the toilet, the country was run by men like Yuri Vladimirovich, who for a reason Olga could not quite grasp, kept hanging around, accompanying her to various mind-numbing functions and driving her everywhere in his official black car. And if he was busy doing whatever a KGB man did in his day job, he would send his Gloomy Gus driver, whose name seemed to be Ivan, and who smelled of sweat and cheap cigarettes and insisted that she sit in the passenger seat beside him.

"Comrade Boss's orders," he told her in ugly Soviet newspeak the first time he came to pick her up. On subsequent occasions, he always held the front door open for her when she came down.

When "Comrade Boss" was around, it was he who rode shotgun, and she was grateful to him for that at least. It would have been torture to have him sitting next to her in the back seat. Yuri Vladimirovich was polite, fairly charming, and tried to act the old-school European gentleman. Yet he made her horribly uncomfortable.

Why was he paying court to her? She wasn't such an important person.

They were not meant to be married, she and Alexei. Their marriage was something of a waste, too. A sweet and tender waste, but a waste nonetheless.

They ran into one another in Crimea, in one of those filthy overcrowded Black Sea resort towns in the days of despair after General Denikin had suffered a horrible defeat on the Don. They spotted each other in a swirling, mad crowd on the embankment, in which the beaten remnants of the Volunteer Army – fresh-faced sub-lieutenants straight out of military schools; rattled staff captains and cynical majors; the tough-as-nails veterans back from fighting the Germans, the Hetman, Daddy Makhno, and the Reds, the Reds, the Reds, always the Reds – mingled with Cossack atamans, blood-thirsty horsemen from the Caucasus, frightened civilians from every corner of the shattered Empire, Tartars, and Red spies. Both had been looking for someone, for people they barely knew or cared about, elbowing their way past men and women with overflowing bags and suitcases and rifles with fixed bayonets, cursing and sweating in the southern sun. What a delight it was to see a dear, familiar face that threw you instantly back to Moscow and St. Petersburg and peace and prewar certainty. The war years had changed them both, but they recognized each other immediately. The ugly duckling kid sister of Alexei's school friend had matured into a striking beauty, while the brilliant Zolotnitsky – a boy all parents used to set as an example to their lazy and wayward offspring – had been transformed into a tired, defeated cavalry officer, covered with dust and dried blood and wearing a mixture of uniforms from long extinct, shredded White armies.

She picked him out of the crowd despite the wrinkles, the untidy, prematurely grey hair, the scars, and the haunted eyes. She saw him suddenly in his parents' spacious apartment on Liteyny, playing Schumann beneath the recently installed electric lights, and the memory, sweeping over her like a wave, clouded her vision. She grabbed him by a tattered sleeve, hid her face in his mud-spattered tunic, and began to cry.

"Don't, Olga, don't," he pleaded, patting her awkwardly on the back and shielding her from the crowd.

She was embarrassed and kept repeating, "I'm sorry, I'm sorry" through her sobbing, but she couldn't make herself stop crying. Had she looked up at that moment, she would have seen his eyes clouding with tears as well.

They found an open cafe and sat under a torn awning on a veranda overlooking the grim, deserted sea. They were silent for a long time, eyeing each other in joyful recognition, habituating themselves to each other's new looks. To their new reality.

"Remember Chekhov?" he said to her at last. *"The Lady with the Lapdog?"*

They laughed bitterly and, once that first sentence had broken the ice, words started to pour out of them in an unending torrent, as if they had both been saving them up for just this occasion.

They sighed and crossed themselves in memory of Nicky, killed in Brusilov's advance in 1915, and again when Alexei told her about his father, murdered by the rioting peasants on their estate outside

Kostroma, but even then they couldn't stop talking. They spoke at the same time and over each other, but it didn't matter. They had no interest in accounting for the wasted years – only in recapturing the old days in the fragile gossamers of memory.

They only had a few memories in common: when Alexei had played the piano in his apartment on Liteyny, and another time, when he had taken her on a wild ride in his father's automobile in Moscow, which had later gotten him into a lot of trouble. But there were so many people they both used to know and love. Their separate memories twined and blended together, becoming one memory about the same people and places, as familiar to them as the dusty, garbage-strewn embankment was not, with its intense blue sky, grimy sea, and sheer cliffs hovering above the surf.

Two hours later, they raised their heads and looked around in surprise, as though waking up from a dream.

The chaos of the first days of defeat was soon overcome, and life in Crimea settled into a semblance of normalcy. Denikin resigned and went abroad. He was replaced by Baron Wrangel, who quickly caught and hung a few Red agitators, while others slipped back into the woodwork, to bide their time. The Whites regrouped and repulsed the early, poorly organized assault on the massive Crimea fortifications, then chased the Reds and their Daddy Makhno allies back to the mainland, recapturing ground on the back of the retreating enemy. For a few short weeks the news from the front fanned a mad kind of hope.

Alexei was mostly at the front in those days, fighting. He shared none of the hope. He knew they were doomed. It was a respite that would last a few weeks or a few months, he thought. They had won it by tricking Fate. The first time he was able to get away from his squadron, he proposed.

They got married in a small chapel in a Feodosia back street. The kind, indulgent God of their childhood was dead. His throne had been usurped by a depraved old coot with a penchant for cruel pranks. Even the priests seemed embarrassed of their new Lord. They were throwing off their vestments, shaving their hair and beards, and melting into the general population.

Nevertheless, Alexei insisted on a church wedding. How else would they know that they were legally married? He found an elderly priest, a refugee from Kharkov, who was willing to officiate.

The air inside the chapel was musty and, on the whole, stank of squalor. The frescoes had been painted by some incompetent local talent and defaced during the short-lived Tavrida Soviet Socialist Republic. Obscenities and crude drawings of genitals had been scratched into the walls, and remained visible under a layer of oil paint. The iconostasis had most of its holy images missing, replaced with ill-fitting pieces of plywood. It had probably been a mistake to try to recapture the old solemnity and sanctity of the ceremony.

She was in street clothes, and Alexei wore the same mismatched mixture of uniforms he had on when they first met, which he made a hasty attempt to dust off. He didn't even have a ring. The only piece of jewelry he owned was a plain silver baptismal cross, blackened by age and the sweat of his body. He was an Urusov on his maternal grandmother's side and, according to a family legend, that tiny cross, given to him by his great aunt who had stood as his godmother, had come down to them from the first Prince, Pyotr, a christianized Tartar khan, and had been taken by him from the body of False Dmitry, whom he had slain.

The cross was beautifully worked, and you could tell it was something special. Alexei had found a red ribbon, and he placed it around her neck as they stood in front of the iconostasis. Whether because the ribbon was old or he hadn't tied the knot properly, the cross slipped off her neck and fell onto the dusty stone floor of the church. While Olga stood there waiting, the groom and the priest crawled on their hands and knees around the lectern, searching for it.

It was a simple ceremony, and it was hard to believe it was a sacrament. The whole thing was more like a wake for a deceased God than joyous nuptials. Their short-lived, chaotic marriage was a mistake. You should never go back to the place where you were happy. They felt awkward around each other, as though they were engaging in an illicit activity, and the baptismal cross around her neck didn't make it any more legitimate in Olga's eyes. There was something artificial about their love-making, about their intimacy. She couldn't rid herself of the feeling that they were on stage, observed while they were making love – by her brother, by their friends, by the people they had once known.

And when Alexei came back after the White's final, irreversible defeat to find Olga gone, he felt betrayed. He was surprised, too. Running away, leaving without him was an act of cowardice, and Olga was anything but a coward. He was disappointed in her, whether they were in love or not, they had a responsibility to each other. He was hurt, but he was happy for her, too, because he wouldn't have wanted her to be stuck in the murderous mousetrap that Crimea had become.

More than anything else, he felt relieved. During the wars, he had learned to take care of himself. He had learned to take care of his men, too, and of other people who for one reason or another became his responsibility, but only up to a point. Ultimately, he was responsible for his own survival, and that was that. Having her on his hands would have been a burden.

He felt he could yet survive on his own, make a run for it. But not if she had been there with him.

When he got back to the rooms they had shared, he was seized by a kind of apathy. He stayed in an abandoned house, rationing his bread, food, and homegrown tobacco, and reading Pisemsky. Waiting for the Reds to come and murder him. And yet, deep down, beneath the apathy, there was an unshakeable belief in his lucky star.

Had she known he was alive, she would have stayed behind and waited for him. As long as it took. Even if he had never made it back. It had nothing to do with love. The thought of leaving him there would never have crossed her mind.

But a week before Crimea fell to the Reds, a man came to see her and told her that Alexei was dead. That man, an officer, had seen him die, had seen his dead body. He even claimed that Alexei's last wish had been that he save her. As a staff officer, he could get her onto one of the last steamers the Allies were running out of Crimea, taking along the remnants of Baron Wrangel's defeated army and whoever else could finagle their way on board. She had to decide at once because time was running out. She accepted.

The journey took five days as their ragtag flotilla waited for permission to pass through the Turkish Straits, and the Allies garrisoning Constantinople inspected and questioned the Russians coming ashore. Five days on a deck thronging with dirty, hysterical humanity with no food or water, not knowing where they were going and where they were going to end up.

During their passage, she began to suspect that the staff officer was no friend of Alexei's. Alexei would not have a friend like that. She also became convinced that he had had an ulterior motive in telling her about Alexei's death, perhaps even lying to her about it. There was nothing she could do about it, and the news that eventually trickled out of Crimea strongly suggested that, if he hadn't died in the fighting, he was surely dead now.

The officer had a loaf of dark bread, and she asked him to share it with a woman and her two starving boys. When he refused, she gave the woman her own portion and was on her own thereafter.

In Constantinople, trading was happening on a grand scale. Family jewels came out of secret hiding places, the sparkling shards of the crushed Empire. They changed hands in payment for bread and moldy feta cheese, the tentative pleading of Russian nobles not yet accustomed to haggling over their valuables adding to the ancient cacophony of Levantine voices, the Turkic, Greek and Bulgarian tongues, and the authoritative English and French attempting to bring a semblance of order to the chaos.

Flesh was on offer on every corner, too – of every age, shape, ethnic background and social class. Whatever else could be said of the dead Empire, it had been diverse. Buyers were few and picky. The war had drawn a sharp distinction in the clientele. The weak had no money and the strong didn't need to pay.

Selling herself was not an option Olga could allow herself to take and she had no jewelry to sell. Just the blackened silver cross she still wore around her neck. What could she get for it when a diamond ring didn't always fetch a skewer of lamb kebab?

She held out for three more days, until she was shaking with hunger. Her body, her lean, muscular dancer's body, demanded lots of calories. It rebelled without food, sickening the stomach that begged relentlessly for something to eat. At last she gave in.

She stood near the side of a squat stone structure by the port that the Allies had adapted for a customs house and police station, and where the Russians had set up an improvised flea market.

For an hour or more, no one paid any attention to her or her tiny speck of silver dangling from a red ribbon. Other Russians had better things to offer, and supply far exceeded demand. The few locals, mostly small-time dealers, circled the area like vultures, stopping to haggle for a few minutes and then walking away. The Turks had gotten spoiled. They were getting wonderful things and paying next to nothing, but they knew they could get them for cheaper still if they waited.

Several times Olga nearly gave up and left, and every time hunger made her stay. She was also worried that the effort of walking to the flophouse where she was staying would be too much for her, that she would faint in the middle of the street.

She closed her eyes to block out the winter sun beating down onto the city. It was when she opened them again – which she did slowly, for even moving her eyelids had become an effort – that her second life began.

At that moment her luck changed – irreversibly, once and for all, forever. So radically, in fact, that it could only mean one thing: one life had ended and another had begun. The kind elderly Russian God of her childhood had died, and there was not going to be a resurrection. Another god had taken His place, a joyous pagan deity, silly and vivacious and vain. This new god placed no restrictions on his devotees and demanded no sacrifices. He didn't want you to change. He liked you the way you were. He rewarded you lavishly and asked nothing in return.

When she opened her eyes, she saw an old man in a black skullcap standing in front of her. He wore a threadbare black kaftan and had curling grey sidelocks. A long beard framed his bony face. He cast a deep midday shadow as he bowed to her.

His sober black clothes clashed with the rich variety of colors in the Middle East street, and his wrinkled white shirt and scuffed shoes, layered thick with white dust, seemed to have come straight out of a town in Galicia. She realized that he hadn't been bowing to her so much as bending over to have a better look at the tiny cross in her hand. She stared at the top of his head, at the flakes of dandruff in his grey hair and on the shoulders of his kaftan, asking herself whether he was a person of flesh and blood or a fairy tale gnome, a hallucination brought on by hunger.

She remembered his distinct smell. It was the smell of a room where many human beings of different ages lived crowded together, of a windowless, never aired space, the pungent smell of soot, melted candle wax, and dusty old volumes.

He spent a long time examining the cross. Still in a trance and not quite realizing what she was doing, she raised her other hand and brushed flecks of dandruff and a few fallen hairs off his shoulder. He turned sharply and straightened up.

"Good day to you, Madame," he said, baring yellowed teeth in what he must have thought was a friendly smile.

He was short. The top of his skullcap barely reached her chest. She didn't respond. She wasn't being rude – she didn't have enough strength left to speak.

"Are you selling this little trifle, Madame?" he asked.

He was addressing her in a broken Russian of the Empire's southwestern provinces. She still didn't say anything.

"Are you selling that which you're holding in your hand, Madame, or are you just taking the airs here by the seashore?" he asked again, elaborating on his previous question.

Five minutes ago, Olga would have been overjoyed to have the old man take an interest in her little cross and would have sold it to him in a second, taking any offer he would have cared to make for it. But when he had looked up at her, taken unawares by her touch, he had not been able to hide the gleam of sheer delight in his eyes. He had seen something special, unique, something he wanted. His grey eyes had turned dull and opaque once more, but the hunger that gnawed at her stomach had imprinted the vision of his delight upon her barely functioning brain. It was the basic instinct of a starving animal.

"Yes, I was thinking about it," she said slowly. "But not very seriously."

"I would like to take a closer look at it," he said. "I doubt it's worth anything. But it's touching in its plainness."

The old man was doing a good job hiding his interest now, but the delight in his eyes had been there. She had spotted it, if only for a fraction of a second, and her starving musculature and her empty, demanding stomach would not let him get away with it.

"On the contrary," she said. "It's a very valuable object, of extraordinary historic significance. If you don't believe it's worth much, I doubt it is for you."

"Are you sure we're talking about the same thing, my young lady?" he asked sharply.

"Yes, quite sure," she said. "I don't have anything else to sell, but I expect to get good money for it. Otherwise it's not worth it for me to part with it."

"And what is your idea of good money, if you don't mind me asking?"

She had never believed Alexei's story about Pyotr Urusov or False Dmitry. Those family legends were for the most part fibs, either ancient, passed from one generation to the next, or very recent. As a matter of fact, Alexei himself had mentioned it more as a joke.

"If you don't have any idea what it is worth, you have no business looking at it," she said and put the hand holding the cross into the pocket of her cardigan.

"Oh, shame on you," the old man said. "You're bluffing. Let's be honest with each other. Just give me a straight figure."

She made her calculations and came up with the highest sum she could think of at the moment, which was 15 pounds sterling. He uttered the words slowly, enunciating each syllable and keeping her eyes fixed on the bushy eyebrows that hung above a pair of pale grey eyes. There was a long pause. The grey eyes narrowed, studying her closely.

"You're insane," he said simply, and started to walk away.

She knew she was – scaring away the only customer she was likely to have.

"That a girl," said a voice next to her, in English. "You did the right thing, Miss. He'll come back, mark my words. How much did you ask, if you don't mind telling me?"

A young man in British military uniform had stopped a few feet away. Her English was rudimentary. She understood in general terms what he had said – or at least she got as far as to figure out that the young officer had taken her side.

"Five pounds sterling," she replied.

She wasn't really lying. She just couldn't bring herself to repeat in English what she had told the old man in Russian. But even a third of that sum struck the Englishman as funny. He grabbed his head between his hands in mock horror.

"You know? I might have been a tad hasty, suggesting that the old boy would be back," he said laughing.

And yet he was right. The old man was back the moment he turned and saw Olga and the Englishman converse.

"It's a deal," he shouted even before he reached them. "I thought it over, my dear. It's just that I never carry this kind of money on me. It's not safe around here."

The Englishman took her by the elbow and propelled her forward. She had no strength to resist, and she had to lean heavily on him as she walked. Her mind, after the intense effort it had taken to focus on the haggling, went blank again. She let herself be guided by the

Englishman. He was very tall and skinny and had exceptionally long legs. She had to take two strides for every one of his.

The old man trailed behind them for a couple of blocks, whining and complaining and accusing the Englishman of stealing his deal.

"I was the first to spot it," he pleaded in Russian, which meant that the Englishman had no way of knowing what he was saying. "It's not fair."

Soon enough, he started to pant and fall behind. Once he had stopped following them, she fainted.

Coming to, she found that she and the English officer were seated on the veranda of a shabby coffee shop.

"You look pale," the Englishman said. "When was the last time you had anything to eat?"

She shrugged.

"Let me order something for you. It may not be great but it's probably edible."

His words were muffled, as though her ears were stuffed with cotton. She smiled and nodded.

"Hey, waiter," he shouted.

She realized that she was still clutching Alexei's cross in her hand. He eased it out of her grip and placed it around her neck. She smiled because his gesture echoed the church wedding in Feodosia and her ill-fated marriage. She'd been a widow for only a couple of weeks, and yet she was already remarried.

That was how Alexei's family heirloom became her talisman and a symbol of her new life.

She and Anthony remained in Constantinople for another month. They spoke to each other in French, which he spoke with an atrocious Albion accent that made her laugh and which he exaggerated for comic effect. He was from a good family and even had some cousins by marriage among Russian nobility, with whom he had lost touch and who were, apparently, refugees in Berlin.

At Christmas, he took her to England. He promised her a passage to Paris and, most importantly, got her a document. Like other Russians evacuated from Crimea, she had no passport, only an enormous sheet of paper with lots of stamps issued by the occupation authorities at Constantinople confirming her status as the subject of a defunct empire. That was not good enough to travel anywhere. To be sure, the Turks would have been only too glad to see the back of her, but no other country would accept her with such papers.

Thankfully, the Italian charge d'affaires in Constantinople happened to be a good friend of Anthony's. As a result, in mid-December Olga was able to board the Orient Express for London, via Sofia, Belgrade and Venice, her freshly minted passport confirming that she was a freshly minted subject of His Royal Highness King Victor Emmanuel III.

The passport was completely authentic, printed on beautiful Italian paper and decorated with lots of red, white, green, and gold, but it felt fake, like her new life.

The first years of her new life felt like a whirlwind – which is probably how the first years of any life should feel. By early January, Anthony was back with his wife and kids in Surrey, and she was in Paris, getting reacquainted with her friends and with a bunch of Russian dancers, and then hugging and crying and being patted sweetly on the shoulder by Sergei Pavlovich. Another six months passed, and she was back on stage. Every night after the performance they went out in a large, boisterous crowd, where dancers mingled with artists and poets, and where admirers in evening clothes footed the bill for champagne and chocolates and bought basketfuls of roses from flower girls. They laughed and drank and smoked American cigarettes in long holders until the wind whipped up and down the steep Montmartre hill, carrying the foul odor of the night in from narrow alleys and making everyone in outdoor cafes huddle more closely together.

Those predawn hours sometimes made her feel sad because they made her think of Russia.

There were beautiful Russian dancers in Diaghilev's company, and there were Russian officers driving black Peugeot taxi cabs. They smoked silently behind the wheel, waiting for the fares and eyeing the beautiful Russian girls and the pretty, effeminate boys, blaming them in their minds for surrendering Mother Russia to Trotsky. Despite it all, they had landed on their feet in Paris and were again drinking and laughing the night away, as they had done in St. Petersburg and Moscow in the golden prewar years.

There were few men in Paris in those days, and a great plenitude of women. Business was bad for the Montmartre regulars. They would have starved if it hadn't been for the war cripples toc-toc-tocking on their crutches through the dark streets, boys changed by the war into broken old men, searching less for beauty than for indifference on which to waste the few francs out of their Ministry of War pensions.

The war cripples were shy in those days, embarrassed by their stumps, scars, and unseeing eyes. Later, about the time Paris began to smell of the next war, they would get defiant.

There were few men around, and yet she had no shortage of admirers. War profiteers, jowly American industrialists, skinny or chubby English aristocrats, and a whole lot of Russians who had somehow managed to salvage their fortunes – or at least pretended they had.

But she and her friends liked Paris artists. If every artist in Paris (and there were hundreds of them now, flocking from the suddenly numerous European capitals to the City of Lights, where they drank, slept with their models, and argued about art and politics) suddenly became famous, they'd have to empty the Louvre of all its paintings and fill it up with their garish cityscapes and distorted nudes. Or perhaps turn one of the city's train stations into a museum.

Pablo was already famous, but not nearly as famous as he would eventually become. He wasn't handsome, but he was extraordinarily attractive. To women, and also to men. There were many men around them who liked other men. Not as many as in St. Petersburg before the war, but enough. Pablo knew about his appeal to them and didn't mind it. But he loved women.

And yet, beneath the patina of Parisian sophistication, he was a very traditional man. Traditional as only a Spaniard, or a Russian, could be.

Other than Hell, a perverted, inquisitorial kind of Spanish Hell, there was very little that he was afraid of.

Sergei Pavlovich told him that if he wanted to have Olga he'd have to marry her. Sergei Pavlovich was very sly and a great judge of character. He knew that was what Pablo wanted to hear.

Pablo took her to Spain. He said he wanted her to meet his friends in Barcelona. The truth was he wanted her to meet his mother. He was pleased that his friends admired a tall, beautiful Russian dancer, but it was his mother's approval that he craved.

She liked Barcelona. It reminded her so much of Moscow during the last wild years before the war, when there was so much art and craziness and money. The city was a precious gem shining amid the sea of poverty and resentment. She wondered if Barcelona would soon go to the dogs as well.

Pablo did her portrait before proposing. She sat for him, and it was a physical experience – like being made love to by his large olive-colored hands, which worked the brushes as if they had a life of their own. After that, there was no question of her not having him. His hands already knew her intimately.

There was the small matter of her marriage to Alexei, but he was dead, and besides, it had happened in another life.

All she had from her old life was her talisman, Alexei's tiny baptismal cross. She wore it around her neck on their wedding day and it felt hot between her breasts, as though it had just been taken from the expiring body of False Dmitry and his life force had flowed into that sliver of metal.

## TWENTY-TWO

"Let me see the pictures of Levkoyev's body," I said to Valera. "The ones that forensics took at the morgue."

Valera pulled out his case file, neatly marked with the case number and date on the front and a list of documents on the inside flap. He leafed through a stack of photographs and typewritten reports, took out several shots and tossed them on my desk.

"A great job," he commented. "Not an easy task to insert the knife so neatly between the ribs. Don't forget that the man was dressed and fully conscious."

That sounded very familiar. I had heard very similar words from the Ramenskoye doctor while we stood over another dead body on the frozen river.

"I've just seen a similar job," I said.

"Yeah? Where?"

I told him about the body fished from beneath the ice on the Moscow River, and also mentioned that we had found the place on the southeastern edge of the city where it had been dumped.

"Do you think it's related to Levkoyev's murder?" he asked.

"The knife wound is very similar," I said. "Maybe forensics could tell us more about the similarities and what kind of blade was used, even though the second body was in the water for a while. But there are differences. The first guy was killed in his apartment and left to lie there, while a lot of care was taken to make sure this other victim wouldn't be found for a long time and identified. Had it not been for its lucky discovery, the body would have drifted under the ice all the way to the Oka."

"So, what do you think?" Valera asked.

"More likely than not, both are pieces of the same puzzle. That brings you in with your Levkoyev investigation, so we're partners once more. To start with, let's see if any young men of Central Asian appearance have gone missing in or around Moscow. There couldn't be too many. We need to identify the victim. Since his murderer was careful to conceal his identity, this should tell us something, right?"

I was about to continue, but Valera interrupted me.

"Central Asian, you say? Dark hair? High cheekbones?"

"That's exactly it. He looked like a Central Asian, and they tend to have dark hair and high cheekbones."

He ignored my sarcasm.

"No identity papers?"

"None whatsoever. I told you, the body was stripped naked. Even his socks were gone."

"No identifiable marks on the face and body?"

"A cross tattooed on an index finger," I said.

"Anything else?"

"The body was damaged in the water, mostly nibbled at by fish, but nothing else that jumps out at you. Except for the knife wound."

Valera didn't like me being flippant.

"I need to think," he said, frowning.

He was absorbed in his thoughts for a while, pulling other files from his desk drawer and going through them one by one. I didn't want to disturb him and went out to smoke a cigarette. He was gone when I returned.

It had started to snow again when I took the suburban train to Zhukovsky. The Air Force base there was secret, so the town was not marked on any map, and its suburban platform was small, dilapidated and called, enigmatically, Station of Rest. Whether or not foreign spies fell for it, every kid knew about the town, which began immediately behind a line of trees running alongside the tracks and was plainly visible in winter, behind their leafless limbs.

In line with the secrecy that prevailed at the base's forensic lab, I was not allowed in until the doctor's no-nonsense assistant came downstairs and confirmed my identity. The doctor was away and was not expected to arrive until later that afternoon.

"Maybe you could answer my questions," I said. "Do you think the victim was already naked when he was stabbed?"

"He wasn't," she replied.

"Any idea what he was wearing?"

"Some," she shrugged. "He wore a cotton undershirt, a flannel shirt – red and white, maybe checkered or striped – and a red wool sweater."

"Phew," I whistled in admiration. "How come so much precision?"

She pulled a small brown envelope from a drawer, shook something out onto a glass tray, and placed it under the microscope.

"See that?" she said, moving aside to let me have a look. "Those are fibers we got from the wound. Just a few, not a lot to go by, but still it's a miracle they didn't all get washed away. White fibers are from the cotton garment, and those dark red flakes are wool."

"Did you find any more tattoos?"

"There was something on the forearm," she said. "But the skin was scraped, and we weren't able to determine what it was. I'd say one of those jailbird tattoos, but it's my own personal opinion, not an official finding."

The next morning Valera showed up at the office even earlier than usual. When I came in at half past eight he was sitting at his desk, beaming at me.

"I think I know who your victim is," he said.

"That's great," I said. "By the way, he was fully dressed when he was stabbed. They must have stripped him naked when he was already dead."

"Last night I figured out why your victim sounded familiar," Valera said. "I had actually been planning on talking to someone who meets his description. A very skilled burglar."

"Oh no, not again, Valera," I groaned. "The Boss isn't going to like it, you hanging around people who turn up dead. He might start suspecting that you are bumping them off yourself."

Valera found nothing funny in my suggestion.

"Not in this case, Pavel," he protested. "This time I hadn't had a chance to meet with him. I tried, but he was nowhere to be found. I checked with his mother last night, in case he had returned, but he's still missing. Apparently it's not the first time he's disappeared, but before he has always turned up."

"There is always the first time," I said. "Besides, he has turned up this time, too."

Of course, I was sure Valera was wrong. It would be too much of a coincidence. Or maybe I didn't want him to be right because then I would have to admit that by playing strictly by the rules, and diligently following official instructions, Valera was getting results, whereas my efforts had hit a wall.

I therefore only reluctantly allowed myself to be persuaded to go with Valera to the address he had for a kid named Mitya Kislitsky, also known by his street name: Kisly. It was still early when we headed out. Budyonny hadn't arrived yet, and we were both relieved that we didn't have to report to him. If it turned out to be the wrong guy, no one would be the wiser, and if Kisly was the victim, we could always tell the Boss then. And of course there was no need to say anything about Valera almost making the kid's acquaintance just before he had been killed.

Along the way, Valera filled me in on Kisly. Some in the trade considered him the best apartment burglar in the city. But he was also highly unreliable. He could walk off a job in progress or become fascinated by some child's toy, and forget why he was there in the first place.

"They say he's like a child himself. And a binge drinker, in the bargain. Every few months he goes on a bender and stays drunk for days. You know the type."

"How come he has just two tattoos, then?" I asked. "If he's such a good burglar. He must have done time a few times by now."

"Two reasons. One, he's unreliable. He's never been accepted into the thieves' fraternity, which would have given him plenty of tattoos. And two, he's never really been caught. He's been brought in a couple of times on suspicion of breaking and entering, but no one could prove anything."

"Don't tell me they let him go because they didn't have enough on him. Since when has that become a reason for our courts not to convict?"

Valera shrugged. He didn't appreciate my sarcasm, no matter whether it was directed at our legal system or at him. But he couldn't deny that there was something unusual here.

"Somehow he keeps getting off the hook. Lucky, I suppose."

"Or else someone's protecting him," I said.

We were having our conversation in a metro car on the red line, pressed against each other by the rush hour crush – a crowd of gloomy men and frowning women, all half asleep on their feet. Our conversation, which we conducted a bit too loudly in order to overcome the rattle of the train as it sped through a narrow tunnel, had started to attract attention.

"As for the rest, they say he's a sweet guy," Valera added softly. "Or at least a gentle soul. Wouldn't harm a fly."

We said nothing for the remainder of our trip. The car emptied out almost completely at the Gorky Culture Park station, where most of the passengers got off to change for the Ring Line. We stayed on as the train proceeded past the glassed-in Lenin Hills platform to Vernadsky Avenue. Opened a few months ago, the station was fresh, functional, and gleaming with light blue and white tiles.

I had expected a kid like Kisly to live in a squalid, two-story, hundred-year-old wooden house, his whole family sharing a dingy room in a communal anthill filled with the stench of burnt lard and the sounds of neighbors squabbling.

It turned out to be nothing of the sort. We exchanged a look of surprise when Kisly's street address brought us to the entrance of a recently constructed cooperative apartment building. The neighborhood was also new, having sprung up in the past year, and it was posh by Moscow standards, although the surroundings were still a bit rough around the edges. Still, a private apartment in one of these nine-story structures, complete with an elevator and piped-in hot water, was something most Moscovites could only dream of.

The doorbell was answered by a woman in her late 40s, somewhat on the heavy side, yet still attractive, with short, greying hair and intelligent, grey eyes. When Valera asked her whether Mitya Kislitsky lived here, she eyed us across the threshold for a very long time.

"He does live here," she replied at last, her voice suspicious and her eyes still watchful. "But he's out now. What do you want?"

Ignoring her question, Valera took a step forward as though he was about to enter the apartment. The woman, suddenly alarmed, was about to slam the door in his face.

"When do you expect him back?" I asked.

"Who are you?"

"We're Moscow Criminal Investigations," I said. "And you?"

The woman let out a deep breath.

"You'd better come in," she said quickly. "I don't want the neighbors to hear us."

"We've moved in recently," she added, once Valera and I squeezed into the narrow foyer. "But the neighbors are already giving us strange looks."

The apartment fitted with the image I had made in my mind of Kisly the burglar even less than the expensive co-op. It was a typical Moscow *intelligentsia* apartment, full of well-thumbed books on bookshelves and with engravings and framed theatrical posters hanging on the walls. There was a whole bank of potted plants by the windows. What made the place less like an *intelligentsia* apartment was the Japanese stereo and a collection of foreign classical LPs, as well as a foreign television set, also Japanese. Such consumer electronics were valuable and didn't often share living space with filled bookshelves. I made a note of it.

With all the books in the apartment, the owner had been hard at work contributing to their number. There was a typewriter on the desk. To the left of it was a stack of typewriter paper and carbons, and to the right two copies of a manuscript and a sharpened pencil on top of one of them. An ashtray sat full of cigarette butts. More butts were in the trashcan under the desk, which was overflowing with torn pages and used carbons. A discarded typewriter ribbon snaked onto the parquet floor.

The setup was somehow all wrong. I had a feeling we had the wrong Kislitsky, and my impression was confirmed by the framed photograph on the desk, showing the owner of the apartment being hugged by a handsome gentleman in a military uniform with the insignia of the Legal Corps. Neither of them looked even remotely Central Asian.

The woman spotted me looking at the picture.

"Yes, Mitya Kislitsky is my son," she said, probably guessing at my train of thought. "Take a look at this picture if you have any questions."

Another snapshot was leaning against the book spines on the shelf. She was some twenty years younger in it and really pretty. She was holding a boy of three or four. He had light hair and a pair of watchful, almond-shaped, Oriental eyes. He hadn't changed that much as a young man, and being in the frigid water hadn't altered his appearance. At least, he was still recognizable. It was definitely the same kid.

"What did he do?" the woman asked, shifting her eyes back and forth between me and Valera.

She was getting worried, and our long silence wasn't putting her mind at ease.

"My name is Pavel Matyushkin," I said at last. "This is my partner, Valery Tumakov. We need to ask you a few questions."

"Yes, of course. My name is Yekaterina Kislitsky. You can call me Katya."

"So this is where he lives?" I asked.

Katya sighed and pulled out a cigarette. I struck a match and held it up for her. I badly wanted a smoke, too, but held back.

"This is where he's *supposed* to live," she said, exhaling a blue cloud. "Half the time I have no idea where he is. Now, for instance."

"When was the last time you saw him?" I asked.

"I don't know," she said. "Let me think. Four or five days ago."

"Can you be more precise?"

"Let me think. What is today, Tuesday?"

She took a minute to think it over.

"It was last Thursday. Thursday night. He said he had to go out for a while. He didn't say when he was going to be back. But that was just as well. You can't trust him. When he tells you he's going out for half an hour, he may be gone for a week."

She sighed.

"I never have any idea when he's going to turn up. I'm used to it. That's how it's always been."

"You don't know where he went Thursday night?" I asked. "Or who he went to see?"

"No," she replied.

She was not a good liar. She had no confidence in her lies and she wasn't convinced she was going to be believed. She kept talking, evidently hoping that the more she said, the more believable she sounded. Her show of counting back in time was just amateur theatrics.

We said nothing and waited for her to continue.

"I assume he's in hot water again," she said, and I winced thinking of the water he had wound up in. "Poor devil. Mikhail Ivanovich said he isn't going to get him off the hook any more. He's sick and tired of it."

"Who's Mikhail Ivanovich?" I asked.

She pointed at the picture on her desk.

"My husband. He works for the Ministry of Defense. Up until now, Mitya has avoided getting in major trouble thanks to my husband, but my husband says he's fed up with Mitya's behavior, that it's got to end."

That at least answered our question how Mitya had avoided jail. It was worth noting – because Mikhail Ivanovich must have had considerable pull at the Ministry of Defense to be able to bail the kid out time and again.

As if answering my question, the woman added, "Mikhail Ivanovich is chief jurist of the Armed Forces. Before that he was in the diplomatic service. He was a military attaché in Belgrade."

"Has Mitya been in trouble a lot?"

"You should know, of all people. It's you he's usually in trouble with."

"Why do you think he may be in trouble this time? Do you know something you're not telling us?"

"No, of course I don't," she replied hastily. "What makes you think I do? I certainly have no idea. It's just he's always in one kind of trouble or another. I'm used to it, and that's why I assumed this time—"

She broke off.

"I'm afraid we have very bad news for you, Yekaterina," I said. "Please sit down."

She grew pale and clutched the back of a chair.

"Oh, my God," she said. She pulled the chair over and sat down.

"Your son is dead, and I think you know something that could give us an idea who killed him and why."

That hit her hard. She screamed and clapped her hand over her mouth. Neither Valera nor I said anything for a long time. She was no longer play-acting. It was genuine horror, incomprehension, and grief. I felt guilty doing things this way, but I knew she had been lying to us, and we needed to get to the truth. For her son's sake – because we needed to find his killer.

She shook her head.

"Do you mean—" she began. "No, it can't be. No. You don't mean it, do you? No, of course you don't. Is this some kind of a sick joke? Are you trying to get some information out of me? No, it just can't be true."

She looked at me, then at Valera, at our grim, set faces. She buried her face in her hands and began to sob.

Her cigarette slipped out of her fingers and fell onto the rug. Valera picked it up and stubbed it in the ashtray.

"You need a drink," I said. "Do you have anything strong in the house?"

She shook her head, still covering her face.

"We don't keep any liquor here. Not with Mitya around. He is a binge drinker."

She broke down again.

"He was," she corrected herself.

I stood over her, waiting for the first attack of grief to subside. She reached for the pack on the desk and shook another cigarette out with trembling fingers. She had trouble striking a match against the side of the matchbox and then placing the flame under the tip of her cigarette. The matchbox had a picture of a riverboat on it and an advertisement for river cruises down the Moscow River. It was like a macabre joke.

"It was bound to happen sooner or later," she said finally, her voice hoarse. "Every time he came up with one of his crazy schemes, he would convince himself that it was finally the real thing. It was going to make him rich, set him up for life. And he trusted people, even dangerous people, criminals of all kinds. He never really grew up."

I pulled out one of my own cigarettes and lit it. Valera gave me a disapproving look. I could tell he didn't like how I had broken the news to Mitya's mother. No doubt I had broken several rules of interrogation.

"Is Mikhail Ivanovich Mitya's father?" I asked.

She shrugged.

"Yes and no. I was very young when I had Mitya, right out of high school. I grew up in Central Asia. My family is German. We were deported from the Volga region during the war. I met Mikhail Ivanovich here in Moscow, during my first year at the university. I'd left Mitya with my parents, and at first Mikhail Ivanovich didn't know anything about him. But he was very understanding when he found out. He's very generous, too. He adopted Mitya and gave him his name, even though Mitya's father was a Kirghiz and Mitya looked nothing like Mikhail Ivanovich. Mitya was still very small then, and we decided not to tell him that Mikhail Ivanovich wasn't his real father. They were close, very close, and I even came to think of them as father and son, despite the differences. But Mitya must have guessed at the truth. It was hard not to. That was his problem. That was why he never grew up. He didn't want to become an adult, to confront his origins. So he stayed a twelve-year-old."

She kept taking long draws on her cigarette between slow, halting sentences, and had now burned it almost to the filter. She put it out and reached for another. The pack was empty.

"Wait, I'll go get another pack," she said.

She tried to get up, stumbled, and had to sit down again, covering her eyes.

"I can't," she said.

I offered her one of mine. She took it, thanked me, lit it, and drew greedily, as if she hadn't just finished a cigarette a moment ago.

"You know how street kids are," she continued. "They're racist, and they have no pity. They never missed an opportunity to taunt him. He so much wanted to belong, and he didn't understand why they wouldn't accept him as one of the guys."

I knew that well. Right after the war, when we came back to Moscow from the Urals, where my mother's factory had been evacuated, I used to belong to a street gang.

"It was my fault," she said. "We shouldn't have hidden from him that his father was a Kirghiz. I should have sat him down long ago, when he was still a vivacious, smart little kid, and told him the truth. The truth is always better, even if it can be bitter. I should have told him about Central Asia, about the Kirghiz nation, what great warriors they were, what a great culture they had. And how they were hospitable to my parents when we were dumped in the middle of their steppes with nothing but the clothes on our backs. They gave us food and shelter and helped us care for our old folks. He should have been proud of his heritage. But Mikhail Ivanovich didn't want Mitya to know. They got along so well when Mitya was small that I let it go. It was my fault."

She smiled bitterly.

"Mikhail Ivanovich and I didn't have other children. He loved Mitya as his own son."

"What did he get himself involved in this time?" I asked.

"I guess I might as well tell you, since it doesn't matter anymore," she said.

She took another one of my cigarettes.

"About two weeks ago, he came home very proud of himself. He said that some important people wanted to hire him to do an important job. It was always like that with him – important people, important jobs. And this time it was completely above board, he assured me. And it was a huge secret. Except he was incapable of keeping secrets. They kept bursting out of him. As I said, he was like a little kid."

"Did he tell you what this job was?"

"I didn't even want to know, because none of his projects ever amounted to much. He said it had something to do with the government. I suppose he was lying. Or else somebody else had lied to him. He was so easy to deceive. When I was skeptical about this new project, he flew into a rage. Ordinarily he was a gentle boy, at least when he was sober, and it was unusual for him to get so worked up. But this time he really believed what he was telling me. He kept saying everything was going to be different from now on, that he was going to be set for life. That was how he imagined things would happen. He had a treasure hunter's personality. Forever dreaming of the Big Score."

"What day was this, exactly?" Valera asked. "When he went out on that job?"

"It was Wednesday, two weeks ago. He went out at night and came back in the morning. Very pleased with himself."

Valera and I exchanged a look. It was the night Olga Khokhlova's suite at the Metropole had been broken into.

"What happened next?" Valera asked, his voice eager, betraying his impatience. All of a sudden, it was his investigation once again.

"He said he had gotten what he had been sent for, and that was of utmost national importance. Now things were looking up. He tried to take a nap, but was too excited to sleep. He kept making himself tea, then saying he was going to get a motorcycle license and buy a motorbike. That was his dream. And he was going to pay off his debts, too. He owed a lot money to a lot of people – mostly bad people, dangerous people – and many times they have sent goons around to beat him up."

She sighed.

"Then he got that phone call."

"Who was it?" Valera asked.

"I have no idea. A man. He asked for Mitya and wasn't nice about it. He sounded angry and impatient."

"What did they talk about?"

"I couldn't hear what the man said on the other end. But judging from what my son was saying, it wasn't a pleasant conversation."

"But you did hear what your son said?" Valera asked.

She nodded.

"Try to remember his exact words. It's very important. It's the only thing we can go by to find his killer."

"I'll try," she said. "At first Mitya sounded defiant. He said, 'No, I don't know anything about that.' Then, 'She's lying.' The man on the other end must have been accusing him of something, something that had to do with a woman, and Mitya was denying it. He was pretty stubborn about it, and he kept saying 'No, that was the only thing. I swear to you.' Then for a long time Mitya said nothing, just listened to the voice in the receiver. And then it was as though the air had gone out of my boy. All his enthusiasm was gone. He started mumbling 'Yes, of course. Sure, no problem. I'll get it. Yes, everything's in one place. Just as you say. Right away.'"

She broke down and began to cry. I went to the kitchen, down a long hallway lined with bookshelves and hung with modernist paintings. I took a coffee mug from a dish rack and filled it with tap water. It took her a few minutes to calm down and stop sobbing.

"When he hung up, he was very upset. Mikhail Ivanovich was home and overheard the conversation, too. I mean Mitya's side of it. He tried to get Mitya to tell him what had happened because it sounded like he had gotten himself into trouble again. But Mitya didn't want to talk, maybe because when Mitya was in trouble last time, Mikhail Ivanovich had told him that he wasn't going to help him anymore, that Mitya could just go to jail if he was so determined to. Mitya put on his coat and was gone."

"And you have no idea where he went?"

She shook her head.

"Did he have anything on him when he got back on Thursday morning?" I asked.

The woman shook her head.

"Did he take anything with him when he went out? A bag or a briefcase?"

"No, he just put his coat on and went out."

"If he had something he wanted to hide, where do you think it would be?"

"He had all kinds of shady acquaintances in the neighborhood. He used to hang out at the garages behind the apartment building. But there are plenty of other places where he could have left it."

"One other thing," I asked as we were leaving. "Was your son wearing a red and white flannel shirt when he went out?"

"Yes, I believe he was," the woman replied after a moment's thought. "Yes, I'm sure of it."

"Why were you asking her about a hiding place?" Valera asked when we left the apartment. "The way I see it, the whole thing is pretty straightforward. After the robbery, Kisly takes the stuff straight to Levkoyev. Then the client threatens him, and he wants it back. He must have thought that the client was a pushover, but the client turns out to be a tough guy. Say, Levkoyev balks, he brings the client to have a talk with Levkoyev, and that client knifes Levkoyev. They don't find the jewels, and so the client kills Kisly, too. What do you think?"

I shrugged.

"It makes sense," Valera continued. "Levkoyev didn't know the client, and so the client leaves Levkoyev's body in the apartment. But he has a murder on his hands. He needs to get rid of Kisly, who could lead us to him. That's why he goes to so much trouble to make sure that Kisly's body disappears and is not identified. This means that Kisly's client is someone he knew fairly well. It shouldn't be difficult to identify him."

"It's a theory," I said.

Valera's theory was good, and we certainly would be looking for whoever had hired Kisly. But there was one problem: the client had been very busy killing Levkoyev and Kisly and hadn't spent any time looking for the missing jewelry. Sure, he might have thought it was a daunting task, but it didn't look like he even tried – whereas Gordeyev and his partner stumbled upon Levkoyev's hiding place within twenty minutes of arriving at the dead man's apartment.

I had to look for a different explanation.

# TWENTY-THREE

Going out of Kisly's apartment building, we turned our attention to the row of rusty sheet metal garages that huddled together on the edge of an unpaved driveway. We spent the rest of the day tracking down their owners, which was no easy task. It turned out that the garages were not registered with the local housing office. No one knew anything about them. They appeared to have been built illegally, and no record of their ownership had been kept anywhere.

That's how our system works. Yury Vladimirovich's agency is supposed to know everything about every last one of us, but there are plenty of people who fall through the cracks. While Valera complained about Russians' perennial lack of order, I kept my mouth shut. Privately, I didn't think it was such a bad thing. People need to have some private space away from the all-seeing eye of the state.

Even after we had tracked some of the owners down, it took us a while to find one willing to talk to us about Mitya. Perhaps they didn't really know him. Those apartment blocks were fairly new, and the neighbors hadn't had time to get decently acquainted. Besides, unlike the tightly packed courtyards in the center of the city, where everyone knows everyone else's business, the yards on the outskirts are more spread out. Plus of course there was also the usual reluctance to talk to the authorities – because you never knew where a conversation might lead. Everyone had something to hide.

"Sure, I know him. He's always hanging around my garage, lying about a Java bike he's about to buy and bragging about his biker friends. If you ask me, he probably can't even ride a bike."

He was a coarse factory worker type, and he had no time for a dreamer like Mitya. Nor was he happy to have been waylaid by two detectives after his shift. He stood impatiently in front of his building, tapping his feet to keep warm. His face and hands were covered with grime, and all he wanted was to get home and wash up.

"Who else is he friendly with in the neighborhood?" I asked.

The man shrugged.

"To be honest, I don't pay much attention to him. I don't think he has too many friends. He isn't quite right in his head."

"Does he know any criminals?" Valera asked. "Any thieves?"

That was a more slippery ground, and the man was instantly on his guard.

"How would I know?" he replied. "I don't associate with them. And if he told me he knew someone like that, I wouldn't believe him anyway. You shouldn't either."

"Any real enemies?"

"He's very irritating, but you can't take him seriously. I'm telling you, he's a bit like a village idiot. Maybe they're all like that, those slant-eyed Central Asians."

"And if he wanted to hide something in one of the garages, who would he go to?" I asked.

The man sneered.

"He doesn't need to ask anyone. He can open any lock and doesn't need a key. That's the only skill he has. If he had brains, he'd make a first-rate burglar."

"Do you think someone could have hired him to use his skills and break into a place?" Valera interjected. "Someone in the neighborhood perhaps?"

"What do you mean? To steal something?"

"Yes," Valera said. "To do a fairly difficult job, to steal some valuables?"

The suggestion seemed to amuse the man.

"You obviously don't know the kid. You can't trust him with anything. He'll either not show up for the job or brag about it to everyone, including the neighborhood cop. You'd only hire him to do something illegal if you wanted to get caught. All he's good for is breaking into someone's garage and stealing some guy's bottle of vodka stashed for a special occasion. Guys hate him for that."

"So there *are* people who hate him?" Valera asked sternly.

"Well, yes, I suppose so. They do kinda hate him."

"Enough to kill?" Valera pressed him.

The man laughed.

"Sock him one in the eye, yeah, for sure. But kill him for a bottle of vodka? No way."

He stopped laughing and stared.

"Wait a second," he said. "Are you kidding me? Do you mean—"

The news about Mitya's death really upset him. He shook his head in disbelief and said softly, "He wasn't a bad kid. Crazy, yes, and a binge drinker, but harmless. Who would have wanted to kill him?"

We eventually sent him home, warning him not to wag his tongue around the neighborhood about our conversation.

Valera was keen to keep looking for other garage owners on the hope that one of them might lead him to Mitya's client, but one was enough for me.

"Well, at least we found out something important," I said.

"Meaning?" Valera asked.

"That the jewelry we returned to the foreign woman wasn't all that was stolen."

"Why not?"

"I have a feeling that something is still missing."

"But I matched all the pieces we found with what was on the list," Valera protested. "It all checked out."

"You drew up the list based on Khokhlova's words, right?"

"Yes, of course. There was no other source."

"So, all she needed to do to conceal the fact that something else was taken was to not report it. Possibly, she forgot to mention it. A simple oversight. But it's too much of a coincidence. I'm actually sure she did it on purpose. It may have been a piece of jewelry, but it may have been something else, too, something entirely different."

"Nonsense," Valera said. "Why would she want to conceal anything from us?"

"Remember I told you after we'd gone to see her on the morning after the burglary that I was sure she was hiding something? This is it. It's the thing Mitya Kislitsky was sent to her suite to steal."

Valera sneered derisively.

"Yeah, sure. I bet she's a spy masquerading as an old woman. Kisly was sent to her suite to get a map of border fortifications she stole from the Ministry of Defense."

I wasn't inclined to joking.

"I doubt she's a spy," I said tersely. "Andropov wouldn't have involved us if it were a spy case. It's a case of burglary that Andropov wanted to be solved quickly, and he thought we'd be able to do it more efficiently than his own people. But the woman wasn't happy when we showed up and, especially, when Andropov introduced us as top-notch detectives. Now I think I know why."

# TWENTY-FOUR

I got home a few minutes before ten. Sevka was still poring over his textbooks, but Tosya had turned in and the light in our room was off. I sat for a few minutes with Sevka, checking his homework and chatting about school.

Tosya's attention was now almost entirely devoted to Nikola, and she was giving Sevka more of a free rein. Before our little one was born, she had taken too much interest in Sevka's schooling, finding it hard to hide her disappointment every time he got less than perfect marks. Fortunately, he was turning into a studious kid. His interests were now centered on biology and chemistry.

I liked hearing Sevka talk about microorganisms and organic compounds even if the stuff he told me was often way over my head. When I was his age, I was hanging around in back streets with guys I would later meet across the interrogation desk. I wasn't proud of it, but it was how my adolescence had been, and it wasn't always my fault. It was a difficult time, right after the war. And growing up back then I learned a few valuable lessons that I would have missed had I spent more time on a school bench. My partner Valera, on the other hand, studied hard when he was in school but didn't become a scientist or an engineer. And he didn't learn any lessons in the mean streets of postwar Moscow, either, and that made his life as a cop a lot more difficult.

"You should definitely become a scientist, Sevka," I said.

"It's interesting, but a scientist's job is really boring. All you do is hang around the lab the whole time. There is no action and hardly ever any excitement."

"Not if you win the Nobel Prize. Then there would be a lot of excitement around the lab."

"You're pulling my leg, Uncle Pavel. Very few people win the Nobel Prize, and they're all real geniuses. I want to be a detective."

"You can be an amateur detective," I said. "You can work in the lab all day and investigate murders in your spare time."

I laughed, and, after pondering whether or not he should pout, he laughed along with me.

I liked talking to Sevka. I wanted us to be a family – not just me and Tosya as a couple, but all three of us, and now all four, counting Nikola. I wanted Sevka to be a real brother to Nikola and not feel resentful or jealous, because everyone always pays more attention to the little guy. I didn't want Sevka to feel that Nikola was my real son and that he, Sevka, wasn't.

"What are you working on, Uncle Pavel?" Sevka asked. "You haven't been talking about your work lately. Still that boring jewelry theft?"

I had told him about the theft in very general terms, complying with Comrade Andropov's orders not to talk about it publicly, but I might have said a bit more to Tosya – I liked telling her about my investigations, and she often gave me solid, common sense advice – but since Nikola arrived, I found it hard to interest her in anything I was doing.

"Boring or not," I said, "it was an important enough case to completely change our new neighbor's behavior."

"I'm glad it did. He's a nice guy, actually."

"So he's no longer rude to your Mom?"

I didn't want Sevka to get too friendly with Boris. I'd dealt with plenty of State Security officers in my time, and I knew they were a vengeful and unforgiving bunch who held grudges and could wait forever for an opportunity to get even with you.

"No, we've got to be real friends. Even Mom has been coming round. He even showed me his service revolver."

"Did he really?"

"And his father's. His father also worked for State Security, but that was before the war. He had a Nagan revolver engraved and personally given to him by Comrade Yagoda. You have never even shown me your gun."

"That's because a gun is not a toy," I said coldly. "Kids have no business handling firearms, and neither do civilians. A surgeon would never give you his scalpel to play with, and neither should a law enforcement officer let you handle his firearm."

"You always say that," Sevka said. "If you don't like guns, maybe they shouldn't have given you one. Especially if you work on silly cases like the theft of some jewelry. Boris has a much more important job. He's got to confront enemies of the state, American spies, and other riffraff. They are armed and dangerous."

I could have told him that my boring jewelry case already included two murders. I also could have told him that most people the KGB goes after are not American spies but unarmed Soviet citizens, like scientists who travel to symposiums in France or Britain, and housewives who talk too much and criticize the government while standing in line at the grocery store. Or ordinary guys like Sevka and me who tell a political joke. Finally, I could have mentioned that in the 1930s the KGB, which was then called the NKVD, shot plenty of innocent people without a proper trial, putting bullets from their Nagan revolvers through the back of people's heads in some dark dungeon, and that Comrade Yagoda had himself been arrested and shot for being too bloodthirsty, even for those bloodthirsty times. But Sevka was too young to be told of such things. He would learn them in time.

Sevka took my silence to mean that his unfavorable comparison of my job with the obviously more dangerous, heroic, and romantic life of a KGB officer had hit home. Sevka had a good heart, and he felt bad about putting me and my work down.

"Did you catch the guy who stole the jewels yet?" he asked.

"We didn't. But I'm working on a different case now. It turned out to be related to the burglary, but we didn't know that until today."

"Was it another theft, Uncle Pavel?"

"No, Sevka," I said. "It's a murder."

"Really?" All of a sudden Sevka was excited. He started asking me all kinds of questions – who got murdered, where and why. I gave him vague answers because I couldn't disclose the particulars, and because I wanted to keep his curiosity piqued, since he was under the impression that my job was so boring.

"I'll tell you more later, Sevka," I said, putting an end to his overeager questioning. "When there's more information and when I'm allowed to talk about this case. You should get back to your homework, and I should go see what your Mom is up to."

"She keeps going to bed early. She's like a little kid herself. But do you at least have a theory who the killer might be?"

"I do," I said. "But it's still a little vague at this time."

I had thought about Kisly and his murder on the way home, and about Levkoyev's murder, too, and I continued thinking about the case until I climbed into bed next to Tosya. Or rather next to little Nikola, because she had placed him next to her in the middle of the bed, and his little red body breathing there by her side now separated us. I leaned over Nikola and tried to kiss her, then started to caress her shoulders.

"You kidding, Pavel?" She hissed angrily. "What do you think you're doing with the baby right here, in-between us?"

"Put him back into his crib then," I whispered.

Tosya ignored me and turned to face the wall.

We now lived together, but our lovemaking had gotten to be less frequent and more complicated, and everything had to be done in silence, since Sevka was right there, too, behind a thin partition. And besides, Tosya has become shy making love around Nikola.

"He's an infant," I would tell her. "He doesn't understand what he sees yet."

"So what?" she would counter. "He's still a person. A human being."

Nor would she accept my assertion that, having been conceived in this manner, Nikola shouldn't find anything objectionable in the act itself. He couldn't have existed any other way.

It was too early to fall asleep. There was still the sound of traffic beneath our windows on Chernyshevsky Street, and occasional voices and muffled footsteps rose up from the snowy sidewalk. I thought about the dead body by the frozen river and Kisly's mother, and then I started to go through everything I knew about the case, and about what I didn't know yet and had to find out.

Start with the identity of Kisly's client. It might have been Levkoyev or some other person, but there had to be someone. Kisly could not have done the job on his own.

"Don't you agree?" I asked myself, then replied in the affirmative.

"What did you say?"

I didn't realize that I had been speaking aloud. Tosya had fallen asleep, and my voice had woken her.

"Nothing," I said. "Talking to myself."

"Tomorrow night," she grumbled, her voice hoarse and full of sleep. "I promise. Wait till tomorrow."

I smiled in the dark. I wanted to kiss her again, but I didn't dare.

Both Levkoyev and Kisly had been murdered by the same person. This followed from the similarity of the wounds. But the man who killed them wasn't necessarily the one who had hired Kisly. In fact, it usually works out that the person in whose possession stolen goods are found so soon after a burglary is directly implicated in the burglary, either as a mastermind or an actual perpetrator. So Kisly's client was probably Levkoyev, working with an accomplice – most likely, his neighbor, Daria Shubina who had been on duty on Khokhlova's floor on the night of the burglary. Kisly stole the jewels for Levkoyev, and that was a straightforward transaction.

However, there was something else that Kisly had taken from the suite at the Metropole but that Khokhlova didn't include in the list of stolen jewelry drafted by Valera. Kisly kept the object for himself, thinking that he could get away with it. Levkoyev demanded that Kisly turn it over. Kisly refused at first but was prevailed upon in the end – most likely, by threats.

At this point, enter a third person. Or fourth, if Daria Shubina is included.

The fourth person is, of necessity, in cahoots with Levkoyev. The two of them kill Kisly and dump the body. But then the two accomplices argue in Levkoyev's apartment, over the object that they took from Kisly, and Levkoyev loses the argument – which is not surprising, considering how skilled our unknown fourth person is with a blade. The killer is only interested in that object and doesn't care about all the jewelry stashed in a secret place in Levkoyev's apartment. Now all he wants to do is get away.

I liked my theory, but it still had holes.

The most important unknown was what kind of object it could have been and why Khokhlova refused to mention it – either before her stolen jewelry was recovered or after.

Lying awake for several hours, sorting out various possibilities, rejecting some and then coming up with others, I finally realized I could ask myself far more questions than I could answer, and that I had to start by having a heart-to-heart with Khokhlova. She had definitely left something out – something that had not been found in the secret hiding place in Levkoyev's apartment.

The problem was that if I tried to talk to her on my own, I was sure to run afoul of Yuri Vladimirovich Andropov, the all-powerful head of the KGB. I would have to try the official channels first.

## TWENTY-FIVE

I waited for the Boss to get us a meeting with Khokhlova, which he had to clear through Andropov.

To my surprise, Andropov didn't refuse my request point-blank but promised to give an answer soon – as soon as he could make an opening in her schedule.

"You know, she's been exceptionally busy," he told the Boss. "There are so many people she wants to meet. Yesterday she spent the entire day with Valentina Tereshkova. It had always been her dream to be introduced to the first woman in space. Today it's Victoria Gubchak, the Stakhanovite coal miner from Donetsk and a People's Deputy elected unanimously to the Supreme Soviet. Olga Stepanovna is learning so much about our country and especially about our Soviet women. It's been an eye-opener for her, after all the anti-Soviet trash she has been fed in France. But I'll let you know the moment she has a few minutes free."

The Boss, ever deferential to his own bosses, assured Andropov that I had all the time in the world and would wait as long as it took.

"I'll have to be present during the interview, of course," Andropov added. "It would be better that way, don't you agree?"

The Boss naturally was in complete agreement.

After that, Andropov disappeared. We waited for him to reemerge for three days and, having heard nothing by the morning of the fourth day, I took a bus to Karl Marx Avenue, walked to the Metropole, and took a seat by the window of a coffee shop.

The weird thing was that it was Valera who had suggested I take action. Valera, who had never in living memory broken a rule or had gone against the will of a superior officer.

Getting to a coffee shop located inside a hard currency hotel sounds easy in the retelling, but first I had to get past the enormous doorman; his practiced eye could not be deceived. He could easily see that I was not a hotel guest and, in fact, not a foreigner.

But at least he didn't recognize me from our first encounter, when I came there on the morning of the burglary. That was a plus.

"What's your business here?" he inquired softly, blocking my way with his giant belly and stabbing me with a chubby forefinger. His hands had the flattened knuckles of a pugilist. "About-turn, buddy, and away with you before you get into more trouble than you've ever seen."

I didn't like being treated that way. I was, after all, a police officer, even though, as a Criminal Investigations detective, I ranked low on our law enforcement totem pole.

"Out of my way, Mustafa," I said, pushing his hand aside. "A Tambov wolf is a buddy to you."

He was the sort of person who treated those "beneath" him like dirt, but who was a boot-licker at his core, scared to death of anyone above him in the hierarchy. If you were rude to him and acted like you had a right to act that way, he accepted it without questioning.

Mustafa stared at me in amazement for a few seconds. In my ill-fitting Soviet-made winter coat and cheap rabbit-fur hat, I didn't look the part of someone who would dare order him around. On the other hand, I knew his first name and that made me an insider. If I had spoken to him that way, it could only mean that I outranked him.

I watched his face struggle with the computations, reading him like an open book. That was why I knew exactly when he made up his mind. A second later, he stepped aside.

Entering the cafe presented a greater problem. A uniformed doorman at the entrance was polite but firm – they only accepted hard currency, and he was sorry to inform me that his instructions were to admit no one who could not produce either a hotel guest pass or any kind of official document confirming the bearer's right to pay dollars, pounds, yen, or West German marks.

"No Mongolian tugriks?" I asked, my face straight and my voice concerned. It was clear that a lot was riding on his answer.

He gave it some thought.

"I honestly don't know, sir," he said. "I'll have to check with the manager, but I have to warn you that it is highly unlikely that your currency will be honored here."

"Well, let's not try to divine something that is above our pay grade," I said. "Let's call the manager. I have no doubt he'll have the answer."

"The manager is a woman, sir," the doorman said.

He went inside, taking care to lock the café's glass door, in case I tried to take advantage of his absence to sneak in. He was gone for a quarter of an hour. It was breakfast time, and a line soon formed outside the door. Everyone in the line looked like they had a right to pay in dollars, pounds, yen, or West German marks. They were lining up patiently, in an orderly manner, occasionally looking up at me in the mistaken belief that I was the doorman and exchanging remarks in their own languages. After about ten minutes, their voices grew louder and I didn't really need to know what they were saying in order to get their drift.

The doorman finally came back, unlocked the door, and waved the tourists in. They didn't complain. On the contrary, they seemed grateful, suggesting that they were getting used to Moscow and to standing in line.

"You're to wait here," the doorman told me, no longer especially polite. The manager must have given him a stern talking to for leaving his post and bothering her with stupid questions about Mongolian currency.

The manager was a very polished lady in a nicely tailored, bright green suit, and sporting a fashionable blonde beehive hairdo. She looked more like someone who should be a theater manager or an art museum administrator than the manager of a coffee shop, even if it was one that only accepted hard currency.

She was not impressed by my Moscow Criminal Investigations credentials, noting that no crime had ever been committed at the Metropole. No person suspected of committing a crime had ever stayed here, either, and the hotel was not, in any case, within my jurisdiction.

I listened patiently and didn't contradict her. All I had to say when she was done was that I just needed a place to sit and wait for Comrade Andropov's Volga. The glass door was promptly thrown open. And I hadn't even lied. I was indeed waiting for Comrade Andropov's Volga, only my plan was to be done and gone just as it arrived.

I found a small table by the window and sat there surrounded by foreigners, inhaling the gentle smoke of their Marlboro cigarettes while staring at the parking area behind the hotel. A few exotic foreign cars – a cute Volkswagen bug, a stately Mercedes-Benz, and a make I didn't know – were being busily cleared of a half an inch's worth of fresh snow by two men in hotel uniforms. From my vantage point, I was also able to keep an eye on the entrance by peeking over the heads of two Japanese couples across the room. No sign of Andropov's Volga yet. I knew I had a wait ahead of me, since Khokhlova, being a ballet dancer, albeit a retired one, wasn't likely to be an early riser. The question was how much time I would have when she came down to breakfast before Andropov was to arrive.

My table was empty. It had been set, and a clean plate stood in front of me on a heavily starched tablecloth. A napkin, also starched to within an inch of its life, had been elaborately folded in the shape of a pyramid and placed on the plate. There was also a tiny glass vase, and the daisy in it was of the same plastic variety that graced the table in the greasy spoon on Petrovsky Gate where my late partner Lenny Urumov and I used to eat. The only difference was that this one was not covered with a thick layer of dust and grime. It even had the price – 15 kopeks – stamped on its green stem.

I had no hard currency, and so I couldn't order anything even if I could afford the prices. The prices, however, weren't much of a deterrent to the foreign tourists, all of whom were eating hearty breakfasts of fried eggs, boiled hot dogs and peas the color of the manager's dress. Everyone was having the same thing, suggesting either the uniformity of foreign tastes spanning national borders, or the paucity of choice on the coffee shop's menu.

After a while, the foreigners began to cast curious glances in my direction, obviously wondering why I was just sitting there not having anything. The manager must have noticed that, too, and sent a waitress over with a cup of tea and a piece of pound cake. The tea was weak, but the pound cake was first rate.

By nine o'clock, Khokhlova had not come downstairs yet, but Andropov's Volga had arrived. As usual, Andropov's driver Ivan was beind the wheel, but there was no passenger in the front seat. Ivan got out, stretched, spat on the pavement, and lit a cigarette. Mustafa came up to him quickly, and Ivan stuck out a limp right hand, which the big doorman shook officiously and with a show of deference. The Japanese couples had left, and my view of the KGB pecking order in action was no longer obstructed.

It was clear that Khokhlova was going to skip breakfast and my plan had to be modified mid-course. I went out of the coffee shop, giving a curt nod to the doorman, and joined Ivan and Mustafa in the freezing sunshine.

If Andropov's driver recognized me, he didn't show it. I ranked well below Big Mustafa. "I think we met before, comrade," I said to Ivan. "You're Comrade Andropov's driver, aren't you?"

The driver gave me a noncommittal shrug and blew bluish smoke through his nostrils. He was smoking a long Bulgarian cigarette with a ring of gold leaf on the filter end. Even though it was a woman's brand, it was popular with the personal drivers of various party and government big wigs. Perhaps it was because they were long and smoking them killed far more time than regular king-size cigarettes during long waits for one's boss.

"Are you here to pick up Madame Khokhlova?" I continued, not waiting for his reply.

He gave me another shrug.

"Excellent," I said cheerfully, electing to interpret his shrugs as affirmatives. "I ought to warn you. The old woman seems to have mislaid her schedule and no longer knows the program for today. She's a bit embarrassed. You know how old people are, always afraid they're going a bit crazy."

I was counting on the fact that, seeing me emerge from the hotel, he would assume I had met with Khokhlova. I was sure he knew that we weren't supposed to talk to her without his boss's permission, but since I wasn't hiding from him – and on the contrary had approached him on my own – he had to assume that his boss was aware of our meeting. My stratagem worked perfectly.

"What's there to know?" Ivan said disdainfully. "First to visit the Likhachev Automobile Factory and then, at two o'clock, back here, to the Arts Club on 25th of October Street."

"Just let her know that discreetly, will you? And warn Comrade Andropov, too."

"The Boss is not with her today," Ivan announced. "The Boss has important meetings."

That was a huge piece of good luck. True, there would be others making sure Khokhlova didn't have some unauthorized or unscripted encounter, but they would be a lot safer to trick than the KGB chief.

"Just don't let her guess that you know she lost her schedule," I said.

"Keep your advice to yourself," the driver said rudely. "I don't need you to teach me tact."

Very pleased with myself, I started back toward the metro station. Just as I was leaving, a man and a woman crossed the street toward Andropov's Volga. Ivan, still smoking his gold-tipped woman's cigarette, greeted them with a condescending nod. They must have been there to accompany Khokhlova to her scheduled meetings and they clearly didn't rank very high at all, since they had to get to the Metropole on their own, by public transport.

I had been just in time. The moment I passed the front door of the hotel, Olga emerged, dressed in her beautiful red coat. A recent acquisition – a Russian wool babushka – covered her head. The babushka looked great in combination with her coat. She managed to make even that plain headgear elegant.

I waved to her. I strongly doubted she knew who I was, but she must have taken it as an expression of goodwill from an ordinary Muscovite and, ever the polite foreigner, waved back to me. I was glad Ivan saw me wave. Back at his post, Big Mustafa applied himself to the heavy revolving door so energetically that it kept spinning for a good minute after she had gone through.

The two newly arrived minders rushed to Khokhlova with an obsequious show of enthusiasm. Even from the distance I could see their saccharine smiles. The man threw the car door open, winning the race with Ivan, who, it should be admitted, wasn't trying too hard.

Khokhlova stopped and shuddered briefly, whether from the morning cold or disgust – it was hard to tell – and sat in the passenger seat. The minders packed into the back and the Volga was off.

# TWENTY-SIX

Our country is socialist, which means that no one is either rich or poor. No one has any money, but no one goes hungry, either. Sure you can make money. People like Levkoyev have money, but sooner or later they get caught doing something illegal and end up in jail. Or dead. Again, like Levkoyev.

In capitalist countries they say money is everything. In our country, money is nothing. Even if you have money, you can't get into a nice place like the coffee shop at the Metropole because it is reserved for hotel guests and other foreigners. No one dares ask why foreigners are so privileged and are treated better than locals.

And even those privileged foreigners, for all their money, couldn't get anything at the coffee shop except fried eggs, bluish sausages, and nasty green peas. And they can't get into the Arts Club because entry is reserved for its members. No exceptions. To be a member of the Arts Club you have to have something to do with the arts. Then you at least have a chance of being admitted, and only after that will you get the privilege of using the restaurant.

There, too, a uniformed doorman in a peaked hat demands to see your credentials.

Through the plate glass windows of the club on 25th of October Street, Valera and I could see into a large, richly appointed dining room and observe a group of diners enjoying plates of steaming winter borscht and generous portions of Beef Stroganoff ladled over mounds of buckwheat kasha. The diners all sat on one side of a very long table, like Christ and his apostles in that famous painting, except there were many more of them and there was a fair number of women among them. They were sitting with their backs to us, partially blocking our view of the table that groaned beneath the dishes and bottles.

That day even a member's card – which we didn't have in any case – would have been of no use. The doorman didn't even ask to see ours before declaring that the club was closed for an important private function and would not reopen until supper.

But the Arts Club was no Metropole Hotel. Our Moscow Criminal Investigations cards still rated here. As well, a couple of years ago I had been taken here by Lenny, who used to be friendly with a junior waitress. Ordinarily, Lenny tended to like waitresses whose good looks and spunky personalities were inversely correlated with the quality of the food at the establishments where they worked. Lenny's all-too-brief courtship of Lyuba, the Arts Club waitress, stood out in my mind as a respite from the usual heartburn.

"Hey, buddy, is Lyuba still working here?" I asked the doorman.

Lyuba, still very pretty but older and more senior in the waitressing hierarchy, recognized me right away. She sighed at the memory of my late partner, but her sadness was more pro forma than heartfelt. It was obvious that she had already found someone else. Lenny, looking down at us from whatever part of the heavens is reserved for good cops and serial adulterers, would have had no right to complain. Lyuba was not the first, nor the last girl he was friendly with – and besides he had a wife, whom he had loved in his own weird way and two little daughters that he genuinely adored.

Lyuba escorted us into a windowless space near the kitchen that the waitresses and busboys used to stack plates on their way out or back from the dining room. It's where she used to feed us in Lenny's day. Not a fancy place by any means, but the dismal surroundings were well made up for by the quality of the food.

"You're in luck boys," Lyuba said. "We're having a reception for some fancy foreign bird. A French ballerina they say, but she speaks Russian better than you and me. Anyway, you're going to be fed well, I can promise you. But keep extra quiet. I don't want to get in trouble for letting strangers in when we have an important foreigner visiting."

I assured her that she had nothing to worry about, but that was before I factored in Valera's excitement at seeing all the famous movie stars gathered at the long table in the main dining room. We had seen them from outside, but hadn't been able to recognize any of them from the back.

Suddenly, Valera was like a kid in an ice cream parlor. He pointed out one guy to me, then another, and then an older woman with a wrinkled face and closely cropped grey hair. He was completely bowled over and couldn't stop dropping their names and shaking his head in disbelief. It was all he could do to keep himself from running into the dining room to ask for their autographs.

Tosya, who is crazy about the movies, would have been just the same. But Valera was a grown man and a Criminal Investigations detective working a highly sensitive assignment. And yet he acted like a groupie on the sidelines of the Moscow Film Festival.

"Oh my, look over there!" He was having trouble keeping his voice down. "It's Rolan Bykov, I swear. Oh, my Lord, I honestly can't believe my eyes. And look, Ktorov. Wait till I tell my Mom. She thinks Ktorov is God. And Anastasia Vertinskaya, too. You really don't know who she is? She was in *Scarlet Sails*. And she's chowing down on Beef Stroganoff just like you and me."

"And the same Beef Stroganoff, too," I observed, pointing to our plates.

Actually, I was the only one eating. Valera was too excited to touch his food. He was completely star-struck.

"Please, boys, keep your voices down," Lyuba told us as she passed by. "You're going to get me in trouble."

Before he saw all the famous actors, Valera had been very unhappy about the clever stratagem I had used to find out where Khokhlova would be having lunch. He had even refused to go to the Arts Club at first, and had changed his mind only at the last moment. And yet, he had been the one urging me not to wait for Andropov's permission to talk to Khokhlova.

I was less taken with the actors and spent my time observing Khokhlova's two minders. She was sitting between them in the middle of the table, the position occupied by Christ in that painting I mentioned. The two of them were doing justice to the white fish, black caviar, marinated mushrooms and other dishes on the table, and not forgetting to refill their glasses after every toast. The toasts were numerous. The actors took turns getting up and declaring that they wanted to drink to the arts, to the theater, to Franco-Soviet friendship, and to Mother Russia – old, new and eternal.

There was plenty of false cheer around the table – these were professional actors, after all – but Khokhlova looked tired and annoyed. She took the tiniest of sips after each toast so that her male minder sitting to her right and wielding the wine bottle never needed to top off her glass. However, he made up for it by filling up his own and that of his female colleague on Khokhlova's left.

Khokhlova wasn't eating much either.

A few minutes later, a heavily made up man sporting a greying pompadour and wearing a black sequined shirt emerged from somewhere near the kitchen. He was accompanied by a skinny, middle-aged woman in a dress.

"These are the artists," Lyuba explained to us. "They'll do the entertainment for the foreign bird."

The woman sat at the piano in the corner while her companion, positioning himself in front of the dining table, raised his hand and froze. After holding a dramatic pause for a few minutes, giving time for the actors to stop chewing and set down their knives and forks, he started to sing, performing several Russian folk songs and gypsy romances. He wasn't that bad, I thought. The actors gave him a nice round of applause.

After that, he bowed to Khokhlova and announced, "For you, Madame. Especially."

He arranged his face into a strange, plaintive expression, then sang something lyrical in a foreign language. It was probably French, and, judging by the sappy melody, it had to be about love and heartbreak.

This part of the performance was not a resounding success. The movie stars listened politely, but you could see that they wanted to get back to their eating and toasting. As for Khokhlova, for whom the foreign song was sung, she turned away and, once the singer started in on a second French ballad, got up and apologized to her minder, who had to get up to let her pass.

There was a brief commotion. The singer stumbled and went silent. His accompanist played a few measures before realizing that the singing had stopped. Both minders made as if to follow Khokhlova to the bathroom before giving up and sitting down again.

In Khokhlova's absence, a sudden change came over the dining room. The actors, who had been sitting with grim faces as if they were at a funeral, suddenly turned to each other and started to chat all at once. The minders, the singer and the woman at the piano all joined in. They were like kindergartners whom a teacher had left unsupervised. Accordingly, the moment Khokhlova returned, they fell back into character. The singer, too, returned to his interrupted song.

Khokhlova clapped once or twice when the singer was done and glanced at her watch. She looked relieved once the waiters gathered the plates and started to serve dessert.

As they passed our little anteroom, the performers looked crestfallen, as if they had been booed off the stage. I felt sorry for them. It probably had nothing to do with Khokhlova. She was just getting tired and annoyed at all the public events her hosts had heaped upon her.

In another ten minutes, Khokhlova got up and thanked everyone for a delightful lunch, and then started toward the door. Her minders followed her, falling two steps behind so as not to look like prison guards escorting a prisoner.

That was my cue. I left the storage space at the same time as Khokhlova left the table and headed for the door, arriving there just ahead of her. I held the door open for her, and she gave me a surprised look, recognizing me as a familiar face and wracking her brain trying to place me. Valera was right there, too. He let us through and then shut the door behind us. Turning to Olga's minders, he took out his Criminal Investigations ID and told them to remain in the restaurant. It was a routine police investigation, he explained. He was probably thrilled to have all the film stars in his power, if only for a few minutes.

I linked arms with Khokhlova and led her toward the front door.

"How dare you!" came a steely female voice from behind the closed door of the restaurant. "That woman is a French citizen. You'll have to answer for it."

A male voice, very authoritative, joined in, "Out of my way, man. I'm a KGB officer."

That was when I knew that we were going to get very little lead time. Valera was not the kind of guy who would be able to resist such a voice. And there would certainly be hell to pay for our prank.

"Let's go somewhere where we can talk, Olga Stepanovna," I said and, seeing that Andropov's Volga limousine was waiting at the curb, steered her in the opposite direction.

Ivan, standing by his car, stared at us.

"We had better walk fast," I said. "Fresh air will do us good after such a filling lunch."

Khokhlova didn't resist. On the contrary, my sense of urgency infected her. She realized that we were escaping and picked up her pace. We headed up 25th of October Street toward the History Museum. The Kremlin's St. Nicholas Tower loomed straight ahead. A minute later, I turned and gave a quick look back.

As expected, Khokhlova's minders had prevailed over Valera and were now outside of the Arts' Club. The man had started after us, rudely shoving passersby out of his way, while the woman was pointing us out to Ivan, ordering him to join the chase.

"We've got to hurry," I told Khokhlova. "They're on our tail."

We broke into a trot. She was very light on her feet, and it was me who got out of breath before long. My heart was pounding, half from the run and half from the excitement.

The sidewalk was thick with pedestrians, and we couldn't be quite as unceremonious in making our way through as our pursuers. The distance between us was narrowing by the second. "Come," I shouted, pulling her into the human vortex streaming in and out of the GUM department store.

The GUM was a warren of shops strung along three long arcades that were connected by short transverses. Each arcade had three levels. It was always crowded with Muscovites and visitors who came from every corner of the country to shop here. People were constantly getting lost, and a loudspeaker periodically instructed them to meet their lost party near the octagonal stone fountain in the middle of the central arcade.

Thank God for the GUM, I said to myself once we pushed our way in. Thank God for its thousands of shoppers and its numerous exits. There was no better place to lose one's pursuers.

There, pressed by people from all sides moving in every direction, we could no longer run. Nor did we want to – that would have created a commotion and given us away. Instead, we blended in, walked further into the center of the building, found a dark corner next to a small shop selling knitting supplies, and stopped to catch our breath.

"What a nice red coat you have, girl," a middle-aged shopper observed as she waddled past us, a heavy shopping bag in each hand. Seeing Khokhlova only from the back, she had assumed that someone with her slender figure had to be young.

"Lord, she's older than I am," she gasped as she took a better look. "How do you like that? A young man carrying on with a pensioner."

"Come," I said to Khokhlova. "Let's get out of here."

But I had underestimated the skills of our pursuers – or rather their KGB training. Bursting into the GUM, they didn't start running around aimlessly as most ordinary people might have done. They headed straight for the top level and split up, each taking a position overlooking one of the three arcades and scouring the crowd from that vantage point.

They spotted us the moment we emerged into the open. First we heard a shrill whistle, which cut through the hubbub of voices like hot steel through butter. I looked up and saw Khokhlova's female minder. Leaning over the lacey grillwork of the banister, she kept pointing at us. In the next arcade, her partner was trundling down the stairs. We had been heading for the exit, but now we had to change course and take one of the transverse passages, moving away from the woman's accusatory finger silhouetted against the glass roof. She saw what we were doing and gave two more of her whistles, which was clearly a signal to the others that we were now in the central arcade. She, too, moved to change her observation post.

Khokhlova's red coat was what had given us away. We had no chance of escaping while she was wearing it. But the red coat was also an opportunity, because that was what the woman looking down from the third level would be expecting to see.

"Give me your coat," I told Khokhlova when we were under the walkway. I helped her unbutton it, and we folded it with the lining out. I then stuck the sizeable bundle inside my own coat.

"You look like you're in your eighth month," Khokhlova quipped.

"I hope that's what everyone else thinks, too," I replied as we headed back to arcade number three, where we had just come from. "Because what they're more likely to think is that I'm a shoplifter. Let's hope they won't decide to call the cops."

This time we were successful. On the third level balcony the female minder was scurrying this way and that, hovering now over one side and then the other, peering down at the crowd. Just as I had hoped, she hadn't guessed that Khokhlova might remove her coat. She was still searching the grey mass of shoppers for a splotch of bright red, now safely tucked beneath my coat. Her frantic running had stirred up a couple of pigeons who had made the GUM their home, and they were now circling beneath the glass roof.

We were almost at the Kuybyshev Street exit, me pushing my way through the crowd, leading with my bulging stomach and pulling Khokhlova in my wake, when we ran headlong into Andropov's driver.

I stopped abruptly and started to back away. Slowly, very slowly, trying not to attract his attention by a sudden movement.

"Watch where you're going, goddamn you," a woman shrieked behind me. I must have inadvertently stepped on her toes.

There was no way to get out of the crowd that was carrying us inexorably toward the exit door – and toward Ivan, too. Fortunately, instead of looking around to search for us, he stared straight ahead, his eyes fixed. We tiptoed past him, almost touching him with our elbows and keeping our heads down. Another thirty seconds, and we were out in the street.

We walked quickly toward the corner and felt out of danger only when we were some thirty meters away from the GUM, shielded from view by the crowd on the sidewalk.

"Phew," Khokhlova exhaled noisily. "That was a close call."

She liked being pursued and giving our pursuers a slip. Her eyes were bright and her cheeks were flush with excitement. Suddenly, she looked twenty years younger.

"Yes," I said. "We were damn lucky."

I had a strange feeling about our miraculous escape that I couldn't quite shake. It was the nagging suspicion that Ivan had seen us but kept looking the other way on purpose. That he had let us get away.

# TWENTY-SEVEN

"Thank you," Olga Khokhlova said, catching her breath. "This is the best thing that has happened to me since I arrived. Otherwise, it's one dreadful function after another. This afternoon was the worst. I thought I was going to die of boredom. I hate actors. I'd rather lunch with a fake combine driver who sits on the Supreme Soviet, I swear."

We were now at a bread store with a little café attached to it, standing at a marble-top table in the back. It gave us the view of the street outside and the front door, but we couldn't be seen inside the dimly lit space if someone looked in. I had purchased and brought over a stale sweetroll and two cups of really atrocious coffee in leaky paper cups. Neither of us was hungry, but Olga had walked almost the entire length of 25th of October Street without her coat and was still shivering. She needed something hot to warm her up. Besides, they wouldn't have let us stand there and take up an entire table without ordering anything.

"Back home I would sometimes go into a store and shoplift," she said. "To a big department store, not a mom-and-pop shop. It was the greatest thrill, being able to get away with it."

She sighed.

"It's unfair, of course," she said thoughtfully. "I'm not taking a real risk. No one is going to put me behind bars if I get caught. It would be easy to explain it away, to say that I simply forgot to pay for the merchandise, that I'm a forgetful old lady. If it were some poor wretch with no money, they would drag him off to the police station. But it still gives me an adrenaline rush. It makes me feel alive, somehow, which is not such a bad thing at my age."

Suddenly, she caught herself.

"Oh, my! Look at me, confessing my crimes to a police detective. Swear to me you're not going to turn me in to your Paris colleagues?"

She gave me a coquettish smile that, despite her being more than twice my age, somehow managed to look completely natural. The thought of writing to the Paris police department about Khokhlova's shoplifting struck me as funny. But I also had to get to the point, and I had to cut all that frivolity short. I didn't know how much time we were going to have before they caught up with us. The KGB had a way of finding people.

"What was it that was stolen from you that you didn't report?" I asked softly.

Bringing it up abruptly and without warning was my best chance for getting results, and it worked. My question hit her right between the eyes. Her smile faded in a flash and a haggard look swept over her face. But I underestimated her. She recovered almost instantly. Had I not been watching her closely, I might have missed her reaction. She would have made a very good spy or secret agent.

"I don't know what you're talking about," she said, screwing up her features in a fake smile.

"How would you?" I said. "You reported a number of your jewelry pieces stolen. You provided us with a list of what had been taken and a detailed description. Two days later, everything you reported stolen was recovered, and you declared yourself to be completely satisfied. Is that correct?"

She nodded, staring at me.

"But you didn't report the most important item, the one that was never recovered. It was the very reason the burglary had been conceived. It's too much of a coincidence, in my opinion – you not reporting it and it not being found among the pieces we recovered. My question to you is what it was and why you didn't report it."

"I don't know what you're talking about," she repeated stubbornly.

"I think you do."

She lowered her eyes and looked away. I could see that she was scared. But I was also pleased to know that I was on the right track.

"Are you accusing me of covering up the theft of my own jewelry?"

"So it was a piece of jewelry," I said. "I wasn't sure."

That was a mistake. My sarcastic tone gave her an excuse to be offended.

"I think you're forgetting yourself, young man. If this is some kind of a joke, it's gone too far. If it's a provocation by Soviet authorities and if the performance and escape from GUM was staged, I'm warning you, I'm going to pack my bags and go back to Paris. You can pass that on to Yuri Vladimirovich."

"I don't work for Yuri Vladimirovich, Madame," I said. "Comrade Andropov knows nothing about this conversation and when he finds out that I have effectively kidnapped you, my partner and I are going to be in hot water with the most powerful man in Russia."

"Good," she said. "I'll make sure Yuri Vladimirovich is informed about the particulars of this conversation. Now, I have no idea where we are. Please find a way to get me back to my hotel. I need a rest. I'm not a young woman."

But now I was mad.

"Look, lady," I said, speaking slowly, deliberately, and keeping my voice down, so as not to let my anger get the better of me. "This theft from your hotel room is serious business, not a childish bit of shoplifting from a Paris department store. Two people have been murdered, and we may not be at the end of it."

She gasped, clapping her hand over her mouth.

"Who were they?" she cried out.

Her shock was genuine, and so was the horror in her eyes.

"I'm pretty sure that one of them was the young man who broke into your room."

"And the other?" she asked quickly.

"The other one is trickier," I said. "He was an antiques collector and a sometime black market dealer. Probably a fence. Your jewelry was discovered in his apartment. All the pieces you reported stolen, at least."

She ignored my reference.

"How old was the collector? Was he about my age? A little older?"

I took my time responding.

"Does it really matter how old he was?"

"It does. Very much so. I need you to tell me."

"He was in his early forties."

She gave a sigh of relief.

Meanwhile, we were starting to attract attention. Two young men at the next table stopped talking and were staring at us. Khokhlova's pale face and our conversation, conducted in soft, urgent whispers, were raising their suspicions. But I had no choice but to press on.

"So you're protecting someone, Madame," I said. "A man of your own age. Is it an old friend? Was he the one who broke into your room? Are we wrong to believe the thief was the murdered kid?"

She shook her head.

"No," she said. "The boy was the thief."

"I see," I said. "You saw him then, is that it?"

She nodded.

"But you also think that your old friend is the one who sent the kid to break into your room?"

"I do," she said.

"And why is that? Because of what was taken from you?"

She nodded. She was silent for a long time. I knew she was about to tell me something really important, and I let her take as much time as she needed to be ready, without further prompting her. The two young men at the next table grew bored, gave up listening to us, and returned to their own conversation. They finished their coffee and left, and still she hadn't said a word. When she finally broke the silence, I was almost startled.

"It was a silver baptismal cross," she said. "That poor boy went into my bedroom and took it. I always wore it around my neck. It was my talisman. The other jewelry was in the study. He went there first, but I think he was just lost. He was trying to get to my bedroom."

"Did you talk to him?"

"No."

"Why didn't you call for help?"

"Because the boy knew exactly what he was looking for and where to find it."

"Is it valuable?"

"It might be. But it doesn't look valuable. It's a small silver cross on a red string. Very dark with age."

"I don't understand," I said.

"It's very simple, really. There is only one person in the world who could have known that I had that cross. It's my first husband, a Russian, and a former officer in Baron Wrangel's White Army. The little cross used to belong to him, and he's the only person in the world who would want it. We lost touch. I knew he might be here in the Soviet Union, but I thought he had died a long time ago. I absolutely don't want him arrested. But I would love to see him again."

"Are you sure?" I asked. "He's a cold-blooded murderer. He has already killed two people. Seeing him could be very dangerous."

"He is not a murderer," she said. "He never became a murderer, even though he fought in many brutal wars."

"People change," I said. "Someone murdered those two men. In cold blood, too, and very skillfully. Your first husband's background fits very well with the way they were killed."

"He's not a murderer," she repeated. "He killed plenty of people, but that didn't make him a murderer."

"You don't know what you're talking about, Madame. Your life may be in danger."

She shook her head.

"I would give anything to see him again."

## TWENTY-EIGHT

Alexei Zolotnitsky didn't die in Crimea, and he didn't die fighting with the Foreign Legion. They just couldn't kill him. He became good at everything he touched, and he was very good at war. Being very good at war meant, among other things, staying alive. Not letting them kill you.

He reappeared in the mid-1930s, still small, skinny, sinewy, but also sunburnt to a crisp, which made him look like an Arab or a Hindu. His hair, which had turned grey, was closely-cropped, and there was a bald spot peeking through the top of his head, round as a tonsure.

He had been to Africa and Southeast Asia and had had malaria. His smile was still boyish, but it bared two rows of metal teeth, and there was something joyless and wolfish about it.

By then, he had nearly two decades' worth of continuous war in him. War was blood, sweat and excrement, and he was full of it. Its stench clung to him.

He found her in Paris. She wasn't difficult to locate. The times were dreary, but Paris was still the most exciting city in the world, and she was at the very center of it, married to the most prominent artist in the most exciting city in the world. She had stopped dancing after she had had a child. The family lived in the country, an hour outside Paris by motor car.

Her marriage, successful on the surface and glowing with the same aura that surrounded everything her squat Spaniard ever touched, had started to unravel.

She had borne him a son, but she knew it wasn't enough to tie him to her. Nothing was going to stop him once he decided he wanted to leave her. Her two husbands were very different. Alexei the soldier always came back and Pablo the artist left, once and for all. Alexei was full of compassion for her – for everyone he met – while Pablo didn't know the meaning of the word.

Alexei didn't reproach her for leaving him in Crimea. He didn't ask for an explanation, and when she told him about the staff officer and his lies, Alexei accepted it with a shrug. She told him nothing about her sudden feeling of liberation or about her new life that had commenced back then, on a Constantinople embankment. Their marriage had been a mistake. Alexei could never have been the man for her. Pablo was.

Alexei offered her a divorce or an annulment. She didn't want either. She didn't want anyone to know that Alexei was alive or that she had never been a widow in the first place. She was nervous about her relationship with Pablo and worried he would use it as an excuse to question the validity of their marriage. He might be genuinely horrified at the discovery that she had been a polyandrist. He was a Spaniard, after all. A devout Catholic lurked just below the agnostic.

As to Alexei, who had once been Russian Orthodox, he had stopped caring long ago. He didn't mind staying married to her. He had no plans to marry again. Nor did he have any wish to bring a new life into this world.

But he did want his baptismal cross back, his family heirloom that had stood in for her wedding ring, and that was a problem. It had been her talisman, her good luck charm, and now she needed it more than ever.

He tried to reason with her. She acknowledged that he had the right to have it back. They were no longer married in any practical sense.

"But, technically, we *are* still married," she insisted.

"We're still married only because I've consented to your request not to annul our marriage."

"It makes no difference why. It's a fact."

He laughed, called her reasoning "woman's logic" and gave up.

"We'll talk about it some other time," he said.

He had sensed that it was the wrong moment for him to insist on getting the cross back. He was highly attuned to other people's feelings. It was his nature. And it was why he was such a great officer. It was easier to send men to their death if you knew what drove them.

Even though he had no formal training, he quickly got a job as an engineer at a Peugeot factory and then, a year later, moved to Germany. He thought that the Nazis, for all their insanity, were better able to deal with the threat of Bolshevism than the Anglo-Americans and certainly better than the French.

"At least they understand its nature," he told her.

Both his grandmothers were of German origin, even though their families had lived in Russia for several generations. He had also had the good fortune of being born a few miles west of St. Petersburg, in a town that was now Finland, which allowed him to prove his Teutonic roots to the German Reich. As to speaking German – well, he excelled at everything he cared to put his mind to.

She came to see him in Berlin in the summer of 1939. She was still formally married to Pablo, but their marriage had unraveled. She now had two sham marriages.

Alexei was in a foul mood. He hated Germany. He hated the Germans.

"They're as stupid as the Russians," he said. "They believe everything they're told by that buffoon. They're goose-stepping to the slaughterhouse. And, mark my word, they will drag many of us there with them."

"At least they're happy while they doing it," she said. "Look at their bright eyes and ecstatic smiles. Whereas we're choking on our own bile as we watch them."

"That's the thing, they're incorrigible. You'll have to kill a few million of them before the rest start to get it."

Above all, he hated Hitler.

"All that's left is for him and Stalin to make an alliance. I'm sure the Devil in Hell is putting finishing touches on a pact between the two of them even as we speak. If it weren't for the Jews in the Bolshevik government, they would have jumped into bed with one another long ago. They are identical in all respects. And they both hate the English and the French. Except an alliance between them won't last. They'll try to double-cross each other and will fall out. That's our only hope."

He also told her that a war was coming. A big war. A war to end all wars.

"Don't be ridiculous," she said. "After the last war, there are no men left to fight another one."

He shook his head.

"Yes, lots of men were killed in the last war, but the ones who survived didn't get their fill. They liked it in the trenches, and they can't wait to get back into them."

She had come to Berlin to talk about his baptismal cross. She still had no intention of parting with it, even though it had failed in helping her keep Pablo's love. Nothing could do the trick, not amulets, good luck charms or potions – not even black magic. Pablo's obsession with his art and, by extension, with his own passions, was stronger than all that.

Exhausted by pointless arguments about the cross and depressed by the political mood, they ended up spending a night together. He was sweet and tender as he made love to her. He had not been a good lover back in Crimea – when he would come home dirty, exhausted, and with too many things on his mind, and would stay a couple of days between military engagements – but he was now. It didn't surprise her. He was good at everything he put his mind to.

Their passion sated, they lay in bed with the light of the early morning trickling through the venetian blinds on his windows. He caressed her breasts and felt the silver cross with his fingers. He held it in his hand, but didn't attempt to remove it. They were married once again, she felt. They had been thrown into each other's arms for a second time, by a new storm that was brewing over their lives, and now the cross was legitimately hers.

Before they parted in the morning, she brought up the subject again and, taking herself by surprise, offered a trade.

"I'll send you something in exchange," she said. "I own something that is quite valuable. You'll see. I'll send it to you when I get back to France, darling."

A couple of weeks later, a notice was delivered to him by a uniformed Reichspost employee, specifying that he had received a special package from Paris, France, and that, on the date stamped below, he was to present himself with his identification papers at the Central Post Office to claim said package upon inspection by the appropriate authorities. There was a long wait at the post office and many forms to fill out, but in the end a large rectangular object wrapped in cotton and packaged in rough brown paper, opened and carefully resealed and covered with Customs and Postal Service stamps, was released to him. When he opened it at home, he found a portrait of Olga painted by Pablo Picasso.

Zolotnitsky knew the work well – and not only because he had a personal connection to it. It was one of the most famous paintings by the most famous living artist in the world. Obsessive as ever, Picasso had done it in the early days of his courtship, when he, love-sick and determined to be married to this beautiful Russian ballerina as soon as possible, had taken her to meet his mother. Done in a style reminiscent perhaps of Francisco Goya, it was unlike anything else he was doing at the time. It was almost like he wanted to make a statement that experimentations in his art were one thing, but when it came to marriage and family, tradition was still the rule.

Hitler had declared Picasso a degenerate artist. He was not a Jew, the Nazis said, but he was foisting Jewish art on the public, emasculating the Volk. It was to stick it to the Nazis that Zolotnitsky was happy to have it, and he hung it in his living room. Other than that, it was too expensive an object for him to own, and it wasn't even a fair exchange for his silver cross. Olga had no use for the portrait and she was glad to be rid of it.

She thought of him a lot over the ensuing months. She tried to write to him several times, but she couldn't find the right words. Their second wedding night in Berlin haunted her dreams and kept showing up in her daytime thoughts.

And then it was suddenly too late. The war Zolotnitsky had predicted broke out. He knew war intimately, and he couldn't have missed its smell in the air. It was every bit as horrible a war as he had predicted, and it went on for six interminable years.

Soon after it ended, she was introduced to a Soviet liaison officer with the Free French government. After the war, the Soviets seemed a lot friendlier and more civilized, even displaying a certain polish. They were not at all the murderous Bolsheviks of the Revolution. During the war, everyone had rooted for the Red Army, not only the French, but also most of the White émigrés in Paris. The news of Stalingrad had passed between them gleefully, in whispers, while the Germans dismissed it as lies and Jewish propaganda. Yet it was readily confirmed by the grim faces of senior German officers and party functionaries, and it had warmed every heart in France during the brutal winter of 1943.

The Soviet officer reassured her that the Soviet Union had been transformed. She would never recognize the miserable backward Russia of her youth in the wide avenues of Soviet cities and the happy smiles of everyone she saw marching down them. Yes, there was plenty of war damage and the Soviet people would have to work even harder to rebuild, but he for one was confident that their new cities and factories would be even more beautiful than the ones the Germans had destroyed.

"You've got to come and see for yourself," he told her. "You'll never want to leave."

She told him she wanted to find Alexei Zolotnitsky in Berlin, which was occupied by the Soviets. He wrote down Zolotnisky's address and promised to help. But before he could do anything or get any information, he was transferred elsewhere.

As soon as it became possible to travel through war-torn, occupied Europe, she went to Berlin and came instead upon the pile of rubble that used to be one of Europe's great cities. She was too late, his landlady told her, eyeing her suspiciously. Herr Ingenieur had been taken to Russia along with his armaments plant.

"The swine dog Russians, ja." She described how they took apart what was left of the plant and loaded it onto German train cars and took everything east. Reparations, they called it. Was her nice radio set part of the reparations, too, the one they stole from her? And her bicycle that a Neanderthal ripped from her grip on Unter den Linden in plain daylight? And her dresses and only pair of good shoes? And her daughter, who was taken by drunken soldiers and never seen again? And yes, they took Herr Ingenieur along. They gave him two hours to pack his suitcase, and two soldiers stood over him while he packed. They needed Herr Ingenieur to reassemble the factory in their steppes and then to work the machines. Because they're barbarians and all they know how to do is rape and steal.

Did she know that her tenant was Russian, too?

"Ach, of course he wasn't. He was German. A good man."

And, in a whisper, "The Führer was so right about the Russians."

## TWENTY-NINE

Della, Budyonny's secretary, lay in wait for me by the elevator. I didn't become aware of her until she swooped upon me, being very much preoccupied with my own thoughts. And yet I should have expected some kind of ambush, considering what Valera and I had done that afternoon.

So Alexei Zolotnitsky, Olga Khokhlova's first husband, was alive and living in Russia. Clearly a tough customer, a former Nazi. He had hired Mitya Kislitsky to break into Olga's suite and to steal the silver cross that he felt belonged to him. Then he murdered Kisly because Kisly was the only link between him and the Metropole burglary. He killed Levkoyev, too – the hand that wielded the knife with such deadly skill was identical. Why? I had no answer.

Catching me off guard, Della marched me to the Boss's office, looking every bit as triumphant as an Indian villager who had succeeded in capturing a dangerous man-eating tiger.

Valera and I had made a mistake. We should have set a place to meet outside the office before coming in, rather than drifting back and facing the music separately. Lenny and I used to meet on a bench behind the monument to biologist Timiryazev at Nikitsky Gate, where we would make sure that our stories matched. We called it "swinging by Timiryazev."

And now, while walking down the long hallway under Della's guard, I was trying to think quickly how to lie to the Boss. Most likely, he had already spoken to Valera. Khokhlova and I had spent more than two hours talking at the café. I had then taken her to the corner of the Maly Theater and, watching from across Karl Marx Avenue, saw her two handlers run out of the hotel to meet her, waving their arms for joy as if they had despaired of ever seeing her alive again. They escorted her to the door, flanking her tightly, as though fearing that she would slip away again.

I knew I was in hot water, but I began to suspect the extent of it only when I caught a whiff of cigarette smoke. The Boss had exiled smokers to a tiny windowless room next to the elevator and had instituted a smoking ban in all offices. Having given up the habit last year, he began enforcing the department-wide ban in earnest. Being caught sneaking a puff at an open window now entailed draconian punishments.

That someone was smoking in Budyonny's office could only indicate the presence of a big boss. Moreover, the sweet aroma could only have come from an American cigarette, which gave me an advance warning whom I should expect to see.

The KGB chief was sitting at the low conference table positioned at a right angle to Budyonny's massive desk. During our departmental meetings, the Boss towered over us like God the Father in the religious paintings at the Pushkin Art Museum. Now, however, the Boss was sitting next to Andropov trying to make himself small and unobtrusive.

Andropov acknowledged my arrival with a nod and offered me a seat across from them. Still saying nothing, he surveyed me for a few minutes with interest, exhaling bluish smoke through his nostrils. His placid expression contrasted with Budyonny's, who was frowning and giving me dirty looks. Under different circumstance he no doubt would have been shouting and pounding the desk with his massive fist, but this time he had to defer to Andropov, who was running the show.

Finally, the KGB boss shifted in his chair and offered me one of his foreign cigarettes. I prudently turned it down, even though the look in the Boss's eyes suggested that even if I smoked in his office I wouldn't have been able to antagonize him any further.

"So, lieutenant," Andropov said, breaking the silence. "They tell me that you have now taken to kidnapping our foreign guests. Is it true?"

I giggled obsequiously as though I thought he was making a joke and shook my head.

"Well, you could call it that, Comrade Andropov," I said, trying to sound innocent. "It was something of a coincidence, to run into Madame Khokhlova like that at the Arts Club. It was a lucky coincidence, too, because I needed to ask her a few questions related to the burglary in her room."

"Why did you run away then?" Andropov asked.

"We didn't, Comrade Andropov, I swear. She suggested that we go somewhere where we could talk, and I took her to a café down 25th of October Street. We didn't run away. We were in plain sight. The café is next to the Ferrein Pharmacy and almost directly across the square from the KGB headquarters."

"I know where it is, lieutenant. What did you want to ask Madame Khokhlova about?"

"I asked her to think back and try hard to remember if she had caught a glimpse of the burglar. You see, we strongly suspect that we know who broke into her room."

"I know that, lieutenant," Andropov cut me off. "I have your investigation under my personal control. What else did you ask?"

"We went over everything that was stolen, sir, all the jewelry. I asked Madame Khokhlova whether she was certain that all the missing pieces had been returned."

"Why was that, lieutenant? I thought Madame Khokhlova had already told you that all the pieces had been recovered. You had the list and it all matched up. Am I right?"

"Yes, sir," I said.

"Why were you going over the same ground then?"

"Because I was wondering why the burglar was killed, sir. He wasn't someone who could have pulled something like this on his own. There had to be someone else who sent him to steal Madame Khokhlova's jewelry. Perhaps it was Levkoyev, the antiques dealer, who also turned up dead. There must have been a disagreement between the two of them, and it could have revolved around pieces the burglar picked up at the hotel room but had not delivered to his client."

"It's a bit convoluted," the Boss said, joining our conversation. "Besides, if it was Kislitsky who killed Levkoyev, how could Levkoyev have killed Kislitsky and dumped his body into the river?"

I was about to answer him, but Andropov interrupted me.

"What else did you want to get out of her?" he asked.

"That was all, sir," I said.

"Oh, it's interesting. It took you a long time to ask a couple of questions. I know exactly when you brought the old woman back to the Metropole. It took you more than two hours."

I was ready for that.

"She wanted to take a walk around the city," I said. "She said she hadn't had a chance to walk around, that she had mostly been driven from one reception to the next. Then, as we walked, she needed to stop and rest several times along the way."

"I see," Andropov said. "And in all that time she said nothing else of interest?"

I shrugged. I could lie all I wanted about my meeting with Khokhlova because Andropov wasn't going to check my story with her and, besides, she had promised to keep our conversation secret. But I also knew that Andropov was no fool, and he wasn't buying any of my simple answers.

"Not really, sir. She mostly talked about the police in Paris and how we seemed to be so much more efficient than they are."

Andropov nodded once more.

"You must have been very proud to hear that. And your superior officer here, Colonel Martirosyan, too. I'm sure he's pleased."

We both turned to look at Budyonny. He looked anything but pleased. In fact, it was his near-apoplectic face, red and sweaty, and about to explode with rage, that told me to be on my guard. The conversation was not going well at all. Once again I regretted not having talked to Valera before returning to the office. Who knew what he had told them.

"So, lieutenant," Andropov said dreamily. "It was in order to hear that flattering comparison with your French colleagues that you were willing to make fools of my officers whose responsibility it was to ensure the safety and comfort of our foreign visitor?"

"I didn't make—" I started to say.

I knew I was in trouble, but I wasn't prepared for the sudden change that came over Andropov. The condescending sarcasm fell from his face in an instant. Rising swiftly from his chair, he leaned over, bringing his face to within a quarter of an inch of mine. His eyes hardened and flashed angrily. In that state, he was truly terrifying.

"Don't you try to make a fool of me, lieutenant," he shouted into my face. "I know that you and lieutenant Tumakov conspired to sneak Khokhlova away from her escorts. I know you were asking her about something that you thought had been taken from her room which for some reason she had not reported stolen. Don't lie to me if you don't want to end up behind bars. Tell me exactly what you talked about and don't try to bullshit me. I can spot your lies from a mile away."

So I was right. They had talked to Valera, and he had spilled the beans. I should have assumed that and constructed my lies accordingly. Now, I had no choice but to tell Andropov about Olga's little cross. I could do it without dragging Alexei Zolotnitsky's name into it for the time being. He was a dangerous criminal, but I had given my word to Olga to try to keep him out of it if he wasn't involved, and, until I had found out more about him, I had no intention of going back on it.

The KGB chief's unblinking, bloodshot eyes stared straight into mine, waiting for an answer. "She told me she thought that the burglar had stolen her baptismal cross," I said. "It had great sentimental value for her."

"Why didn't she report it?" Andropov asked, still keeping his shrewd eyes, magnified by the thick lenses of his glasses, fixed upon me. I was trying to look as honest as I could, which was not an easy thing to do beneath his unblinking stare even if I was telling him the whole truth.

"She wasn't sure she'd brought it with her to Moscow, Comrade Andropov. She remembers debating with herself whether she ought to, but could not remember what, in the end, she decided to do. She is quite embarrassed about her memory lapse. You know how touchy old people can be about their minds. It took me all that time to get her to admit it."

I knew I was recycling the same explanation I had used only that morning. Let's hope Ivan hadn't revealed that to his boss. It wasn't a safe assumption, however. Most likely, Andropov had already questioned him, trying to figure out how Valera and I had known where Olga would be having lunch.

"Why didn't you tell me that right away, lieutenant? What was there to hide, I wonder."

Andropov stared at me and so did Budyonny.

"Sir, she made me promise I wouldn't tell it to anyone. She would rather not get the cross back than to admit that she's become so forgetful. Even though she values the little cross very much."

The mistrust written all over their faces had the perverse effect of spurring me on, making me lie even more outrageously. After all, I had nothing to lose.

"Besides, it was insured," I went on. "Had she declared it stolen and filed a claim, she could have been accused of insurance fraud if the cross had been in her house all along. She was worried about that. Insurance fraud is a serious crime in France."

"It is here, too," Budyonny said grimly.

"Is this true?" Andropov asked ominously, still ignoring the Boss.

I shrugged.

"I don't know, Comrade Andropov. That is what she told me."

Andropov shook his head. He took another of his American cigarettes and offered the pack to Budyonny. The Boss hesitated, put his hand up, then pulled it back as if he had been stung, then finally surrendered to temptation. He could never say no to his superiors. And Andropov was as superior as they come – virtually a god in the Soviet law enforcement hierarchy.

Andropov lit his cigarette and slipped a gold lighter back into his pocket, oblivious of the Boss, leaning toward him for a light.

"Remember, lieutenant," he turned to me once more, "your job is to investigate the two murders, not the burglary. Your partner will continue to work on it, and it should not be your concern. If you can't find the killer, so be it. Frankly, I don't give a rat's ass whether you solve those murders or not. All I need from you is to stay the hell out of Madame Khokhlova's way. That's an order. I've warned everyone on the Metropole staff to report to me if anyone – you, your partner, the Devil himself, anyone – so much as tries to talk to her. Watch out, lieutenant. If you try to pull another one of your tricks on me, I swear I'm not going to mollycoddle you anymore. Understood?"

"Yes, sir," I responded with great enthusiasm, which I didn't have to fake. I had gotten off easy this time.

As I saluted them and went out, I was pretty sure that Andropov wasn't going to check my story with Olga – it would have been extremely tactless of him to mention her possible memory lapse. I was probably on safe ground. But I wasn't as far as my partner was concerned. Apparently, Andropov trusted Valera a lot more than he trusted me. And that could mean only one thing, that Valera had agreed to keep him informed about everything I was up to. I would not be able to keep my conversation with Olga secret. I would have to tell him something about it – and my story would have to jibe with what I had just told Andropov.

The only difference was that Valera, unlike Andropov, would know that Olga's silver cross had been in Moscow, that Kisly had been sent into her suite specifically to steal it and that it was the only reason why the burglary at the Metropole Hotel had been conceived.

I pondered mentioning Olga's first husband to my partner. Even if I omitted all the telltale particulars about his past, Valera would have no difficulty making his own inferences about Zolotnitsky's role in the burglary and the murders. That would mean breaking my word to Olga, especially since I knew that Valera would report it to Andropov. I would have to do it eventually, I decided, but not yet. First, I needed to try to find the guy on my own.

# THIRTY

Valera and I were once again working on two different cases, not running into one another much during the day. Valera's schedule was rather fixed, and so I had a good idea when he could be found at the office and when he would be making his rounds in the city. He didn't feel a need to keep me informed who he met with and what they told him, and that was, in turn, making me feel a lot less guilty about keeping him in the dark about my own activities. His regular schedule allowed me, over the course of the next week, to pay several extended visits to the basement at headquarters, without being observed by him. That way I didn't have to explain what I was looking for.

Or rather whom.

The basement contained records of various investigations carried out by our agency as well as by local police investigators around the country. It was perhaps the most comprehensive crime archive in the Soviet Union outside the KGB, containing an alphabetized list of career criminals, along with descriptions of their transgressions and known aliases. There was also information about people convicted of theft, robbery, burglary, rape, and aggravated assault. You could search through historical data on gangs and other criminal associations, including an extensive section on white-collar crime, illegal commerce, black market activities, and theft of socialist property. Much of this was not, strictly speaking, the province of Moscow Criminal Investigations, but it was a useful cross-reference tool since gangs often provided protection to or shook down underground entrepreneurs, and the two kinds of criminal activity often became blended.

Because the archive was in the basement, it was called The Dungeon, and the middle-aged woman who worked in The Dungeon was known as the Witch. The Witch seemed to have been pickled in the paper dust that hung in The Dungeon's stifling air.

If you needed to locate a file or obtain information about a specific person, you had to approach her counter and fill out a request form printed some time in 1950. Even the forms reeked of dust, and the paper fell apart in your hands.

The Witch would then go down to the stacks, which were off limits to everyone else, and therefore a source of great mystery. It was rumored, for instance, that they stretched all the way to the center of the earth, that there were hundreds of levels filled with paper files. Judging by the quantity of materials The Dungeon contained, that might well have been true. The stacks were also said to have no electricity and to be lit by kerosene lamps. Indeed, the Witch smelled faintly of kerosene, and her drawn face seemed to have acquired the pallor of the dark, airless vaults. There was also the outrageous story that she hired beautiful young maidens fresh out of the library college, whom she kept locked in the stacks, but since no one except her had ever been there, it was all idle gossip.

Joking aside, the Witch was a kind woman and could be very helpful if you were nice to her. She liked me, perhaps because I was always respectful and, apparently, was the sole person in our entire building who had gone to the trouble of learning her name and patronymic.

The quick alphabetical search produced two results for Alexei Zolotnitsky, raising false hopes. Those hopes were promptly dashed, since neither Zolotnitsky turned out to be the right one. That would have been too easy. I then changed my tack and searched for Soviet citizens known to have been in the White movement, to have lived in Germany, or to have been trained as engineers. Nothing. Or rather, plenty of information, through which I had to sift over two long afternoons, only to draw a blank.

Next, I shifted to criminals with nicknames like German, White Officer, Engineer, etc. Since "zoloto" means gold in Russian, there were plenty of jailbirds a.k.a. Gold, Goldie, Goldsmith, Golddigger, Goldfinger, Goldtooth, and even Fake Goldtooth. None of them fit Alexei Zolotnitsky's description. I had made the Witch go down to the stacks a total of about sixty times, and in the end, had nothing to show for it.

And yet I had a pretty good mental picture of the man I was looking for, as well as a general idea of what had happened to him. He had been repatriated to the Soviet Union with his armaments plant and at some point arrested and sent to the camps. They all had been, sooner or later. Though convicted under a political statute as traitor or wrecker, he had been befriended by and eventually joined with common criminals who were the camp's aristocracy, lording it over ordinary convicts and, especially, politicals. Such an outcome was not unusual, especially for men with a military background.

Of course, had I been given access to the KGB archive, I would have found Zolotnitsky in no time at all. In Stalin's time, the political police had been scrupulous in collecting such information. The problem was not only that Andropov would never have allowed me near their archives, but that those archives had been sealed. There was no question in my mind that they would remain closed forever.

And then there was the question of what I was going to do if I found him. I had given Khokhlova my word that I would leave him alone, but he was a dangerous criminal, and she had no right to extract such a promise from me. Not finding the man spared me those moral qualms.

Meanwhile, Tosya was preparing for our housewarming party and was, as usual, fretting about it too much. Having guests always made her nervous. She was self-conscious about her lack of domestic skills. She worried what she was going to serve at the party, how she was going to arrange everything on the table, and whether the guests would like it.

"Let's forget about the party then," I said. "We don't have to have it."

She gave me one of her looks, meant to convey that I was mad to suggest such a thing. Didn't I know that you absolutely had to have a housewarming every time you moved? Otherwise you would have nothing but bad luck in your new place.

At least we didn't have to argue over the guest list. That part was easy. We'd have Sveta, her best friend from the orphanage who worked at Yeliseyev's food store, and Lera, Tosya's boss at the Trekhgorka textile plant, who headed the bookkeeping department and who had helped Tosya a great deal when she was just starting out and was pregnant with Sevka.

Then there was Irina Drozdova, whom we had met while I was investigating a series of child murders three years ago and who had become a good friend, and, finally, Raisa, Lenny Urumov's widow, and her two daughters.

All of the guests were women, so in order to diversify the guest list I also invited Valera. We were not good friends, but not inviting one's partner would be bad form.

I could have invited several other guys from work, as well as my two male cousins – who had a drinking problem and so were on Tosya's bad side. But Tosya declared that we had too many people already and that we still needed to invite our neighbor Boris. He had been on good behavior, and our initial fight had been all but forgotten.

My job was to make sufficient quantities of lamb pilaf. I was dispatched to the collective farm market on Tsvetnoy Boulevard with instructions to purchase the ingredients and be sure the vendors didn't take advantage of me and give me rotten meat.

"Maybe we should get married," I suggested. "That way we could also celebrate our wedding, and then you wouldn't have to get all nervous about having guests a second time."

For all of Tosya's worries, the party was a great success. Lenny's little girls adored Sevka, who had been like a big brother to them, protecting them and taking care of them in the difficult months after

Lenny was killed. They had brought their figure skates, and Sevka took them down to the skating rink on Clear Ponds Boulevard. They were eager to show him all the jumps and spins they had learned since last year.

They left before I started serving my pilaf because the girls didn't want to skate on a full stomach. Sevka was hungry – he had been saving his appetite since morning – but valiantly agreed to have his pilaf after the trip to the skating rink, if I solemnly promised to save some for him.

"A lot, Uncle Pavel. You know how much I eat."

There was plenty of food. The table was set in Sevka's room, which required taking his bed out to the hallway and pushing his desk up next to our dining table to fit everyone in. Tosya had made all the traditional appetizers, including the Olivier salad and the *venegret* – which in her case was pretty much the same thing except it had beets, which left purple stains on our only large tablecloth. She had bought two large jars of pickled mushrooms from her old Kirov Street neighbor, who sold them on the side. She served herring with boiled potatoes, garnishing it with green scallions that I had got at the market. When sprinkled with dark-yellow sunflower oil, it was as beautiful and tasty a dish as any woman in the world could hope to prepare.

Sveta had brought white fish from her store, a great delicacy that was never sold over the counter, but which she was always able to procure whenever somebody was having a party. And Raisa, a formidable cook and a great baker, had made two pies, one with minced meat and the other with cabbage and chopped egg.

The pies went first, disappearing in a matter of minutes, almost before I had time to cut and save a couple of pieces for Sevka and the girls. The guests also did justice to Tosya's salads, ignoring the fact that, impatient as ever, my beloved had cut the vegetables a little too thickly.

The food was accompanied by numerous toasts. We drank to our new home, to happiness, to little Nikola, to peace on earth, to the beautiful hostess, and to our great friends. Then I proposed another toast to Nikola because I knew that every mention of the little tyke, no matter in what context, made Tosya happy. The three half-liter bottles of Moskovskaya went quickly.

Boris was the soul of the party, and I was glad Tosya had thought of inviting him. He jumped up every few minutes to raise his glass or to serve the women. He told jokes, flirted with Sveta, and charmed everyone. The general opinion was that we were lucky to have landed such a wonderful neighbor, along with a great apartment, whereas Sveta, having downed a number of shots, began to stare at him with a twinkle in her eyes.

We raised glasses without clicking them to honor the memory of my partner Lenny and then, separately, Irina Drozdova's daughter Tanya.

Just as a melancholy mood set in, little Nikola woke up and started to scream. Tosya went to our bedroom to feed him and then brought him out to be universally admired. There were more toasts to the beautiful baby. Everyone drank to his health, to our great fortune to have given birth to such a big, healthy baby (spit three times over your left shoulder and knock on wood to avert the evil eye) and to his bright future.

In the end, when my pilaf was finally done and I served it, nobody was hungry, having stuffed themselves with appetizers. I felt dejected – after all, I had spent the whole day slaving over the stove, not to mention half of my monthly salary – until Sevka and the girls returned, cold and wet and shaking with hunger, then wolfed down two heaping plates each. Sevka was especially voracious. I watched proudly as vast quantities of rice and lamb disappeared down his bottomless maw.

In the kitchen, where Tosya exiled the smokers, Boris and Valera argued about the relative merits of a Nordic sport known as Russian hockey or bandy. Valera was an avid bandy fan. He spoke excitedly of the open spaces, the skating speed, and the high scoring. He had grown up in Krasnogorsk, a town just outside Moscow where his dad was deputy director of the local manufacturing plant. The plant fielded a bandy team that played in the big leagues. Every kid in Krasnogorsk was crazy about the Zorky Hockey Club.

Boris was dismissive of the sport and complained about the cold in the open-air stadium.

"This Russian hockey of yours has no future," he kept saying, holding the middle button of Valera's double-breasted jacket and slurring his words slightly on account of having had too much to drink. "The days of the masochists are over. People want to be comfortable. They want to stay indoors and have a beer or two while they root for their team. No one has any desire to freeze his ass off—"

He caught a sight of Irina Drozdova smoking by the window, stopped and apologized to her profusely for using profanity. She smiled and shook her head. She had not even heard him. She was in her own world. It happened to her now and again.

"Anyway, try going to the new Luzhniki arena, Valera. That's where they have Canadian hockey matches. It's warm, there are bright lights, there's a roof over your head, for God's sake. You don't care if it's a blizzard outside. You're warm and cozy in there. You can take a babe along to a hockey game, and even she'll have a good time. It's very civilized."

I had to admit that Boris had a point. Every Russian hockey game I had ever attended had been a rough and tumble affair, with fans drinking too much vodka to keep warm and chasing it with cloves of garlic and cutting frozen sausage and bread on concrete seats. By the end of the game you got a bunch of cold, drunken, and foul-smelling blue-collar types looking for a fight. I would certainly think twice about taking Sevka to see an event like that, to say nothing of Tosya.

But Valera was not ready to submit.

"You've got to admit, Boris, it's a graceful game. Canadians don't skate. All they do is stomp around on their tiny rink, shoving each other against the boards. It's a game of goons. It's rugby on ice."

"It's a man's game," Boris objected.

Irina finished her cigarette and started back toward our room. I put out mine and followed her, leaving Boris and Valera to their debate.

She was in the hallway in front of our door when I caught up with her. I didn't want her to be looking inward, thinking dark thoughts.

She needed something to take her mind off Tanya and the tragic events of three years ago.

"I meant to tell you something, Irina," I said, thinking of how I could distract her from her thoughts.

She stopped and waited for me to continue, her eyes dull and withdrawn.

"I met someone recently who you might be interested in. An older Russian woman who used to be married to the French artist Picasso."

That immediately brought her back to life.

"Yes, of course," she exclaimed. "Olga Khokhlova, a Diaghilev dancer."

Irina was an educated woman. She was a graduate of Moscow State University with a degree in Russian literature. If anyone in our acquaintance had heard of Khokhlova, it would certainly be her – but I was still impressed by how readily she knew who I was talking about.

"She's in Moscow now," I said. "Visiting from Paris."

"I would have thought she died a long time ago. It's very exciting. What did you talk to her about?"

"Nothing related to her husband's art or her dancing. You know I'm no good at that."

"It's a shame," she said. "I mean she knows so much about Picasso, Diaghilev and Paris in the 1920s. I'm sorry, Pavel, but the time you spent with her was wasted."

"I know it was," I said. "But she's been going around meeting all kinds of arts people in Moscow. They are in a better position to talk to her about such things."

Irina shook her head.

"I don't think so," she said. "I fear it's one of those mind-numbing official visits. Everyone she gets to see has been carefully vetted. Their job is to brag about the achievements of the Soviet system. Meanwhile, I know someone who would have given her eye teeth to talk to Olga Khokhlova in the flesh. Even half an hour would have been like a gift from God. It's my university friend Martha, who wrote a book about Picasso. Do you think you could arrange for the two of them to meet?"

"Not a chance," I said. "They're guarding her like a national treasure. I'm already in a lot of trouble for trying to see her on my own, without the sanction of the KGB's top man. They tightened security arrangements even more after that."

Irina sighed.

"I feel bad for Martha. Khokhlova witnessed that era first hand, and was an active participant in so many crucial artistic events. Why not let her interview Khokhlova? It's not as if she could worm state secrets out of Martha. Martha would have been devastated if she knew Khokhlova was here. I had better not say anything to her."

"I'm sorry," I said. "I wish there was something I could do for your friend."

"A couple of years ago, Martha had a huge let-down," Irina continued. "An old man wrote to her in response to an article she published in some art journal. She thought at first that he had known Olga Khokhlova personally. But in the end, he turned out to be a senile imposter."

She broke off.

"I shouldn't be boring you with all that. You need to go in and entertain your other guests. Come to think of it, I'm going to go back to the kitchen and have another cigarette. I wonder if those two are still there. They were arguing about something quite passionately."

But Irina wasn't boring me in the least. On the contrary, I was suddenly listening to her with great interest.

"Do you remember his name?" I lowered my voice to a whisper and cast an eye around, to make sure that neither Valera nor Boris could overhear us.

"I don't believe so," she said. "But I'm sure Martha does. I suppose I could ask her."

"Yes, please," I said. "It's extremely important. But please, not a word to her why you're asking. And let's not mention it to anyone else. Not a word."

Irina gave me a look of surprise. She had never known me to be interested in questions of art or history.

The party went on for a while longer. Boris and Valera stayed in the kitchen until they filled it with thick cigarette smoke. After that, they moved to Boris's room, grabbing a bottle of semi-sweet Crimean wine and the rest of the marinated mushrooms. About an hour later, Valera stuck his pale face into our room, waved a silent goodbye and faded away.

Other guests, although less inebriated, began to leave soon thereafter. As she headed out, Irina winked at me and spun her index finger in the air, indicating that she'd be in touch by phone. Sveta asked whether she could stay overnight. She lived on the outskirts, and it would have taken her a long time to get home at this hour. Besides, she was working the afternoon shift the next day and didn't have to get up early. She and Tosya had grown up together, and the two were as close as sisters.

So they sent Sevka to sleep on the floor of our room while the two of them shared his narrow bed. Sevka wrapped himself up in a sleeping bag and began snoring almost immediately. The party and the task of playing an older brother to Raya and Lenny's daughters had drained him. Baby Nikola wasn't bothered by his brother's snoring, sleeping quietly by my side.

In the middle of the night Nikola woke up hungry, so I took him to Tosya in the next room, discovering to my surprise that the other half of Sevka's bed was empty. Sveta was gone.

"Did she decide to go home after all?" I asked.

Tosya could feed the baby without becoming completely awake. Nikola too would go back to sleep with his face against her nipple, waking up every now and again to suck.

"Oh, she isn't here?" Tosya asked, patting the empty half. "Then she must be with Boris."

## THIRTY-ONE

She'd had it. She'd had it with official meetings, with boring lunches and their stupid toasts to friendship, to the great Russia old and new and to the beautiful ladies. (That toast, to the beautiful ladies, men drank standing up, like army officers at a god-forsaken garrison town.) She'd met her fill of smarmy cultural figures and fake workers and peasants. She felt like she was on the set of a bad Hollywood movie surrounded by cliché villains from special casting, their faces plastered with rubber smiles and their glassy eyes glowing out of deepened sockets.

They were like a bunch of vampires, and she amused herself during the interminable laudatory speeches on Soviet achievements by imagining them being extracted from their caskets in the morning, whence they were doled out their rubber smiles and loaded onto a special bus to come meet her.

They lied to her all the time. They talked about how happy they were, and their happiness was invariably measured by material possessions and three-bedroom apartments and dachas that she was never invited to visit. She knew it was a lie, and they knew she knew it, and she was embarrassed on their behalf.

All the while, they complained about the "soulless materialistic West," a place few had visited and that they knew of only from descriptions in propaganda-filled Soviet newspapers.

They never asked her any questions about her life. If they wanted to know anything, it was the price and availability of various consumer goods in France. If she answered truthfully, they gave her a skeptical smile as if to say, "Of course you're lying to us on behalf of your government, the way we've been lying to you on behalf of ours, so there, dear girl, we're all in the same boat, and there is no reason for you to feel superior and put on airs. Everyone is the same. Everyone is a liar and a cheat."

If she tried to talk about art or music in Paris, they listened patiently, but they weren't interested. It was not only the Stakhanovite steel workers or record-setting milkmaids who were uninterested, but artists and actors also seemed bored by such subjects.

When she had decided to come to Moscow, she worried that people would ask her lots of personal questions about Pablo. Maybe that was because it was what everyone in France (and, especially, in North America) always wanted to hear her talk about. American journalists were the worst, hounding her as if she were a criminal, pestering her with questions. Pablo was a celebrity, and Americans were obsessed with celebrity.

Pablo hadn't treated her well, and her life with him was a painful topic. They were still nominally married, but their marriage had long been a burdensome formality. She couldn't think of it without crying, not even of the good times they had had together when they first met and he would come every night to see her dance. He had been obsessed with her in those days.

She had expected the Russians to be curious about everything. About Pablo, about Diaghilev and about Paris. They lived behind the Iron Curtain and were thought to be starved for information. But they weren't. Not in the least. She ended up wanting to tell them about all these things, to insist on telling them – in order to break through their artificial smiles and indifference.

Pablo had moved on, but she couldn't. She would have, if it had not been for the goddamn war, or if Alexei had listened to her and returned to Paris before it broke out. She could have gotten over her love of her second husband, had she had her first husband by her side.

The thought of Alexei ran like a silver thread through her stay in Moscow. It first came to her the day she arrived, before his cross was taken. She felt his presence surrounding her, as if he were watching her, following her, being near her. She could almost feel his breath on her neck. She was absolutely certain she would see him. Every time she turned a corner, she expected him to be standing there, waiting for her.

Of course he was dead, she would tell herself in her sober moments. They'd killed all her people, her family and friends, and had done so systematically, in successive waves, to make sure they missed no one. They had killed all the living, and now only the vampires were left standing. There was no way they could have missed Alexei. He was so full of life.

The burglary – the matter-of-fact way the kid who broke into her suite had removed the cross from her neck – told her in no uncertain terms that Alexei was near, that he knew she had come to Moscow. It was a secret message only she could decipher. And, in case she didn't get the message right away, there was the stratagem with her other jewels – first stolen and then miraculously returned.

Receiving this message from him filled her heart with joy, but also with fear. He obviously could not see her openly. Which could only mean one thing. He was still living in the shadows. He didn't want to be discovered – least of all by the execrable KGB boss Yury Andropov.

Yury Vladimirovich was the worst. Every last vampire fawned before him. The rubbery smiles became even more cloying in his presence, as each tried to outdo the next with their sycophancy. And in his absence, too, whenever his name came up in conversation, they would nod their heads and raise their eyes reverently heavenward, as if he were a deity whose name had magical powers. With her, he was at pains to play the perfect gentleman, jumping out of his limousine each morning to kiss her hand and to hold the door open for her. He was the worst offender at all the lunches and dinners, raising his glass to beautiful women and giving her a meaningful look.

It wasn't that he had fallen in love with her. Or rather it wasn't an ordinary kind of love. She knew that kind well, too. The KGB boss was simply star-struck. He was like those fans, usually homosexual men, who picked a ballerina or an opera diva to worship, and then obsessed about her.

In the Russian ballet world, such people were known as cheeses. Yury Vladimirovich was her cheese. But that didn't make him any less dangerous.

His driver was sour and ill-mannered, yet she was always relieved when Yury Vladimirovich was busy and only his driver awaited her at the front door of the Metropole.

The driver's name was Ivan. Neither of them ever mentioned the incident when she had given him the slip at the Arts Club. He must have gotten quite a talking to from his boss, yet a kind of unspoken bond had been established between them on that day. Now and then she would catch a derisive or, perhaps, admiring glance in his rearview mirror, and he even became a little nicer to her, albeit only marginally so.

On the other hand, her minders, the man and the woman whose names she could not, try as she might, memorize, were mad at her and didn't care to hide their feelings. Hadn't she been warned repeatedly that walking around the city alone was extremely dangerous? That's right, there was absolutely no crime in Moscow, because hooliganism was a capitalist vice and Moscow was not New York City or Chicago, but nevertheless she had been in a terrible danger of getting lost. Yury Vladimirovich had been very angry and upset about her disappearance. She must never, ever, under any circumstances, do that again.

Only the service personnel were alive here, and it was with them that she had managed to have a few spontaneous human interactions. No more than a smile or a friendly gesture, but it was enough to show they were living, breathing human beings. No surprise then, that her minders kept her away from them as if they bore some dangerous illness and might infect her with it.

After about a week, Yury Vladimirovich read her some of his poems. Some were about nature, others about love. A large body of his poetic oeuvre was dedicated to describing the hardships of his day job. God save us from spy chiefs writing poetry, she thought. Let everyone stick to what they do best. She couldn't tell whether his poems were good or not. It was all she could do to keep a straight face.

## THIRTY-TWO

The stairwell smelled of day-old cooking, cheap disinfectant, and cigarette smoke.

It was one of those St. Petersburg anthills Gogol and Dostoyevsky wrote about with such dread: brick walls with tiny, grime-blinded windows, unlit hallways, and a succession of steep staircases with worn steps and cast-iron banisters winding around the perimeters of narrow airshafts. Their chimneys, black with a century's soot, stood out like dead, arthritic fingers against the perennially overcast sky. Misery and broken dreams dwelled beneath the low ceilings, reeking of the wet wool of office scribes' overcoats.

Much had changed over the past century – the city became Leningrad and its old name had become a distant memory – but much had also stayed the same. You almost expected to see a gas lamp swinging near the entrance, flickering in the miasmic air. The wet wind had never left, whipping off the Neva and chilling passersby to the bone. And darkness still came early to Leningrad's straight, barren avenues, the bill that must be paid for the magical white nights of June, and it was settled on those dreary, tubercular winter afternoons.

It also snows a great deal in Leningrad. The copious snow comes down in wet flakes. Then, almost immediately, a thaw arrives, delivering a dense fog that transforms the frivolous, Rococo city into something dark, ominous and full of mystery, where the Bronze Horsemen rides silently through the silvery mist.

It was hot on the landing between the fifth floor and the locked trap door to the attic where I had set up my observation post. The radiators hissed and knocked loudly. The heat, drifting upward, smelled of burned dust.

The old building on Marat Street was alive with the muffled sounds of late afternoon. Kids were laughing somewhere, doors opened and closed, feet scurried down the stairs. The telephone began to ring and then continued ringing for a long time, persistently, until it was answered by a loud female voice speaking some Finno-Ugric language.

The arthritic elevator, a later addition that clung to the building's facade like a glass caterpillar, came to life now and again to take on passengers and to discharge them on higher floors.

Reliable as ever, Irina had phoned me the day after the party to give me a name and an address in Leningrad.

"I asked Martha about the old man," Irina said. "She had gone to see him. She had been very excited because she thought she was going to get lots of completely original first-hand material about life in Paris in the 1920s. But, in the end, she decided he was nothing but a senile old man."

"Do you know what he told her?"

"She mentioned a few things, but I don't remember much. Sounded like a bunch of lies. Too fantastical to be believed. Oh, and he claimed to have been Olga Khokhlova's husband before Picasso. It simply wasn't true. Martha checked it. Olga Khokhlova never had another husband. Granted, he knew a lot about Khokhlova's background and family, according to Martha, but there were also numerous fabrications and inaccuracies. To begin with, he was a German, and no German man meeting his description was ever known to be associated with Khokhlova, the Diaghilev ballet, or Picasso."

I was listening intently, pressing the receiver hard against my ear. A German? It made sense. That was how he had managed to conceal his real identity – from the Germans as well as from us – by taking the name of one of his German grandmothers. It would have been dangerous to be a German in Russia after the war, but being a White émigré who had worked for the Germans would have meant a certain death sentence.

I grinned when Irina said that the old man had been married to Olga Khokhlova. What had made Martha think that he was a fraud was the very thing that told me he was for real.

"Try to be gentle with him, Pavel," Irina added. "Martha says that he's a harmless old fool who has had a hard life. It's no surprise he's not completely right in the head."

A harmless old fool for sure, I thought, wondering if Levkoyev and Kisly, from their early graves, would agree with such a characterization.

Now, hanging around the dingy building on Marat Street, I had to admit that the thug had disguised himself cleverly. A harmless old fool living out his twilight years in a place like that, in a communal apartment.

I had gone to Leningrad in secret, leaving the office on Wednesday afternoon, claiming to have a high fever and imitating a deep-throated cough.

The pretense had to be maintained not only at the office, but at home, too, for Boris's benefit. Despite recovering from his injuries, he continued to loiter around the apartment, showing no intent of returning to work. Deceiving him fell to Tosya and Sevka, with the help of little Nikola. During the day, I was supposed to be sleeping off a bad cold, so Tosya had to stay out of our rooms so that I couldn't give the cold to Nikola. Once Sevka returned from school, his job was to imitate my cold by coughing into a pillow and blowing his nose. I practiced it with him before leaving and coached him how not to overdo it.

It was a naive trick, especially when deployed against a KGB operative trained to see through far more sophisticated deceptions, but I figured that Boris would not expect me to resort to such childish tricks. Besides, I was going to be away for just one day, and would return with the killer in tow.

Traveling overnight on the Red Arrow train, which covered the 600 kilometers in just seven hours, I arrived in Leningrad full of strong tea – served by the female conductor with platinum hair and gold teeth – and well rested from my night in the sleeper cabin. It was still very early when I stepped out of Leningrad's Moscow Station – an exact replica of Leningrad Station in Moscow – so I took a brisk walk down Nevsky to St. Isaac's Cathedral and watched the winter sun rise over its tarnished golden cupola. Then, shivering against the bitter wind and worrying about catching a cold for real, I followed the usual tourist route, from portly Peter the Great astride his steed to the vast parade ground in front of the Winter Palace, where the wind seemed to be blowing from every direction at once, swirling around several swaddled female figures who methodically swung their brooms back and forth, sweeping cigarettes butts from the cobblestones, then headed back toward Nevsky through the Admiralty arch.

Leningrad is a beautiful city – and very different from Moscow. Tosya and I had been talking about traveling here for a long time, and Irina Drozdova had told us what we absolutely had to do while in the city, and what to see at the Hermitage and the Russian Museum. But now, what with little Nikola, the trip would have to be postponed indefinitely.

I took my time sipping a coffee at a small café on Bolshaya Konyushennaya, warming my frozen hands against the paper cup. I still had a lot of time to kill before heading over to Marat Street, only a ten-minute walk from Nevsky.

It was 11 a.m. when I rang the bell of the fifth-floor apartment. Responding to a young woman's look of surprise when I asked for Comrade Knorring, I said I was the son of a distant cousin, passing through Leningrad while en route from Volgograd to Vyborg. That got me another questioning look, now tinged with suspicion.

"Not at home," she replied rudely and tried to shut the door in my face.

"Hey, wait a second," I called out promptly. "Are you his daughter?"

"His daughter?" she repeated in astonishment. "Me? Of course not. I'm a neighbor."

She was wearing a house dress that was too large for her. Frankly, I had not been prepared to see a neighbor – and a young and pretty one at that – and I had been flustered by the look of surprise and suspicion in her eyes. I realized I had already made a few mistakes that deepened both her surprise and suspicion.

"You see, my father died a long time ago," I said. "We have not been in touch. I know nothing about Comrade Knorring except that he's a distant cousin. Other than him, I don't know anyone in this city and I've never been here before. I'll stop by again before I have to catch my train."

"He'll be back later," she said.

She was starting to warm up to me, but not enough to remove the chain. I didn't think I could get any information from her about his living arrangements or habits, and I decided not to try.

"What is your name?" she asked as I turned to leave.

"Stanislav."

I felt her eyes on my back while I waited for the elevator. She continued watching me through the narrow crack in the door and shut it only when she saw me get into the cabin. I rode all the way to the lobby, waited a few minutes and climbed the stairs to the landing above the fifth floor, tiptoeing past Knorring's door.

I wondered whether talking to the girl had been a mistake. My fears were reinforced when, a quarter of an hour after my fake departure, Knorring's front door flew open and my young acquaintance emerged on the landing. She had changed out of her house dress and was wearing a short shearling coat and an even shorter skirt beneath it. She was holding an elegant leather briefcase. I was quite sure she wouldn't be able to see me in the dark stairway above the landing, and she didn't even look. Not bothering to wait for the elevator, she ran down the stairs, her high heels beating a spirited tattoo on the stone steps.

She might be off to warn him, I thought, and wondered whether I should follow her, but with her flying down the stairs like that, I had no way of catching her without being noticed.

Once the door of the building slammed downstairs and the echo of her footsteps died down, the fifth floor sank into inactivity for a long time, and so did, by and large, the entire stairwell, with just a few comings and goings on the lower floors. I waited in my dark and increasingly hot ambush, the strange behavior of Knorring's young neighbor nagging at me unpleasantly.

I couldn't allow myself to leave my observation post, and of course smoking in my hideout was out of the question. The yearning for nicotine was the worst thing about waiting.

There was a sudden burst of activity once the workday came to an end. The elevator was now running almost continuously. It ascended to the fifth floor several times, and I kept my service Makarov on my lap, just in case. None of the returning tenants went into Knorring's apartment, but I knew that sooner or later someone would. Perhaps even his young neighbor.

She was still bothering me. She was so stylishly dressed and so confident. And her surprise and even concern at my arrival had been very evident. What if she wasn't his neighbor at all, but a young mistress. Sure Zolotnitsky – if it was indeed him – was very old, fifty years older than the girl if he was a day, but poor students had been known to be kept by old gangsters. Jailbird romanticism could have a mesmerizing effect on a young, unformed mind, and intimidation could also play a role

Then, as I was pondering this possibility, which might result in my quarry slipping from my grasp, a middle-aged woman exited the elevator, stopped in front of Knorring's door, and fumbled for the keys in her purse. She unlocked the door and entered. She was shortly followed by a man about her age. He was thickset and muscular, and two decades younger than Zolotnitsky. He rang the bell, and the woman promptly let him in.

Another hour passed and the stream of new arrivals to the building gradually slowed to a trickle. Then, finally, groaning as though it were tired out from a busy day, the elevator reached the fifth floor and the door opened.

I'm not sure whom I had expected, but I must have been mentally prepared to see a tall, burly old man with a full head of thick grey hair – like an aging war movie Nazi. Instead, Knorring was small and sinewy, all skin and bones. As he stepped out of the elevator, he removed his cheap wool cap to reveal a completely bald head.

He walked with difficulty and a heavy limp, leaning on a stick. Crossing the landing was a visible effort for him. A knit bag containing a bottle of kefir and something wrapped in wax paper hung off the hook of his walking stick. The empty left sleeve of his shabby winter coat was tucked into its belt.

He was the picture of poverty and lonely old age. You could not have come up with a less likely suspect for organizing a burglary at the Metropole and stabbing two able-bodied men. I put away my Makarov, but I still had to make sure.

I stood up, stepped out of the shadows and spoke softly, "Good evening, Comrade Zolotnitsky."

The old man had just leaned his walking stick against the wall and was pulling out his keys. Turning his deeply lined face toward me, showing its cataract-tainted pupils, he bared a pair of pink, toothless gums in a bitter smile.

"So, you found me at last," he said. "By God, I always knew you would."

# THIRTY-THREE

The brief winter day had come to an end, and the Northern night had fallen, but the small room, with its low ceiling and a narrow window overlooking an airshaft, would have been dark even in daytime. It was tidy and clean. Possessions were few, but everything had been neatly arranged. The furniture was homemade – simple, functional and solidly built. It was a Spartan environment and very orderly, very German. Somehow, it managed to be a pleasant and comfortable place, despite its evident poverty.

"Just one moment, officer, if you permit me," he said as we entered. "I need to put away my shopping before it spoils, and then I'll be completely at your service."

He was a pleasure to listen to. He had the same old-style St. Petersburg accent as Olga Khokhlova, but without the softer consonants that betrayed her Ukrainian origins. He also managed to be polite without being obsequious, and deferential to authority without seeming to be scared. You could see that he was a man who respected others because he had respect for himself.

"Let me help you with the latch," I said, seeing that he was struggling to open the window. But I was too late. He had undone the lock of the inner frame by leaning on it with his shoulder, had taken out the kefir and butter from its knitted bag, and placed them in the space between the double frames.

"There we go," he said, closing the window. "This is my icebox. It works only too well in winter, less so in summer. To what do I owe the honor of your visit, officer?"

"I see you have no photographs anywhere," I said. "No previous life?"

He chuckled.

"Yes, it won't do to tell you that my eyesight is failing, so that I no longer recognize anyone in my pictures. Since you know my real name, you must know a lot about my previous life. I have been living here as Andreas Knorring, but it is clearly Alexei Zolotnitsky that you are now interested in."

"Not exactly," I said. "I know about Alexei Zolotnitsky, and he doesn't concern me."

"Really?" He sounded genuinely surprised. "May I ask you how you have come by this knowledge?"

"Let's leave that out for the moment," I said. "Let's talk about more recent events. What I want to know is when you were last in Moscow."

"In Moscow? Why, not very recently." He gave it some thought. "It must have been more than ten years ago. Yes, it was in 1955. When Stalin finally died and there was an amnesty for many of us imprisoned under Article 58 of the old Penal Code. I was traveling from the Kolym-Lag, and I was headed for Leningrad. I stopped over in Moscow for a few days."

It still didn't prove anything. He could have been a good actor. He'd had many lives, and pretending must have been second nature.

"Moscow had changed a great deal since the days of Alexei Zolotnitsky," he said. "I'm not sure if all the changes were for the better. But I had changed too – and certainly for the worse."

"And never since 1955?" I asked. "Not, say, in the past couple of weeks?"

"I don't get to go anywhere these days, officer. Except to the grocery store and the Summer Gardens, to sit on a bench by the front gate and watch the Neva flow. I'm an invalid, and I don't have much money. And, frankly, I've traveled enough for one lifetime."

Article 58 made him a political, an enemy of the people as they were called back then. Kolym-Lag, the notorious labor camp, was exactly the kind of place where you met people who could organize a jewelry heist and would not hesitate to murder everyone involved in order to mop up.

"How about your friends? Do you keep in touch with anyone? People come to visit you now and then?"

He giggled.

"I'm sorry, officer," he said, taking out a clean, carefully folded handkerchief and wiping his eyes. "I'm not laughing at you. Rather, I'm laughing at myself. You're the first person to visit me since 1955. I don't have any friends, and I don't expect to make any more for the rest of my days."

"What about your neighbors?"

I thought about the girl. No wonder she had been surprised when she answered the door. She had never seen anyone calling on Comrade Knorring.

"How do you mean? Do you want to know whether they would eavesdrop on our conversation?"

"That, too."

"There is a nice family living next door. Both are engineers. We have a lot in common. I used to be an engineer, too, before I lost my arm in Kolym-Lag. They have a daughter, a nice girl. You can check with them to see whether I travel much or receive any visitors. They will know all there is to know about me. I mean about Andreas Knorring and his geriatric habits. There are three other rooms here. It's a big communal apartment, like most others in the center of Leningrad. I'm on good terms with them, but not overly friendly. Not my kind of people, if you know what I mean."

"I saw a young woman leave the apartment," I said. "She seems to know a lot about you. Is that your neighbors' daughter?"

His lips spread in a smile almost in spite of himself. His pleasure in speaking of her was evident. He had a nice smile, which almost made you forget the toothless mouth.

"Yes, that must have been Emilia. She's studying to be a ballet dancer."

"Quite a coincidence," I said. "Did you put her up to it?"

The smile faded as suddenly as it had appeared, and his face was cold and hard. His blue eyes became watchful. You could tell he had been a soldier – and you could see him being involved in a murder. Two murders if necessary.

"What if I did?" he said slowly. "In what way is it a coincidence?"

"It just seems as if you're surrounded by ballerinas. Your neighbors' daughter is studying to be a ballet dancer, and your first wife was one as well."

"How do you know that?" he asked.

"Let's do this differently. Why don't you tell me how you found out that Olga Khokhlova was in Moscow? Did she communicate with you?"

"What are you talking about?"

It didn't matter whether he was leading a double life and living in character. No one was such a good actor that they could pretend to be so surprised.

"About your baptismal cross. Did you have it stolen from her?"

He stared at me.

"Speak man," I shouted, bringing my face close to his. "Did you?"

He waited a long time before shaking his head.

"You're very well informed, officer. A lot better than I. You have gotten me very confused. I don't quite follow you."

"This is how it happened, Citizen Zolotnitsky," I said. "Khokhlova got in touch with you, letting you know she was coming to Moscow. You arranged for her room at the Metropole Hotel to be broken into and the cross stolen. You figured it belonged to you, and she had no right to keep it. Except things went wrong, and the man you hired stole more than he had been told to steal. Because of that, two men were killed. The first because he turned out to be too greedy, and the second because he had the misfortune to buy the stolen jewelry. Was Levkoyev killed because he refused to give up the loot? Collectors are crazy, and he might very well have preferred to die rather than part with such wonderful trinkets. Or did you leave the body in his apartment rather than dumping it into the river because you figured we'd find the jewels sooner or later?"

Zolotnitsky batted his eyes.

"But at least you've got your cross, don't you? I don't believe you would be so dumb as to wear it around your neck. Otherwise I'd ask you to unbutton your shirt collar."

Zolotnitsky began to laugh. He kept laughing for at least two minutes, and, unlike his smile, his laughter was not pretty. His face became wrinkled, his jaw got twisted, and the cavity of his mouth was dark and empty. His eyes were not laughing.

"I don't know who fed you this nonsense, but it is very convoluted. Yes, I once gave my baptismal cross to my wife in lieu of a wedding ring. It was the only piece of jewelry I owned at the time. But we had made a trade for that cross, and I have no right to it any more, having surrendered all claims of its ownership to her. As to being in contact with Olga – well, I haven't seen her or heard from her since before the war."

I didn't want him to keep laughing.

"How did you end up at Kolym-Lag?" I asked, changing the subject.

Alexei put his hand down on the dining table and began drumming a nervous tattoo on the oilcloth. His hand was rough and strong and surprisingly large for such a small man, with long fingers and clean fingernails. I wondered how he took care of his nails.

"It was Dalstroy at first, a labor camp outside Magadan," he said. "Since you're so well-informed, there is no point hiding anything. After the war, the German munitions factory where I worked as chief shift engineer during the war was disassembled by the Russians and shipped east from the Berlin suburb where it had been located. I was considered essential personnel. They needed me to reassemble and run the equipment at the new site, and so they took me along. You may consider it as if I was looted along with the plant, even though they preferred to call it war reparations."

He grinned.

"The new site was in Nizhny Tagil, in the Ural Mountains. I continued to work there for a while, doing pretty much what I had been doing in Germany, except there were no Allied bombs falling on my head. Then, in January 1949, all of us they had brought over from Berlin were arrested and put on trial. To be honest, I hardly noticed the difference. We had been living behind barbed wire, anyway. They fed us at the plant cafeteria and didn't allow us off the premises."

"Did they know you were Russian?"

"God no. They would have hung me on the spot as a traitor. To the end, I pretended not to speak a word of Russian, even after my other colleagues started to pick up a few phrases here and there. I kept claiming I had no ear for languages. In general, I quickly figured out that playing an idiot was the best survival strategy here. You Soviets kill everyone sooner or later – the good, the bad, the thieves, the bastards, what have you. Only idiots have a chance of surviving."

I shrugged.

"You don't agree, officer? All the other Germans who worked with me were shot. It didn't matter that some of them had spied on their comrades for the NKVD or joined the Communist Party. I'm the only one who survived. Because I played it dumb."

"What did they charge you with?"

"Wrecking and sabotage."

"And were you wreckers and saboteurs?"

He laughed.

"They said we were unreformed Hitlerites who had formed a clandestine National Socialist cell at the plant. That we had recruited a bunch of Russian workers and engineers who worked with us. We had been preparing an armed rising in Nizhny Tagil. It was complete nonsense, of course. They all denied it at first, but admitted everything under torture and were sentenced to be shot."

"But not you. Why?"

"Perhaps because they thought I was too dumb to make a good showing at the show trial. But, in truth, there was never any rhyme or reason. They beat me every bit as badly as the others during the interrogations, and they could have shot me just as easily as the others. There was a young girl, Lina, working at the library – they had a library for the workers at the plant, which was no different from the way the plant had been run back in Germany, and Lina was in love with me. They arrested her, too, and she even eventually testified that I was a Hitlerite. She got shot, and I got off lightly. If that's what you call a twenty-five-year sentence. Even now I would have had another ten years left to serve if Stalin were still alive."

"I'm hard to kill," he concluded, chuckling after a moment's reflection. "Many people have tried, but it didn't work on me. I'm starting to think something is wrong with me. Either the Lord is saving me for some greater purpose, or else I'm never going to die at all. That would be a terrible thing."

"Once they let you out of the camps, you could have gone to East Germany," I said cutting short his musings. "But you didn't. Why not?"

He sighed.

"I didn't want to go for a number of reasons. First of all, I didn't want to attract attention to myself, which would have been unavoidable if I had applied to leave. Once they started to dig into my past, they might have found out that I wasn't a real German. They would have charged me with treason, and, even though Stalin was dead, I could have still been hung. Besides, I had had enough of living in Germany. I had made a mistake going there in the 1930s and didn't want to repeat it. Finally, and perhaps most importantly, this is my country. Since I had been repatriated, I wanted to end my days here, even if it were under an assumed name."

"But you still wanted that baptismal cross back," I said quickly.

"You're trying to knock me off balance, officer. I know the trick. They all use it, the Reds, the Gestapo, and the NKVD. Do you really think that if you spring a question on me unawares I'll admit to a crime I know nothing about?"

"Very well then," I said sharply. "Since you know the drill, maybe you can level with me without us wasting any more of one another's time?"

"Look," he replied. "I don't know what crime you're talking about and why you keep dredging up all that stuff from the past. I told you I have not been in touch with Olga for more than twenty-five years, and that's the truth. I didn't even know if she was alive. When you told me she's in Moscow, I got excited – more than I would have thought possible. But that is neither here nor there, because I have not been to Moscow since 1955, and I have no money to go there."

"And what about your baptismal cross?" I asked.

"What about it? I haven't thought about it a single time in all these years. As you can imagine, I had other things on my mind – and other, far larger losses to mourn, had I been inclined to do so."

"So you didn't arrange to steal it from Olga Khokhlova, and no one did it on your behalf? Do you have any idea who might have done all this? Anyone who knew about the cross?"

"What is there to know about it? If it's my family's cross you are talking about, it's not valuable. There is some kind of a family legend associated with it, but who knows whether it is true? Most likely my grandmother invented it. It once held sentimental value for me, but no longer. As I said, officer, I've lost so much – my country, my friends, my loved ones, even my name. When the head is lost, what's the use of crying over the lost hair?"

I had to admit that he was right.

"What about Olga?" he continued. "What is she doing in Moscow?"

"It's some kind of official visit."

"I think I would like to see her," he said slowly, after a long silence.

"I think she would like to see you, too," I said. "Once she knows that you're alive."

Now he shook his head.

"Actually, no. I can't see her. Look at me. She'll be upset when she sees me like this. I would appreciate it if you didn't even mention to her that you saw me, officer."

We sat in silence. Alexei again started drumming a tattoo on the surface of the table.

"So Olga was robbed in Moscow?" he asked at last. "And someone stole my baptismal cross? This means she was still wearing it. It makes me happy to know that. It's strange. I've been all alone in the world for a long time, since your damn Revolution. I have no relatives, no friends, just me, and I like it like that. I survived on my own, barely. Taking care of another person would have been impossible in my situation. Ever since my failed marriage to Olga, I've avoided love and friendship. And yet it warms my soul to think that someone in Paris cares for me."

"She thought it was you who took the cross, and that was why she told no one about its loss. She didn't want you to be caught, even if it had been you who sent the burglar. She protected you."

He chuckled.

"It's nice to know. Still, she must have thought I had changed a great deal since when she was married to me. In those days, gentlemen didn't steal."

It was getting late, and I had to go. I needed to get to the station in time for the nine o'clock Red Arrow.

"Let me know if you change your mind and decide to see Madame Khokhlova," I said, getting up. "I could try to arrange it for you, even though it won't be easy. You would have to come to Moscow."

I left Zolotnitsky's apartment with time to spare, but still ended up almost missing my train. Exiting the elevator on the ground floor, I ran into his young neighbor. I could see now that she was a ballerina – she had the characteristic build of a dancer and held her head in that upright, almost supercilious way. She must have been coming back from a rehearsal, because she looked drained and her hair, gathered into a ponytail, was dark with perspiration.

She recognized me right away.

"So you did manage to see your cousin?" she asked.

"I did. I suppose he doesn't get too many visitors?"

It's a nasty habit cops have, never letting an opportunity slip to see if a story checks out. We are a suspicious lot, and we always assume that everyone is lying. But it is important. If you catch a guy lying to you in the small things, you know you can't trust him in more important matters, no matter how plausible he might sound.

"You're the first I can remember," she said.

"Does he stay in touch with anyone?" I said. "By phone or by mail?"

"No, he doesn't. And he has no friends or family. He's all alone."

"Do you feel sorry for him?"

"I do. Of course he's German and the Germans invaded us, and lots of Leningraders died in the Siege, but it is a terrible thing to grow old like this, in a foreign country. I've never heard him mention any cousins, either."

She was obviously a clever girl, and it was time for me to identify myself.

"You're right. I'm not his cousin," I said. "I'm a police detective."

I pulled out my ID. She glanced at it briefly and said nothing, waiting for me to go on.

"I want you to do me a favor," I said, pulling out a twenty-five-ruble bill. "Comrade Knorring may need to go to Moscow at a moment's notice. If he does, I'll ask you to buy him a ticket on the Red Arrow and put him on the train. Can you do that?"

She nodded.

"And one other thing," I added. "Take down my phone number. If something happens to him, make sure you give me a call right away."

"Nonsense," she exclaimed. "What would happen to him? He's a harmless old man. His life is very regular. He goes out in the morning, buys a newspaper, and sits on a park bench in the Summer Garden, reading it and watching the boats go up the river. He's as punctual as you would expect a German to be."

"I'm sure there is nothing to worry about," I said. "It's just a precaution. Write down my home number, too. And let me know if anything strange or unusual happens. It's important. Will you do that?"

I was speaking softly, so that we were not overheard by her neighbors, but I was insistent. Emilia grew serious, swayed by the urgency in my voice.

"Is there something in particular I should watch for?"

"Anything at all. A visitor, a phone call, a strange person hanging around the building or the courtyard, asking about him. Keep your eyes open and report to me right away if you see any suspicious strangers."

"Somebody like you, in other words," she giggled.

"Yes, exactly."

"May I ask you what it is all about?"

She was serious once more.

"I'm not sure," I said.

It was true. It was just a hunch, a vague suspicion, but I had decided to act on it. Better safe than sorry.

I was back in Moscow early the next morning, arriving at six o'clock and having to take the first metro train by full frontal assault, battling a crowd of commuters from villages outside the city.

By the time Boris left his room three-quarters of an hour later, I was sitting in our communal kitchen, wearing a ratty bathrobe and Tosya's wool scarf, unshaven and pale, with black circles under my red-rimmed eyes. I definitely looked ill and was genuinely exhausted, because I had forced myself to stay awake all night, battling the irresistible, soporific effect of the snowy darkness outside my window and the monotonous rattle of the wheels. I was drinking strong black tea with honey and lemon that Tosya had made for me and coughing furiously at regular intervals.

"How are you doing, buddy?" Boris asked.

He fried two eggs with kielbasa and ate this appetizing concoction directly out of the frying pan, standing before the stove. When I was single, I used to do the same thing in order not to dirty a plate for no reason, but after we moved in together, Tosya put an end to such brutish behavior.

"Did I keep you awake with my coughing?" I asked, arranging my face into what was supposed to be an expression of concern.

"No more than your baby," Boris said, winking at me. "Actually, I didn't hear a thing. I've been sleeping like a baby myself. You really look awful, old man."

"Actually, I'm starting to feel a lot better," I said. "The tea is helping. I must have drunk twenty cups of it during the night."

"Good. I don't want to catch your cold. I need all my strength at the office and at night as well."

He winked at me, but the full meaning of his words became clear only later.

It was the first time I had seen him go to work since we had had our fight. He was still walking with a slight limp, but otherwise had recovered completely.

He left, and was soon followed by Sevka who had been, as usual, impossible to get out of bed. This time he used, as an excuse for oversleeping, the assignment I had given him to wake up every hour or so and imitate my cough for Boris's benefit. Be that as it may, he was now late for school and his mother was not pleased about it.

Having finally pushed her first born out the door, Tosya fed the baby and took him out for a walk.

Being alone in the apartment – and in the daytime, to boot – was an unaccustomed luxury. I enjoyed the silence and the privacy it afforded me and was in no hurry to return to our rooms. Eventually, I got into bed – after all, I was supposed to be ill with the flu, and besides I had had a sleepless night.

But I couldn't make myself go to sleep. My mind was working feverishly, and I kept reviewing the details of Olga Khokhlova's case. It was the first time I had had an opportunity to think about it quietly and at my leisure.

The little silver baptismal cross had to be the key to the whole thing. That much was clear. Whoever had arranged the burglary was after that cross. Why? For its own value perhaps? Was the Zolotnitsky family legend true, and was it a valuable historic artifact? Possibly, but who could have known that, except for Zolotnitsky and Olga?

There had to be another person then, who not only knew about the legend but was aware that Olga would be wearing the cross around her neck. Only the KGB could have been in the possession of that knowledge, but the KGB would have plenty of other ways to lay its hands on it. It certainly wouldn't have needed to employ a basket case like Mitya Kislitsky.

And, moreover, Andropov wouldn't have brought us in to investigate.

Let's leave the identity of the person with the knowledge about the cross aside for the moment, I told myself. Let's focus on the reason for stealing it. What could it have been?

To let Olga know that Alexei Zolotnitsky was alive?

That made sense, because Zolotnitsky was the only one who knew she would have the cross and who cared about it.

So the unknown person – I called him Comrade X, as I always did when I tried to visualize the criminal while investigating a crime – hired Mitya Kislitsky to break into Olga's suite and steal the cross. Was he then going to impersonate Zolotnitsky? That was unlikely. Olga knew him too well. Had he expected her to do something once she realized that Zolotnitsky was alive and in town? If so, he would have been disappointed, for Olga had done nothing – at least as far as I could tell. She hadn't even reported the cross stolen.

And what about the jewelry in Levkoyev's apartment? What was Levkoyev's role in the burglary? How was that haul of valuable trinkets connected with the cross? Wasn't it curious that everything Olga reported stolen was found in Levkoyev's secret hiding place *except* for the cross? In a way, the fact that all that stuff had been stolen and then returned reinforced the message Comrade X was trying to send to Olga. That was something worth bearing in mind.

I was still fairly confused, but one thing was clear, somebody was playing a complicated game. A burglary and two murders were part of it, and, by the look of it, it would end with harm coming to Olga

Khokhlova and Alexei Zolotnitsky. But it wasn't clear what kind of game it all was, and whether I could help either of them avoid what might be coming. Or, for that matter, whether I should even try.

When I had left for Leningrad, the case looked straightforward. I was convinced that I would return having collared Mitya's and Levkoyev's murderer. Now, all of a sudden, I didn't know what to think.

# THIRTY-FOUR

Valera came to check on me in the early evening. I had finally fallen asleep, exhausted by the sleepless night on the train and my nagging thoughts about the case. Tosya had brought little Nikola home from his walk, fed him, and put him at my side. We were both sleeping peacefully, oblivious to the rustle of pages and the scratching of Sevka's pen as he worked on his school assignment at his desk.

"How is it going?" Valera shouted from the threshold, bursting into the room in a cloud of cold winter air.

"Keep your voice down, Valera," I groaned. "You'll wake up the baby."

He bent over the bed, cast an eye over Nikola, and declared him to be looking more and more like me.

"Poor kid," he added, rubbing his hands. "How's your flu?"

"Much better, thanks. I'm thinking of going back to work tomorrow. I'm bored here."

"I wouldn't if I were you. No doctor would recommend that you go out in this weather. Besides, there isn't much for you to do at the office."

"We'll see about that," I said.

Valera glanced over Sevka's shoulder.

"How're you doing, kid?" he asked. "What's that you're working on? Math? Very good, you need to study hard to avoid being an ignoramus like Pavel and me."

"I still want to be a detective when I grow up," Sevka declared. "Like Uncle Pavel and you."

Valera patted him on the head.

"Be like me, not like Uncle Pavel," he said. "I'll make you my partner instead of him. He keeps getting sick on me."

"That's true, be like Valera," I said. "He has a logical mind and he gets results."

Valera knew I was kidding, but he was pleased nonetheless.

"It's too bad you've got the flu," he said after a moment. "Boris and I are going to a bandy match tomorrow night."

"Are you talking about my neighbor Boris?"

Valera nodded.

"It's Zorky against Krasnoyarsk. A huge game. I'm sure Boris will get a kick out of it even though he says he won't like being out in the cold for two hours. He says he'll bring Sveta, just to prove that it's no place to bring a date.

"Wait a minute," I exclaimed, forgetting my warning to Valera to keep his voice down lest he wake up the baby. "Do you mean he and Sveta—"

"Where have you been, Uncle Pavel?" Sevka said, laughing. "They haven't parted for a second since they met at our party."

Now the meaning of Boris's remark in the morning about him needing all his energy became clear. I was always the last one to wise up to such things.

"Anyway, I would love for you to come along with us to the game, but it's not a good idea in your condition," Valera said.

"Nonsense," I said. "I'm ready to go. Fresh air will do me good."

"As you wish. You're a responsible adult. Just don't blame me when you come down with pneumonia."

Valera pouted. He was defending common sense, and losing.

"Anything new in your investigation?" I asked, in order to deflect him from concerns about my health.

"Nothing really," he said. "Anything to report on your end?"

I shrugged.

"I was told to get off the case. Comrade Andropov was convinced that Olga and I gave the slip to his agents on purpose. I told him that we weren't even aware we were being followed, but he didn't buy it."

"Well, I don't think you can put off the KGB chief with a primitive lie like that," Valera said sternly. "You didn't even tell me what you found out."

"It wasn't much," I said. "There was in fact a piece of jewelry the victim didn't report, but it was only a silver baptismal cross."

"Was that all?"

I nodded.

"Baptismal crosses are worn all the time," Valera said. "No one takes it off for the night. Could it have been taken off her neck?"

"I don't know," I lied.

"I see," he said thoughtfully. "It's a very strange story then."

"Why?" I asked, trying to sound innocent.

"Look, we've got Mitya Kislitsky breaking into Khokhlova's suite at the Metropole to steal something on someone else's orders. He commits the robbery at night, when the guest is certain to be there. We initially assumed that he had to take this risk because that was when his associate was on duty. Now Khokhlova tells you that he stole her baptismal cross. Obviously that was the thing he had come to steal. That means that he needed her to be there. Was it valuable?"

"I don't know," I shrugged. "It definitely had sentimental value. It was given to her by her first husband. A White officer by the name of Alexei Zolotnitsky. The interesting thing is that he ended up in the Soviet Union after the war and—"

"Is this what you've been working on all this time?"

It was Sevka. We both turned to see him staring at us, his eyes glinting with curiosity. We had forgotten all about him and were discussing an ongoing case in his presence.

Valera turned away, a pained expression on his face. He hated breaking the rules and, having done so unintentionally, was mad at himself.

Dismissing his protestation that I had to stay in bed to get better, I walked Valera to the front door.

"I don't believe Khokhlova's first husband had anything to do with the burglary," I said.

"Why do you think so?"

"I'll tell you later," I said. "It's a long story."

Later that night I got a call from Zolotnitsky. I had half expected it.

He began from far away. He was speaking slowly and haltingly. He was having difficulty finding the right words and then getting them out.

"You might think me a fool," he said. "I'm usually not so inconsistent. I don't change my mind so readily. I feel like a blushing girl out on her first date."

He went on like that for a few minutes. It was sweet to hear an old man, a tough military officer, and a veteran of a bunch of bloody wars, talk this way, but eventually I wanted him to get to the point.

"I take it you decided to come to Moscow to see Olga?" I said, cutting to the chase.

"Well, I don't know," he mumbled on the other end of the line. "In a word, no. What I meant to say was, yes, I would very much like to come down to see her."

"Do you have money for a Red Arrow ticket?"

"Not quite. I mean not really. No. But I don't need to come by the Red Arrow. It's too expensive. I can come by a local train."

"Emilia will buy you a ticket and put you on the train," I said. "It's been arranged. You will have to come by the Red Arrow, and you'll have to do so on short notice. As soon as I can fix the time and the date, I'll let both of you know. Understood?"

I was speaking in short, clipped sentences, making myself sound like a military officer. If it sounded like an order, I figured he was more likely to act. He tried to protest some more, but it had been decided, and I hung up in a very good mood.

Now there was the small matter of getting in touch with Olga, making sure she still wanted to see him, and arranging their meeting. And ensuring that no one was aware that I had found Zolotnitsky and that—

It had been staring me in the face. It was a completely crazy idea, but it was the only one that made sense. The cross was supposed to be a message to Olga, but its ultimate recipients were Valera and me. If she had played by the rules, she would have reported the theft of the cross and told us at the same time that it used to belong to her first husband, who might have ended up in Russia after the war.

We were *supposed* to find Zolotnitsky. Of course. Whoever was looking for him knew he was in Russia, but didn't know under what name.

Who was looking for him? For what purpose? I had no idea. It seemed completely crazy, but it was the only possible explanation. And, naturally, a person who was willing to murder two people to get at Zolotnitsky, my mysterious Comrade X, was unlikely to bear him any goodwill. And I may have led him to Zolotnitsky's place in Leningrad already, even though I had taken every precaution. It was only a hunch then, but I was glad I had asked Emilia to keep an eye on the old man.

And of course bringing Zolotnitsky to Moscow was a huge risk – which I now had to take, since I had promised him I would arrange his meeting with Olga. He was clearly so eager to come.

# THIRTY-FIVE

Valera met us on the platform of the Krasnogorsk station. I rode in the last car of the suburban train out of Moscow. By the time I walked all the way to the front of the long green caterpillar, everyone was already gathered, waiting for me – Valera, Boris and Sveta.

The weather had turned even colder toward evening. The northwesterly wind off the Baltic that had chilled me to the bone two days before in Leningrad had arrived on the outskirts of Moscow. Sveta, swaddled in a wool shawl over a long sheepskin coat, was clinging tightly to Boris, both to keep warm and to display affection for her man. Boris, showing no sign of being cold in his half-length shearling, occasionally passed the back of his hand over her cheek and pulled gently at a blonde strand of hair breaking loose from under her fur hat.

Every time his fingers passed over her lips, they would linger for a second – long enough for Sveta to kiss them.

"Phew," Boris whistled when he saw me. "You've made it. The power of Russian hockey healed our Lazarus."

He laughed and Valera joined him, even though his laughter had a reproachful undertone, as though he was not yet fully convinced that I should have been out and about, much less out of doors.

"Seriously," Boris said, breaking off his laughter. "I'm glad you decided to come, old man. We'll keep you warm. Sveta has provisioned us well. We've got sausage, bread, Dutch cheese, even some red caviar. Not to mention plenty of beer and vodka. We're ready."

They were holding large bags bristling with various packages and bottles, as well as a sizable length of smoked sausage.

"But you'll have to wait until the intermission," Valera said. "We'll be sitting with my Krasnogorsk buddies. They'll lose respect for you if you eat during the game."

"What, they don't even drink?" Boris exclaimed in mock horror.

"Drinking is a different matter. You can start drinking before the game and you can drink until the end – or until you run out, whichever comes first."

By the time we got to the stadium and paid our 20 kopeks for the tickets, the referee had whistled the start of the game. The stadium belonged to the Krasnogorsk Mechanical Plant, and its red brick buildings loomed across a wide, snow-covered field. The windows of the plant were lit red and, despite the freezing weather, were wide open, releasing clouds of steam and the clangor of machinery into the night sky. The evening shift was hard at work.

Bandy is played on a huge ice field – the size of a soccer pitch. The stands of the Krasnogorsk stadium ran the length of the field along the sidelines. The seats were wooden and had no backs. They looked uncomfortable and cold. The stands were mostly empty and only a small section near the center line was thick with fans, which was where we headed, as well. Everyone huddled together in the wind, talking loudly and cheering the home team from the moment the tiny ball was put in play. They also sounded like they had started drinking quite a while ago.

Valera went to each person in turn, and they shook hands. They were his childhood buddies, from school, the neighborhood, and youth hockey. They patted him on the back and commented on how rarely he came to see them.

"You never show up to root for the team, either," they said reproachfully.

Frankly, I was pleasantly surprised by how many friends Valera had, and how they genuinely liked him. He wasn't so popular at Moscow Criminal Investigations.

Valera kept telling them that he was busy at work and that the city was far away. It wasn't really – much closer than I had expected – and his buddies were ribbing him, telling him the distance was, if anything, purely mental. Once you were a Muscovite you no longer wanted to have anything to do with your hometown crowd.

They were probably right. I don't know about myself, but Boris and Sveta looked like a big city couple, and they certainly stood out.

The Krasnogorsk team had had a few patchy years. They had been demoted, and this was their first year back in the top league. But they had a new coach and lots of homegrown, fast-skating talent, whom Valera and his friends seemed to know on a first-name basis.

Krasnogorsk soon scored, and everyone around us went wild. Valera was especially jubilant, hugging a grey-haired old man who ran up to him from a few seats over.

"This is my Dad," Valera said to us once they stopped hugging. "My partner, Senior Lieutenant Pavel Matyushkin."

"Vasily," the man introduced himself. "Vasily Petrovich."

We shook hands. Valera introduced him to Boris and Sveta, too, but then the old man turned to me.

"I've heard a lot about you," he said. "My son says you've cracked a couple of hard cases over the years. Valera thinks you're a lucky so-and-so."

"Dad," Valera said, blushing. "I never said it like that. I said I was lucky to have him as a partner."

"No, you did say he was lucky," the elder Tumakov insisted. "I'm an old man. I went from apprentice, when I started here at fourteen, to lathe operator and finally shift foreman. I didn't get all that way by telling lies about people. I always tell it like it is."

"I'm retired now," he added.

"Your son was right," I said. "I've been pretty lucky. And I had good partners, like your son."

"Is he good?" he asked, a note of pride in his voice. "Is he really?"

I glanced at Valera. He was standing like a schoolboy whose grades were being discussed by his teachers.

"We're a bit different," I said. "I tend to break the rules, and Valera keeps more to the straight and narrow. It's good when partners complement each other."

"It's good that he keeps to the straight and narrow, like you say, and that you're a rule-breaker. I like that. As to luck, listen to me, young man. I tell you from experience, you've got to be good to be lucky."

Valera's dad was set to go on for a bit longer, but Zorky had been awarded a penalty shot near the visitors' goal. Yenisei set up a wall, a Krasnogorsk player took a vicious curving shot, the ball soared over the wall and slipped into the far corner. The goalie leapt desperately off his skates, but he had been beaten.

"That's the second one for you," the old man shouted to me in a high falsetto, as though I had ever doubted that Zorky could score twice. He then hugged me and kept hugging everyone while the Yenisei goalie, who had come down hard to the unforgiving surface of the ice, was being helped to the locker room.

Boris tapped one of our vodka bottles and pulled out a few small glasses. He filled them up and passed them around.

"I needed that," Valera's dad declared after downing his. "I was getting cold."

With so many eager hands extended from the stands toward Boris, and Boris passing the glasses to everyone who wanted them, the first bottle was finished in no time.

"How do you like it?" Valera asked Boris. "It's a great game."

"It's not bad," Boris conceded. "Very fast. But not as dynamic as the Canadian game, of course. And it's cold out here. And dark. And too far to travel for just a game."

As to Sveta, she got into it right away. She rooted for Yenisei because, she told us, she always rooted for the underdog.

"What if Yenisei scored three times all of a sudden?" Boris asked her laughing, kidding her. "Would you consider switching your loyalties?"

"I don't know," Sveta shrugged sweetly. "Probably not. They're from Siberia, they're three thousand kilometers from home, and they have none of their fans here. They need my support."

"God forbid they score," Vasily said, downing a second shot of vodka. "We need every point."

Unfortunately for the home fans, Boris proved prophetic. The visitors got on the board, making Sveta scream with delight. Her screams were met with boos and catcalls and hostile glances toward our group.

Before halftime, the teams exchanged goals. First Zorky went up 3 to 1, but then Yenisei cut the difference in half. Zorky was still up when the teams repaired to their heated locker rooms for a well-deserved rest.

While Valera and Boris went to the bathroom, I stayed behind to help Sveta unpack and lay out the food. We sliced the bread and cut the sausage. While Sveta was putting the two ingredients together to make sandwiches, I pulled out boiled eggs and potatoes. Sveta was very skilled with the knife, but then it was, of course, her profession. After the orphanage, she went to the retail trade vocational school for a year, and had been working at a grocery store ever since.

In the bitter cold, our sausage had hardened to the consistency of vulcanized rubber, and could only be chewed with a generous mouthful of hot tea from thermoses, which everyone had in abundance.

While we were alone, Sveta began thanking me for introducing her to Boris.

"He's so wonderful, if you only knew. So sweet and gentle – but a real man, too. Tough and stubborn when he wants to be."

I shrugged.

"I didn't do a thing," I said. "He's not even a friend, just a new neighbor."

"Still. I never thought I'd meet someone like that. Someone—" she stumbled for a second. "Someone so perfect."

Sveta was just like Tosya. Voicing such feelings didn't come naturally to her.

"That's great," I said. "But I really had nothing to do with it. The two of you met and fell in love. It's an accident that you happened to meet at our party."

"Maybe we were meant for each other," she said. "Maybe it wasn't an accident after all."

I grinned. Once she had overcome her aversion to saying sappy sentimental things, she had apparently decided to go all the way.

Our picnic was a great success. Valera's friends munched on our sandwiches and drank our beer and vodka, and they all flirted with Sveta – not only because there were few other women in the stands, but also because she was young and genuinely pretty and glowing with her newly found love. I'd noted that before: whenever a woman falls in love, she immediately attracts other admirers. Love is like misfortune. It never travels alone.

They were regular guys, Valera's hometown buddies – blue collar guys with down-to-earth manners. Sveta was used to that sort of courtship and brushed off their lewd remarks with practiced ease. She was carefully saving food for Valera and Boris to make sure we didn't run out.

The two of them were taking their time in the bathroom. When they finally returned, they looked like they had had a fight. They were mad at each other, and Valera, sighing deeply, whispered to me something about people who couldn't sit back and enjoy a game without criticizing everything.

Boris ignored Valera's theatrical whisper.

"What, no more cheese left?" he asked Sveta sharply.

"I'm sorry," she replied. "Pavel and I saved you a smoked sausage sandwich. I thought you liked it."

"I hate smoked sausage, and you know that very well, woman."

"I'm sorry, darling. I didn't know you wanted cheese."

"Well, now you do. But it's evidently too late."

Valera's friends had finished all our sandwiches and only the food they had contributed was left, spread out on a piece of old newspaper. Boris surveyed it with disgust.

"I get it now," he said slowly. "You gave them my cheese sandwiches and got a pile of shit in exchange."

Using the tips of his fingers, he picked up the corner of an old newspaper and tossed it on the ground.

"What made you think I was going to eat other guys' scraps."

"I'm sorry, darling," Sveta repeated.

Heads started to turn even though the second half had already started. However, at that moment Zorky scored again, and they all jumped up and began to cheer, forgetting all about Boris and his nastiness. Valera joined in the cheering, whereas Boris turned away and spat on the ground. He seemed to have lost all interest in the game.

"It's damn cold out here," he growled. "I knew I was going to freeze my ass off."

Sveta ran up to him, an open thermos bottle in hand.

"Here, darling, have some hot tea."

Boris grabbed the thermos out of her hand. He took a sip and spat it out at once.

"It's boiling hot, you idiot. I burned myself."

Sveta tried to explain that she was going to warn him had he not—

"Oh, do me a favor, woman, shut your trap."

For the rest of the game, Boris drank vodka, mixing it with beer and commented on the stupidity of the game in nasty asides. He vented his foul mood on Sveta at every opportunity.

It was as though the old Boris, the one who had met us in our new apartment and with whom I had had a run-in, had made an unannounced return during halftime.

This new-old Boris ended up driving Sveta to tears. She actually started to cry – something I had never seen a person from an orphanage do – when he leaned over and slapped her face.

It happened after Yenisei had first tied the score and then, with two minutes left, had pulled ahead, 5-4, on an individual effort by their star player and the league's top scorer Nikolai Durakov.

Sveta, who was still rooting for the visitors, couldn't resist jumping up and down, shouting, "Did you see that? Did you see that? He was like a figure skater. He went around their entire team! What a goal! Go Yenisei!"

Her outburst was met with dead silence from her former admirers. Since she absolutely had to release her enthusiasm, she first tried to hug Valera, who was sitting next to her, and then threw her arms around Boris, kissing him on the mouth.

That was when he slapped her.

"Shut the fuck up," he said loudly.

Valera's buddies were crestfallen by the changing fortunes on the field, and they hated Sveta for rooting for Yenisei, but they couldn't tolerate a man beating a woman in their town.

"Hey, buddy, take it easy," said a big fellow whose embroidered Ukrainian shirt showed through the open front of his winter coat. "You can beat the shit out of your woman at home if she lets you. You're in public here, so behave yourself."

"Aw, go fuck yourself, you and your shithole town."

Boris was drunk – a sordid and unhappy kind of drunk, with aggression glowing in his eyes.

The Krasnogorsk guys weren't easily put off. When we came out of the stadium and started toward the main road and the bus stop, a group of them caught up with us. The huge Ukrainian led the way. He looked even bigger in the dark, and he meant business.

"Hey, come over here," the Ukrainian called out to Boris. "I'm going to beat you up."

It wasn't my business how Boris treated Sveta if she let him do it – and especially if she thought he was the Prince Charming of the State Security establishment. And I wouldn't have minded if the local guys had socked him in the eye. But the moment their leader led with threats, I knew it wasn't going to happen. It's always one or the other. You either throw a punch or talk tough.

Boris knew that, too.

"Listen you, shithead," he said quietly, advancing on the Ukrainian along the narrow footpath. "If you don't turn around and go home this second, you and your band of clowns will be very sorry. This is advice, not a threat. I'm counting to three."

The Ukrainian was about to say something, but Valera intervened.

"You'd better go home, Taras," he said, sounding conciliatory. "And you too, guys."

He lowered his voice and added, "He knows what he's talking about. He's KGB, you know. So go home, please."

It was as though they were instantly deflated of the air that had puffed them up. They stood around for a moment, shuffling their work boots on the dirty snow and trying to pretend they were not intimidated. Then one after the other they turned and headed back. A dozen dark, dejected silhouettes stretched out in a long line against the white snow. The windows of their factory glared red in the background.

His buddies gone, Taras lingered.

"So, you're with them now, Valera," he said bitterly. "Once a cop always a cop."

In an instant, Boris was upon him. He kneed the giant in the groin and then threw a savage uppercut that caught him on the chin. Blood began to run down the embroidered front of his shirt. The kid groaned and sunk into the snow. Boris barely looked down at him, turned around, and headed for the bus stop.

"Let's go," he tossed at Sveta over his shoulder, and then, a moment later, when she didn't move, "Are you coming or what?"

"I think I'll go check on my Dad," Valera said reluctantly. He was shuffling his feet the way his childhood buddies had done a moment ago. "He hasn't been feeling so well lately."

The prospect of spending an hour on the train with Boris and Sveta held no appeal.

"I'll stay with you," I said, turning to Valera. "I'll catch a later train. We've got some work stuff to discuss."

"As you wish," Boris shrugged and resumed walking. Sveta hesitated for a moment and then started after him. The headlights of a bus appeared on the road, rushing toward Krasnogorsk and the train station, and Boris picked up the pace. Sveta broke into a run to keep up.

We waited to give Taras time to get up, shake off the snow, and get about a hundred paces ahead of us. We stood in silence. Neither of us wanted to discuss Boris and his nasty behavior.

Valera spoke first when we started walking.

"That man you told me about," he said.

"Which man?" I asked, even though I knew perfectly well who he meant.

"I mean Alexei Zolotnitsky, Olga Khokhlova's first husband."

"Oh, yes. What about him?"

"Are you sure he's not the one we're looking for? It is all very suspicious. Surely he must be the one who organized the burglary."

"How did you figure that out?"

"Come on. He's the only one who knew she had the cross. And the only one who would have a motive to steal it. Given that she had all that other, more valuable jewelry in her suite."

I waited a few moments before replying.

"You know, Valera, I think you're absolutely right. Why didn't I think of it myself?"

That made Valera happy. He knew he was smarter than me, and he liked it when I admitted it.

"So that solves all our problems," I continued. "We just need to find him."

"I looked," he said. "He's not in our archive."

"We should ask Comrade Andropov for access to KGB files. If he's a former White officer, he's certain to be there."

"He's not there either" Valera said.

That was a revelation. So I was right. My partner had a direct line to the KGB chief behind my back. I chose not to comment on that interesting piece of information.

"That makes things more complicated," I said.

We walked on in silence. I was thinking about the implications of Valera's connection to Andropov and what it meant for our further cooperation. I didn't know what Valera was thinking about. We passed the factory and entered the neighborhood of old wooden houses interspersed with five-story apartment buildings recently constructed to house workers. Neither Taras nor any of his friends were anywhere in sight.

"This is where my Dad lives," Valera said, stopping by one of the newer buildings. "He got an apartment here just before he retired. It's small, but it's plenty big for him and my sister. Our Mom is dead. Do you want to come up?"

I thanked him and said that it was getting late, and that I wanted to get back. Valera was going to stay with his Dad and catch an early train into the city.

"Hey, Pavel," he called out to me when I turned to go. "Maybe you should spend some time looking for Zolotnitsky, too. You're resourceful, and you do that sort of thing quite well."

"I'm lucky, too," I responded without breaking my stride. "But they took me off the case, and I don't want to get into any more trouble."

## THIRTY-SIX

It was a strange thing, the more Andropov kept warning me to stay away from Olga, the greater need I had to see her. I was getting to be quite a pro at avoiding the wall of security he had built around her.

The Karl Marx monument was a large grey chunk of rough-hewn granite tapering toward the top and, as it did so, it morphed into the shape of the founder of scientific communism. It stood in the middle of a small park across the street from the Bolshoi and next to the Metropole. The park was always well-tended, and after every snowstorm, the snow was promptly gathered into tidy mounds by sturdy old women in grey quilted jackets. After all, it was one of the country's high-visibility public spaces. However, it tended to be empty even in spring and summer, except for a couple or two on park benches cooing in the monument's imposing shadow. It was a perfect location from which to observe the hotel entrance. The problem was that this is what two of Andropov's men also did from there, on a round the clock basis.

One of them walked next to me for a couple of minutes as I rolled Nikola's carriage early the next morning around the Karl Marx monument.

"It's nice to see a father taking a walk with his baby," the man said. "Is it a boy or a girl?"

"Hush," I replied in a whisper. "It's a boy. You'll wake him up. I barely managed to get him to sleep."

He glanced into the carriage. There was nothing to see there except a bundle of wool blankets with a pair of shiny nostrils sticking out into the air.

"How old?" the man asked.

"Almost three months."

"I've got a one year-old at home. A girl."

I nodded, rocking the carriage gently as we walked.

"Look how you've swaddled him," he observed after a minute. "And it's not even that cold outside."

"I know," I said, still keeping my voice down. "His mother wouldn't let him out any other way. He's just getting over a cold, and she's down with it. Usually she takes him out."

Andropov's man nodded and went to rejoin his partner. Indeed, it wasn't that cold out, but they had been on duty all night and looked frozen.

I was glad he hadn't decided to carry his inspection so far as to lift the blanket off the baby's face. Because if he had, he would have seen the red porcelain cheeks and the chipped chin of my little sister's doll Sonya. My dad had brought it back from East Prussia the last time he came to visit from the front. Mom was pregnant then and Dad really wanted a girl, and so he brought back a beautiful porcelain doll the size of a two-month old baby, with blonde hair and blue eyes that opened and closed. He must have picked it up somewhere as they were fighting their way west. He would get his wish, because Mom had Natashka, but Dad got killed before she was born. Sonya was her favorite toy when she was growing up. Actually, her only toy. Then, when Natashka disappeared on the day Stalin was buried, Mom couldn't look at the doll without tears welling up in her eyes. She wanted to give it away, but I couldn't bear to part with it. I saved it and I thought that if Tosya and I had had a girl, Sonya would go to her. And now the doll had come in handy.

Earlier that morning Tosya and I had had a fight. When I suggested that I would take Nikola for a long walk, she had stared at me suspiciously.

"Where are you going to take him?"

"To the park around the Karl Marx monument," I replied reluctantly.

"Why all of a sudden?"

"Well," I admitted. "I have a surveillance job to do. The baby will provide the cover."

Tosya went off like a stick of dynamite.

"Have you lost your mind?" she shouted. "There is no way in Hell you'll use your own son in some stupid surveillance job. Never in your life. Forget it."

"But there's no danger," I objected. "No danger at all. It's routine surveillance."

It was impossible to reason with her

"No way, Pavel. Do you hear me? Never. You'll have to kill me first."

"Come on," I said. "Why are you so mad?"

"If you don't understand why, it's useless to explain."

She went out of the room muttering under her breath, shaking her head in disbelief. I was glad Boris wasn't there to overhear our argument. Recently, he had been spending most of his time in Sveta's room on the outskirts of the city.

In the end, I persuaded Tosya to let me use Nikola's carriage, into which we placed Sonya, swaddling her thoroughly in Nikola's blankets. I took the carriage on the bus, trying to maneuver its bulk through the rush hour crowd. Fortunately, even the normally rude Muscovites turn sweet and helpful when they see a baby. Especially if the baby is with a clumsy, good-for-nothing dad.

I felt guilty deceiving them like that and taking advantage of their kindness.

Sonya and I arrived at the Metropole at ten minutes to ten, expecting a short wait. Nights were long in winter, and the sky had only recently been brightened by daylight. The sun, still hidden behind the tall buildings, was sending pink rays into the clouds over the towers and belfries of the Kremlin.

Ten o'clock came and went, and nothing happened. The clouds dissipated, and the sun rose on its low wintry trajectory, creating an elaborate play of lights and shadows on the mosaic façade of the Metropole, and sending sparkling needles into the mounds of fresh snow between black tree trunks.

I waited for another half hour, and my clever ploy with the carriage was starting to backfire. There wasn't a loving father anywhere in the universe willing to roll his sleeping baby round and round the Karl Marx monument for so long. Had Andropov's men not ended their shift and been replaced by two identical ones, their suspicions would certainly have been aroused. I was about to give up when the familiar black Volga limousine made a sharp illegal turn across the avenue and came to a screeching halt in front of the hotel.

It was twenty-five minutes to eleven and, by the look of it, Andropov's driver Ivan was late picking up Olga. I had to hurry if I hoped to intercept her before she got into her car. And even that would have had to happen in plain view of Mustafa the doorman, who no doubt had been instructed to report to the KGB chief if I ever tried to approach Olga again.

That was when having the carriage became a liability. Dispensing with my original plan and shedding the carefully cultivated image of a loving father, I parked it behind Karl Marx's granite bulk and, under the horrified stare of an older passer-by, crossed the street on the run. Slowing down in front of the hotel entrance, I peeked into the lobby as though I was seeing it for the first time and tried to look suitably impressed.

In the end, it turned out that I had timed my run perfectly without even trying. Mustafa pushed the revolving door open, and Olga stepped out into the street. I didn't even have to break my stride to walk beside her. Speaking softly, I asked her where she was going to be that evening.

She reacted quickly.

"At the Bolshoi. Why?"

"I need to see you. How can I do it?"

"Get there at eight thirty," she said. "I'll meet you by the coat check. I'm going back to Paris tomorrow."

I stopped, letting her get ahead. Ivan was out of the car, holding the door open for her. I pulled out a cigarette, then patted my pockets for matches. I inhaled deeply, listening to my own heartbeat.

A man now stepped out of the hotel and brushed past me. Despite the cold, he was wearing no overcoat. Tall and bulky, he walked with the awkward gate of a weightlifter, pushing his massive chest forward. I recognized him once he stopped and turned his face toward me. I couldn't think of his name, but I knew it was the KGB colonel in charge of Metropole security. His face could not be mistaken as anyone else's: a long ugly scar ran down its length from the left temple past the corner of the mouth, then came to a point at the chin.

He had been nice to me at our previous meeting, but now his disfigured face was twisted with rage. He must have caught my brief exchange with Olga, even though he couldn't have overheard the words.

"You again?" he hissed, his one eye flashing.

Olga got into the car. Ivan slammed the door and turned toward me.

"Get into the passenger seat," he said. "I'm taking you to my boss."

Under the circumstances, the best thing for me to do was to pretend I hadn't heard him. I turned around and began crossing the street back to the Karl Marx monument. Big Mustafa took a couple of steps after me, and I thought we were in for an ugly fight in front of a hard currency hotel. But Ivan stopped him with a dismissive wave of his hand, "Let him go. He won't get away."

He had a point. There was nowhere to hide from the KGB.

## THIRTY-SEVEN

It was seven o'clock, and the performance was about to start. The square was bright with lights, the snow glistened yellow under the streetlamps, and I was carried by a well-dressed crowd flowing around the base of the famous Bolshoi colonnade in a cloud steaming from breath, cigarette smoke and perfume.

"What is the performance tonight?" I asked the girl at the box office.

She gave me a contemptuous smile. I had come by motorbike, riding through the half-melted mixture of salt and sand that winter roads can turn into. Plus, I had had a minor breakdown near Pokrovka Gate that I had been able to fix, but which had left my coat splattered with mud and my hands black with grime. Certainly with my oil-stained face and wet hair I looked out of place in that festive environment.

"You mean you don't know?" she asked, her voice dripping with snobbery. "It's Glinka. *Ivan Susanin*. It's an opera theater, in case you're curious. They mostly sing there. You'd probably be bored."

She was just a kid, putting on the supercilious airs of a theater professional. But she was fresh-faced and sweet, and you just couldn't get angry with her.

"I'm not going in," I said, winking at her. "I'm going to a steam bath with a bunch of buddies. But I want to have a ticket stub to show my mother-in-law when she asks me where I spent the evening. Give me the cheapest seat you got."

She didn't find this the least bit funny. She must have thought I was serious, seeing that I didn't, in fact, go into the foyer once I purchased my ticket and pocketed the change, but headed back into the street. I was afraid she thought even less of me.

It had started to snow, but the temperature had risen and the thick, wet flakes were not dancing in the light of the streetlamps but coming straight down, heavily, melting almost before they hit the ground.

I turned the corner and had to draw back sharply to avoid running into Olga and Andropov. Their Volga limousine stopped at the side of the building, by the special entry reserved for guests of honor. Ivan jumped out and, opening an umbrella, jogged around to the passenger side. He held the door for Andropov first, keeping the umbrella over his boss's head. Spry as a young boy, Andropov was out of his seat and helping Olga, who had started to get out of the back seat without waiting for anyone's assistance. Ivan now held the umbrella over both of them, walking a step behind until they got to the door. He then folded the umbrella and went back to the car, ignoring the snow.

An hour and a half later – time I spent drinking coffee and chain-smoking at a café on Gorky Street, where I had also reserved a quiet table for two for later that evening – I was back at the Bolshoi, my cheap ticket in hand.

The ticket taker was a middle-aged veteran. She had seen all kinds of theater-goers in her time, and she didn't judge them by the kind of clothes they wore. My disheveled appearance, which I had been able to improve only marginally in the café bathroom, made her compassionate, not disdainful.

"You're very late, young man," she said. "It's the middle of the second act, and I'm afraid they won't seat you until second intermission."

"It's not a problem," I replied. "I know the story. I'll wait over by the coat check."

The music was almost as loud in the foyer as in the theater. For a while, it sounded as though the chorus on the stage was worried about something, male and female voices twining in anxiety. Then a baritone became threatening, and was answered by a tenor. However, in the end the danger appeared to have been averted and everything ended on a happy note. There was a lot of clapping, and the audience began to file out. Women and young people ran toward the snack bar, quickly forming a line. Equally long, but not as joyful, was the line to the rest rooms, while smokers rushed down the dimly lit stairway to the basement smoking lounge.

"You had better check your coat and get to your seat," the ticket taker reminded me, seeing that I was still standing by the coat check, doing nothing. "You're all the way up in the fourth circle."

I nodded just as I spotted Olga.

I knew she was a clever woman. I had no doubt she'd be able to get away from her companion, even though he was the all-powerful chief of the KGB. My heart began to beat faster. Even though I had planned it all out, we needed to act quickly and hope that our luck would hold.

"I'm glad I've been able to see you before I leave." She was almost shouting in order to be heard over the hum of many voices filling the foyer. "But we don't have much time. I've got to get back."

"I was going to ask you to come with me," I said.

"Is it going to be another adventure?"

"Yes, I believe so. Let's get your coat."

I headed toward the coat check, where there was a small line of people leaving early.

"Wait. I don't have it here. We're in the Imperial Box. That's where I left my coat."

Damn, I hadn't thought about that.

"You'll have to put on mine," I said. "It's warm and it's better to wear it, anyway, when you ride a motorcycle in this weather."

She stared at me.

"Are you serious? Are we going to take a ride? Where are we going?"

"I'll explain in a moment," I said. "We've got to go."

"Let's go then," Olga said readily. "I'm game."

"You won't be able to re-enter later if you leave now, comrades," the ticket taker told us. "And you're crazy to be going out without your coat. It's February."

"Don't worry," Olga replied to her. "You don't know me. I'm used to the cold."

We stopped under the colonnade, and I took off my coat.

"Put it on," I said.

It wasn't very cold, but the air was humid and heavy, and a chill was blowing in the wet wind.

"I left my boots upstairs," she said. "My good shoes will get ruined. Oh, never mind. Let's go."

I turned around to make sure we weren't followed and spotted the box office girl. Her shift must have just ended, and she was coming out of the theater. Seeing me helping a tall, distinguished-looking lady into my ratty coat froze her in the door, and she stood staring at us until someone trying to get past her shoved her out of the way.

My Zundapp was parked on the side of the Maly Theater.

"Is this what we're going to ride?" Olga asked. "What a magnificent pile of junk."

"Don't insult it," I said. "It's World War II. German. It runs like a song."

I helped her into the sidecar and covered her with a few layers of old blankets, and we were off.

"Where are we going?" she shouted through the roar of the engine.

"To the Leningrad Station," I replied, also at the top of my voice.

"Are we going to Leningrad?"

"No. We're meeting someone who's coming to Moscow."

I had acted fast after seeing Olga that morning. I had to. We were running out of time. The first thing I did was phone Leningrad. Zolotnitsky was out on his usual rounds at the Summer Garden, but I was lucky to get Emilia at home. I asked her to get Zolotnitsky and to put him on the next express train to Moscow. An hour and a half later she called back to report that he was on the train, scheduled to arrive at half past nine.

We got to the Leningrad Station a quarter of an hour early. Olga cast a nervous look around.

"This is the St. Petersburg Station. I remember it well. It hasn't changed all that much. Except for that thing."

She pointed to the marble bust of Lenin in the middle of the vast, rectangular hallway.

"It wasn't here in my time, of course."

"I assume you have guessed who we're about to see, Olga Stepanovna," I said.

A shudder ran through her body. She gave me a brief nod.

"You wanted to see Alexei Zolotnitsky, Olga Stepanovna," I said softly. "He'll be here in a few minutes."

She shook her head.

"I don't know," she said slowly. "It's not nice of you to spring it on me like this. I needed to be prepared."

"But you do want to see him, don't you?"

"I do, of course. Very much so," she replied. "But I don't want him to see me. The way I am now. In this leather coat. I must look ridiculous."

I grinned.

"That's pretty much what he said to me about seeing you."

"Well, it's a natural reaction. You can't blame either of us for thinking this way."

"Sure," I said. "Except while you were living in Paris, he was doing hard labor in Magadan."

Suddenly, she was scared.

"Does he really look awful? Do you think he'll resent me for having it so easy?"

"I doubt it," I said. "But you should prepare yourself to see someone who's a physical wreck compared to people like you. You should also know that he's an invalid. He lost an arm in the camp. You shouldn't show surprise or aversion. It would upset him very much if you did."

"I'll try," she said.

She turned away and was silent until the Leningrad express was announced.

"Yes, you're right," she said. "It's stupid of me to worry about my own looks."

A few moments later, Zolotnitsky appeared at the end of the hallway. He cut a dissonant figure among the prosperous passengers who travelled by the Leningrad express. He was walking with a limp, and the empty left sleeve of his coat was tucked into his belt, the way I had seen him before.

"Oh, my Lord," Olga muttered under her breath.

He saw her too, and there was suddenly a spring in his step. He was trying hard to hide his limp as he approached us. They were a strange pair, a small man dressed in hand-me-down clothes that made him look like a beggar, and she, much taller than he, elegant and beautiful, with a string of pearls around her neck. She managed to make even my leather coat look elegant. They stood still for a second, and then she stepped forward and hugged him. He too put his arm around her and they kissed.

It was as though the entire station gasped, not knowing what to think. Everyone stopped in their tracks and stared. Not me, however. I turned away and went to look at the magazine covers on the back of the newspaper kiosk. I read every word on every cover, and when I turned around ten minutes later, the two lovers were still kissing.

## THIRTY-EIGHT

"Oh, my Lord, it's a Zundapp," Zolotnitsky exclaimed as we approached my motorbike. "I haven't seen one in years. The last one I saw was in Berlin in—"

He caught himself. He came up to the motorbike and patted the synthetic rubber of its seat. He bent down to examine the engine. He used his mouth to pull the knitted mitten off his one hand, and his long elegant fingers ran over its parts as though he was trying out a piano.

"Not too bad, not bad at all," he kept muttering under his breath. "Taking into account its age and lack of competent service. What a nicely engineered machine. So simple and yet so elegant."

The inspection, in its precision and competence, was a work of art. I made a note to consult him next time something went wrong with the bike.

Olga was starting to shiver in her wet pumps.

"We don't have much time right now," I said.

"Yes, of course, I'm sorry," he said hurriedly, cutting short his inspection and straightening up. "I tend to forget myself around those internal combustion things."

Next, I tried to pack him into the sidecar.

"No," he said firmly. "The lady gets the sidecar. Don't worry about me, officer. I can hold on with one hand. I used to be a pretty good horseman in my time."

"Where are we going?" Olga asked.

"I'll take you to a café on Gorky Street," I said. "You'll have a quiet corner where you'll be able to talk."

Zolotnitsky screamed with delight once we took off. I hadn't expected so much enthusiasm for riding a motorbike from a worn-down invalid.

"I love bikes," he shouted in my ear. "I never thought I'd get another ride in this life. And on a Zundapp, no less."

We stopped at the light before turning into Kalanchevka. I turned and took a quick look at Olga. She had her eyes on Zolotnitsky, and they shone with joy. She loved seeing him, and she loved seeing him so excited about the motorcycle ride.

I turned into Orlikov Lane, crossed Garden Ring and on to Kirov Street. The rush hour had ended a long time ago, and the road was clear. I gave it a bit of gas, and we zoomed toward Boulevard Ring, splattering melting snow in all directions. We were in a rush, after all, and I wanted the old man to get even more enjoyment.

"It's changed a lot," Zolotnitsky shouted again as we crossed the Boulevard Ring. "Even since the mid-fifties. Before the revolution it was an exciting place to be. A lot more happening here than in St. Petersburg."

"And now?" I shouted into the wind.

"What now?"

"Is anything going on in Leningrad?"

"Nothing. It's a museum."

He continued a few minutes later, while we were stopped at a light again. "Moscow was getting elegant before the war. The Great War, I mean. It had plenty of style. Not so much now, I'm sorry to say. St. Petersburg was the Empire, and it was always boring. Moscow looks ridiculous when it tries to be like St. Petersburg."

I accelerated past the main post office on the left and my old apartment building on the right. Zolotnitsky shouted something, but I couldn't hear him over the roar of the engine and the headwind.

I had to slow down again as we entered the traffic circle on Dzerzhinsky Square.

"So this is the famous Lubyanka," he shouted. "I've seen a lot of it, but never from the outside. And rarely above ground."

He laughed and gave me a poke in the ribs, as though being interrogated at the Lubyanka prison had been the funniest thing under the sun. I didn't find it funny at all. Considering that someone – and possibly even KGB chief Yuri Andropov himself – was looking for him and had cleverly arranged for me to find him, it wasn't out of the realm of possibility that he might end up there yet again.

I took a shortcut down Pushechnaya Street on the side of the Children's World department store – not so much to avoid passing by the Bolshoi where Andropov was probably still sitting in the Emperor's box, wondering what had happened to Madame Khokhlova, but to save time. Within two minutes, we were on Gorky Street off Pushkin Square, at the café where I had already spent part of the evening.

They sat down at the table, still flushed and frostbitten from the ride, but now suddenly oblivious to everything around them. They stared at each other for what seemed like an eternity.

"Should I order something for you?" I asked. They didn't reply. They didn't even hear me.

"You're still beautiful, Olenka," Zolotnitsky said at last.

"Please, Lyosha, we're too old for compliments."

She reached out across the small table, took his hand in hers, and raised it to her lips.

I left them there and went outside. I smoked a cigarette and watched the trolley car pass by, still full of passengers. Looking over my shoulder, I could see them through the plate glass window, talking excitedly and waving away the waiter when he came over to take their order. I went back in – I was getting wet under the steady snowfall – and asked the waiter to get them coffee and ice cream. They thanked him when he put the order on the table but didn't touch anything, leaving the ice cream to melt in its metal serving dish.

All other tables were taken – and a line had started to form outside.

"What are you, some kind of a chauffeur?" the doorman asked me.

I nodded.

"Is she your boss's wife?"

He pointed to Olga. Doormen at such places were even more nosy than old ladies who spent their days sitting on benches in Moscow courtyards, with nothing better to do than gossip about other tenants. I nodded again in reply, not feeling the need to give him an exhaustive account of who Olga Khokhlova really was.

"A fine looking woman," he said. "If only my Dusya looked like that, I wouldn't be chasing skirts like I do. But she looks like shit even though she's fifteen years younger than your boss's wife. I wonder what she has to do with the old invalid.

I shrugged.

"I do, too."

I gave them another twenty minutes and went over to say that Olga had to go back if she hoped to salvage the situation. I was thinking of myself, too. If she wasn't at the theater when the performance ended and they started to look for her, Andropov would get my description from the ticket taker and would know who was responsible for Olga's disappearance. My job at Criminal Investigations would be lost, but that would be the least of my troubles. It might be me, not Zolotnitsky, who would next see the inside of the Lubyanka prison.

"And you, too," I told Zolotnitsky. "You've got a train to catch."

I didn't want him to hang around Moscow. And, with Boris as a neighbor, I was wary of letting him spend the night in my place.

They hugged in silence. As they locked arms in a tender embrace, there was a lot of similarity between them. What was it? Breeding? Upbringing? Human decency?

Their shoulders were heaving, and I thought at first that they were weeping. But when they raised their faces toward me, they were convulsed by laughter.

"And at the cemetery, remember?" she exclaimed.

"How can I forget?" he responded, his voice going into a higher register and becoming almost a squeak as he giggled like a schoolgirl. "Reinickendorf, the Russian graveyard."

"The Church of Saints Constantine and Helena? That was where you kissed me that time."

"Nonsense," he objected. "It was you who kissed me first."

They roared with laughter.

"Don't mind us," Olga explained, wiping her eyes. "We're just a pair of *vieillards* talking about the olden days. Two very old people. Yes, we were young once, too. Young enough to kiss. It was back in '39, just before the war broke out. Alexei did kiss me first, and it was right in front of the elder Nabokov's tombstone."

Zolotnitsky shook his head.

"Fine, let it be the way you tell it. I never went back there. I thought of going there a lot during the war years. Of going to the church to pray. Except I no longer knew how to pray, and war is not a good time for praying. The cemetery is in the Western zone now. It would be easy for you to visit. Think of me if you do."

She grew serious.

"I've got to go," she said, suddenly matter-of-fact.

They hugged again, briefly this time and not laughing. He pushed her away, and she made a sign of the cross over him.

The doorman stared. He wasn't used to customers being religious. It wasn't done in the Soviet Union.

We dropped Olga off first, in front of the Bolshoi. There was no more hugging. She gave Alexei a nod and thanked me before stepping into the shadow under the colonnade.

"I'm glad I met you," she said. "You made my stay here halfway bearable. I hope you're not going to get into too much trouble on my account."

Alexei was quiet all the way back to the Leningrad Station. I was still driving fast, even though we had time to spare until his train.

"I never thought you could go back to the past," he said when we got to the station. "I've had so many pasts, and they are all gone, without a trace. Except for Olga. My past with her keeps popping up. Come to think of it, our past together is all I have. The early years before the war and Revolution, the Civil War, Paris, Berlin. And now here. Thank you, officer. I know it wasn't you who organized this meeting. Divine Providence did, using you as its instrument, but thank you all the same. I'm forever in your debt."

I shrugged. We had arrived early, and we had time before the train was to leave.

"It's a nice feeling, to be an instrument of Divine Providence," I said. "But if you want to repay me, perhaps you could do me a good turn, too."

"Me?" He was surprised. "What could I possibly do for you?"

"You can tell me why anyone might be after you. You must have some idea who's looking for you and who's so eager to find you that they sent a burglar to Madame Khokhlova's suite at the Metropole and then murdered two people."

"You're right, officer. I do. It's another one of my pasts, and it once again involves Olga, if only tangentially. But it's a long story."

"We have time," I said.

"There was a painting, *The Muse*. Olga's portrait by Pablo Picasso. One of the most famous paintings in the world. She gave it to me when she came to see me in Berlin in 1939. I'm sure I killed the two men who were after it, but perhaps there had been others, their associates, that I wasn't aware of at the time."

## THIRTY-NINE

The war ended, and Berlin was divided into four occupation zones. Alexei Zolotnitsky concealed his Russian nationality – or rather, he continued living under his grandmother's name, which he had assumed since coming to Berlin more than a decade before.

It had been a wise decision both under the Nazis and, especially, under the Soviets. He had seen Soviet political police arrest and repatriate Russian women who had been brought to Germany and made to work at his factory. It wasn't their fault – they had done what they were told by the Germans, and if they had refused they would have been shot or sent to a concentration camp. He had been friendly with some of them during the war and had brought them food and medicines on the sly. And now, after they had been supposedly liberated by their own Red Army, they were sent home under armed guard and in cattle cars. He had heard also about Soviet prisoners of war charged with treason for the crime of not dying on the battlefield, and allowing themselves to be captured.

Being a German engineer contributing to the German war effort was bad enough. Being a former Russian national working for the Germans and carrying a German passport would have been suicidal.

He was pretty sure he could get away with it. The munitions plant where he worked was being dismantled and packaged for shipment to the Urals. He, along with other engineering staff, had been told by the Soviet authorities to help with the dismantling. He planned to cross over to the French or American sector the moment the work was finished.

All those plans went awry when two men in Soviet military uniform showed up on his doorstep. One was an older man and had a major's single star on his epaulets. He was well-mannered and suave, but Alexei took an immediate dislike to his fake smile and creepy friendliness. He had the bearings of a scoundrel. The other was a burly young kid in the rank of junior lieutenant. Both had blue borders on their peaked hats, which Alexei would come to know well. It was the color of the NKVD.

The major addressed him in French, calling him by his Russian name.

"*Pour l'amour du Dieu, M. Zolotnitsky*," he protested when Alexei, responding in Russian, asked him whether they had come to arrest him. "How can you say that? We're your compatriots. We're Russians, not Gestapo. Why should we arrest you? Is there any reason that we don't know?"

Ever since he came to Berlin more than ten years before, Alexei had lived in a room in a large apartment, sharing it with his landlady and several of her other boarders. Every other building on the street had been bombed and then damaged further by artillery fire during the Russian assault on the city and the hand-to-hand combat in its streets. Their building suffered too, and only their first floor was still habitable.

As soon as he let them in, they turned nasty. The kid struck him in the face, knocking him down, and proceeded to kick him viciously, aiming for his head and kidneys. The major pulled out his revolver and threatened to shoot him, pressing the barrel to the back of his head, squeezing the trigger and laughing when Zolotnitsky involuntarily shuddered and pushed forward at the soft click over an empty chamber. He never got tired of the game, claiming that he had loaded his gun with a single bullet and suggesting that Zolotnitsky, as a Whites officer, had been used to playing the Russian roulette.

"Scum! Traitor!" he kept shouting. "You deserve to hang. You were living high on the hog among the Nazis, serving them, while they killed and pillaged your motherland. What did you do during the war?"

They didn't seem to know where he worked. Otherwise there would have been no end of sanctimonious wailing about the bullets he had made killing their comrades-in-arms.

"Answer me," the major shouted while the lieutenant gave him a savage kick in the stomach. "What was your occupation?"

"A teacher," he groaned gnashing his teeth.

"Teaching little Nazis to kill Russians?" the major asked.

But all that was just for show, as Alexei soon realized. It wasn't what the Russians were after. When he decided they had softened Alexei sufficiently, the major brought up Olga's portrait.

"We know you've got it. I don't see it here in the room. You'll need to fork it over. Surrender it to the motherland, and I'll let you go."

Alexei didn't believe for a second that the major wanted the painting for some Soviet art museum. The greedy gleam in his eye told Alexei that he was interested in the Picasso purely for his own personal profit. Moreover, the guy was probably contemplating an escape to the Western occupation zone, because that was where a world famous, museum-quality Picasso would fetch real value.

That was when he hatched his plan. It was a long shot, but it was worth the try. What did he have to lose? He knew the two would kill him once they got the painting. The major didn't need a witness. And the young lieutenant was going to be eliminated, too. Why share the proceeds if you could avoid that?

Alexei pretended he was scared – he wasn't really, he knew they wouldn't kill him until he gave them the painting – and started to plead for his life. He would take them where he kept the painting, but they had to promise that they wouldn't hurt him.

"I give you my word of honor," the scoundrel major declared. "The word of honor of a Soviet officer. I assume you will not doubt its validity. Now where is the painting?"

"It's not here, obviously, comrades," Zolotnitsky said. "I've been keeping it in a safe place."

They went out, watched by the frightened landlady through the crack in her door.

"Make sure he doesn't try anything funny," the major told the lieutenant. "Shoot to kill if he does."

He turned to Zolotnitsky.

"Did you hear that? We'll shoot you like a dog if you make a run for it."

That Alexei had no doubt about. Killing a German civilian wouldn't have been considered a serious offense by the Soviet authorities.

He led them through the bombed out city, where residents gathered by bonfires on street corners, drawing water seeping from ruptured pipes or eating American canned beef, past checkpoints and Russian tanks, impromptu flea markets, and Allied patrols.

After about half an hour, they reached a completely destroyed section of town. The buildings had been fire-bombed, so that nothing was left of them except a pile of rubble overgrown with new grass and young trees. Back in '43, it had been an elegant block of villas and townhouses, one of which belonged to a friend, a fellow engineer working at the same plant. Their house had burned. The engineer, his wife, and their two daughters had perished in the fire, and Zolotnitsky had been using the work space that the friend had made in his basement as his own mechanical shop. It had good tools, and he had found that working on motors, clocks, and other mechanisms was a way to keep his sanity during the final months of the war.

The added advantage had been that he didn't have to leave during air raids. The basement, with the rubble of a bombed out house on top of it, was a perfect bomb shelter.

They went down several broken, soot-covered steps, and Zolotnitsky unlocked and lifted the steel trap door he had fitted over the entrance to the basement to keep out hungry kids scavenging in bombed-out areas. All the while, the two Soviets kept close to him, pressing the barrels of their handguns against his back.

Zolotnitsky hadn't been there for a few weeks. There was now a small hole in the ceiling through which a bit of rain had gotten in. Water was sloshing under his feet, and the place smelled of mildew.

"I'm going to light a kerosene lamp," Zolotnitsky said. "We will need it to get the painting."

"Stay where you are," the major ordered him. "I've got a good flashlight. American. Don't move."

But Zolotnitsky no longer needed to. He had already seen all he wanted to see in the thin light from the hole in the ceiling and had formed a plan of action.

There was a thick steel plate lying on the floor, which he and the owner of the house had brought from the factory back in 1941, before there was a steel shortage. The man had been planning to reinforce the underside of his Horch motorcar, but it was soon requisitioned for war needs.

"Give me a hand with it, will you?" Zolotnitsky said to the young lieutenant.

The two of them tried to lift the heavy plate, struggling with it in an inch of water on the floor, but it wouldn't budge. The major stood over them, holding the powerful flashlight in one hand and a gun in the other.

"Is this where you keep your Picasso?" he inquired.

Zolotnitsky, pretending to strain under the weight of the plate, nodded.

"I just hope for your sake it didn't get ruined by rain water."

"It didn't," Zolotnitsky replied through clenched teeth. "It's safe. Believe me."

Seeing that they were making no progress, the major, a squeamish look on his face, placed the flashlight on the work table and joined in, trying to keep away from dirt so as not to stain his uniform.

Together, they succeeded in lifting the plate ever so slightly off the ground – especially since Zolotnitsky was faking the effort.

"We're going to push it out of the way," he said. "Just hold it like that."

Before either of them could figure out what was happening, he leapt to the side, snatched an ax hanging on a hook, and flung it at the major's head. It wasn't a perfect throw. The edge of the ax glanced the man's head sidelong, but it was sharp and heavy enough to still chip his skull and send him reeling against the wall. The beefy lieutenant, left alone to hold up the plate, dropped it. It smashed heavily on the floor, catching him on the toe and raising a splash of dirty rainwater. He howled in pain and, before he had time to recover, Zolotnitsky was upon him, grabbing a screwdriver and slashing his face with its sharp edge.

In just a couple of seconds, it was all over. He paused for a minute to catch his breath, then crouched in a puddle and crawled under the worktable. Glued to its underside was a flat, rectangular package carefully wrapped in oil cloth. He took it out, stuck it under his arm and climbed out into the bright summer sunshine. He thought of locking the trap door but changed his mind. If someone found something useful inside, they were welcome to it. As to the two Russians, they weren't going to crawl out of there, that's for sure.

Once outside, he stopped for a few minutes and looked around. There was rubble all around and not a living soul except a couple of cats rooting around in the distance. He inspected his clothes and used muddy water from a ditch to wash off the blood that had splattered on his safari jacket.

He had long ago made an escape plan, and now it was time to put it into operation. He went back to his room and undid the oilcloth of his package. It contained a folded canvas and another, smaller package wrapped in a length of cotton fabric. When unwrapped, it turned out to contain a wad of currency, mainly British pounds and American dollars, adding up to a substantial sum. He divided the money, put one half of it in his pocket and rewrapped the rest in fabric and, along with the canvas, into oilcloth the way it had been before. The money was for the Soviet captain in charge of dismantling the plant. Zolotnitsky needed him to sign the official form allowing him to leave the Soviet occupation zone.

It was a good plan, but he ran out of time. The same afternoon he was placed under NKVD guard. The first tranche of equipment had been loaded onto platforms to be taken to the Soviet Union, and he had been selected by the higher-up to accompany it.

That was what the captain told him. He had taken Zolotnitsky's money but professed inability to help him. Perhaps it was even true.

There was a lot of talk in the next few days about the disappearance of two Soviet officers. The major was apparently with the Allied Liaison Service and had just come from Paris. The Russians spoke freely with Zolotnitsky around, since they thought he couldn't understand them. Apparently, the two officers had gone to arrest a Russian, a former White officer. A giant manhunt had been organized in all four occupation zones, but the officer had somehow slipped through.

## FORTY

I walked Zolotnitsky to his sleeper car, and we shook hands.

"I don't think we should be in touch," I said. "I'll call you if I need you, but you should lay low for a while."

He grinned.

"It would be hard for me to lay lower than I already do," he said. "And don't worry about me. I'm not easy to kill."

I had a lot to think about when I got home, to sort out what Zolotnitsky had told me and to fit the new information into what I already knew. But my eyes were heavy with sleep, and the thoughts began tangling in my head the moment I got into bed. The case was moving toward resolution – even though I didn't expect to like the way it would be resolved, and I wasn't going to get any accolades for solving it. Rather, the other way around. But I felt good about bringing Olga and Alexei together, and I was flattered by being compared to – what exactly was it? Oh, yes, Divine Providence.

Nikola was sleeping in our bed, between me and Tosya. He shifted in his sleep and sidled closer to me.

"Is that you?" Tosya asked in her sleep. "I've got to tell you something."

"Go ahead. I'm not asleep."

"But I am, Matyushkin. Don't bother me."

"It's you who wanted to tell me something," I objected.

"Hush. You'll wake up the baby with your loud voice. We'll talk tomorrow."

As I was dozing off, I thought about Olga leaving for Paris the following morning. I was going to miss her.

It was still dark when Boris woke me up by tiptoeing through Sevka's room and shaking me by the shoulder. It was still snowing outside. The cold had returned and the snow had started to stick again, covering the bottom of our window panes.

"What's the matter? What time is it?"

I glanced at the phosphorescent face of the alarm clock ticking on the night table next to Tosya. It was almost seven.

"Get up, quickly."

I wrapped myself in a blanket and followed him to the brightly lit hallway. He was wearing pajama bottoms and an undershirt and had also been roused out of bed.

"There's a phone call for you," he said.

"Hello."

I was hoarse from sleep, and angry. I had expected to hear Valera's pedantic voice, for I suddenly remembered that we had made an appointment to meet at the office early to discuss plans for locating Zolotnitsky. Instead, there was a click, and a professional female voice came on.

"Long-distance operator," she said, identifying herself. "Leningrad calling. You have three minutes, and you've already wasted fifty seconds. You can speak now."

"Who's this?" I shouted into the receiver, suddenly awake.

Instead of a reply, I heard a loud sob.

"Emilia? What happened?"

Instead of going back to his room, Boris was standing in the hallway, not even pretending he wasn't listening. I didn't care if he did, but a wave of disgust and anger suddenly washed over me, so that I had to turn away in order to focus on what Emilia was saying. She wasn't easy to understand through her tears.

"It's Andres Karlovich," she said, making an effort to speak coherently. "I came to the station to meet him. He wasn't on the train."

It took me a few seconds to figure out who she was talking about. I had forgotten Zolotnitsky's German alias.

"I was waiting in the station, and when he didn't come out, I went to see whether he had fallen asleep or needed help," Emilia continued. "He wasn't there."

"That's strange," I said. "I definitely put him on the train. Could you have missed him?"

"No, I couldn't have, and he had definitely travelled in his compartment, no question."

"Did he share it with someone?"

"I don't know. It was empty when I got there."

"Did you talk to the conductor?"

"That's what worries me," she exclaimed. "She says she didn't see a thing and that she doesn't even remember Andres Karlovich being on the train, but she's lying. She's lying, I'm sure of it. She couldn't even look me in the eye, and when I asked her about him, she just started to yell at me. And she told me not to call the cops. She definitely knows something."

"Perhaps he got off at a stop to stretch his legs and was left behind?" I suggested.

"No he didn't," she shouted, outraged. "His compartment is soaked with blood. They killed him."

I realized that it wasn't just Zolotnitsky's disappearance that had upset her. She was, more than anything else, terribly scared.

"There is so much blood, and it wasn't even dry. Who would do such a thing to Andres Karlovich? He was such a sweet old man."

She began to cry. I was shaking when I got off the phone, but I got a grip on myself. I hoped I looked calm when I turned to face Boris. There was no point in having it out with him. He was nothing but a little wheel in a much larger machine.

"Who was it?" Tosya asked when I rushed into the room, threw down the blanket, and began to get dressed.

"I'll tell you later," I said. "I'm in a rush now."

"Just listen," she said, and what she began to tell me caught my attention.

"Boris beat up Sveta last night. Badly."

"What happened?" I asked, stopping with half a pant leg on and balancing on one foot.

"They came here yesterday afternoon, and she made supper for him, served it, they ate, and he seemed just fine. Then, someone called him on the phone, and he was a changed man after that. Everything went to hell. All of a sudden he turned on her. He started screaming. I have no idea what he thought she had done wrong. And then he started slapping her face, and she let him do it. I never thought she'd let a man hit her. She used to be such a proud girl."

I recalled the scene at the hockey match and shook my head. It always starts like that, with the thin end of the wedge.

"Then he just told her to get out. It was getting late and it was starting to snow. I told her she could stay with us, but she wouldn't. She didn't want to make Boris angry, she said, because he wanted her out of his apartment. Can you believe it?"

"She's fallen hard for him, I suppose," I said. "Love is a tough master. They'll probably reconcile."

I had finished dressing while Tosya was talking and was now about to leave.

"They probably already have," Tosya said. "Boris was upset too. The moment she left, he ran after her."

"Did she come back?"

"No, but he was out for a long time."

I stopped.

"Really?" I said. "When did he come back?"

She shrugged.

"I don't know for sure. I was tired, and I went to bed early. Taking care of the baby exhausts me."

I rushed to the other room and woke up Sevka. It was time for him to get up for school anyway.

"Do you remember when Boris came home last night?" I asked, keeping my voice down to make sure Boris wouldn't hear me.

"It was after eleven," Sevka replied after pondering my question. "That's right. I was still doing my history reading. Probably about twenty minutes before you."

## FORTY-ONE

I would not recommend going to the Vnukovo Airport by motorbike after a wet snowstorm that has frozen into a lunar landscape of ruts and ridges hidden by a fresh dusting of snow. The windshield provides protection from the biting wind, but the cold still gets deep into your clothing, stiffening your limbs and sending numbing pain into the tips of your fingers. And if you are late, you ride at full speed, passing slow-moving vehicles in the narrow median separating you from the oncoming traffic, keenly aware of how flimsy your bike feels compared to an on-rushing five-ton truck.

I arrived just in time. No sooner had I positioned myself by the outgoing passport control in the main hall than the electric schedule overhead flipped a few times to announce the Air France flight to Paris. The same information was conveyed over the loudspeaker by a melodious announcer speaking French and English, but no Russian.

A group of Soviet tourists headed toward passport control, looking nervous. They kept close, like a flock of sheep, rubbing shoulders and stepping on each other's heels. The similarity was reinforced by the presence of two men in identical, half-length shearling coats and red scarves. Their faces were identical, too, and as keen as those of two German Shepherds. Their presence on the perimeter of the group held it together, making the tourists huddle ever tighter. They were operatives from Comrade Andropov's agency going along on the trip to Paris, where their job would be to keep an eye on everyone, prevent defections, and make sure no one got recruited by foreign intelligence services.

The group would have been through the customs and border control promptly – they had been cleared many times, starting months before their travel date and, most recently, before boarding the bus for the airport – but then a French family arrived, consisting of a grey-haired gentleman, his much younger wife, and their three little girls. The Russians were unceremoniously shunted aside, and as they retreated, Andropov's men began to circle their flock to make sure none broke away.

There was no sign of Olga.

And then I realized that my plan had a fatal flaw. They probably had a special entrance reserved for high government officials and other VIPs, where Andropov had undoubtedly taken her.

I came up to one of the men in a shearling coat, who had just finished barking at a straggler, and asked him softly, so that only he could hear, "I have an urgent message for Comrade Andropov. He's here at the airport, accompanying a foreign guest to her plane. They've gone through the VIP entrance and are in the lounge over there. Get me to him."

He surveyed my mud-splattered coat and raised an eyebrow.

"What are you talking about, buddy? What business do you have with Comrade Andropov?"

He had that special taunting cop's voice designed to put members of the public in their place.

His colleague was instantly at my side, sensing a situation and preparing to lean into me. They were moving smoothly, stealthily, and their body language contrived to convey a threat while remaining easy and elegant.

"What does he want?" the second man asked.

"He wants me to get him to the VIP lounge," the first one replied. "He says he needs to see Comrade Andropov."

The two of them exchanged meaningful glances.

"Show me your papers, buddy," the second one said. He seemed to be the senior of the two.

"Not now," I said coldly. "I don't have time. Take me there or tell me how I can get there."

My manner took them aback, which was what I had intended it to do. Men working for Andropov's agency were not used to being talked to like that by a civilian, and they naturally assumed that I was more important than I looked.

"Do you realize it's beyond passport control?" the senior one asked after a moment's hesitation.

"That's why I need your help. We're wasting valuable time."

"Nevertheless, you'll have to wait and answer my questions. Why do you want to go there?"

"Comrade Andropov is taking a French visitor to her plane," I said. "I need to see him before she boards. And let's do it quickly. It's a matter of national security. "

I didn't know for sure that Andropov had personally taken Olga to the airport. In fact, now that they had gotten Zolotnitsky, there was no longer any need for him to pay court to her. But I didn't have a choice. If there was any hope of getting Zolotnitsky out of their clutches, I had to see Olga, and I needed Andropov to be there.

"Let's go then," the senior man finally said, shaking his head as he made the decision. "You start processing the group, Kamyshov, if I don't come back in time. You can handle them on your own."

He pushed past the French family who were still getting their passports stamped and, waving to the border guard, practically ran down a narrow corridor. There was a door in the wall without any markings, and he turned into it. Behind the door was a guard, at whom my companion flashed his KGB card and who let us through without a word. The next corridor was longer and equally narrow. As we hurried through it, a voice over the loudspeaker again said something in French and English.

"Hurry up," the KGB man shouted, turning to me and breaking into a trot. "They're about to board."

There was another door and another guard, an armed one this time.

"Is Comrade Andropov here?"

We were both out of breath. The guard said nothing, staring at us.

"Is he here?" I asked him again.

The guard remained impassive, as though he hadn't heard me.

"Is he here?" the KGB man said, repeating my question.

"Not yet," the guard replied. "They may be going directly to the plane."

Not bothering to thank either of them, I ran outside, and I saw them right away. Ivan was holding the back door open for Olga. Two men were taking her suitcases out of a second Volga, parked directly behind the first. Their coats and scarves matched those worn by the two officers shepherding the tourists. Andropov stood on the sidewalk, putting on gloves.

"Olga Stepanovna," I shouted as she and Andropov were about to enter the building.

Both turned. Ivan stepped forward to intercept me and slipped his hand into his pocket.

I stopped. I had no intention of being shot.

"What are you doing here, lieutenant?" Andropov asked.

His voice was cold, and his eyes were boring into me through the thick lenses of his glasses.

"I need to speak to Olga Stepanovna," I said, still not moving. "It's important. Both of you have to hear me out."

"Didn't I tell you to stay the hell away from Madame Khokhlova, lieutenant?" Andropov said, but Olga interrupted him.

"Yes, Pavel," she said. "What happened?"

"Please, Madame, we don't have time," Andropov said. "We're late. They won't hold the plane for you."

Now I took a step forward, and Ivan's right hand was out of his pocket in a flash. He was holding a small foreign-made automatic.

Olga remained completely calm.

"Ask your driver to put the gun away, Yuri Vladimirovich," she said coldly. "I need to hear what this man has to say."

"But the plane," Andropov tried to plead with her. "You're going to be late."

She ignored him.

"Olga Stepanovna," I said. "Alexei Zolotnitsky was kidnapped last night on his way back to Leningrad. He may be hurt and is certainly in serious danger. I wanted you to know that this man, Yuri Vladimirovich Andropov, is responsible for his kidnapping."

The same foreign language announcement reached us from the airport building, its end overwhelmed by the roar of a landing aircraft.

None of us said a word for a very long time. Olga had turned to Andropov and was glaring at him.

"Is it true?" she asked at last.

Andropov held her stare and turned to me. He looked surprised, almost vulnerable. Had I not known what kind of training KGB people go through, I might even have been convinced that he had no idea what I was talking about.

"I have no idea what you're talking about," he said finally. "Who's Alexei Zolotnitsky?"

"He's a friend of Olga Stepanovna," I said. "A friend from the old days living in the Soviet Union."

"He's my first husband," she said. "I was married to him before I married Pablo."

"Let's not play this game," I said. "Comrade Andropov knows perfectly well who he is."

"I don't, lieutenant. Don't say what you don't know."

"And what about the *Muse*?" I asked.

"A muse? What muse?"

"A painting by Picasso," I said. "A portrait of Olga Stepanovna which he gave her as his engagement gift to her?"

"Oh, that," Andropov said. "Yes, I've heard about it. It disappeared during the war, I think. It was looted by the Germans. I have no idea why you're talking about this painting, and in any case, it is not the best time to discuss art history. Olga Stepanovna is going to miss her flight."

"What about my baptismal cross?" Olga asked him. "What about the burglary in my suite?"

"What about it?" Andropov asked, putting on a stupefied look.

"What about the two men killed after the burglary?" I asked. "The only reason for that entire charade was so that I would locate Alexei Zolotnitsky for you, wasn't it?"

"You're mad, lieutenant. And, Madame, with all due respect, I think he's leading you astray. I don't know what his game is, but I'm going to find out soon. Let me take you to your plane."

Ivan took a step towards me and grabbed me by the arm. He had an iron grip that I could feel even through my leather coat and two layers of wool sweaters. Olga spotted his move and stepped down from the sidewalk.

"I'm not going anywhere until I see my husband," she said calmly. "You can arrest me if you wish."

✳

It was early afternoon, and we were still sitting in the VIP lounge at Vnukovo Airport. Andropov had told his staff to give us some privacy, and they disappeared in an instant, as if they had never been there in the first place. The guards were gone as well, replaced by Ivan and two men in shearling coats whom I had seen unload Olga's suitcases. Olga's plane had left without her. Andropov had sent word that she would not be on it, and her suitcases were brought back.

I had told him everything I knew about the burglary – hiding nothing this time – and it was obvious he was hearing it all for the first time. Or at least that he had never given any thought how it all fitted together: the break-in, the theft of Olga's baptismal cross, the disappearance of her other jewelry, the first murder, the recovery of all the jewelry except the cross, the second murder that was not intended to be discovered – the entire sequence of events.

He also wanted to know about Zolotnitsky – and I let Olga tell him the story of their marriage, her escape from Crimea, his near-execution and survival, their meeting in France and, finally, in Berlin.

And that was how we got to the *Muse*.

I was reluctant to recount to Andropov what I had heard from Zolotnitsky the previous night – after all, he had murdered two Soviet NKVD men and even now could be tried and sentenced to hang – but it was our only chance of finding him.

"How are we going to look for Alexei?" Olga asked.

Andropov shook his head thoughtfully.

"We need to find Comrade X first," I replied and then explained, seeing their mystified faces. "This is what I've been calling the person who wanted me to find Zolotnitsky. I was convinced it was you, Comrade Andropov."

"But you were wrong, lieutenant."

"What else was I supposed to think, since you had my partner, Senior Lieutenant Tumakov, spying on me."

Andropov gave me a sidelong look.

"I did no such thing," he said. "What gave you that idea?"

"Then who was he spying on me for?"

Andropov and I looked at each other.

"I'd like to use the phone." I said.

Two minutes later we were on our way. We zoomed past the few minor traffic tie-ups in the city by using the center lane reserved for government vehicles. Traffic cops on Kutuzov Avenue seemed to recognize our Volga and nodded to Ivan as an old friend – except with a lot more respect than any friend ever gets, especially from a traffic cop.

We arrived at Petrovka 38 headquarters barely half an hour after leaving the airport. As before, Andropov headed unceremoniously toward Budyonny's desk, while Olga, myself and the Boss sat down at the conference table. The Boss kept giving me his trademark suspicious glances. He had no idea what it was all about and, knowing me, suspected mischief.

Della was sent to fetch my partner, and Andropov instructed her not to say a word about who was waiting for him in the Boss's office. He only said a few words to her but she left as intimidated as though she herself were the criminal.

We waited.

Valera came into the office, took one look at us, and immediately grew tense. With Andropov hovering from the height of the Boss's desk, he looked like a judge in a courtroom, the three of us being the jury.

I would have done it differently if I could. I would have come into our office and chatted with Valera informally, hoping to catch him off guard. I was sure I would have gotten a lot more out of him that way.

But we didn't have time for such niceties, and in the end, we still got everything we needed and got it quickly.

Andropov grabbed the bull by its horns right away.

"Have you been spying on your partner?" he thundered from his seat.

Valera raised his eyes to glance at the KGB chief and looked away.

"What do you mean, Comrade Andropov, sir?" he asked.

"What's the matter with you, lieutenant? You don't understand the Russian language? I want to know whether you have been informing on Senior Lieutenant Matyushkin."

Valera now turned to me to give me a quick sheepish glance.

"I haven't been spying on him," he replied. "I have been providing updates on his investigation."

"And what kind of updates have you provided?"

Andropov put a sarcastic emphasis on the word "updates."

"Not much, sir. He has not been very open with me lately. He probably suspected something."

Budyonny guffawed sarcastically, and I grinned. Andropov remained dead serious.

"Can you be a little more specific?" he inquired.

"I filed a report on his private conversation with Madame Khokhlova, for instance, at least as much as he had told me about it.

I filed another report when he told me about Alexei Zolotnitsky. He claimed he had no idea where to find him. However, I'm convinced he wasn't being straight with me."

He glanced at me again. He was more perceptive than I had given him credit for.

He was going to add something but changed his mind.

"Who did you pass those reports to?" Andropov asked.

"Certainly not to me," Budyonny thundered, turning purple with rage. He had now understood that my partner had done something wrong and that the head of the KGB was annoyed, and even though he didn't yet know what it was, he was already mad at Valera.

"Not me either," Andropov said. "Who was it then?"

Valera squirmed under his steely gaze.

"But surely sir—" he started and broke off. "Can I speak freely?"

"I wish you would," Andropov said coldly. "And hurry up with it, too. Don't waste my time."

"Didn't you send me the instructions to—"

"I did no such thing," Andropov interrupted.

Valera stared at him in horror. Whether or not the powerful head of the KGB really hadn't sent him any instructions or was merely denying that he had, Valera now realized that he was in trouble. A thin line of perspiration appeared on his upper lip, and he licked at it nervously, his tongue darting in and out of his mouth like a lizard.

There was a tense silence in the room that I broke by asking Valera a question – even though by then I had figured out the answer.

"To whom were you submitting those reports for Comrade Andropov?"

Valera was still looking sheepishly at Andropov while replying to me.

"Why, to Boris, of course."

"Who the fuck is Boris?" Andropov exclaimed and then, suddenly turning crimson, apologized to Olga.

I had no time or inclination to be amused by the head of the KGB being flustered by his use of a profanity in the presence of a lady. I was already by the Boss's desk, dialing a number.

"He's my neighbor," I said while the line was ringing. "A KGB officer."

Andropov was going to ask me something else, but I stopped him. Tosya had picked up the receiver on the second ring.

"I have no idea whether he's in," she said. "I don't give a damn whether he lives or dies. I was out with Nikola all morning, anyway."

"Please go and see whether he's in," I said. "And call him to the phone if he is."

"I told you I'm mad at him."

"Please," I said. "Do as I say."

She covered the receiver, and I heard her muffled cry into Boris's end of the apartment.

"Boris, you're wanted on the phone."

"He doesn't answer," she came back in a moment. "He must be out."

"Please go and knock on his door," I said, getting exasperated and feeling four pairs of eyes watching me quibble with my girlfriend.

Tosya didn't like being ordered around and ordinarily she would have made her objections known. But now she must have sensed the urgency in my voice. She went away, putting the receiver down, and was back almost immediately.

"You need to get here right away," she said, her voice suddenly soft and hoarse. "I just hope to god it wasn't Sveta."

"I don't think so," I said. "Take Nikola out. I'll call an ambulance."

"It's not going to be of much use. At least not to Boris."

"I'm sorry," Valera said. "I honestly didn't know. I thought—"

"You just wait," the Boss bellowed.

"It was not Lieutenant Tumakov's fault," I said as Andropov and I headed out of the office. "He was tricked."

# FORTY-TWO

"Now what?" Andropov asked.

I had nothing to say.

We were sitting at the Metropole coffee shop where I had waited for Olga a few days before. We were now waiting for her again. The coffee shop was closed, and we were there alone, sitting at a table that had been set for the next morning's breakfast.

"We're at a dead end, lieutenant," he added.

"That was why Boris was murdered," I said. "He was the only link to our Comrade X. He's quite good at eliminating links that might lead back to him."

"Do you think Boris committed the first two murders?"

I shrugged. "I don't know."

"It looked like the same hand, but it could have been Boris and it could have been the person who killed him. Whatever you say about us, we teach our people well. The exquisite skill in wielding the blade."

We had just come from my apartment, where we had found Boris's body lying on the floor of his room in a pool of blood, stabbed through the heart the same way Levkoyev and Kisly had been.

"This means that another person from your agency is involved," I said.

Andropov chuckled.

"That's true, lieutenant. There was nothing special about the wounds. Fairly generic stuff. You learn this in the first month of KGB training."

"But I bet Boris was the one who approached Eduard," I said.

"Who's Eduard?"

"A black market real estate broker. My fiancée and I had been looking to swap our two rooms in different apartments for two rooms in the same apartment, because we were going to live together. About a month ago, he suddenly found us an apartment. That was how we became Boris's neighbors."

"Wait a second. This means that the operation has been in the works for a long time. Since it became known that Khokhlova was coming to the Soviet Union. This Comrade X of yours is definitely working for me – and he's not small fry. Boris, for instance, had no way of knowing anything about her."

I nodded.

"In any case, lieutenant, we've got to question this Eduard."

"We could," I agreed. "But even if he's still alive, he only dealt with Boris and knows nothing."

We were sitting close together at a small table, and Andropov, leaning towards me, gave me a shove in the ribs. He was facing the door, and it had now opened to admit Olga. The guard had been instructed to admit her while keeping everyone else out, including the hard currency-paying hotel guests. I felt privileged. I had precedence over foreigners in my own country.

Andropov and I stood up to greet her.

"Did you find him?"

Olga had been crying. She was pale, and her eyes were puffy. She had been shocked by Zolotnitsky's disappearance, but I wouldn't have expected her to cry.

"Sit down, Olga Stepanovna," Andropov said.

"You have to tell me what happened to Alexei."

"We don't know yet. But I wouldn't have much hope. We're dealing with a ruthless killer. We questioned the conductor on his train. She didn't see the man or men who were in your husband's compartment. They told her to stay in her cabin and not stick her head out. She was scared of them."

"Why didn't she call the police?"

"They claimed they worked for the KGB, but I assure you—" Andropov broke off.

"I understand," Olga said. "I thought you might have found out something. It's better to know, even if it's the worst."

"In the meantime, Olga Stepanovna, I would strongly advise you go back to Paris."

"I am not going until Alexei is found," she said firmly. "Dead or alive."

"But there is nothing for you to do here," Andropov pleaded. "You cannot help us in any way. I give you my word as a communist. We'll do everything in our power to find your husband. And I will keep you informed daily by telephone. Please, Olga Stepanovna, go back tomorrow. You know, your visa to the USSR is about to expire. You can be forcibly removed – or even go to jail."

"Is it a threat?"

"Of course not. It's you I'm concerned about. I don't want you to be upset if we find out—"

"Very well then," she said abruptly. "I will go home tomorrow. But I want you to know that I'm doing it under duress."

We didn't have to wait long for the resolution, which unfortunately didn't come as a great surprise. Late the next morning, while Andropov was still at Vnukovo, where he had taken Olga for the second time in two days, we got a phone call from the town cop in Likhoslavl, a Karel-populated regional center some three hundred kilometers from Moscow and halfway to Leningrad. A railroad guard living in one of the brick huts along the tracks that dated back to Nicholas I and the construction of the Moscow-St. Petersburg line had been walking his dog and stumbled upon a dead body in the woods about three hundred meters from the tracks. The reason he discovered it was the trail of blood leading into the woods.

I sent our medical expert Sasha Grigoryev ahead to the town of Tver, the nearest large city with a suitable morgue, where the body had been taken for identification and autopsy. Grigoryev went by train and got there well ahead of us, since I first had to wait for Andropov.

It was only late evening when we got to Tver, but the place felt dead, sunk into an immutable provincial torpor. It was an old town, comprised of street after street of two-story wood and brick houses bristling with television aerials, their slate roofs buried beneath two feet of snow, and five story apartment buildings of more recent vintage, also covered with snow and bedecked with icicles. Streetlights were sparse, and as we drove down the empty main drag, unimaginatively named Soviet Street, a ferocious chorus of dogs barked from every darkened yard.

The hospital was at the northwestern edge of town, on the road to Leningrad and across the bridge over the Volga. The river is still very narrow here and the bridge is narrow, too, the roadway having been reduced to a single lane by snowdrifts creeping in from both sides. Ivan took it very fast, avoiding an oncoming truck by a few millimeters, occasioning its driver to roll down the window and shout nasty profanities into our wake.

We pulled up to the main entrance of the hospital, where Ivan got out and made a few inquiries at reception. We then made a couple of wrong turns in the darkness among still more snow piles and found a two-story addition in the back of the main building.

Grigoryev was waiting for us by the closed door, smoking a cigarette and pacing in the narrow space to keep warm. The building reeked of formaldehyde, excrement, and disinfectant. Andropov made a face. The KGB dealt with death on a daily basis, but the head of the organization didn't seem to be used to its smell.

"Is it Zolotnitsky?" he asked Grigoryev.

Grigoryev shrugged.

"I have no idea. My job is to tell you what he died of and in what condition the body was found. You'll have to decide for yourselves who he is."

Grigoryev showed no deference to Andropov. He was known as an independent guy and a free thinker who tipped his hat to no one. A reputation is a thing of value, and he had to maintain it even before the head of the KGB.

The basement was even colder than the first floor, and after three hours of near total darkness, it took us a few seconds to get used to the stark bright light bathing the white tiled walls. Andropov shuddered when an attendant pulled the handle of one of the steel drawers and a gurney trundled out, containing a blue and yellow human body, stark naked. He took a quick look at it and turned to me.

"Is it him?"

He looked queasy.

I nodded. The face was discolored and swollen beyond recognition, and smeared with clumps of dry blood from a savage gash running from the left temple to the edge of his mouth. But it was certainly Zolotnitsky, there could be no doubt. His delicate right hand had formed into a fist, and there was a scarred stump in place of a crudely amputated left arm.

"Lot of bruises," I said.

"Yes, and if you take a look his legs, you'll see that both tibias and the left fibula are probably broken. That must have happened when he jumped or was thrown from the train."

"Was he thrown off the train?" Andropov asked. "Or did he jump?"

Grigoryev shrugged.

"The guy was an amputee, and he wasn't that young, either. He's past the age when guys hop off fast moving trains lightly. Even if he jumped on his own, it wouldn't have been of his own free will. It wouldn't have been easy for him to keep his balance and not to land awkwardly. But I have no idea. I wasn't there. All I can say is that he was a pretty strong old geezer, to crawl as far as he did when it was minus thirty. Losing so much blood, too. Look at that cut."

"He was a survivor," I said. "Lots of people tried to kill him over the years."

"Well, he bled to death, if that makes you any happier," Grigoryev said.

"Everyone has to die sooner or later," Andropov observed philosophically. "You can't survive life."

"This is what I find more interesting though," Grigoryev said, turning back to the body. "See these dots here on his arm?"

Zolotnitsky's arm was bruised and had a kind of reddish-black rash on the skin from the shoulder to the wrist.

"What are they?" Andropov asked.

"Cigarette burns."

Andropov and I looked at each other.

"That makes sense," he said.

"In what way?" Grigoryev asked.

"We know what they were trying to get out of him," Andropov said. "What we don't know is whether they got the information they wanted. And, of course, we don't have any idea who they were."

"I think we're getting closer," I said.

They both looked at me.

"What do you mean?" Andropov asked.

"I think I know where to find Comrade X. We had better get back to the city."

# FORTY-THREE

Andropov's Volga was waiting for me at the entrance to our courtyard on Chernyshevsky Street.

I was staying alone in the apartment. Tosya and the kids were still at Sveta's, keeping the kids out of an apartment where a murder had been committed and comforting Sveta. Sveta was devastated by the double blow of Boris's murder and the discovery that he had only been interested in her because he was spying on me.

"It checked out," Andropov told me when I got into his car. "You were right, lieutenant."

Unlike Budyonny, the KGB boss was free with his praise and made sure he gave full credit where it was due.

"And there has been another piece of news," he added. "You'll find out in time."

He turned to Ivan. "Let's go. We're going to the Metropole."

It was like going back to the start of the case. We arrived at the hotel, where everyone from beefy Mustafa at the door and the old man running the elevator, to a cleaning woman we ran into when we got to the third floor, and the concierge who was on duty, all saluted Andropov and stood at attention. We were still a threesome. There was no Valera with us this time, but I suggested we ask Ivan to come up in case our conversation with the man we were going to see turned nasty. Andropov thought it was a good idea and told Ivan to carry a large briefcase he had taken from the car.

We went to the door of Suite 319, where the concierge produced a passkey and let us in.

"Go get Major Yershov," Andropov told her. "Tell him to join us here."

The suite had been cleaned up, reverting to its sterile, nondescript state and waiting to receive its next guest. I sniffed the air, hoping to catch a whiff of Olga's perfume, but there was nothing but the slight smell of disinfectant and perfumed soap. Every sign of Olga had been expunged. She was back in Paris and out of our lives, most likely, forever. The real distance between Paris and Moscow was much greater than the two and a half thousand kilometers that physically separated us.

We were waiting in silence. We were not guests but interlopers, disturbing nothing in the suite. Andropov and I had no desire to speak. And it wasn't Ivan's place to speak without being addressed first.

About five minutes later there was a knock on the door.

"Come right in, colonel," Andropov said softly.

I grew tense while Ivan, on the contrary, relaxed and pushed back in his armchair, watching from under half-closed eyelids as the draperies over the door swayed open and Major Yershov made his appearance.

He looked bulkier than I remembered. He was in civilian clothes and his jacket hung a little loosely over his muscular body. He goose-stepped into the room and stopped at attention. Even as he goose-stepped, I noticed a slight limp that he was trying to hide.

"At your service, Comrade Boss," he reported smartly.

He was tense.

"We have a couple of questions for you, major," Andropov said, pulling out a dog-eared file from his briefcase and leafing through it. "You started your service in '45, is that correct?"

"Yes, sir. I was drafted the day I turned eighteen, and comrades at the draft board accommodated my preference to do my service at

SMERSH. I joined state security two months before the war ended. I have risen through the ranks."

"Very good," Andropov said. "I see that your first posting once you completed your training was Berlin."

"Yes, sir."

"But it didn't start very well," Andropov said. "You were attacked when you went to make an arrest and nearly died. Your commanding officer was killed. Is it not so?"

"Yes, sir. Major Balashov and myself, sir, we came to arrest a traitor, a White Russian who had spent the war living among the enemy in Berlin, the Fascist nest, while we were struggling to defeat the aggressor. Unfortunately, I was inexperienced back then, and he turned out to be a sly fox. He caught us off guard, and Major Balashov was killed. I was severely injured, and the American doctors who treated me said it was a miracle I survived. They said I had a very strong constitution. They called me a Russian bear."

Yershov was getting nervous about the direction the conversation was taking, but the only way HE showed it was by talking too much.

"What happened to the man you had come to arrest?" Andropov asked.

"He disappeared," Yershov said. "He slipped through our fingers and most likely ran off to the Western zone of occupation. We were blamed for letting him get away, and I was detained. However, the investigation determined that it had been Major Balashov's fault. He had been in cahoots with the traitor. He was sentenced posthumously to be shot, and his family back in Russia was arrested. I was released and reinstated in SMERSH."

"And you never saw or heard about that man again?" Andropov asked. "Never tried to find him and take your revenge on him for disfiguring you?"

"I did not, sir. I didn't— I mean, I didn't know where he was. I don't believe—"

Andropov was suddenly on his feet.

"And yet you kept tracking the man all your life. You kept looking for him everywhere. You did not in fact believe that he had slipped into the Western occupation zone. You knew he was in the Soviet Union, but you had no idea how to find him. Because you didn't know the name he was living under."

"I'm sorry, sir, I don't know what you're talking about."

"Don't you interrupt me, colonel. And don't lie to me. When you learned that Olga Khokhlova would be coming to Moscow and, moreover, staying at the Metropole, you thought you had your chance. That's because Major Balashov had met Madame Khokhlova when he was stationed in Paris and had learned about the portrait of her by Picasso and about her baptismal cross. She was hoping Balashov would help her locate Zolotnitsky, but Balashov only wanted to get the painting, because he rightly believed it to be extremely valuable. How does that sound so far?"

The colonel turned away and stared out the window. His jaw was set, his face was pale, and the disfiguring scar traversing its left side was as red as a fresh welt.

"I'll let Senior Lieutenant Matyushkin continue the story from here, since he knows it firsthand."

The colonel stared at me with barely disguised hatred. I shrugged and began reluctantly.

"There isn't much to tell, sir," I said. "Yershov came up with a plan to have us, at Moscow Criminal Investigations, help him find Zolotnitsky. First, he got me to move into the same apartment as Boris, an officer who worked for him. Boris tried to intimidate me at first, and then pretended to be my friend. Once Madame Khokhlova moved into her suite, Yershov arranged to have her place broken into. He hired a disturbed kid to do the burglary. His job was to take only her baptismal cross, which would have tipped Madame Khokhlova off to the fact that her first husband was alive and living in the Soviet Union, and had sent the burglar. But the kid stole more than he had been told to, thinking that he could get something for himself and no one would be the wiser. To correct the damage, Major Yershov had to return all the other jewelry, except for the cross. He planted it in Levkoyev's apartment and murdered him to make sure the jewelry would be found – smashing a window in Levkoyev's apartment, so that it would happen sooner. And he probably always intended to kill the burglar to cover his tracks."

"He was a moral degenerate," Yershov muttered under his breath. "A retard."

"Well," Andropov stepped in. "Since you admit that it was you, there is no need to go into further details, which as you can see we know perfectly well. All I want you to tell me is why you were so stupid as to slash Zolotnitsky exactly the same way he had slashed you. We might never have gotten to you if it hadn't been for that detail. It was the senior lieutenant here who made the connection."

As ever, Andropov was generous with the credit.

"I wanted the bastard to know what it felt like," Yershov said angrily. "I slashed him, and I threw him off the train. I wanted him to be alive when he landed, and I'm betting he was. He's like a cat. He had nine lives."

Andropov laughed.

"You wanted the old man to live with a scar on his face? But there's a difference being disfigured at eighteen versus seventy, don't you think?"

"I wanted him to know what it felt like," Yershov repeated stubbornly through clenched teeth. "What it felt like bleeding to death from your face, tasting your waning life on your tongue. I'm happy I shared that experience with him, and I'm glad he croaked."

"How do you know he's dead?" I asked him quickly.

He stared. We sat there waiting for him to answer, but he said nothing.

Andropov shook his head disapprovingly.

"Anyway, for that childish revenge you threw away all the money you were going to make from the sale of Picasso's *Muse*," he said.

"You know about that, too?"

"I told you I know everything, and lying to me will do you no good. And don't you try hiding anything from me either. It will make matters worse."

"I'm not hiding anything."

"Then how can you explain this?" Andropov asked.

He reached into his briefcase again and pulled out another folder. It contained two sheets of very thin, nearly translucent paper.

"This is a report from our embassy in the German Democratic Republic. There was an attempted robbery at the Russian Orthodox Church in the Tegel district of West Berlin. The night watchman spotted a man who apparently hid in the cemetery during visiting hours and was trying to break into the church. The watchman let him get in to see what he was up to, since the church had nothing valuable to steal. Once inside, the watchman told the West Berlin police, he started counting the stone slabs on the floor and, having chosen the one he wanted, used a crow bar to lift it. The young man was so absorbed in his task that he didn't hear the watchman lock the door before going to get the police. When the cops arrived, the man was still digging – even though there was nothing there to dig for. They thought he was mentally ill – there are many such characters in West Berlin – except he spoke in heavily accented German, and when they searched him they found an East German identity card in the name of Hans Dietrich Oedenbach. They decided to detain him."

He turned to Yershov.

"Does this story mean anything to you?"

Yershov shrugged, "Not really."

"Well," Andropov said, sounding disappointed. "Maybe this one will."

He replaced the first sheet and pulled out the other.

"This is a report from the head of the Dresden KGB section. He reports the disappearance of one of his officers, Lieutenant Lukin, who went missing two days ago. Naturally, it is a major incident when an officer goes AWOL, especially in Germany, where we're surrounded by enemies and constantly under threat from West German and American spies. A thorough inquiry was conducted, and it was discovered that Lukin issued a permit to cross into West Berlin to a man named Hans Dietrich Ödenbach, even though he had no authority to do so without informing his superior officer. The man Ödenbach made the crossing seven hours later – plenty of time for Lukin to travel from Dresden to Berlin. Do you know anything about that, colonel?"

Yershov didn't answer.

"And yet you *should* know plenty about it," Andropov said, taunting him. "Because some time before leaving for Berlin, on the day of Zolotnitsky's murder, Lukin received a telephone call that was traced to a secure line in your office. Now, what happened to your determination not to hide anything from me?"

There was a tense silence in the room. The sound of traffic outside, on Karl Marx Avenue, reached us faintly through the double panes.

"I wasn't doing it for myself," Yershov said after a while. "Obviously we were going to get the painting and give it to the Soviet government."

"Is that so?" Andropov said. "Was that why Lukin also had on his person the addresses and phone numbers of a pair of contemporary art dealers in West Berlin? Shady ones, known to deal in stolen art?"

"I know nothing about that, I swear. That was strictly on his initiative. If that's what he was thinking of doing, he was a traitor. That wasn't how we planned it."

His indignation was almost too strong to be genuine, but then again strong emotions often look faked.

"We'll know soon enough how you planned it," Andropov said. "Lukin is already in East Berlin, and he's being sent here, to the Lubyanka. Anyway, Zolotnitsky had the last laugh at your expense. He tricked you. The Picasso wasn't in the church."

There was another tense silence. Andropov turned to Ivan.

"Take him downstairs," he said. "I have a car waiting for him, a Black Maria, along with a couple of guys. You're under arrest, Yershov."

"Actually, it would be better if you tell those guys to come upstairs, sir," I said to Andropov.

He looked at me.

"Why is that, lieutenant?"

They'll also need to take your driver."

"What?" Ivan bellowed at me. "What did you just say, you scum?"

"Sorry, didn't you hear me? I've just suggested to your boss that he make sure you're arrested for complicity in all the crimes we've been discussing."

"I'm going to kill this guy," Ivan shouted.

"Now, lieutenant," Andropov said. "Let's be reasonable. What evidence do you have against my driver?"

"He has nothing on me," Ivan screamed.

"I first started to suspect him when Madame Khokhlova and I were trying to get away from her handlers after a lunch at the Arts Club. We were at the GUM, and we were cornered. I thought at the time he let us escape on purpose, but I wasn't sure and I couldn't figure out why on earth he would do that."

"Exactly," Ivan interrupted me again. "Why would I want to get in trouble with you, sir, for letting him and the foreign bird get away?"

"Yes, lieutenant, why would he want to do that?" Andropov asked.

"Madame Khokhlova never reported her baptismal cross stolen," I said, still ignoring Ivan and addressing Andropov. "Perhaps she didn't get the message. Perhaps the theft of the other stuff had muddled her perception. But when the other jewels were returned to her, and she still said nothing about the cross, even though she surely couldn't have missed the significance of the cross not being among them, Yershov decided to give me a hint. Which he did with my partner's help. But that required arranging for me to see Khokhlova on my own, so that I could extract from her the admission that her cross had been taken and that it was Zolotnitsky who had taken it. That was the reason why Ivan pretended not to see us."

"That's pure speculation," Ivan said. Andropov nodded his agreement.

"I thought so, too," I said. "That was why I never said anything about it. But now your accomplice has given you away."

"How so?" Yershov asked, piping up for the first time. He had been standing in front of us seemingly indifferent to our conversation.

"You had no way of knowing that Zolotnitsky was dead. Only the medic at my office knew that, and he had been told to keep it secret. The only person who could have told you was Ivan."

"I should have shot you at the airport when I had a chance," Ivan hissed. "The world would have been a better place with you pushing up crocuses."

"Now, now," Andropov said, grinning. "Violence is not the answer. Easy does it. We have a saying in Russian, a sweet calf gets to suck two cows."

He reached into his briefcase yet again and pulled out what looked like a piece of fabric rolled and tied with a couple of ribbons. He undid the knots and let it unfold. We all stared at it.

I shook my head and had the urge to rub my eyes. Olga was back in her suite, with the same kind smile and slightly mocking eyes but younger, without wrinkles, and with long dark hair pulled tightly back in a bun. Around her carefully detailed and lovingly painted figure was a blank canvas deliberately left empty, as though the artist was only interested in her and nothing else in the world was relevant.

"What is it?" I asked.

"It's *The Muse*," Andropov announced and continued pedantically, "One of the world's most famous and expensive paintings. Pablo Picasso's portrait of his wife, the Russian ballerina Olga Khokhlova. Painted during his courtship of her in Paris and Barcelona and given to her as his engagement present. Believed to have been lost during World War II, but recently recovered in Leningrad."

The striking first impression had worn off, and, as I kept looking at it, I realized that I liked it less and less. It wasn't the Olga I had come to know. Her lips were prim and proper and didn't have the mocking, capricious and, despite her age, still sensuous curve. And her eyes, too – there was so much more to them than Olga's second husband had tried to capture – so much more depth and feeling. The woman in the picture was more shallow, there was more vanity in her and not enough steel. Zolotnitsky wasn't the world's most famous painter – and as far as I knew painting wasn't one of his many talents – but I was sure that, had he put his mind to it, he would have painted a very different Olga. He would have painted an Olga that was like him – a survivor.

But it was still a very good painting. You could do a better portrait of the real Olga, but only after looking at this fake one and rejecting it.

"What's the matter, lieutenant? You're not asking me how I got it."

Andropov's eyes were laughing at me from behind his thick lenses. He was very proud of himself and couldn't hide his self-satisfaction.

"I figured you would tell me how you got it if you felt I needed to know that," I said.

"I certainly think you do," he said. "It might be a good lesson for you in the future."

He paused, enjoying his moment of triumph.

"By the way, are you finished looking at it? May I put it away?"

He rolled it up carefully and retied the ribbons.

"You see, lieutenant, when I learned about the existence of this painting and the story behind it, I was absolutely sure that, if it still existed, Zolotnitsky would have wanted Olga to have it. And in fact I was right. He had brought it to the Soviet Union and hid it in Nizhny Tagil. Once he was released from the camp, he went back there and retrieved the painting. When they met, he told her where he had hidden it in Leningrad and said he would give it to her when she came here next time. Not that she was eager to tell me that. I think she was hoping to come back and to get it out of the country herself. In other words, to smuggle it out of Russia. But I got it out of her in the end."

"How did you manage that?" I asked.

"First I told her that she could forget sneaking it out of Russia. If she came back for it herself, we'd keep an eye on her at all times and search her luggage thoroughly when she left. And if she tried to send someone else to recover the painting, they would risk a very long, very tough sentence if they were caught trying to smuggle it across the border. That made her think hard about it, but she still wasn't ready to give in. She said that since it belonged to her and she had no intention of donating it to the Soviet State, she would leave it where it was, in the secret place Zolotnitsky had hidden it. This way, no one would have it."

"And you did get around that?"

Andropov laughed.

"Look, lieutenant, she's a woman, and all women are constructed in the same way. They're a two-dimensional bunch. This is how evolution created them. So I told her that, if the painting were lost – and it *was* going to be lost – her role in Picasso's oeuvre and his life would be greatly diminished. But if she surrendered it to us, it would hang in the Hermitage and people would talk about her and remember her for centuries. That was the argument that swayed her. *Vanity, thy name is woman.* I think it was Shakespeare who said that. But we've been wasting a lot of time here. Let me call the guards, and let's get out of here."

"But Boss, Comrade Andropov, you have the painting," Yershov exclaimed, his voice pained. "It's very valuable, and it is now the property of the Soviet State. And you wouldn't have known anything about it had it not been for me. You've got to take this into account."

"I will," Andropov said coldly. "To be frank, I don't give a damn about the people you murdered. They were scum – a total waste to the Soviet State and the communist cause. One an aesthete, a collector of antiques and a black market dealer. Another, even worse, a burglar. Boris was a KGB agent, but he was willing to go rogue, and I would have personally kicked him out of the service had he survived. And, finally, Zolotnitsky. A White officer, a traitor, and a Nazi collaborator. He should have been hung long ago. But that's not why you're going to jail."

"Why then?" Yershov asked.

"Because you failed. If it hadn't been for me, you would have never gotten close to this painting."

Throughout this discussion Ivan said nothing, staring grimly in the corner.

And I kept thinking that Picasso might have been right in his view of Olga, and I might have been wrong. I wished I could take another look at the painting, but I wasn't going to ask Andropov to show it to me again. Up until that moment, we had been working on the same case, and we were, if not equals, at least partners. But now the case was closed, and he was suddenly the all-powerful head of the KGB again and the distance between us was once again immeasurable.

And so if I wanted to see Picasso's Olga again, I would have to wait until she was hanging on a wall at the Hermitage. All the more reason for me to act on Irina Drozdova's advice and take Tosya to Leningrad some day soon.

# ABOUT THE AUTHOR

Alexei Bayer is a New York-based author, translator and, by economic necessity, an economist. He writes in English and in Russian, his native tongue, and translates into both languages.

His first novel, *Murder at the Dacha*, was published in 2013. The second, *The Latchkey Murders*, followed in 2015.

Bayer's short stories have been published in *New England Review*, *Kenyon Review*, and *Chtenia*. His translations have appeared in *Chtenia* and *Words Without Borders*, as well as in such collections as *The Wall in My Head*, a book dedicated to the twentieth anniversary of the fall of the Berlin Wall, and *Life Stories*, a bilingual literary anthology to benefit hospice care in Russia.